THE TWELVE

THE TWELVE

CINDY LIN

HARPER

An Imprint of HarperCollinsPublishers

Library of Congress Control Number: 2018968294

ISBN 978-0-06-282128-7

Typography by Molly Fehr

20 21 22 23 24   PC/BRR   10 9 8 7 6 5 4 3 2 1

❖

First paperback edition, 2020

TO MY MOTHER,
FOR HER LOVE OF STORYTELLING,
AND MY FATHER,
FOR BEING THERE TO LISTEN.

EARTH

"Within every branch of the zodiac resides the Earth element, for out of it everything is born."

—Book of Elements, from *The Way of the Twelve*

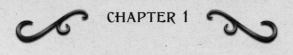

CHAPTER 1

RICE RUN

USAGI CROUCHED IN THE DIRT, praying to the gods that the falling dusk would hide her from the Guard. She pulled some fern fronds from the forest floor and stuck them in her dark braids, then crept closer with her foraging sack to the edge of the rice fields. Tall bundles of harvested rice stalks had been left there to dry in the late summer heat, dotting the landscape like a regiment of the Dragonlord's troops. Her mouth watered at the thought of a steaming bowl of rice. Hardly anyone got to eat rice these days. Most of what was grown in their island's rich soil was sent to the neighboring empires that had invaded Midaga. The rest went to the Dragonlord and his Guard.

Her stomach growled and she pressed a hand to her hollow belly, trying in vain to silence it. It had been days since she'd had a decent meal. On the other side of the fields was her friend Tora, whose vision remained sharp even in the dark, as befitting a youngling born in the year of the Tiger. The Guard always marched the workers back to the town of Goldentusk at day's end. When the quilt of rice fields was clear, Tora would give the signal.

In the fading light of the hour of the Dog, the workers gathered under the watchful eye of the Guard, who roughly inspected the sleeves of the workers' tunics and made them remove their broad straw hats to make sure not a single grain left the fields. Usagi shifted impatiently, hiking up her long, patched skirt to stretch out a leg at a time. The last thing she needed was for her limbs to fall asleep right before a rice run. Her little sister, Uma, was waiting with Tora on the other side of the fields, ready to take whatever Usagi could grab and run it to safety, fast as a horse. Usagi's job now was to make use of her own zodiac powers and listen, her hearing sharp as a rabbit's.

Beyond the buzzing drone of the cicadas and the rustling creak of the forest canopy, Usagi could hear the distant footsteps of the night watch marching from town toward the fields. She caught the squeal of the pigs in the town sties, and the rattle of wheels in the dusty streets. Farther still was the sigh of waves crashing onto shore, the sea barely a dozen miles away. If she filtered out those sounds, reeling in her focus, Usagi's sensitive ears could detect the fluttering heartbeat of the squirrel perched on the branch above her, hear the plop of a wood frog in the irrigation ditches, listen to the tapping legs and gnashing jaws of the shiny black beetle crawling at her feet. The beetle's dark shell reminded her of the armor worn by the Dragonlord's elite force, the Strikers. Rumor was they hauled younglings with zodiac powers away, by special order of the Dragonlord himself, and punished them horribly—torturing some to the point of death. They'd caught so many that she, her sister, and Tora were the only ones left around here.

Twee hee, hoo hoo.

Usagi stiffened at Tora's birdcall. It was time. She tilted her head in the direction of the fields, listening, and heard quiet. Tora was right, the workers and the day Guard had left. There would only be a brief moment where the fields would be clear, the Guard's night squadron not yet fully dispersed around the borders. She cupped her hands around her mouth and replied. *Twee hee, hoo hoo hoo.*

She straightened and backed up a few steps into the forest, rubbing at the tiny wooden rabbit she wore around her neck for luck. Squinting at a stack of drying rice in the middle of the field, Usagi took a few skipping steps before launching herself at the pile of rice bundles. The ground fell away as she soared into the air past the treetops, catching a glimpse of the setting sun as it slid toward the horizon in a pink-tinged sky. Usagi's laugh slipped out in the summer dusk. She'd leaped like this countless times, and it still felt like a miracle.

"There she is!" Uma's excited whisper carried across the fields.

"Yes, I see her," came Tora's reply.

Usagi tore her gaze from the sunset. She still had to land, which was tricky. Focusing on a spot near the rice stack, she reached out a tentative toe and held her breath, steeling herself as the earth rushed up to meet her. With a jolt, Usagi hit the ground, crumpling into a heap like a rag doll. "Oof."

"Awww." Both Tora and Uma let out groans of disappointment.

"Thanks a lot," Usagi muttered, though she knew they couldn't hear her in return. Grimacing, she rolled to her hands and knees. It wasn't her fault that she hadn't yet mastered all her animal talents. Back when Midaga was still protected by the Twelve, those with such talents were honored and celebrated. She would have gone to one of their schools as soon as her rabbit leaping had presented itself. She'd have been *trained.* Her mother might even have been one of her teachers. But that was five years ago, before the war, when Usagi was seven. Her hearing had just begun to change when the island was shaken by an earthquake, beset by tidal waves, and invaded soon after. Though the Warriors of the Zodiac had shielded Midaga from outsiders for centuries, a warlord known as the Blue Dragon and his troops breached their forces and those of the king's court in the space of a few weeks. And now the Blue Dragon sat on King Ogana's throne (may his spirit rest), calling himself Dragonlord.

Usagi's ears pricked. The night watch was getting closer—no farther than a hundred paces away from entering the fields. She needed to get out fast. She grabbed a bundle of rice from the drying stack, still warm and scented of the sun, the long golden heads of grain dangling from their stalks like so many bead necklaces. Stuffing the bundle into her foraging sack, she dashed toward the trees on the other side of the fields, where she could hear Uma and Tora urging her on. It'd be safer to make a run for it instead of trying to leap again, for she couldn't see where she'd be landing, and one bad crash was enough for the day. Passing the last stack of rice at the edge of the fields, Usagi couldn't resist snatching up another bundle. Who knew when they'd get another chance at this harvest?

But the straw binding around the stalks tore open, and the heavy bundle scattered to the ground in a cascade of grassy stems and rattling rice husks. "Spit and spleen!" Usagi swore. Hurriedly she picked at the fallen stalks, jamming them into her burlap bag as quickly as her shaking fingers would allow. If she left the scattered rice behind, the Guard would know that someone was stealing—and an alarm would be raised. Security around the rice fields would be tightened with increased patrols, and then they'd never be able to get rice again—even with all their zodiac powers between them.

The marching footsteps of the approaching Guard grew

louder. Two dozen of them, from the sounds of it. She glanced up to see their torches glimmering in the twilight at the far end of the fields. Just a few more handfuls and she'd get it all.

"What are you doing?" hissed Tora. Her friend stalked out of the shadows, sleek and lithe as a cat, her amber eyes glinting. Crouching beside Usagi, she swept up the remaining rice stalks and dumped them, dirt and all, into the bag. She grabbed Usagi firmly by the arm and together they ran for the trees, where Uma stood waiting, hopping from foot to foot, her wide-set eyes anxious in her thin face.

Tora thrust the bag at Uma. "*Go.* We'll meet you at the turtleback." With a nod, Uma took off like a shot, her dark hair streaming behind her as she disappeared into the forest. Usagi's sister was not quite yet nine, but she could run circles around Usagi, who was a fast runner herself. Even Tora, who at thirteen was a year older than Usagi and often acted like she'd seen everything already, was impressed when Uma first began to run as fast as a galloping horse. Uma now could run so quickly that if you tried to keep eyes on her, she'd be but a blur.

"That was close," Tora muttered, unconsciously rubbing the scars on her arm, slashed across her tawny skin in pale stripes. She shook her head as they moved deeper into the forest. "What were you thinking?"

Shamefaced, Usagi glanced back at the fields, filling with the bobbing light of torches. "I figured I was already there and had room in my bag. Just in case we couldn't do another rice run."

"You didn't need to risk it. There's going to be a third planting," Tora told her, frowning. "The Empire's rice grows so much faster than Midagian rice. We'd have another chance at a run." She softened and pulled the fern fronds from Usagi's hair, sticking one in her own unruly locks. "Look, I'm glad we got that extra rice, but that bag's twice as heavy now. Let's make sure Uma got to the grave safely."

They broke into a jog, weaving around moss-covered trees and stands of bamboo, their worn rope slippers hushed on the leaf-strewn earth. With the help of Tora's sharp vision in the deepening gloom, they ducked under low-hanging branches, steered past prickly shrubs, and hopped over wayward roots and fallen logs. It was near dark by the time they made their way to the turtleback hill deep in the heart of the forest.

Rising almost to the treetops, the hill was a mass grave where more than a quarter of the township was said to be buried. After the Blue Dragon destroyed the Twelve, the invaders had rounded up every soul they could find with animal talents and elemental gifts. Few people nowadays went near the giant mound, and even the Guard avoided it on their patrols, as though the grave of those with zodiac powers frightened them. Maybe the Guard thought that the ghosts of their victims, with all their powers intact, would come back to punish them.

If only.

For Usagi, it was a place of comfort, for her parents were buried in that grassy knoll. She whispered a silent greeting to them as she ran up the slope, and sighed with relief to see Uma. Her sister was waiting at a craggy knot of rocks that she and Tora had arranged around a small hollow. It was there that they hid their stash of rice. They'd begun braving the fields last year when Uma started displaying her talent for incredible speed, and it still worried Usagi to let her sister do something so dangerous. But Uma was perched happily on the largest stone with a handful of mustard flowers, chewing on the stem of one and weaving the rest into a crown.

"What took you two so long?" Uma's thin cheeks were flushed from her run, and her long hair had become a tangled mess.

Tora collapsed onto a rock beside her with a mock groan. "It's not us. You're just getting faster and faster."

Uma beamed. "Fast enough to become the Horse Warrior?"

"You'd have to be the Heir to the Horse Warrior first," Usagi snorted. Before the Twelve's demise, a few younglings were chosen to compete for the honor of becoming an Heir and apprentice to a Warrior. They were always excellent students from one of the schools, often with multiple powers or the rare combination of both animal talents and elemental gifts. Her sister would have been a good Heir, what with her incredible speed and her abilities with fire. But such a competition only happened when a Warrior died or stepped down, and the new Warrior needed to find an Heir of their own. With no Warriors left, there were no Heirs either. Usagi pulled a comb wrapped in tattered silk from the folds of her belt. "Here, Horse Girl. I'll fix your mane."

She unwrapped the wooden comb carefully. It was the only thing of her father's she'd managed to keep, besides the little charm around her neck. She'd had to trade the rest of his fine carvings and his woodworker's tools for food and clothing. Just before the invaders had come sweeping through Goldentusk, her father had given her the intricately carved comb. "No matter what happens to me or your mother, you must look after Uma," he'd told her, looking unusually serious. "She's only three and you're a big girl of seven. Right?" He gave her an encouraging smile, but it was crooked and his eyes were red. "And whatever you do, keep this comb close. It's very special—full of great magic from Mount Jade. I can't tell you much more, but it's not to be played with. Don't drop it, for that will unleash its powers, and don't ever let it out of your sight. Can you promise me that, my rabbit?" He'd made her swear on the Twelve. Back when there was a Twelve.

With a sigh, she traced the circle of zodiac animals on the handle. As the moon brightened in the sky and fireflies began to wink their greenish glow in the warm evening air, Usagi ran the smooth, wooden teeth through her sister's tangled mane. "Sorry," she soothed as Uma yelped and grumbled. She tied her sister's hair into a neat tail and crowned her with the wreath of mustard flowers. "There you go." Her stomach rumbled again and she peered into the hollow. "Any chance we can taste a bit of this rice? I'm starving."

Tora swatted her lightly. "We need every bit for trade."

"But I got us an extra bundle," Usagi pointed out.

"Winter will be here before we know it, and we'll need warm clothes that aren't falling apart," Tora replied. "And your shoes are a mess."

Usagi wiggled her toes, tied snugly in loops of fraying rope. Her straw sandals were barely holding together, it was true. They all needed new shoes, especially Uma, who was wearing through her slippers in a matter of days, not months. Even the hand-me-downs her sister wore were more patch than whole cloth. She glanced down at Uma and smiled. "I'll just eat your flowers then."

Giggling, Uma thrust a mustard blossom at her, and Usagi bit off the frilly yellow bloom. "Mmm, peppery." It would take a lot more to quell her hunger. If only her sister had thought to pluck the more substantial leaves.

Tora pulled out a small sack and shook it. "There wasn't anything in the traps today, but I did find us a few beetles and grub worms."

"I'll get us a fire going and we'll toast them!" Clapping her hands, Uma jumped up.

Usagi stopped her. "Is that such a good idea? It's already dark. What if the Guard see the flames?" It was challenge enough to keep their zodiac powers under wraps, but a fire was especially hard to hide, even in the depths of the forest. It had only been since the start of summer that her sister had begun to display special abilities with fire. She was still exploring what she could do with her fire gift, which made Usagi nervous.

"Maybe I can get it started faster this time," Uma protested. "I'll keep it tiny—just enough to roast the grubs. They'll taste so much better."

Tora opened the sack. "It won't take long—there's not a whole lot. I'll try to catch us a frog later."

Biting her lip, Usagi listened hard, searching for the marching footsteps of a patrol nearby. In the distance, she could hear the sounds of the workers' convoy shuffling back to town, punctuated by an occasional swear by a Guard and the crack of a whip. In the forest around them, though, it was quiet. She relented. "Okay, but make sure it's not too big."

"I'll try." Uma began to rub her hands, softly at first, then faster, her wide brown eyes narrowing in concentration till they were nearly shut. At last a small flame sprang up between Uma's palms, and she cradled it as painlessly as if it were one of the mustard blossoms. "I did it!" she crowed, her face alight in the glow. "Here, give me the bugs."

Tora emptied the sack into Uma's cupped hands, where the grubs and beetles quickly roasted with a sizzle and a pop in the dancing flame.

"Do you remember how to put it out?" Usagi asked her sister.

"Of course!" Uma pulled her hands apart over a large rock, letting the roasted bugs fall to the rough surface, and shook her hands as if she were trying to dry them. The flame disappeared, sparks flying everywhere as Usagi and Tora ducked.

"Make sure you never do that around any kindling." Tora chuckled. She bent and scooped up the scattered grubs and beetles, popping one into her mouth as she divided them into equal portions. "Well done, Fire Horse."

Sitting on the grassy slope of the hill grave, Uma crunched on her beetles, and Usagi did the same. There was a time when they had meals that looked like feasts to her now, with plenty of rice alongside the savory dishes her mother would make. Back then, the mere sight of a bug disgusted them, and Uma would wail while Usagi flapped her hands and squealed for their father to crush it and sweep it out of sight. But now grubs and beetles were precious morsels. Roasted, they were warm and nutty-tasting, and softened the empty ache in their bellies. They'd more than once fought over them. "Mama and Papa would be proud," Usagi told her sister. "You'd be a star pupil at the School of the Twelve for sure."

"As good as Mori, the second Horse Warrior?" Uma asked. "He was born under the sign of the Fire Horse too."

Usagi raised an eyebrow. "Mori was the model Heir to all Warrior Heirs. Don't get full of yourself!" She tweaked the crown of flowers on her sister's head. Ever since they'd lost their parents, Usagi had dutifully recounted the stories her mother had told her about the Warriors of the Zodiac. She would huddle together with Uma and Tora and tell them like dream tales before they all fell asleep. In those moments, they would forget that they were hiding in the forest, hunted for their powers, with no family left to protect them.

Screams and shouts erupted in the distance. Usagi stiffened at the high-pitched cries. "Do you hear that?"

"All I hear are cicadas," Uma piped up.

"Gods, those bugs never stop," Tora said, annoyed. "We should collect a few for dinner." She paused and looked more closely at Usagi. "What is it?"

"Something's happening by the rice fields."

A loud bang cracked the evening air, echoing through the trees. "I heard *that*," Uma gasped. "A firecannon!" She trotted down the hill.

"Where do you think you're going?" Usagi scrambled to her feet. "Uma, get back here!"

"I'm just taking a quick look," Uma called over her shoulder. "I'll be back before you can blink!" Her spindly legs kicked into a run and she darted into the trees.

"Uma, no!" Usagi called.

But her voice only echoed in the darkness. Her sister was gone.

CHAPTER 2

THREE MASKED BANDITS

UMA VANISHED. FEAR COURSED THROUGH Usagi as she ran after her sister through the forest, Tora hard on her heels.

"That girl," Tora panted. "Tell her she's got talent enough to be a Warrior and she loses all sense."

Usagi couldn't answer. Panic squeezed her throat. She heard angry shouts and the clang of metal. Whatever was happening in the rice fields, it didn't sound like something to be running *toward*. She stumbled over an exposed root, but Tora caught her. Hand in hand, they raced through the trees, moonlight splashing silver patches on the forest floor. Usagi followed the quick patter of her sister's feet, which led them to the edge of the forest overlooking the flat expanse of the fields. With the help of Tora's tiger vision, they found

Uma in the shadows, crouched behind a boulder. They knelt beside her, and before Usagi could start scolding, Uma pointed to the torchlit fields. "Look!"

Three figures, dressed all in black, were fighting with the Guard. Their faces were covered so that only their eyes could be seen, and they weren't wearing any armor. The Guard outnumbered them four-to-one, their curved swords gleaming as they surrounded the masked figures. Usagi stared, astonished. The masked ones didn't have swords—no one but the Dragonlord's men were permitted to carry weapons—but two were keeping their foes at bay with a wooden flail used for threshing and a pair of harvesting sickles. If they were field workers, they were either supremely foolhardy or incredibly brave.

The figure with the wooden flail whipped it about so the sentries couldn't find an opening to attack. One who tried was clipped in the face and jerked away with a yell. Another Guard thrust his sword at the figure with the harvesting sickles, who hooked the blade aside with one sickle and slashed at the Guard's arm with the other, forcing him to drop his sword, howling. The third figure threw something that flashed in the moonlight and made a tiny whistling sound. It struck a charging Guard, who stopped short and collapsed as if he'd run into a wall.

Usagi gasped. "What was that?" How were these masked men overcoming the Guard, with nothing but their simple tools? She felt like she was watching a dream tale come to life—the underdog heroes defeating a powerful enemy. The masked figure threw again. With a whistle and a thud, another Guard fell with a moan.

"Blades," Tora hissed. "They look like little metal stars—dipped in some sort of potion."

Uma pulled on Usagi's sleeve. "Over there—the Guards with firecannon are down." From the far end of the field, where the men lay, came the buzzing sound of snoring.

"A sleeping potion?" Usagi wondered.

A roar erupted from three Guards as they raised their swords and attacked the masked man holding the wooden thresher. The figure waited, still and silent. When the Guards were as close as a whisker, he ducked into a somersault, jumped up behind them, and swung the flail hard. Their helmets rang like a set of temple bells. Usagi clapped her hands over her ears.

"Nicely done," Tora murmured. The Guards swayed, then toppled like felled trees. Uma gave a delighted giggle. Usagi herself couldn't help but grin.

Transfixed, they watched as one by one the night watch was knocked out, the three masked figures moving almost in unison, ducking and blocking every attack with hard kicks and sudden blows. The number of assailing Guard shrank as the figures in black fought, until they were the only ones left standing.

"They did it!" Uma whispered excitedly.

"Every single Guard is down," Usagi marveled. It was incredible. She'd never seen anyone dare to challenge the Guard, let alone fight them and win. Who were these people?

The masked trio pulled out empty sacks big enough to fit a grown man and began stuffing them with bundles of rice.

"Bandits," Tora observed. "They're getting enough rice to feed a whole town."

Usagi let out a low whistle. "That could fetch a lot of shoes."

"Or gold," said Tora.

They watched the bandits strip the drying racks until the sound of marching feet caught Usagi's attention. "That firecannon shot must have alerted Guard headquarters," she muttered nervously. "They've sent reinforcements." A whole host of men appeared at the far end of the fields, flaming torches aloft. A loud crack sounded and a plume of dirt flew up near the bandits. "And they've brought more cannon!"

The new squadron poured onto the field. With silent efficiency, the figures in black hauled up their bags and came barreling in Usagi's direction.

"Run!" she shouted to the others. But before they could move from behind the boulder, the masked bandits swept right past them. Despite carrying bulging sacks of rice large as a Guard in full armor, the bandits ran at a dizzying speed.

A breeze left in their wake ruffled the fine hairs around Usagi's face. "Zodiac powers," she whispered.

As the black-clad figures melted away into the darkness, she heard one of them whoop, sounding like an excited boy. Another voice—a young woman's—floated back. *"Hush, Nezu! Not till we're out of the woods!"*

Usagi started. The bandits sounded like younglings— and at least one of those fighters was female. She craned to hear more, but her sister grabbed her arm.

"The Guard are getting close," Uma said, pointing at the approaching torches. Shouts and the thunder of pounding feet filled the air.

"Back to the grave mound," Tora ordered.

They hurried into the depths of the forest, retreating toward the safety of the turtleback hill. There, they hunkered by the rocks that hid their rice stash, holding themselves still and quiet while Guard units lumbered through the trees with torches aloft. For once, Usagi was thankful that the Guard had been angered, for their cursing and shouting made them easy to track. Several times a unit would draw close and Usagi would squeeze Uma's and Tora's hands to warn them. But as soon as the men neared the clearing and saw the dark rise of the grave mound, they would bellow and back away, too quickly to notice three younglings crouched in the shadows.

As the hour of the Rat approached, signaled by the moon

rising directly overhead, the Guard moved elsewhere and the sounds of patrols faded. At last they could make their way safely to the shack they'd built themselves in the forest. Not far from a small brook that meandered off the forest stream, where the outer reaches of Goldentusk melted into dense tree growth, they'd fashioned a lean-to of thatch and discarded bamboo poles against an exposed outcropping of rock. It was tall enough for Uma to stand in, and if Tora and Usagi, both a head taller, hunched over, they could at least stretch their legs. More importantly, it was just wide enough for the three of them to lie down, protected from the elements.

"Home sweet home," Tora murmured, lifting the thatch door.

A weary Usagi crawled inside after Tora and Uma. She tucked a threadbare blanket around her sister, who couldn't stop talking about what they'd seen.

"They must have been workers, with those tools," Uma guessed. "I never thought you could use them as weapons!"

"If the Dragonlord catches wind of that, he'll ban them too," said Usagi, yawning.

Tora scoffed. "Then everyone will have to pick rice with their bare hands. Ol' Blue Dragon won't have the patience."

"But did you see how they fought?" Uma sounded awed.

Usagi rubbed her eyes. "I don't think they were ordinary workers. You saw how fast they ran with those enormous sacks of rice. And I heard their voices. They're younglings with zodiac powers, just like us."

"No younglings could fight the Guard the way they did." Tora tossed and turned on the hard-packed earth. "Those bandits took so much rice, they might as well have taken all of it," she grumbled. "Thank the gods we got there before they did."

Usagi's heavy eyelids cracked open. "And got the extra bundle." She propped herself up on an elbow. "Uma, we might be able to get you a coat for the winter!"

Her sister made a noise halfway between a happy squeal and a sleepy sigh. "I want new shoes," she murmured.

Curling herself around her sister's small form, Usagi gave Uma a squeeze. "Then that's what you'll get," she promised. As she drifted off to sleep alongside the others, Usagi touched the carved wooden rabbit at her neck and smiled.

Several days later, Tora retrieved their rice from its hiding place and threshed the heads off the stalks with an old flail she'd salvaged long ago from a garbage pile. She twirled it experimentally over her head, nearly clipping her own ear. "If I used this like those bandits, think I'd stand a chance against the Guard?"

"At least one of them," said Uma loyally. "Maybe two."

Tora gave a mock snarl and bared her teeth. Two of them had grown in rather crookedly, looking almost like fangs.

She called them her tiger teeth.

Usagi grinned back. After the invaders had "cleansed" Goldentusk of those with zodiac powers, more than a dozen orphaned younglings had taken refuge in the forest, their homes looted and razed, and the three of them had been among the youngest. Though Tora was just eight at the time, she was fierce and skilled with catching small game in a way that made even the older ones include her in their hunting runs. Her ability to sneak about quietly was like no one else's. Helped by Usagi's increasingly keen hearing, it was why, after so many others had been caught, they'd managed to stay free.

Pouring the threshed grains into small bags, Usagi tied some to their legs, hiding them beneath their skirts. She stuffed them in their pockets and beneath their wide belts, thickening their middles.

"Look, I'm a juggler!" Uma threw several bags into the air at once, trying to catch them as they fell. One tumbled to the ground and burst open, spilling golden heads of rice.

"Uma! Those aren't toys," Usagi snapped. "This isn't a game!" She took a deep breath to calm herself. There was no pinning down a girl of the Horse year. But one of these days her sister would get all of them in trouble. "Clean that up now."

Uma bent down and quietly picked up every last grain, her lower lip pushed out as far as it would go. Tora put an arm around her. "Come on, Fire Horse. Let's see what we can do about getting you some new shoes."

They emerged from the forest, waddling somewhat under the bulk of the stolen goods, into the town of Goldentusk. It was still the seat of Stone River Province, long famed for its rice even before the Dragonlord introduced faster-growing plants from the Empire of Hulagu. But the formerly fine buildings that lined Goldentusk's streets were in various states of ruin and disrepair, some abandoned with shredded paper in the windows, others taken over by Guard officers, who liked to practice their shooting on the ornamental figures that graced the roofs.

Nearing the town center, Usagi spotted the high, peaked rooftop of the former School of the Twelve and grimaced. It was headquarters for the Guard now. Hacked stumps and ugly gashes remained where the carved figures of the Twelve once stood. Someone had painted over the stumps with blackened pitch, but the roof was horribly disfigured. It made Usagi want to cry every time she saw it. Her father would be devastated by the destruction of his handiwork, her mother aghast at the occupation of invaders who'd razed the attached shrine to the ground. Usagi's stomach twisted and she slowed to a stop.

"What're you staring at, lass?" A Guard's hissing Hulagan accent startled her. He was leaning against the nearby wall of the Tusk & Bristle. The old inn had become a pub frequented by Guards. Now the townsfolk secretly called it the Squealing Pig. The Guard before Usagi rather looked like one, with a broad, flat face and beady eyes. His metal helmet was cradled in his arms, which were covered with thick leather sleeves, and his iron breastplate barely covered his enormous belly. Usagi glanced nervously at the curved sword he wore and said nothing. He pushed off the wall with a grunt, picking at teeth stained bloodred with the juice of chew-nut. Usagi tried not to wrinkle her nose at the reek of stale garlic and rice wine as he got closer. "What's the matter? Your head nothing but an empty dumpling skin? Ghost got your tongue?"

"Something like that, sir," Tora said quickly. "She was . . . born mute—just like old King Ogana."

May his spirit rest. Usagi bit her lip to keep from blurting it.

The Guard spat. "Backward islanders. How you allowed a man who wasn't even whole to be king is beyond me. Lucky the Dragonlord's in charge now. He got rid of that useless king and his demon warriors, started trade with the twin empires—and look how well off this little island is now!"

Usagi and Tora nodded uncertainly. Uma piped up, "Yes sir. More rice in the fields than ever!"

"That there is," said the Guard. He peered at the three of them with his piggy eyes. "We should put the three of you to work out there, ragged as you are. You look able-bodied enough. Even you, mute girl." Usagi squirmed and looked down at her feet. Piggy Eyes laughed until his face was as red as his teeth. "The looks on your faces!" He coughed and waved a lazy arm. "Get out of my sight before I take you to the next work detail."

Without a word, they hurried away, the Guard still laughing at them. Uma slipped her hand into Usagi's and squeezed. Usagi squeezed back gratefully. She smoothed her belt, heavy with rice, her heart pounding so hard she could hear nothing else.

"Come on," muttered Tora. "Let's go see Aunt Bobo."

It was late afternoon, well into the hour of the Monkey. Many were still in the fields or preparing harvested crops for transport. But there was one person who didn't work the fields, and always purchased whatever they brought her. Everyone called her Aunt Bobo, a midwife who lived with her young son in the workers' quarter, where she dispensed herbs and salves for people's pains and ailments.

The cramped quarter had been hastily built after the war, after many of the people who'd farmed on their own in the province had been herded into Goldentusk, along with those whose villages had been destroyed. They lived in rows of modest homes raised on stilts, known as "floating houses." Chickens pecked in the dirt beneath them, while goats tied to the houses' stilts stood impassively chewing. Communal pig sties, built of sturdy scraps of marble and granite from

Midagian quarries, were filled with pungent droves of hairy pigs rooting in the mud.

As they passed one, Usagi spotted a chunk of sugarcane that had missed the pigs' trough, lying in the dirt just outside the sty. Sugarcane was even harder to come by than rice. It was half dried out and covered in ants, but what a treat it would make! She picked it up and quickly brushed it off before squeezing it into her already full pocket, then hurried to catch up with Tora and Uma, who'd slipped through the door of Aunt Bobo's floating house.

Inside the one-room hut, drying herbs that hung from the slatted bamboo walls chased away the pig sty smell seeping through the quarter. Aunt Bobo had them sit on cushions nearly as round as she, and poured them cups of watery green tea. "It's been a while since you three came by," she said with a gentle smile. She tucked a loose lock of silver-streaked hair into her careless bun. "I hope you've brought some good additions to my bitterroot stock. I've been running low."

They'd first met Aunt Bobo right after the war, when she was in the forest hunting for herbs and fungi to replenish her store of medicines. She'd just arrived in Goldentusk with her baby, and was thinner then, with a haunted look in her eyes. Usagi still remembered how startled she'd been upon coming across a pack of younglings in the forest, and yet she never screamed or alerted the Guard. Instead, she left little gifts of food, and invited them to collect plants for her. As people in town flocked to her for remedies and help with birthing, she received plenty in barter that she then would trade with the younglings from the forest. If it weren't for Aunt Bobo, they'd have been barefoot and stark naked long ago.

Now her son, Jago, was six, wiry and browned with jet-black hair that stuck straight up from his crown like so many feathers, and bursting to tell the latest news.

"My bottom tooth is loose!" he exclaimed, showing them. He bounced up and down. "And everyone's got rice! There was a bag of rice at every door this morning!"

"Every door?" asked a disbelieving Tora. "That can't be."

"How big a bag?" Uma asked.

"But . . . *we* brought rice," Usagi said, dismayed.

The laugh lines around Aunt Bobo's mouth deepened. "It's true, there was rice left outside every home in town—enough to feed a household for a month if stretched with millet and beans. I've not seen such generosity since the days of King Ogana, may his spirit rest." She showed them the burlap sack, which was the size of a roasted chicken.

"Where did it come from?" Uma's eyes were round.

Jago danced about, kicking up his bare feet. "No one knows! It showed up in the middle of the night! We had to bring it in before the Guard saw it!"

Usagi thought of the masked bandits, and the bulging

sacks of rice they'd carried off. Could it possibly have come from them? But what sort of thieves would just give away their loot? She showed Aunt Bobo the rice they'd collected. "We were hoping you'd be able to take this in trade."

Shaking her head regretfully, Aunt Bobo weighed the rice in one hand. "With everyone in town suddenly flush with rice, I won't be able to give you as much as usual. But I'll take it if it's all you have."

Disappointed, Usagi nodded, but Tora put a hand on her arm. "Maybe we'll hold on to it for a while. When rice gets scarce again, we can get more for it."

"Spoken like a shrewd merchant," Aunt Bobo laughed. "That's why I like dealing with you three." She offered them some roasted seeds rolled in honey, which Uma devoured in two bites before going off to play with Jago. Tora ate hers delicately and licked her fingers, while Usagi couldn't help stuffing as many sticky clusters in her cheeks as they would hold. As she tried to chew through them, Aunt Bobo asked how her sister's fire gift was developing.

"Word is that Strikers captured another youngling last week in River Bend," Aunt Bobo told Tora and Usagi. "A youngling of the Snake year. Apparently the Dragonlord wants them brought directly to him now. You girls had better be careful out there. I don't know that Jago has any zodiac powers, but he's starting to lose his first teeth. Until his voice changes and I know he's safe, I'm keeping a close eye on him."

"Did anyone in the family have talents?" asked Usagi through a mouthful of seeds.

Aunt Bobo paused and glanced at Jago, who was showing Uma his rock collection. "His father didn't. And I certainly don't. But there were relatives who were gifted. So we'll see—you can't help how you're born."

A far-off quavering note, like that from a flute somewhere in the distance, caught Usagi's attention and she turned her head. It was a beautiful sound rarely heard these days. It seemed to be coming from the Ring Road, the great big thoroughfare that circled the entire island. More notes followed, jaunty and inviting, over the snap of a drumskin. "Music!" she exclaimed. She sat stock-still, listening greedily.

Aunt Bobo frowned. "I don't hear . . ." Then the twin grooves between her brows softened. "Ah, your gift."

"Animal talent," Usagi corrected. "I wish you could hear this! Traveling entertainers must be coming!" She bobbed her head a little, in time with the distant melody.

"Oh please, can we go see?" Uma asked. Her cheeks flushed with excitement as she and Jago abandoned his rock collection to lean out the window, trying to hear what her sister was hearing.

"It's a wonder the Blue Dragon lets them keep performing," Aunt Bobo said dryly. "They're lucky they haven't been shipped off to the mines like everyone else."

Uma threw open the door. "It can't hurt to go have a listen. The Guard won't send people to the mines for that."

Usagi grabbed her sister's arm. "But they will if they see our abilities. You have to remember, you can't do anything out of the ordinary in front of the Guard."

"You act as if I'm the only one with powers." Uma rolled her eyes. "What about you?"

"I know better than to leap in front of anyone," Usagi said sternly. "And it's not like people can tell if I'm eavesdropping."

"It's so unfair." Uma sighed, then pointed at Tora. "You never say anything about Tiger Girl sneaking around in the dark."

Tora raised an eyebrow. "That's because no one'll ever see me coming. Your sister's right. You can't be careless. No running, no fires."

"Enough talk!" Jago pushed past them all. "Let's go find the music!"

CHAPTER 3

THE FLYING BOY

THE MUSIC WAS LOUDER NOW, clearly heard by all, the drum like an insistent heartbeat, while the flute sang an invitation to the town center. Usagi hurried with Tora and Aunt Bobo from the workers' quarter toward the music, chasing after her sister and Jago. The little boy could barely contain himself. "Do you think there'll be puppeteers? Or maybe jugglers?"

"I hope so! It could be the tumbling acrobats from last time," Uma speculated. "Remember the pyramid they made?"

"Even a few songs would be a lovely treat." Aunt Bobo sighed. It was true—entertainment troupes appeared but once or twice a year nowadays, when before the war they'd come through at least once a month. Usagi guessed it was because there were fewer of them now. Plenty of entertainers had had animal talents and elemental gifts that allowed them to do things like spit fire in elaborate shapes, lift an ox over their heads, and conjure items out of thin air. They'd brought such joy—it hurt to think of them wiped out by the invaders. At least the surviving entertainers still traveled around the island, though their shows weren't nearly as spectacular as the ones of old.

A crowd was gathering in the marketplace, where a life-sized bronze statue of the Dragonlord presided. Depicting a grim-faced man in an elaborate helmet and scaled armor, the sculpture had weathered to a dull shade of blue green, including the bronze plaque on the stone base proclaiming the Dragonlord's greatness. Usagi didn't know which stories were actually true and what was exaggerated, but many whispered that the Dragonlord had powers of his own, allowing him to become larger than the sun or so small that he was invisible. Some said he could summon wind and rain with a wave of his hand—that he was so powerful that looking at him in the eye would strike you dead. A few even insisted that an actual dragon was at his command up on Mount Jade, Midaga's highest peak, and that was how he destroyed the Twelve.

The stone base still showed marks where an older statue once stood, celebrating the very first Warrior of the Zodiac from the province, Bulugan the Boar Warrior. Old Bulugan had been there forever—a symbol of the Warriors' protection. Usagi remembered climbing on him and rubbing his boar's head helmet when she was very young.

Too young to imagine that Old Bulugan wouldn't be there forever.

Now a trio of traveling entertainers stood before the new statue. In contrast to the townspeople in their drab dun and faded indigo clothing, they wore crisp whites with brightly patterned belts and jackets that signaled their occupation. One was a lanky boy who couldn't have been more than fifteen, carrying a large pack on his back. His hair was cropped so closely you could see his scalp, and there was a shadow of dark fuzz on his upper lip where he had just begun to grow a few sparse whiskers. When he turned and shrugged off his pack, Usagi saw that he had a long rat-tail braid running from the base of his skull down his back. He pulled some sections of thick bamboo from his pack, fitting them together with metal joins till they formed a long pole.

The flute player was a boy who looked just a couple of years older, with an overabundance of shaggy dark hair that flopped low over his forehead and hid his eyes. Though he had a rather melancholy air, the music he played was lilting and jaunty. Already some younglings in the crowd were dancing along, Jago and Uma among them.

A young woman with a pale, inquisitive face and alert brown eyes stood between the rat-tailed boy and the flute player, carrying a double-headed drum. Her hair was the color of chestnuts, tied tightly in a high topknot wrapped with ribbon that matched her multicolored belt. She tapped a steady beat on the drum, watching the crowd grow larger. Many were chatting excitedly, cheered at the prospect of a show.

A few Guards placed lit torches around the marketplace, while others stood around the perimeter. Some came out of the nearby headquarters to stand on the steps, craning their necks to see. Even they liked a bit of music, it seemed. A phalanx of field workers returned along with their Guard escorts, and instead of dispersing, everyone milled about the town center, waiting to see what the troupe would do.

"A snakebox!" Tora exclaimed. Sure enough, the boy with the rat-tail braid had pulled out a boxy lute, made of snakeskin and bamboo, with a carved wooden snakehead at the end of the neck. Strumming its three strings experimentally, he frowned and tightened them. He strummed again, and Usagi could hear the notes fall into place. The boy's face lit up with a flashing grin, and he nodded at the young woman and the shaggy-haired flute player. The music stopped and the crowd quieted.

"Greetings, Goldentusk!" the entertainers shouted. The young woman stepped forward and bowed. "Thank you for indulging us with your attention this fine summer evening. We hope to make it worth your while." As she gestured to an empty basket on the ground and invited the crowd to contribute what they desired, Usagi cocked her head. Her voice sounded familiar. But before Usagi could place it, the show began.

First, the two boys took the long bamboo pole and set it on their shoulders. The young woman swung onto the pole and slowly got to her feet. Then she began to walk back and forth on the narrow pole, displaying her balance. Without warning, the boys threw the pole up and the young woman shot high into the air to gasps from the crowd. She executed the splits before landing nimbly back onto the pole, which the boys brought back onto their shoulders to sighs of appreciation. During a series of flips and tumbles, Usagi squinted at the girl's movement. Had she seen this performance before? The boys began walking in a circle, the pole like a spoke in a wheel, while the young woman continued to do acrobatic tricks across the moving pole. When she finally somersaulted off the pole and landed neatly on her feet, the crowd cheered.

After the entertainers set the pole aside, they put on brightly painted masks of wood pulp. "And now, a story," said the young woman, sounding slightly muffled behind the face of a surprised-looking red monkey.

"A thousand years ago, there lived on the island of Midaga twelve different tribes, each with a claim to the tallest mountain at its heart, Mount Jade. Each tribe worshipped the mountain, and the goddess that was said to live within it.

"'The goddess has blessed our tribe,' declared one,

'because we have among us members who can swim like fish.'" At that, the boy with the shaved head pretended to swim, his face hidden behind the mask of a grinning green rat. The audience laughed and the young woman continued.

"'No, the goddess blesses *our* tribe,' insisted another, 'for some of our members can run like the wind.'" The shaggy-haired boy made whooshing noises behind his yellow dog mask, which was decorated with purple spots. He ran in circles around the rat-masked boy, who went on making swimming motions.

"The tribes warred for many years," said the young woman, "pitting their strongest and bravest against each other. Every tribe was convinced of the rightness of their cause, and sent those who had special talents and gifts into battle."

At the mention of talents and gifts, Usagi stiffened, and heard a few sharp intakes of breath around the marketplace. The crowd around her shifted uneasily. To openly mention such things in front of the Guard! Had the young woman lost her mind? The grinning rat and the spotted dog pretended to fight, their hands clenched in fists, and as they bobbed and feinted, Usagi realized who the three of them were.

"Those are the bandits," she whispered to Tora.

Tora's amber eyes widened, then she quickly frowned. "There's three of them, and I suppose they're around the same size—but what makes you so sure?"

"I heard their voices, remember? And look at the way they move—who else could it be?" But the two boys in their animal masks began weaving and throwing clumsy punches, looking like a couple of Guards who'd had too much to drink at the Squealing Pig. Their audience guffawed.

Tora shook her head. "I don't see it."

"Eventually," said the red monkey, "one of the wisest warriors realized that tearing each other apart was doing nothing but weakening them all. With his great talent for persuasion, he unified the warriors of the other tribes, and together they lay down their arms and refused to fight. They established a treaty among the twelve tribes, and agreed that Mount Jade belonged to no one—that in fact, they all belonged to the mountain. Each tribe sent their best warrior to represent them in a council, and for many centuries after that, this council of Twelve kept the peace in Midaga."

As the green rat and purple-spotted dog bowed to each other and patted each other heartily on the back, murmurs went up from the crowd. Several Guards began to make their way toward the three masked ones. Usagi felt a stab of alarm.

"If those entertainers go any further with this story they're going to get themselves arrested!" Aunt Bobo said worriedly. She looked about. "Where's Jago and Uma?"

"Up in front," said Tora, pointing. They were standing

with a few other small younglings, in hysterics at the antics of the green rat, who had swept the dog up in his arms and was dancing around. Usagi tensed. Should she wiggle through the crowd and fetch them?

The red monkey held up a hand. "Of course, this is only an old fable, as our supreme leader the Dragonlord might tell you." She turned to the bronze statue behind her and dipped in a little bow, and the rat and dog did the same. The approaching Guards exchanged glances and stopped. Usagi held her breath. The young woman removed her mask and smiled. "But even old fables need not be forgotten, for every story has something to teach us." The Guards scowled, but stayed where they were. Usagi started to breathe again.

The young woman took up the drum and started a solid beat, while the boy with the rat mask pulled it up over his shaved head like a hat. He grabbed the snakebox lute and plucked at its three strings in an insistent rhythm. The shaggy-haired boy left his dog mask on and played the first few notes of an old Midagian folk song on his flute. Cries of approval went up around the marketplace.

"'The Welcome Song.'" Aunt Bobo sighed. It was a song traditionally sung to visitors, inviting them to the table for food and drink. It could get very merry, as there were two parts for men and women, and they would sing at each other in boisterous rounds.

Singing in high, clear voices, the young woman and

the boy with the snakebox smiled as others lustily joined in. Before long people were singing in a call-and-response, their voices ringing through the town center, while glowering Guards rocked on their feet, arms crossed. Most of them were either Hulagan or from the other neighboring empire of Waya, so the song wasn't part of their tradition. Aunt Bobo linked arms with Usagi and Tora, and they sang at the top of their lungs, while people around them began to dance, stomping their feet on the hard-packed earth. The warm evening air vibrated with raised voices and the beloved old tune, and Usagi felt every note, more joyful than she'd been in a long time.

A scream cut through the music and the singing quickly died. Usagi and Tora looked around uneasily in the silence. "What happened?" Aunt Bobo asked.

Gasps went up from the crowd. "Spirits save us, look!" Tora said.

In front of everyone, Jago was rising into the air, floating steadily higher. Eyes wide, he flapped his arms frantically as if he were trying to grab on to something, but it only made him move higher still. "Mama!" he cried. "Something's happening to me!"

"Jago," Aunt Bobo breathed, the color draining from her round cheeks. She tried to get to him, but Jago had already risen high above their heads and was hovering by the rooftops. Screams and shouts echoed through the town center.

Tora grabbed Usagi. "His zodiac power. We better get out of here before the Guard start sweeping every youngling up."

"No, wait. I don't see Uma." Usagi frantically scoured the crowd, trying to find her sister in the chaos. Guards were running and shoving people out of their path, their eyes on Jago as he hugged the tiled roof of an old assembly hall.

"Stop right there, you demon freakling!" bellowed one.

"Grab me a ladder!" yelled another.

"Get the commander!" brayed a third.

Panicked, Jago lifted off again, swerving through the air until he landed on a different building. A dozen Guards swarmed at its base, shouting. The entertainment troupe had quietly packed up and disappeared, while parents were snatching up their younglings and hurrying them from the marketplace, as if what was happening to Jago was somehow contagious. Other townspeople, enjoying the show, called out unhelpful advice. "Fly higher! Fly away! See if you can spit on the Guard from here!"

Jago flew to yet another building while Aunt Bobo screamed at him to calm himself. But it was too late, for Usagi could hear him sobbing hysterically. Then she heard a familiar voice through the chaos.

"Don't be scared, Jago!" Uma shouted. "It's just your animal talent!" In the midst of the agitated crowd, she stood unruffled, looking up at Jago with her hands cupped around her mouth. "Jago, think of the Twelve! Don't you see? You've got rooster flight!"

Tora followed Usagi's horrified gaze. "What is she doing?" she hissed.

"Spit and spleen," Usagi swore. She started for her sister, pushing past the gawkers staring up at the rooftops, fear and anger coursing through her. Why oh why hadn't she kept Uma by her side? If Uma exposed herself as having powers, she was done for.

On the steps of the Guard headquarters emerged a tall man in armor, his breastplate and helmet streaked with silver lacquer. His nose looked as if it had been broken several times, and he had the heavy beard that many Wayani wore. He took one look at the scene and began issuing orders.

"Get the fly-nets!" he barked. "And you, send a messenger bird to the Striker outpost immediately!"

"Yes, Commander!"

Guards ran to get firecannon and load them with fly-nets. They could be shot from a good distance, and when one landed on its target, the fly-net would become stickier than a weeping pine. Jago would be trapped like a bug in amber.

"Jago!" Uma called. "It's all right! Look, watch me!" She began to rub her hands, preparing to create a flame.

"No!" Usagi tackled her sister, sending them both tumbling to the ground.

Uma kicked and struggled. "Let me go! What are you doing? I'm trying to help him! He doesn't understand!"

"You'll get yourself captured," Usagi said furiously. "We're getting out of here. Now! Before you make things worse!" She hauled her sister to her feet and dragged her away, ignoring her pleas, while half a dozen Guards positioned themselves around the marketplace, mounting firecannon to their shoulders. Jago flew frantically about, swooping from rooftop to rooftop, until finally he landed on the Guard headquarters itself.

"Fire!" roared the Guard commander.

CHAPTER 4

CAPTURED

THE EXPLOSIONS FELT LIKE A punch to Usagi's ears. She threw her hands over them, stumbling at the edge of the marketplace. Uma and Tora bent to help her. They hustled away from the chaos and didn't look back.

Usagi's heart squeezed. What would happen to Jago? Would the little boy be brought before the Dragonlord? Thrown in some horrible lockup? Put to work in the mines—or worse?

Tora led the way through the evening dark back to their forest hut. Dried pine needles underfoot enveloped them in a powdery perfume as they traipsed along a makeshift path through the trees. Midway there, Usagi realized something.

"We forgot our rice," she said. "It's still at Aunt Bobo's."

"She's lost her son. Let her have it," Tora replied softly.

Usagi stole an anxious glance at Uma, who lagged behind them, silent and brooding. It was unlike her to be so quiet. Feeling through her pockets, Usagi dug out the lump of sugarcane and offered it to her sister. "I found it outside the pig sties. It'll still be sweet when you chew it."

Uma swatted it away. "It's not fair!" she burst out. "Jago didn't even understand what was happening."

Tora sighed. "I know. He's even younger than you were when your talent first began to show. And I don't think Aunt Bobo prepared him for it."

Usagi thought of her father, and the last night she saw him. He'd told her to take care of her little sister, even given her something for safekeeping, but never prepared her for living in a world without him. How much had he known? If he thought he might die, why didn't he say so? Why wasn't *she* prepared?

At least her parents had always talked to her about her powers. Her mother, born in the year of the Horse just like Uma, liked to tell the story of how her own horse speed had appeared when she was five. "My big brother and I were on a walk, when he thought it'd be funny if he hid behind a tree. I thought your uncle had gone and left me behind, so I started running as fast as I could, trying to catch up with him. He said I disappeared in a blink. By the time he found me, I'd long since reached the seashore!"

And when Usagi began to hear things that others couldn't, like snatches of their neighbors' conversations and the cries of newly hatched chicks in nests clear across town, her father made a pair of ear mufflers out of sheep's wool, presenting them to her over a special feast her mother had cooked for the occasion. "Until you get used to hearing more," he'd said, beaming.

Now when your powers emerged you were taken away like poor Jago. Usagi had seen it happen so many times with the younglings who'd hid in the forest with them. One by one, they'd been caught using their talents, often because they were careless. Usagi dreaded the distinctive clack of the Dragonstrikers' black lacquered armor, which made them look and sound like giant roaches. She worried that one day the roaches would come for the three of them, hauling them off to gods knew where.

Entering their tiny shack, Usagi breathed a sigh of relief. For tonight, at least, they were still safe. "I wish we hadn't gone to see those entertainers," she said, feeling guilty.

"Still think they were the bandits?" Tora asked. "They ran off as soon as the Guard moved in."

Uma kicked the door panel shut, shaking the hut hard enough to rattle the thatch. "We should have done more to help Jago."

"Don't bring down the roof, Uma," Usagi chided.

Tora spoke over her. "Even if there was something to be done, it's too late, little one. By now the nearest Striker post has gotten the messenger bird that the Guard sent. They'll be in Goldentusk for him by morning."

Usagi tried comforting her sister. "Maybe it won't be so bad. If younglings are being brought straight to the Dragonlord, it means they're taking them to the capital. That's better than the mines, right?" She offered Uma the piece of sugarcane once more. "Here."

"I'm not hungry," Uma groused.

"Well, save it for later, then." Usagi pressed the sugarcane into Uma's hand. "Now try to sleep."

Uma sat pouting for a while, but eventually lay down. She continued to toss and turn, while Tora emitted a gentle snore. Wedged between them, Usagi stared into the darkness, thinking.

What did the Dragonlord want with these younglings? If he were half dragon, as some whispered, perhaps he would eat them for their talents. Maybe that was what the Strikers had been doing all along—bringing him younglings as snacks. Usagi clutched the tiny wooden rabbit at her neck and prayed that the three of them would never find out. As her little sister became still and her breathing at last grew even, Usagi found her own eyelids getting heavy, and her thoughts gave way to sleep.

∽

Soft rustling sounds roused Usagi from a fitful slumber. She drowsed, lying curled on her side, till birds in the forest began trilling their greetings for the day. Usagi cracked open an eye, squinting as pale fingers of morning light reached into the makeshift hut.

With a chilled shiver, Usagi rolled over, grimacing from the cricks and aches that came from sleeping on a packed dirt floor. She stared at the cold empty space beside her. Her sister was gone. Listening hard, a knot of worry formed in her stomach. She turned and shook Tora. "Wake up! Uma's not here."

"What?" Tora blinked at her, her voice thick with sleep.

"Uma's gone—I can't hear her anywhere in the forest."

"Boils and blisters," Tora groaned. "Are you sure?" Sighing heavily, she got up. Together they did a quick search around their corner of the woods, Tora peering through the shadows, Usagi scanning every sound for a sign of her sister, but she was nowhere nearby.

Tora frowned. "You think she went back to town? To help Jago?"

"She was so upset—she might have." The knot in Usagi's stomach tightened. "We've got to stop her before she gets caught herself."

They raced back to town in the gray dawn, hoping to find Uma before the morning patrols of the Guard began. As they scurried through the quiet streets, Usagi caught the

47

sounds of a boy crying.

"I hear Jago," she muttered to Tora. The crying grew louder as she led them to the town center where the main building of the Guard headquarters loomed. "He's somewhere in there."

"What are we going to do? We can't just march up the front steps," Tora said.

"Around back," Usagi whispered. They wound through back paths and byways until they were looking over a low, tree-lined wall into the dusty grounds of what had once been Goldentusk's School of the Twelve. Guard barracks had been built over the razed shrine that adjoined the school, and stables and outhouses sat on the former gardens and training fields. A steady stream of Guards, slipping on their helmets and adjusting their scabbards as they left, were setting off to escort the field workers and start early morning patrols of the town. Usagi tried not to gag at the fetid stink of horse manure mixed with stale rice wine and the fumes from the outhouses.

She spotted a row of cages by the stables, a good hundred paces away. Just large enough to hold a single prisoner, they were made of thick bamboo poles reinforced with iron bands, and were designed for transport. All were empty except one, in which Jago crouched miserably. A Guard stood watch, leaning against the trunk of an enormous old banyan tree that shaded the grounds. He hardly glanced at Jago, instead idly trimming stray hairs off his beard with a knife and examining them.

"Where's Uma?" Tora asked. "I don't see her anywhere."

"Maybe I was wrong," Usagi said, perplexed but relieved. "Maybe she didn't come here at all. Let me listen for her." She closed her eyes and cocked her head. Not far from them was a fidgety rustling and the familiar pattern of her sister's breathing. Usagi's heart sank. She led Tora along the low wall till they came to an unruly hedge. Her sister was half hidden in its foliage, peering over the wall into the grounds. "Uma!" Usagi whispered.

"So you decided to help," Uma said happily. She pointed to the bored Guard. "I don't know what that Guard ate, but he goes off to the outhouse every few minutes. I've been watching. When he wasn't looking, I snuck Jago the sugarcane you gave me. The cage is locked, of course, but if I used my fire gift, maybe I could soften the lock enough to break it open."

"You'll do nothing of the sort," Usagi told her. "You're not thinking this through. You don't have full control of your gift yet."

Tora nodded, exasperated. "Besides, it would take forever to melt a lock open."

"Well then, why don't you buy me some time? Distract

49

him for me?" Uma shot back.

"Because I don't want to be locked up with Jago and turned over to Dragonstrikers!" Tora's tiger teeth glinted as she grimaced.

Usagi stiffened. "I can hear the Strikers," she warned. The faintest clack and clatter of their armor sounded in the distance, signaling the approach of the Dragonlord's most elite fighters. She calculated quickly. "They'll be here in less than an hour. Come on, we need to go." She grasped her sister's arm and tried to help her out of the bushes.

Uma jerked away. "No!"

Frustrated, Usagi threw up her hands. "For the love of the Twelve, Uma, why are you doing this?"

"Why?" Her sister looked incredulous. "Because what if that were me?" she demanded. "Would you just shrug and turn your back? 'Oh well, nothing we can do, it's too late now.'" Her dark eyes filled with furious tears. "Would you?"

The words stung. "Of course not!" Usagi said. "I would never leave you."

"There's so few of us with talents left," Uma sniffled. "If we don't help him, who will?"

Helplessly, Usagi looked to Tora. But Tora was staring at something behind them.

"There's someone up in the tree," she muttered, narrowing her gaze.

"What?" Usagi turned to look. Perched high in the branches of the banyan tree was a masked figure dressed in black.

"Is that one of the bandits from the other night?" Tora scanned the grounds, frowning. "What are they doing here?"

The bearded Guard under the tree appeared not to notice the figure above him. He stuck the knife back in his belt and ambled toward the outhouses.

Uma brightened. "The Guard's walking away!" She vaulted over the wall and sprinted off. In an instant, she appeared next to Jago's cage. Scowling in concentration, she rubbed her hands. A blaze of fire sprang up and she cupped her hands around the lock.

"No! She'll be caught!" Usagi fretted. "I've got to go get her."

"There's not enough time to run," said Tora. "Use your rabbit leap."

But before Usagi could move, the Guard on duty turned back and spotted Uma.

"Oi! Some freakling is trying to free the prisoner!" He ran to a nearby bell and rang it frantically.

Usagi's mouth went dry and her breath stopped. If she didn't fetch Uma now, it would be too late. She launched into her rabbit leap, flinging herself into the air. She soared up, up, up—too high! Spitting spirits, she'd jumped too hard. Rising far above the banyan tree, Usagi thought she glimpsed two masked figures in black on the roof of the Guard headquarters.

A shout went up from the ground. Looking down, Usagi saw two slack-jawed Guards pointing at her. They dove out of the way as she hurtled straight toward them.

Crash! A stack of empty rice wine barrels broke her landing. "Gods, that hurt," Usagi moaned.

"Eat my foot, there's more than one of 'em!" exclaimed one of the slack-jawed Guards. His face was peppered with blemishes.

"A demon jumper!" said the other. He had an eye that turned away from his nose, as if it were looking for his ear.

They drew their curved swords and shuffled closer, approaching her cautiously. Usagi staggered to her feet, aching and bruised. Her leap had gone horribly. Across the grounds, she saw Uma, her hands ablaze, still working on the lock on Jago's cage. The bearded Guard who'd sounded the alarm drew his sword. Usagi screamed a warning at her sister just as Tora streaked from the wall and jumped onto the Guard's back.

At the sound of a grunt, Usagi looked back as Pimple Nose and Wall-Eye lunged at her. In the nick of time, she sprang over their heads. Clearing a short distance, she tumbled into a heap upon landing, just ten paces away. Usagi silently cursed herself. Her zodiac power was hardly helping.

She'd be better off running. Usagi scrambled up and looked about in a panic.

Guards streamed onto the grounds from all directions, responding to the alarm bell with urgent shouts. Tora was surrounded, but fought back with a ferocity Usagi had never seen before. The two snaggleteeth that had always looked like little fangs seemed to have grown suddenly, and when she swiped at an approaching Guard, she clawed right through his leather sleeves, leaving bleeding slashes. "I hope that leaves a nice scar," she hissed. Usagi's eyes widened.

"Come on now, freakling," said Pimple Nose, taking a few steps toward her. "We won't hurt you."

"Then why are you pointing your sword at me?" Usagi countered. Behind her was the crunching sound of dirt beneath tiptoeing boots. She ducked just as Wall-Eye rushed to grab her. He collided with Pimple Nose instead, while Usagi turned and ran. She sprinted as fast as she could toward the stables, with additional Guards giving chase. But where was Uma? Her sister had disappeared, though a terrified Jago still remained in his cage. Half a dozen bloodied Guards were in the midst of tying Tora up, even as she snapped her fangs at them.

The bearded Guard who'd sounded the alarm yelled at the Guards chasing Usagi. "The fire freakling's run off! Don't let that one get away!"

Usagi faltered to a stop. Uma had run away? Her mind

went blank and she looked at a still-struggling Tora. What should she do now?

Tora caught her staring, and her feral gaze grew steely. "Run, Usagi! Run!"

Like she'd been kicked in her backside, Usagi jolted forward. She could barely feel her limbs, and her racing heart was all she could hear. With a desperate heave, Usagi tried leaping one more time, springing as hard as her legs would let her. Staring blindly into the heavens, she soared up as the sun crawled higher above the horizon, up over the Guard headquarters, up past the blackened stumps on the roof. No masked bandits crouched there—she must've imagined them. The statue of the Dragonlord in the town center caught her eye, and she began falling toward it. Usagi braced herself as she plummeted, praying that she wouldn't collide with the bronze figure. She hit the ground with another bone-rattling jolt, rolling several times before coming to a stop.

Groaning, Usagi raised her head. A few townspeople in the marketplace had stopped to stare, but averted their gaze and hurried away. Most of the Guards in town had run back to headquarters at the alarm, but it wouldn't be long before they'd be out in the streets looking for her. She had to get moving. Usagi pushed herself to get up. Her whole body felt heavy and slow, aching from her terrible landings. The distant clacking of the Strikers' armor had gotten louder. They would be in town soon, and between them and the Guard, she'd have no chance. She needed a miracle to save her now.

Then she remembered. With shaking hands, she pulled out the tattered silk square she kept tucked in her belt and unfolded it to reveal the carved wooden comb her father had given her.

It's full of great magic from Mount Jade. Don't drop it, for that will unleash its powers, her father had said. Holding her breath, Usagi dropped the comb.

CHAPTER 5

THE WARRIOR HEIRS

THE WOODEN COMB HIT THE dirt and stuck there, quivering, its finely carved teeth biting into the earth. The ground beneath Usagi rumbled and shook. Sprouting all around her, trees pushed their way up through the hard-packed soil of the old marketplace, their leafy branches blotting out the morning sun. The buildings around the town center disappeared from sight, leaving Usagi and the statue of the Dragonlord in a dense thicket.

"Spirits," Usagi gasped. The comb had magic, all right. She gulped for air, trying to catch her breath. The roar of blood rushing through her ears subsided as her pounding heart slowed. Cautiously, she got to her feet. She was surrounded by tall trees as far as she could see. She reached out and touched the rough trunk of a boxwood, its snarled branches covered in glossy green leaves. All this from a little comb? To think she'd been carrying a forest in her pocket.

She rubbed the wooden rabbit charm at her neck and listened. The steady clacking of the Dragonstrikers' armor was growing louder as they marched toward Goldentusk. While the copse of trees had quieted, there was commotion outside it, with exclamations from townspeople and Guard alike.

"Earthquake! A small one, but I felt it!"

"Where did all these trees come from?"

"It's from that demon jumper—the one that cleared the building like a human cricket!"

"Commander got word back from the Dragonstrikers. They'll be here before the hour of the Snake. Says if we can't get this youngling or the one with fire, then they will."

Usagi's stomach twisted. Tora had told her to run—not attract the notice of everyone in town. She bit her lip and tried to stay calm. There had to be a way out of this. At least her sister was still free. Usagi thanked the gods for Uma's horse speed. Surely she'd outrun the Strikers.

Her ears pricked at the sound of rustling and angry voices, and she turned to see movement through the tangle of trees. The Guard were coming. Alarmed, she moved in the opposite direction, and bumped into a masked figure dressed in black, who grabbed her. Usagi screamed.

"Hush!" whispered the figure in black. "I'm not here to hurt you." Usagi recognized the voice and stopped struggling. She stared at the alert brown eyes peeking over the face mask. It was the young woman from the entertainment troupe.

"You were in the rice fields!" Usagi breathed. "I knew it!"

The young woman's eyes twinkled. "Now how would you know about something like that?" She pulled down the mask and smiled. "We haven't much time, but I think we can help you. Do you trust me?"

"Did you leave rice for everyone here in town?"

The young entertainer's eyebrows shot up. "Why yes, we did. But how—"

"Then I trust you. You're better than the Blue Dragon's men," Usagi interrupted. Time was short. The Guard were hacking their way through the copse of trees with their swords, and she could clearly hear the clattering armor of Strikers approaching.

The young woman looked relieved. "Good." She pulled the mask back up. Her eyes darted about the ground. "Where did you plant the comb?"

"You—you know about that?" Surprised, Usagi pointed. "It's over there."

The bandit took Usagi by the hand and brought her to the bronze Dragonlord, the comb stuck in the ground before it. A shaft of sunlight illuminated its carved spine with the twelve zodiac animals. "Listen carefully. I'm going to pull this comb from the ground, and the moment I do, we'll be exposed. There's Guard all around the marketplace now, so the only way out is up. I'll have to carry you." She put Usagi's arms around her neck, draping Usagi across her back. "I want you to hang on to me like this, whatever happens. Can you do that?"

"Y-yes," Usagi stammered. "But don't lose the comb. My father gave it to me."

"Believe me, I won't," promised the bandit. "Ready?" She reached down and with a swift flick, tugged the comb out of the earth. The trees around them vanished, sliding into the ground even faster than they sprouted. For an instant, Usagi saw the Guards who'd been trying to find her, their swords slashing at nothing as the branches before them disappeared. A flash of bright light flitted across the Guards' faces, making them squint and cover their eyes. Then a bang sounded, and the town center rapidly filled with acrid, choking smoke. The Guards coughed and shouted in the confusion, unable to see.

"Hold on!" The young woman lunged toward a nearby building and nimbly climbed up its side, while Usagi tightened her grip. Before she could even blink, they were on the tiled roof. Below them, a series of small explosions went off in the swirling smoke, sounding like firecrackers or cannonshot. The young woman leaped to another rooftop, then another, Usagi clinging to her back like a baby monkey. As they traversed across town on rooftops of thatch and tile and bark, Usagi caught snatches of astonished cries from the streets below.

"What was that?"

"That was no bird!"

"Has Aunt Bobo's little flying boy escaped?"

Reaching a building on the outskirts of town, the bandit stopped and let Usagi off her back. She motioned to stay low, pointing to the Ring Road.

Usagi flattened herself on the rooftop tiles. From their vantage point, she could see the wide ribbon of highway leading into Goldentusk. Broad enough to allow six horses to ride abreast, the Ring Road wound all around Midaga, linking the island's towns and villages to the capital. In a show of each region's wealth, parts were paved with marble, smooth river stones, fired clay tiles, metal plates, or timber. In Stone River Province, the rich dark soil had been display enough, and had been beaten till it was packed hard and smooth.

Now in rows five deep came a squadron of Dragonstrikers clad in shiny black plates of lacquered leather that clicked and clacked with every movement. The roaches marched in precise lockstep, looking straight past the low brims of their horned helmets, carrying long spears or firecannon in addition to their swords. In their midst rolled a horse-drawn cart for transporting Jago's cage to the capital. As it went by, Usagi cried out.

Uma lay in the back of the cart, curled on her side with her hands and feet tightly bound. She appeared fast asleep, but Usagi had seen Strikers use dreamfumes to knock out the younglings they'd taken away in the past. It kept them from struggling and using their zodiac powers to escape.

The bandit clapped a hand over Usagi's mouth. "Quiet! Do you want them to find us?"

Usagi pointed with a shaking finger, and pushed the young woman's hand aside. "They've got my sister!"

"Keep your voice down," ordered the young woman. Eyes narrowed, she stared after the cart. "Your sister—she's got a fire gift, no? Along with animal talent?"

"Horse speed," whispered Usagi.

"Right," the bandit replied. "Unfortunately, when she showed up, she put sand in the rice pot for us. We were going to try to get that little flying boy out."

"I saw you in the tree at Guard headquarters!" Usagi felt a spark of hope. "Isn't there anything we can do now?"

"Against Strikers?" The young woman shook her head. "We'll be lucky if we can get out of here without attracting their notice."

Usagi helplessly watched her sister and the cart proceed farther into the town. She moved to spring off the roof, but a wiry arm yanked her back.

"Do you want to join her as their prisoner?" asked the bandit, not unkindly. "Look, I know how you feel. But you don't know what you're up against. You'll have a better chance of helping your sister and your friends if you stay free."

The clack and clatter of the Dragonstrikers and the horse-drawn cart receded as the procession turned a corner. Usagi blinked back tears. "How?"

"First we need to get out of here." The young woman helped Usagi up. "Hop on," she instructed. After a moment's hesitation, Usagi wrapped her arms around the bandit's neck. They swung off the edge of the roof and the young woman climbed them down to the ground. They were met by two other masked figures in black. "Nice work with the smoke screen and decoy firecannon back there," the bandit told them.

"The smell of the smoke nearly knocked me out," muttered one. A shaggy lock of hair poked out from beneath his hood. "But there's a bigger problem. We saw them capture that youngling in the cart. One of the Strikers had horse speed of his own—ran her down in no time."

"What?" said the young woman in disbelief. "The Dragonstrikers have zodiac powers now?"

"I wouldn't have believed it if I didn't see it," said the other bandit. His voice cracked in a squeak, as if it had newly deepened.

"A Striker with animal talent is a disturbing new development," added the bandit with the stray lock of hair.

"Could that be what the Blue Dragon is doing?" the young woman asked, half to herself. "Recruiting his own prisoners?"

"I heard he eats younglings with powers—and his Strikers torture the younglings they take," Usagi interjected, feeling frantic. "That's my sister they have in that cart!"

"I'm sorry about your sister," said the bandit with the squeaky voice. "If it makes you feel any better, I don't think he actually eats them. But the stories about torture . . ." Trailing off, he looked away.

The young woman shook her head. "Let's get into safer cover before we say anything else."

With dread in her chest, Usagi followed the three black-clad figures as they stole away from the town, crossing the Ring Road and diving deep into the forest. She was unfamiliar with this part of the wilderness, untouched by farming and filled with old growth. Usagi stumbled a few times as she tried to keep up with them, her mind racing as fast as the bandits. If Uma was caught by a Striker with zodiac powers—what did that mean? Was the Dragonlord turning prisoners with powers against their own kind?

Finally, they reached a small clearing where a camp had been set up. It was the hour of the Horse and the sun was straight overhead, but only a few stray beams of light reached through the thick canopy. A ring of stones surrounded the charred remains of a campfire, and several traveling packs were tucked behind the fat trunk of an enormous old camphor tree. Usagi saw three wood pulp masks—of a red monkey, green rat, and a spotted yellow dog—hanging from one of its branches.

The young woman pulled off her hood and tucked a few stray chestnut strands back into her topknot. "My name is Saru," she said. A smile lit up her pale face as she gave Usagi a formal bow of greeting. "Born in the year of the Earth Monkey."

Usagi bowed back awkwardly. "I'm Usagi. Year of the Wood Rabbit."

"Ah, rabbit talents!" The squeaky-voiced bandit pulled down his cloth mask and flashed a grin, his teeth gleaming white against his tanned skin. "Good to meet you, Usagi. I'm Nezu, and I was born in the year of the Water Rat."

The bandit with the stray lock of hair took off his hood and ruffled his shaggy mop till his dark eyes were nearly hidden again. "Inu," he said gruffly. "Dog year, ruled by the metal element."

Usagi glanced at the colorful masks that the bandits had worn the previous night when they were performing, then scowled at the three of them. "You're thieves. Thieves pretending to be entertainers so you can travel around and steal."

"That's a serious charge," said Inu, his dark eyes flashing with indignation. "Where would you get such an idea?"

She pointed at the black hood in his hand. "I saw you earlier this week. The three of you were dressed just as you are now, and you got away with quite a lot of rice. And then your fake show got a little boy in trouble, and now my sister and best friend are prisoners too!" said Usagi, getting louder.

"Fake!" said Nezu. His voice cracked in surprise. "We worked hard on those routines. Without using our zodiac powers, I'll have you know."

Saru put a calming hand on the boy's shoulder. "Look, I told you, we felt bad about the little boy, and we were going to try to free him. But when your sister triggered an alarm and all the other Guards showed up, it became too risky."

"Too risky? The three of you knocked out more than a dozen Guard on the fields the other night," Usagi protested.

"That was a good fight," agreed Nezu, grinning again. He removed his hood and pulled out the thin, long rat-tail braid stuck under his collar. "But we had the element of surprise and the cover of darkness to help us. And regular Guards aren't half as fierce as Strikers." He smoothed the fuzz above his lip, becoming serious. "If the odds aren't in your favor, you pull back—otherwise you won't be able to fight another day."

Usagi sagged. "I can't fight at all." Tora could fight—what a sight she'd been, with those newly sprouted fangs! Even so, she'd been overpowered. And Uma, who could run faster than any grown man—she'd looked so helpless and small, tied up in the back of the Strikers' cart. What if Usagi never saw them again? Her chest grew tight and she choked back a lump in her throat. Should she go back onto the Ring Road and try to find them, use her rabbit hearing to locate the Dragonstrikers? Even if it meant getting captured herself, at least then they'd be together.

Saru put an arm around Usagi and sat her on a low stump. "You could learn."

"Learn what?" asked Usagi.

"How to fight, of course!"

"From you?" Usagi frowned. "You said I'd be able to help Uma and Tora if I stayed free. Are you saying I should become a bandit too?"

"We're not bandits," said Inu irritably. He stuffed his black hood into one of the packs beneath the camphor tree. "We don't steal. We give to the people the things they deserve. That rice belongs to them."

"So if you're not thieves, what are you, then?" demanded Usagi.

The young woman exchanged glances with Nezu and Inu. "It's complicated. And dangerous. It's not the sort of thing we go around telling people."

"I trusted you enough to come along with you when you asked me to," said Usagi. "I let you hold my father's comb—which I want back, by the way."

"Right." Saru nodded. "I suppose that's true."

"We're not bandits," Inu repeated. He hesitated, twisting a horn ring that he wore on his thumb.

"Just tell her," Nezu exclaimed. "If we're going to do what

we talked about, she'll need to know."

Inu scowled. Intrigued, Usagi leaned forward.

"We're Warrior Heirs," said Nezu, puffing out his chest. "I'm the Heir to the Rat Warrior, Saru's the Monkey Heir, and Inu is the Heir to the Dog Warrior."

Usagi slumped and rolled her eyes. "That's ridiculous. Why would you lie at a time like this?"

"It's true," Nezu insisted. "I was chosen to become the 49th Rat Warrior. I'd be known as Nezu the Seventh upon promotion."

"You dishonor the Twelve!" Usagi rose with a huff. "The Warriors of the Zodiac are all dead, and so are their Heirs. The shrines are gone, the schools are gone, all the teachers—my mother was one of them. You're not funny."

"He isn't joking," said Inu firmly, pushing his hair out of his eyes. "There's still a few of us left—and the most important shrine was not destroyed."

"Its priestess still remains," Nezu informed her.

"What shrine is this?" Usagi challenged.

Nezu waved vaguely north. "The one on Mount Jade, of course. It's the one place on Midaga that the Blue Dragon can't conquer."

"You're not really the Dog Heir," Usagi insisted to the shaggy-haired boy.

"I am." A spark of pride flared in Inu's dark eyes. "For six years now, in fact. Ever since I was eleven. I would have been the forty-eighth Warrior in the line."

Saru lifted her chin. "I would have been the 46th Monkey Warrior. My master, Gausana the Third, was the forty-fifth, and he died fighting to save the king. I saw it all with my own eyes."

"A few of us managed to escape to Mount Jade," said Nezu. He removed a small drinking gourd from his belt and uncorked it. He took a long draft, then wiped his mouth with the sleeve of his tunic. "Horangi—who was the Tiger Warrior before becoming guardian of the shrine—took us in. I was one of the youngest Heirs ever, not even eleven years old at the time, and only just started. She's taught me almost everything I know." Nezu offered the flask to Usagi. "Water?"

Usagi shook her head stubbornly. "If any of that's true, and you're actually Heirs of the Twelve, then why didn't you become Warriors after your masters were killed? Isn't that the whole point of being Heirs?" Not only did these three bandits cause trouble, but they apparently believed she was stupid.

"It happened so fast. There was no Twelve left to speak of by the time the Blue Dragon seized power. There was just a few of us Heirs, and the priestess." Saru's bright eyes dimmed and her face seemed to crumple. "She saved us by sheltering us at the shrine."

For a moment Usagi almost believed her. But even if it

were all true—she had other things to worry about now, like tracking down Uma and Tora. She stood. "I think I should go. Thank you for helping me escape the Strikers. I'd like my comb back now, please." She held out her hand.

Saru reached inside her tunic for the wooden comb. Turning it over with careful hands, she examined the fine carving of the twelve animals of the zodiac, circling in perpetual order: rat, ox, tiger, rabbit, dragon, snake, horse, ram, monkey, rooster, dog, and boar. She held it up. "It's lovely. You said your father gave it to you? Where'd he get it?"

"My father was one of the best wood-carvers in the kingdom," said Usagi, annoyed. "He must've made it. He said to never let it out of sight."

Glancing at Inu, Saru tilted her head and made a strange gesture. "I see. We've actually been looking for this comb for a long time. I have a feeling it was given to your father for safekeeping."

"That can't be," Usagi said sharply. She moved toward Saru. "The comb is his. I promised to take care of it."

Saru took a step back. "And you did. But it's not really yours to keep. It belongs to the Twelve."

Furious, Usagi lunged for the comb, but Saru dodged her. "It belongs to *me*! How dare you use the Twelve as an excuse to steal!"

"I told you," Inu said. "We don't steal." Usagi turned to see him holding a tiny brass bell. He rang it once and a clear high note pealed. It hung in the air for a long moment, then deepened until it became an enormous thrumming sound that seemed to shake the earth. Usagi clapped her hands over her ears, but it was no use. She could hear—no, *feel*—everything. The quavering hum sent vibrations through her so powerful that they rattled her teeth. It seemed to go on forever. "What's happening?" she cried.

"Stand by me and you'll see!" Nezu shouted over the din. "We've summoned the Tigress."

CHAPTER 6

A SUMMONING

THE UNEARTHLY VIBRATIONS SHOOK USAGI to her teeth. She clenched her jaw to keep them from chattering. Hurriedly, the three self-proclaimed Heirs arranged themselves so they faced each other. As the resounding thrum faded into the surrounding forest, Nezu turned and yanked Usagi forward to stand in a wide circle with him, Saru, and Inu. The air within the circle rippled like the space above a hot flame, distorting and undulating. A pinpoint of light appeared, growing steadily in size and shape.

Transfixed, Usagi shrank back, her ears still ringing. This was not a firefly, nor a spark from a torch or fire. It was something she'd never seen.

The morphing glow took on the shape of a great tiger nearly the height of a horse, standing tall over them. It gave off a cool light, and had greenish orbs for eyes that glimmered as its saucer-sized ears swiveled back and its glowing tail twitched. It was as if a piece of the moon had come into the forest—in the form of a giant cat. Usagi rubbed her eyes in shock. What sort of strange magic was this?

"Honored Teacher," said Saru, bowing. "Thank you for answering our call."

Inu and Nezu followed suit and bent low. "Honored Teacher." Nezu looked up briefly and flashed a quick smile. "It gladdens the heart to see you, Mistress Horangi."

Usagi jumped as the enormous glowing tiger spoke with an old woman's croak that echoed through the trees.

"I wish I could say the same, youngling. The protocol is that I summon *you* for regular reports. To ring your Summons Bell indicates grave danger."

"No, Teacher—we are safe," Saru assured the tiger.

"For now," Nezu interjected, his voice cracking with excitement. "But we've made an urgent discovery about the Dragonstrikers. Inu and I saw one of them use animal talents to capture a youngling."

The tiger let out a deep growl that rumbled beneath Usagi's feet. "The Blue Dragon's forces now include those with zodiac powers?"

"At least one that we know of, Teacher," said Inu. "We witnessed a youngling with horse speed caught without the use of fly-nets or spidertraps." He shook his shaggy head. "A Striker ran just as fast as the youngling and overtook her."

"It was my sister," Usagi volunteered. "Uma. She's not yet

nine but has both horse speed and a gift with fire."

The tiger swung its great radiant head around. Its eyes narrowed into green slits. "Who is this youngling? I see from her spirit form that she is born in the year of the Rabbit. What in the name of the gods is an outsider doing in a Summoning Circle?"

Usagi's mouth went dry. She probably wasn't supposed to speak. Now what? In a panic, she looked at Nezu, who gave her a rather sheepish smile.

"This is the only youngling with talent who didn't get caught by the Dragonstrikers today," he told the tiger.

Saru held up the comb. "Teacher, she was carrying one of the Treasures."

The tiger's luminescent ears swiveled forward and it lowered its great nose, as if to sniff the carved wood piece. "The Coppice Comb," it snarled. "On that you have done well. I am glad it has been recovered. But I do not see why you had to reveal yourselves to the youngling."

"Her father gave her the comb. She promised him she'd keep it safe. And since she has talent, we couldn't just take the Coppice Comb from her." Saru took a deep breath. "Teacher, we want to bring her to you."

With a growl, the tiger reared back. Its tail lashed back and forth. "Bring her to the Shrine of the Twelve? An untested, unschooled youngling?"

Usagi's breath was so shallow that she was dizzy.

A priestess with the power of a tiger had manifested right here before her.

It was impossible to deny the truth of what the three bandits—no, Heirs—had been saying all along. The Twelve had not completely been wiped out. A Warrior still lived.

Those with zodiac powers were not alone after all.

"If the Blue Dragon is capturing these younglings for his strike force, we'll be at a greater disadvantage than ever before," Saru said to the luminous tiger.

"It's not enough for us to try to keep the Treasures out of his hands," said Inu, his dark eyes stormy. "We must keep talented younglings from him as well."

Usagi's chest grew tighter and tighter. "But my sister and our friends . . . they all have powers and they've already been caught by the Strikers! Can't any of you help?"

"It is not so simple," the tiger snapped. "Even when the Twelve was whole, we were never invincible. That is why a Shield of Concealment was created for the island in the first place. With our tattered remains, thwarting the Blue Dragon has been the bleakest of battles." The giant cat began to pace within the circle. "Even if you Heirs locate younglings of talent and bring them to Mount Jade safely, they still must pass the Running of the Mount. None of us can force the mountain goddess to accept them."

"But if they succeed in getting to the shrine," said Saru, "it only makes sense to teach them all that you've taught us. And we found one today, carrying one of the Treasures, no less. It's a sign from the gods—we have to try. We can't let the legacy of the Twelve die." She tucked the comb into her tunic. Usagi's fingers twitched, wanting to snatch it back.

"Yes! Don't you see?" Nezu's voice cracked. He cleared his throat and spoke in a deeper register. "This could be our chance at rebuilding the Twelve. Once there are enough of us, we can take on the Warrior mantle. The Warriors of the Zodiac can rise again. Isn't that what you want?"

"Enough," thundered the tiger. "Return to Mount Jade, and bring the youngling—if you can. It is up to her to make it to the shrine. If she does, then I will teach her." The form pulsed with a white glow, becoming so bright it hurt to look at. Usagi cowered, shielding her eyes. In a great flash of light, the tiger disappeared.

In the dim and quiet beneath the forest canopy, Usagi blinked, dazed. Inu put away the little bell he'd used to call upon the glowing tiger, wrapping it in cotton wool and placing it in his pack. He glanced at her and his mouth quirked up. "Still don't believe us?"

Usagi shook her head. It hardly seemed possible, but three Warrior Heirs stood before her. What next?

She was to go with them. The Tigress had said that she would teach Usagi—if she made it to the shrine with the Heirs. Perhaps she'd finally learn to master her talents. And from an actual Warrior of the Twelve! How proud her parents would be!

Usagi sank back onto the low stump. If she studied with the Tiger Warrior, she would surely find a way to help her sister and Tora. It certainly sounded better than going after them alone, just to get captured herself.

"This is a lot to take in, isn't it?" Nezu flashed a sympathetic smile. "I don't know about you, but I'm famished. Let me make a quick porridge—it will settle us after the morning we've had." After murmurs of agreement from the others, he retrieved a small burlap bag from one of the packs under the camphor tree. "Lucky we didn't give all the rice away."

He brought out an iron pot and poured in some of the rice, followed by water from his drinking gourd. While he washed the rice, Saru had Usagi help gather dry wood, which they stacked in the blackened ring of stones for a cookfire.

From his pack, Inu removed an unstrung bow of bamboo and horn that was curled in an open circle. "I'll see if I can't hunt down some meat."

"A bow!" Usagi stared. It had been a long time since she'd seen anyone other than a Guard or Striker with such a weapon. Bows, swords, and spears had been confiscated after the war, even though they were mainly used for hunting or handed down as family heirlooms—at least before the arrival of the invaders. In some parts, even knives had been banned, with only a communal knife chained to a post in the middle of villages.

Usagi pointed. "Why didn't you use that when you were stealing in the rice fields?"

Inu snorted. "Show up with a forbidden weapon? Sure. Because *that* wouldn't raise any alarms."

"When you're outnumbered by well-armed foes, it's best to use stealth tactics," Saru told her. "It's why we used hidden blades and farm tools."

"Hidden blades," said Usagi slowly, thinking of the night she'd first seen them. She remembered hearing the whistle of something that flashed in the moonlight, of Tora telling her the bandits were throwing metal stars dipped in sleeping potion.

"At first the Guard didn't know they were being attacked," said Inu. "It might have bought us only a little more time, but that little bit can make all the difference. To get you and Saru out of the town center, we used the sun's reflection, smoke bombs, and firecrackers to distract the Guard." He attached a sinewy string that pulled the bow's arms into curved wings. With his thumb ring, he gave the string a twang, then slung a small cylinder of arrows over his shoulder. "I won't be long." He slipped into the trees.

Usagi stared up at the masks that hung from the branch above her. Her head was flooded with questions, and she hardly knew which one to ask first. "There are still things

I don't understand," she said to Nezu and Saru. "The comb my father gave me. You said it was a treasure, and that tiger seemed awfully interested in it."

Nodding, Saru drew out a firestarter and struck it above a pile of kindling. "The Coppice Comb is one of Twelve Treasures, created centuries ago at the shrine on Mount Jade. Each possesses unique and useful powers and was passed down from Warrior to Warrior. Most of the Treasures were lost when the war began. We've been hunting for them ever since." A spark flew into the kindling and flared. Saru blew on it gently.

"How many have you found so far?" asked Usagi.

"We've recovered two on this mission." Nezu smoothed his whiskers. "Including yours. At the shrine are two others."

Usagi cocked her head. "Why is it so important to find them?"

Saru sighed. "It's a long story. For now, let's just say that they were very important in keeping Midaga safe for many years. They hold even more power together than individually, so we want to make sure they don't fall into the wrong hands."

"Like the Dragonlord's?"

Saru nodded, frowning. "Especially his."

Usagi thought about the fearsome tiger of light that had stalked around the clearing. "So the talking tiger—that was . . ."

"The 42nd Tiger Warrior," said Saru. "Horangi. We call her the Tigress. You saw her spirit. In a Summoning, you don't see the person—you see the animal that hides in their heart."

So Horangi had seen her in rabbit form. Usagi wondered what sort of rabbit the Tigress had seen. Probably not a particularly ferocious one. She tugged at her ears, which were no longer ringing. "That little bell made an awfully big sound."

Nezu laughed. "That was the answer—from the Summoning Bell. It used to hang at the Palace of the Clouds, and kings would ring it when they needed to call for their Warrior Council. Luckily Tupa smuggled it out and got it to Mount Jade. Can you imagine being at the Blue Dragon's beck and call?" He shuddered.

"Tupa?" asked Usagi, confused. "Who's that?"

"He's the other surviving Heir—to the Ram Warrior," Saru told her. "He's been on a long mission in the north, but hopefully you'll get to meet him someday. It's just been the four of us, and the Tigress, since the Blue Dragon came to power."

Usagi's head swam. Four Heirs and a retired Tiger Warrior. "My sister is just eight years old. Do you really think the Blue Dragon wants her for his strike force?"

"I think we have a way to find out," said Saru thoughtfully.

Nezu nearly knocked over the pot of porridge. "The Mirror of Elsewhere!" he exclaimed. "Of course!"

"Inu has it," Saru told Usagi. "We'll have to wait till he gets back from hunting, but he's carrying the other Treasure we recovered. We found it in the village of Sea View. It will give you a way to see your sister again."

Hope sparked in Usagi for the first time. "Really?"

Saru nodded. "Swear by the gods."

Impatient for Inu's return, Usagi listened for him, rubbing the carved wooden rabbit at her neck. A thought struck her. "How would my father wind up with one of the Treasures?"

"Someone must've entrusted him with it," said Nezu. From a small pouch, he threw a pinch of seasoning into the pot and gave it a stir. "He seemed to know it was important, no? You said he'd made you promise to keep it in sight."

"He did," said Usagi. She'd bent her forehead to his hand and swore to him that she would.

She'd also swore to him to take care of Uma. What a failure she was.

I'm sorry, Papa. Her voice grew small. "So if it's truly one of the Treasures, does it mean I'm not getting the comb back?"

"You won't be breaking your promise to him," said Saru gently. "If you come with us to the shrine, you can keep an eye on it all the way there."

Usagi nodded, but she was doubtful. How would she ever get up Mount Jade? In prewar days, when the time came to find a Warrior Heir, only the best students in the kingdom were allowed to attempt climbing its slopes. Whoever was the first to reach the shrine on Mount Jade received the honor of becoming Heir. Usagi's mother used to tell stories about spectacular failures during a Running of the Mount—terrible falls, broken bones, encounters with wild beasts, even momentary blindness and strange hallucinations. "The Tigress didn't seem to think I could make it to the shrine."

"Don't you worry about that," said Nezu stoutly. He smoothed the sparse whiskers above his lip. "We'll do everything we can to help you prepare."

Usagi heard snatches of a tune in the distance. Someone was humming "The Welcome Song" softly under his breath. "Inu's on his way back. He should be here in a few minutes. I think he's caught something."

"How would you know that?" asked Saru, squinting at Usagi.

Shrugging, Usagi pointed to her ears. "Year of the Rabbit, remember? I can hear him coming—and it sounds like he's in a good mood."

"That would be a first," said Nezu with a chuckle. He sliced some wild mushrooms and added them to the pot. A warm, earthy fragrance filled the air.

Inu's humming grew louder, then stopped as he strode into the campsite, his bow and quiver slung over one shoulder. A fat pheasant flopped over the other. "Anyone for a bit of meat in their porridge?"

Saru clapped her hands, her pale face alight. "That's a handsome catch. It'll fortify us for our journey."

While Nezu began preparing the bird, plucking its feathers and exclaiming over its size, Usagi approached Inu, who was putting away his bow and arrows and looking pleased with himself. She stood by until he looked up from his pack, his dark eyes quizzical. "Yes?"

"Saru and Nezu said you had one of the Treasures on you," Usagi ventured. "A . . . a mirror? They said it might help me see my sister again."

Inu's face cleared and he gestured for Usagi to sit down beside him, brushing dead leaves and sticks from a patch of mossy earth. Reaching into his tunic, he produced a small bronze disk. The gilt back of the mirror was cast in an elaborate raised design. Twelve animals of the zodiac paraded around a small knob, a handle embossed with swirling shapes like fish chasing each other's tails.

"This is the Mirror of Elsewhere," he told her. "Cast in the province of Iron Tree, blessed by Mount Jade at the Shrine of the Twelve, and carried for generations of Dog Warriors. When war broke out I helped my master, Seta the Second, hide it in order to keep it from the Blue Dragon. I was looking forward to recovering it on this mission." He turned it over and held it up in a beam of sunlight. Light glinted off the mirror's face onto Usagi's sleeve. "Look," Inu smiled.

A pattern of twelve animals, cast in sunshine, danced on Usagi's tunic. It was the exact same pattern from the mirror's back. Usagi blinked in surprise. "It's like the mirror is transparent. Can you see through it?"

"Something like that," said Inu. "It can be used as an ordinary mirror, but if you hold it at a certain angle while thinking of a specific place, person, or thing, the mirror will show it to you. It might not be the clearest picture, but it can give you a general sense of the thing you're thinking about. It's how we came to Goldentusk. The mirror showed us that the comb was here, but we couldn't quite see who was carrying it or the comb's exact location." He gave a wry smile. "Until we caught you using it. But the mirror still helped."

He rubbed the front of the disk against his tunic and put it in Usagi's hand. It felt heavy and warm, and fit perfectly in her palm. "Hold it by the handle. Put it just in front of your face, at the level of your chin. Angle it slightly up to the sky, so that you don't see your eyes," he instructed. "Now think of your sister."

The image in the mirror grew cloudy, going from a glimpse of Usagi's forehead to a faint moving form. It was if she were looking through a tiny window covered with a sooty piece of glass. Usagi squinted, then gasped. Uma was no longer asleep, but crouched in a bamboo cage, her hands still tied. Her long mane of hair was completely undone, half hanging in her tearstained face. She looked miserable. "They've got her in a cage," Usagi whispered. "Oh, Uma."

She wondered if Tora was with her sister, and another face immediately floated into view, in a cage next to Uma's. "There's Tora!" Her long fangs had disappeared, but her amber eyes looked fiercer than ever. She raised her bound hands as if she were reaching for Uma and said something, but jerked back and stared angrily at someone outside her cage. The cages jittered and shook on a jouncing cart—the same one that Usagi had first seen that morning, coming for Jago. As Usagi thought of Jago, the image expanded to show him in a cage on the other side of Uma, his face streaked with dirt and tears. Were they on the Ring Road with the Strikers? As if in answer, a phalanx of black-armored escorts marched into view behind the cart.

"What do you see?" Inu asked.

"They're all in cages," Usagi choked. "My sister, Tora, and Jago. I think the Strikers are taking them to the capital." A tear slipped down her cheek as she stared at the faint image of her sister. "I'm so sorry, Uma. I'll come for you. I promise."

WATER

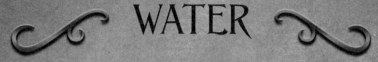

"Water seeks the most direct path, and changes to fit every circumstance. But do not mistake its flexibility for weakness, for even mountains can be dissolved by Water."

—Book of Elements, from *The Way of the Twelve*

CHAPTER 7

FAR FROM HOME

BEFORE THE DAYS OF THE Dragonlord's rule, people often traveled the island's Ring Road on foot or by cart, bringing goods to market in the capital and other provinces, or making pilgrimages to shrines. It was a source of pride to stop and visit some of Midaga's most beautiful wonders—like the Dancing Dunes, Butterfly Kingdom, Staircase of the Sea, and the Rainbow Wood—along the way.

But this was back before the war, when people weren't stopped at Guard checkpoints to show their travel permits, and trade within the kingdom still existed. Nowadays no one was able to move freely from town to town without questioning or harassment, except for entertainers and temple monks.

So the Heirs put on their brightly colored coats and gave Usagi a bold patterned belt to wear over her shabby tunic. They taught her a quick song and dance routine, in case they were stopped by the Guard. Saru gathered some of their gear and a spare bedroll, and tied everything into a bundle for Usagi to carry. Then they set off for Mount Jade, deep in the heart of the island.

Because Usagi still had trouble with landing her rabbit leap, they traipsed through the wilderness like ordinary people instead of using their zodiac powers to travel more quickly. After trekking through untamed forest and dense brush for nearly a week, Usagi's already ragged slippers became wisps of straw, barely offering any protection for her feet as the thongs unraveled and the soles wore thin. The hem of her long skirt was filthy and there were countless new rips and hanging shreds from snagging on scrub and thorns.

With envy, Usagi admired the polished walking sticks that the Heirs carried. Maybe those were why, even without using their animal talents, they traversed rough terrain with ease. She tripped on a rock and stumbled, and the heavy pack on her back lurched and nearly took her down. "Spitting spirits!" Scowling, she crouched and rubbed her throbbing toe.

A drop of sweat trickled off her nose and splashed on the offending rock. Usagi smeared her face against her sleeve and tore off a dusty strip of her skirt. She tied her slipper more tightly to her foot then tried to stand. The pack she carried tipped her on her back like a hapless turtle. "Blasted blisters!"

She heard a stifled giggle. Saru came and offered her hand to Usagi. "Are you all right?"

Usagi gritted her teeth and nodded, grunting as Saru helped her up. An encouraging smile crossed Saru's pale face. "You're getting so strong. Look at how much you're carrying compared to when we started out. By the time we get to Mount Jade, who knows? Maybe you'll be carrying all of us."

"If I make it that far," Usagi muttered. She grimaced and wiped her face again. "And I'll still have to get to the shrine." The thought tied her stomach in knots.

"We'll help as much as we can," Saru promised. "When we get to our next camp, expect a bit more training than carrying a heavy backbundle."

Usagi paused. "Is that why the three of you keep loading more into my pack?"

"Strong *and* smart." Saru's smile grew wider. "You'll get to the shrine yet."

But when? Usagi couldn't stop thinking about her last words to her sister—they still rang in her ears as if she'd just said them out loud. *I would never leave you.* But wasn't that exactly what she'd done? She had to get back to Uma and Tora soon, before they lost all hope.

Nezu caught up and pulled out his water gourd, offering it to Usagi. She took a tentative sip, then drank more deeply, the cool water flowing down her throat, washing away the dust and the late summer heat. Sighing, Usagi wiped her mouth with her sleeve and gave the gourd back, refreshed as if she'd taken a nap in the generous shade of a banyan tree.

"The water tastes so sweet—and it's always cold and never seems to run out. Is your canteen one of the Treasures?" she teased.

Nezu flashed a grin. "No, but I've got a cloud in there."

Usagi stared at the worn flask, which looked completely ordinary, and raised a skeptical eyebrow.

"It's from Mount Jade," he insisted. "A wisp of a cloud from the top of the mountain. Took me ages to get it. Every week for a whole year, I'd climb to a little nook chiseled into the south side of the peak and try to capture a cloud. I tried everything—sneaking up on one with a bag, trying to suck one in with a reed straw, rigging fancy traps. When I finally managed to get one into the flask, it wasn't by force at all!" Nezu shook his head. "Turns out I just needed to win it over with some flattering compliments—it was easy to coax in after that."

"It sounds like magic," Usagi marveled.

"The invaders might say that, but they wouldn't mean it as praise," Nezu chuckled. "What do they like to call us? 'Demon freaklings'? But water ruled the year and the month I was born, so it's a friend to me—it listens to me."

"You have an elemental gift." Usagi's hand strayed to the wooden rabbit at her neck. Her sister, born on both a day and an hour that was ruled by fire, had a gift with that element. Their mother had dressed Uma all in red for her first birthday, with a matching little cap embroidered with flames of gold thread. "So that the god of fire may grant your baby sister a fire gift," her mother had laughed. And apparently it worked, for her mother's wish came true. But though Usagi was born in the year of the Wood Rabbit, sharing an element with her father, a Wood Dragon, she'd never felt any unusual connection with the forest. Trees never bent her way or responded to her touch, and while her father could shape blocks of wood into marvelous objects, her own attempts at carving always left her with nothing but a pile of splinters. She rubbed her pendant. No matter. She had her rabbit hearing and her rabbit leap.

Looking at his battered gourd, Nezu gave it an affectionate pat. "It's been so long since I've thought about it, but I suppose it's hard to believe that there's a fragment of cloud in here, and that it's always raining inside."

"That's nothing." Usagi shrugged. "I've been known to carry big blasts of wind." She waved a hand vigorously behind her.

Saru and Nezu stared at her for a moment in shocked silence. When Usagi grinned, they threw their heads back and guffawed.

"Oi," called Inu. "Can you speed it up or are you having a tea party? I want us at the lake before nightfall." He strode back to them with an impatient frown.

Her pale face flushed from merriment, Saru wiped her eyes. "She's worn out, Inu." She peered at the sky. "It's midway through the hour of the Horse now, and we haven't had a rest since dawn. Surely we can stop for a moment. We'll still make it to the lake before sundown."

Usagi hitched her backbundle higher on her aching shoulders. "No, I'm fine. I just tripped and lost my step there for a moment. Let's keep going."

"A short break might do everyone some good," said Nezu, offering his flask to Inu. "We're well inland from any settlements, and haven't seen another soul for days. It's only going to get rougher as we get to higher ground, so we should conserve some strength."

Inu opened his mouth as if to speak, then shrugged and took the gourd. He drank thirstily, strands of his shaggy black hair plastered to his neck and forehead with sweat. As he passed it to Saru, Usagi saw that they all looked tired. Even Nezu's cheerful face was gray with fatigue.

Saru gave Usagi a gentle push toward a large rock in the shade. "Sit."

Relieved, Usagi sank down gratefully and slipped off her pack, not even caring that the rock's jagged surface pricked though her worn skirt. While they rested, Nezu handed out bits of salted dried squid. As Usagi nibbled on the stringy morsels, Inu squatted beside her and began scratching something in the dirt, muttering to himself.

"Half a day more till we reach Sun Moon Lake. Rest and hunt, train three days. To the Sea of Trees, it's two days travel from the lake . . ."

Usagi leaned over for a better look. She'd heard about Sun Moon Lake—it supposedly had waters so glassy and calm that the lake glowed from the moon at night and shone like the sun during the day. Few went there because it was far from any road. Inu had drawn a rough map of Midaga, the island shaped like a smoke leaf or, as some said, a sweet potato. Several *x* marks were scattered across his drawing. She pointed to a circle. "What's this?"

"That's where we should be tonight," Inu said. "Sun Moon Lake. We'll find good shelter there, and refresh our stores of food. We'll also go over the Running of the Mount with you, and try to get you ready before we move on in a few days. I wish we had more time, but I don't think the Tigress will take kindly to us dragging our feet much longer. We're taking a while to get there as it is." He dug a shallow hole and pulled a small straight pin from his belt. With a scrap of silk from his pocket, he rubbed the pin vigorously. "Rat Boy, could I get a splash from your canteen here?"

"What are you doing?" Usagi asked, puzzled.

Inu held up the pin and squinted at it. "Making a compass."

After Nezu had poured water into the shallow hole, Inu placed the pin on a dead leaf and floated it in the center of the puddle. The leaf spun around, then stilled and came to a halt. "As I thought," Inu nodded, and pointed in the same direction as the pin. "That way's north. We're going to go a bit more east."

Usagi was impressed. "Is that a gift you have with metal?"

Inu cracked a half smile. "Not exactly. Just a little something we learned in school. Anyone can make one of these—even you."

For the thousandth time, Usagi wished she'd had the chance to go to school. There was so much that she didn't know. She squared her shoulders. If she made it up to the shrine on Mount Jade—no, *when* she made it up to the shrine—she'd finally get a chance to learn, and from a Warrior of the Twelve, no less. After she figured out the best way to help her sister and their friends, of course.

They shouldered their packs. Usagi felt much better after their brief stop, and was almost able to keep up with Inu's brisk pace, even as the path wound through the hills like a meandering snake. They passed a clump of bamboo, the green stalks standing tall, dagger-shaped leaves swaying gently in the warm breeze. Saru paused, drawing a porcelain-handled knife from her belt. She cut a long pole and stripped away the spindly branches, then presented it to Usagi.

"Use this as a walking stick," Saru advised. "It'll take some of the weight off your legs and help you balance."

The bamboo pole jutted above Usagi by nearly three heads. Despite its length, it nestled comfortably in Usagi's hand, her fingers and thumb just meeting around the smooth stalk. She thunked it on the ground as she walked, and found that it did make her more sure-footed, each step less arduous. "It's like having an extra leg," she said after a few minutes.

"Exactly," said Saru, smiling. "And you'll find other uses for it too."

The path became steeper and the air cooled. Wisps of fog appeared. Usagi was grateful for her new walking stick, leaning on it heavily as the ground pitched higher. She kept her eye on Inu's back, trying not to lose sight of him as he led them into a dense growth of trees and plants. These were of a kind Usagi had never seen. The trunks of the trees were covered in shaggy mosses and lichens in countless hues of orange, green, and yellow, while moisture dripped from dangling vines that trailed from branches overhead. The howl of monkeys and the call of birds echoed around them, while the smell of damp wood, earth, and wild orchids filled the air. From time to time, brightly colored feathers would flash against the verdant canopy, or a long, curled tail would slip behind a tree trunk. A pale face framed with golden fur peeked out from a veil of leaves and watched them with dark eyes.

"Is that a monkey?" asked Usagi, trying to contain her wonder.

"Clowns of the cloud forest," Saru replied. "A good sign. It means there are no leopards around."

Usagi had never seen a live monkey, for none lived in the lowland forests by Goldentusk. But this one reminded her of one that her father had carved and gilded with gold, with a bright halo of fur and a tail curling delicately about its haunches. The monkey carving went to crown a litter for the king, who'd paid her father handsomely. Papa had gotten her mother a new silk scarf with the earnings, and slippers with tiny silver bells on them for Usagi and Uma. The two of them had danced and stomped around the house, their new slippers chiming with every step, making their parents laugh. Together they'd feasted on braised pork and crackling duck, with sweet dumplings stuffed with sugary bean paste at the end of the meal. A lump came into Usagi's throat. They would never be that happy ever again.

The animal caught Usagi staring and ducked back into the foliage. Usagi was so preoccupied that she didn't notice that they had stopped. She bumped into Saru, who lurched into Inu. "Sorry," said Usagi meekly.

"Pay attention," grumbled Inu. Shaking his head, he

turned back to the path before them. He sniffed the cool wet air.

Nezu came up behind them. "What's wrong?" he asked.

Inu frowned. "I don't think we're alone."

CHAPTER 8

THE WOOD DOG

STOPPED IN THE DAMP CLOUD forest, Usagi felt her skin prickle. For the first time since they'd set off from Goldentusk, Inu's sensitive nose had caught something that he couldn't seem to identify, and he looked worried. He yanked a hand through his shaggy hair. "I can't tell who or what it is." He sniffed the air around them again. "But it doesn't smell right. Be on the alert."

The Heirs grasped the tops of their walking sticks and pulled. Usagi stared in astonishment as the sticks slid open to reveal weapons hidden inside. Nezu drew out a long sword. Inu tipped his hollowed stick and poured out a sharp claw hook attached to a long chain. Saru transformed her wood staff into a spear-like weapon with a wicked-looking curved blade. "Ready," she said, her jaw set.

They resumed walking. Usagi clutched her bamboo pole and eyed the newly revealed weapons the others carried.

Spitting spirits, if only a weapon were hidden in her stick! Her ears scanned the unfamiliar sounds in the cloud forest: the shrieks of monkeys, the chirp and boom of tree frogs, the songs of strange birds, the clicks of unseen insects, and the constant drip of accumulating moisture.

And then she heard it—the unmistakable sound of a huffing snuffle and the padding of several sets of heavy paws on the damp earth. "At least three animals stalking us," she warned. "And they're not small."

"I smell them," Inu said grimly. "Wild dogs." Hurriedly he returned the hook and chain to their hiding place in his walking stick. Pulling out his bow, he strung it in a fluid motion and nocked an arrow. He nodded and they pressed on.

Nerves tingling with every step, Usagi listened for the dogs. They were closing in, tracking them as she and the Heirs went deeper into the cloud forest. It wasn't long before she noticed another set of footsteps that didn't sound like an animal's. "I think . . . a *person's* with them," she hissed.

Inu grunted. "Whoever it is hardly smells human." He stopped and shouted. "Oi! We know you're out there!"

Growls erupted and three wild mountain dogs came charging out of the mist. Their brindle bodies were lean and muscular, their wolflike ears erect. Sickle-shaped tails curled over their backs. They snarled at Inu with sharp white fangs, their black eyes fixed on his every move.

As Nezu brandished his sword and Saru tilted her bladed

shaft at the dogs, Inu kept his bow drawn, ready to let an arrow fly. He growled back at the dogs, glaring, until they stopped snarling and tilted their heads quizzically. With a snort, they wheeled and ran back into the cloud forest.

"What was that?" Usagi gaped at Inu. "Do you speak Dog?"

"Since I was a pup of four," Inu said offhandedly. He didn't relax his hold.

Impressed, Usagi was about to ask him what he'd said to the mountain dogs when she heard a rustle in the surrounding foliage. She pointed. "Someone's still out there!"

"Steady," said Saru, tightening her grip on her weapon.

A shaggy mass of leaf-strewn moss emerged. "The gods take my pants," it croaked. "You dare call yourselves Heirs?"

Usagi blinked. At first glance, it looked like a moving, talking shrub, but upon closer examination she saw that it was an older man whose gaunt face was half hidden behind a long, mud-smeared beard. He was dressed in barkcloth with a jacket of moss, and his overgrown hair matted into long, dense strands beneath a leafy helmet of intertwined vines. He stared at them with wide bloodshot eyes, grasping a thick, gnarled branch like a club.

Inu didn't lower his bow. "That would be us. And since I only told that fact to your dogs, it's clear you have animal talents of your own. Identify yourself, sir."

"You can call me Yunja," the man said warily. "Born in

the year of the Wood Dog." His voice sounded rusty, as if he hadn't used it in a while. "My boys tell me that you ordered them to bring their master before the Heirs of the Twelve." The three wild dogs spilled out from the bushes and surrounded the man protectively, their eyes trained on the Heirs and Usagi. The man reached out a mud-crusted hand and scratched one of the dogs behind its ears with his long-nailed fingers. "I'm their master. If what my dogs say is true, then you've got more than just zodiac powers—you probably have trouble on your tail."

"Your dogs aren't wrong," Inu replied calmly. "But there's no one following us—we're just passing through."

"Dogs don't lie. People do."

Saru kept the curved blade of her pole arm raised. "What is your affiliation with the Blue Dragon?"

Yunja hawked and spit. "Do I look like I have any affiliation? I'd be dead if I didn't have the sense to run when all hell broke loose." He shrugged, rattling the dried leaves entangled in his hair. "Till now, I thought I was the only one with sense." His gaze sharpened and he raised his club. "You keep pointing your weapons at me, I'm going to start thinking you're the Blue Dragon's spies, sent to finish me off."

Saru and Nezu lowered their weapons, and Inu relaxed his draw on his bow and arrow. "We have nothing to do with that turncoat," he growled.

"I didn't think so, but you never know," said the hermit.

He rested his club on his shoulder. "But if you're the Heirs of the Twelve, then you're a sorry lot. I don't see even half of twelve here."

"At least he can count," Nezu muttered to Usagi.

Yunja's bloodshot eyes narrowed. "Yes, I can, and I'll thank you to keep your smart comments to yourself."

"I—I didn't," Nezu stammered.

"Whoever you claim to be, you're not welcome here," said the hermit angrily, giving his club a shake. "I've managed to stay alive this long and I won't have you younglings exposing me."

"Forgive us, sir," said Inu, shooting a glare at Nezu. "We haven't presented ourselves properly." He gave their names and ruling animals to the hermit. "You don't have to believe our claim of being Heirs, but we're trying to stay away from the Blue Dragon's men—just like you. We don't mean to intrude like this, but we didn't expect anyone to be here."

"I wasn't going to show myself until I was sure you weren't one of his," the man admitted. He grinned, exposing a gap-toothed smile riddled with brown-stained teeth.

Saru bowed. "We only mean to stay at the lake for a few days. We'll make sure not to disturb you, and wouldn't mention your existence to anyone—as long as you do the same for us."

Yunja barked a laugh. "Who would I tell? You're the first people I've laid eyes on in five years." He turned his gaze to

Usagi, who squirmed and looked down at her rope slippers. They were soaked from the dripping moisture in the cloud forest, mud caking her toes.

The hermit grunted. "Is she an Heir too?"

Saru put a hand on Usagi's shoulder. "This youngling isn't an Heir, but she does have talent. It's rough and undeveloped. We're hoping to change that."

"Hmphf." The man scratched his neck, dislodging a patch of crusted dirt, and pointed ahead through the thick foliage. "Follow my boys and they'll take you down to the lakeshore. There's decent fishing and a few spots where you can stay pretty dry." He half growled, half yelped at the three wild dogs, made some clicking noises at the back of his throat, then abruptly turned and disappeared back into the trees.

"That was unexpected," Nezu commented. He eyed the dogs. "Think there are any more like him hiding on the island?"

Inu slung his bow over his shoulder. "Hermits with powers? Who knows? In all our missions, he's the first we've ever come across."

The dogs trotted ahead, looking back from time to time to make sure the Heirs and Usagi were following. Inu would occasionally rumble at them and get a huff or a shake of the head in response.

"According to the dogs, Yunja's been their master for five winters—since they were pups. They've never seen any other people up here," Inu reported.

Usagi wondered what it would be like to live alone for years at a time, with no one to talk to but a trio of dogs. She couldn't talk to any animals—not even rabbits. If she'd stayed in the woods outside Goldentusk and avoided all people, she probably wouldn't have lasted very long before craving company. She'd been lucky to have her sister and Tora. Sighing, Usagi shifted her pack and leaned on her walking stick. Her sore shoulders throbbed and every muscle in her legs cried out for a break.

"Spirits be praised!" said Saru. "I can see the lake."

The steep pitch of the path veered downward, and the waters of the lake glimmered through the trees. The sun was sinking, and the red glow it cast across the sky was reflected on the lake's surface, throwing a rosy light over everything. "Beautiful," Usagi breathed.

The dogs watched as they set up camp in a little clearing by the lake, then trotted away into the cloud forest as Inu barked at them. Usagi looked at him curiously. He shrugged. "Just telling them thanks."

They left their packs beneath a bower of trees, and went looking for food. Saru found a stand of fig trees, the branches heavy with fruit—and an entire troop of golden monkeys clutching half-eaten figs in their sticky paws. The monkeys shrieked and bared their teeth at Usagi, but Saru swung easily into a tree and waved her arms, hooting until they scampered away.

"You're not the only monkeys around here," Saru shouted after them, and laughed. She tossed fig after fig to Usagi until they'd gathered a whole sackful.

Usagi couldn't resist sneaking a taste, sinking her teeth into the honey-sweet flesh of a juicy purple one and crunching on the tiny seeds. She'd never had a fresh fig before—only dried ones, and even those were worth their weight in gold. Next to this, sugarcane was as bland as straw.

Uma would love these. Usagi's heart twinged as she remembered how her sister would carefully divide up any precious sweets they found, always making sure everyone had at least a taste of honeysuckle nectar or wolfberry. Even that shriveled piece of sugarcane Usagi scavenged for her—Uma had given it away to Jago. How were they faring now?

She resolved to try for another peek in the Mirror of Elsewhere. Ever since she'd had the chance to see her sister through it, Usagi had pestered Inu for another look. If she could, she'd be checking in on Uma every moment of the day. But the Dog Heir had refused.

"If you're not careful, you start spending all your time looking Elsewhere, and stop paying attention to your actual surroundings," he'd told her. "The 19th Dog Warrior was forced to step down after he stopped eating and drinking— he wasted half away from doing nothing but staring into the Mirror."

At the campsite, they showed their pickings to the boys, who'd come back with a couple of fat ducks. Nezu soon had a cookfire going, and set about wrapping some of the figs in meat and spitting them on sticks to roast. Usagi took off her shoes to dry near the heat of the flames. She held up a foot in the warm air and wriggled her mud-crusted toes.

"Oi, get your muddy paws away from dinner," Nezu grimaced. "Wash off, will you? Unless you're going for the hermit look."

Usagi waggled both feet at him. "Maybe I am! It'd save me the trouble of bathing." She ducked as Nezu threw a handful of feathers in her direction.

"I'll come with you," Saru said. "You too, Inu! A swim would do you good."

Inu finished cleaning his hunting gear, then stretched. "All right," he said, and ambled behind Saru and Usagi as they made their way to the shore. A gibbous moon rose, glowing three-quarters full, and brightened as it drifted higher in the sky, its light bouncing hard off the lake's glassy surface.

Dipping her hands into the cool water, Usagi briskly rubbed her arms and face. It felt so good to wash off the dust and sweat of their travels. She noticed a motionless, dark shape in the lake. From this distance it looked like a whale floating on the surface of the water.

She pointed it out as Inu and Saru sloshed in. "What's in the middle of the lake?"

Inu squinted. "Wolf Snot Isle. A big rock, really." He took a breath and dove briefly beneath the surface, popping up a few seconds later. "Gods, that does feel good."

"Funny name," Usagi commented.

Saru laughed. "It's from the tale about the Wolf and the Wind God. Each night the Wind God would throw the moon through the heavens for his loyal companion to catch, until the Wolf dropped it on this spot, where it stuck fast. The Wolf pawed and pawed till great hills of earth rose up all around the moon, but still it wouldn't come out. When the sun appeared for daytime, there was so much light that everyone nearly went blind. The seas began to boil, crops couldn't grow properly, and no one slept a wink. The Wind God had to put the moon back in the sky and promise the other gods that the Wolf would never play with it again. It made the Wolf so sad that his tears filled the hole left by the moon, turning it into this lake. But the gods would not be budged. To this day, the full moon will set a pack of dogs howling."

Inu waded over and splashed Saru. "That's enough of the old yarns. One of these days I'll tell the story of how the Monkey caused so much mischief that he was banished by the gods to clean up after the horses in their stables. To this day, a monkey will still throw poop when he's angry at you."

Saru flung some water back at Inu, and before long the three of them were kicking and splashing at each other, laughing and screaming, until they were neck-deep in the lake.

Usagi heard Nezu's voice in the distance. "We're being called for dinner."

Inu cocked his head. "I don't hear anything." He sniffed. "I do *smell* something though. Meat's definitely done."

Back at the camp, they found the hermit Yunja seated by the cookfire, tearing into a skewer of roast duck while his three dogs sat at a polite distance, drooling. The hermit barely stopped to wave, so intent was he on his meal. Occasionally he would stop and throw a morsel at one of his dogs, who would snatch it out of midair with a flash of sharp teeth and a slavering gulp.

"He stopped by to check on us, so I invited him to share our meal," Nezu said cheerfully. "You might want to hurry before he eats everything." He frowned at the three of them. "You're soaked. Were you trying to drown yourselves?"

Smiling, Saru lifted her arms. "A little help, if you please, Water Rat."

"Hold still," Nezu commanded, and raised his palms. Furrowing his brow, he circled his hands slowly in the air. With a sudden flick, he threw his arms wide.

Usagi felt a pulling sensation and then a spray of water

shot from her in all directions. The clammy wetness against her skin disappeared. She looked down, then checked behind her. She, Saru, and Inu were standing in a circle of damp earth, and their clothes were bone-dry. Usagi touched her hair. Also dry, and no longer plastered to her forehead. "What a useful gift," she marveled.

"Oi," spluttered the hermit from behind them. "That's a nice trick you got there, but you could have directed it away from me." Yunja was covered in a sheen of water that beaded on his hollow cheeks and dripped off his mud-smeared beard. He shook himself, flinging muddy water from his tangled locks.

"Sorry," laughed Nezu. He lifted his hands and made a sweeping motion toward the lake. There was a sizzling sound, and the water he'd pulled from Usagi and the others flew out of the clearing like a cloud of steam, leaving the hermit and the ground dry once more.

"That's better," Yunja grunted, and resumed eating.

"How old were you when you first knew you had a gift with water?" Usagi asked Nezu, replaiting her braids.

He stroked his upper lip, thinking. "I was about three when I came down with a bad fever. My mother had to stay up all night to tend to me, feeding me sweetened ginger water from a cup. At one point she fell asleep. I was so thirsty, I made the water rise out of the cup and come to me." Nezu reached out an arm and crooked a finger to demonstrate.

"But I was so surprised at what I'd done that I dumped it all over me. I didn't get to drink any of it, and my crying woke my poor mother. She had to clean up the mess I'd made and calm me down." He shook his head.

"Our poor mothers indeed," Saru said with a wistful smile. "My mother found me high up in an old cypress tree when I'd just turned two. She said an enormous wild boar was scratching itself against the trunk, shaking the tree while I screamed from the branches. But it wasn't until a few years later that I began climbing up high whenever I could—on the roof, trees, anything I could get my hands on."

Inu scoffed. "At least your mother didn't threaten to cane you if you didn't stop sharing everything with the family dog. She put up with me eating from the same bowl as the dog for a while, but she put her foot down when I started peeing on the trees around our house."

As they all laughed, Usagi thought of her own mother and how her wide brown eyes, so like Uma's, had lit up when Usagi first complained that frogs in the forest had kept her up all night with their croaking. "Your talent is showing itself," her mother had said, beaming. Usagi swallowed a sudden lump in her throat, and saw that the others were lost in thought as well.

The hermit broke the spell. "Oi, if you're going to tell stories all night," Yunja hollered, "d'ya mind if I eat the rest?"

They helped themselves to sticks of roasted duck and

figs, which had turned out beautifully. The figs were cooked into a jammy sweetness that oozed out with each bite, and the duck skin was crackling crisp. It was the first fresh meat they'd had in a while, and they ate until not a single morsel was left.

Nezu gave a groaning sigh and began combing and replaiting his rat-tail braid. Inu gnawed on the sticks for the last bits of meat. Saru leaned back against an old stump and licked drippings of fig juice off her fingers, her pale face pink in the light of the fire. Usagi couldn't remember the last time she felt this full.

The hermit let out a loud burp and wiped his mouth daintily with the ends of his matted hair. "Gods' guts, that was delicious. I don't know if it's because it was a meal cooked by another . . . or . . ." He stopped and cleared his throat, then started to sniffle. "Or because I didn't eat it alone." A strangled sob escaped him and Yunja hunched over, hiding his face in his hands.

One of the wild dogs whined and pushed up against Yunja. "Oh, you know what I mean," the hermit choked, burying his face in its flank. "With people!"

"You're certainly welcome to eat with us as long we're here," said Saru. Her eyes glistened more brightly than usual.

With vigorous nods, Usagi and the boys voiced their agreement. "Please do," Usagi urged.

"Can't let good food go to waste!" Nezu said, his voice cracking.

"You know this place so well, we could use your guidance," Inu added.

The hermit lifted his head and dragged his face against a ragged sleeve, wiping away the mud. His eyes were still wet. "That's mighty kind of you younglings. Mighty kind. I must say, since the war, I've wondered if I'd ever come in contact with a friendly soul again."

"Poor Yunja!" Saru reached out and patted his back. "Of course you would. You're not alone." A determined look came into her eyes as she looked around at everyone. "Those of us with zodiac powers must take care of each other."

That night, after everyone had collapsed into their bedrolls, Usagi waited, wide awake. When Inu began to snore, she tiptoed over and quietly felt around his pack, searching for the Mirror of Elsewhere. After a fruitless hunt, she remembered that he kept it close. Gingerly, she slid a hand beneath Inu's pillow.

His eyelids popped open. "What do you think you're doing?"

"I'm sorry," Usagi whispered. "I can't stop worrying about my sister. Please, can't I look in the mirror? I swear I won't ask again if you let me."

Inu groaned. He reached inside his tunic for the bronze disk. "Make it quick."

"Thank you!" Usagi took the mirror over to the dim light of the dying campfire. Peering into the polished surface, she waited till her sister came into view. She caught her breath. Uma was sleeping. Usagi couldn't make out much more since she appeared to be in a darkened room, but her sister looked peaceful. She stifled a sob.

"Soon." Usagi touched the image of Uma's face. "I will come to you soon."

CHAPTER 9

HUMBLE WEAPONS

USAGI WIGGLED HER TOES IN her new slippers, admiring the intricate pattern of the sturdy straps in the late morning light. They were a gift from the hermit Yunja, woven from reeds and grasses he'd gathered, and the soles were remarkably thick and springy. In the few days they'd been at the lake, resting and preparing Usagi for the climb up Mount Jade, he'd become a regular fixture at their camp. The hermit brought fruit he'd picked and game his dogs had brought down, and shared all his meals with them. In the evenings, they swapped stories by the campfire. The Heirs even unpacked their instruments, and together they sang "The Welcome Song" and others in their repertoire, while Yunja's dogs howled along. He'd brought over the slippers last night, and smiled a delighted gap-toothed smile when Usagi pronounced them a perfect fit.

In these shoes, she might just manage to make it to the

shrine. Provided she didn't get crushed by boulders, fall off a cliff, get eaten by a wild animal, or worse. Checking on her sister in the Mirror of Elsewhere had been a relief. Even if she didn't know exactly what was happening with Uma, she'd appeared to be in good health, and that had eased the knot of worry that sat in Usagi's chest. But the Heirs' warnings about the Running of the Mount made the knot tighten up again.

"Everyone who ascends for the first time is tested by Mount Jade in different ways. The mountain will bring out your strengths, but also your weaknesses."

"Make sure you practice your leap—you're going to need it. Pity you haven't trained in swordplay or archery."

"You'll be forced to use every talent at your disposal, and your wits as well. People have been known to lose their minds on the climb."

Talk like that made Usagi quail. Maybe attempting to go with the Heirs up Mount Jade was a bad idea. But what else could she do? Stay here with old Yunja and his dogs? Return to Goldentusk? Go to the capital on her own—straight into the Strikers' cages?

No. If she made it to the shrine, the last Warrior of the Twelve would teach her to master her talents. She'd have a better chance. Usagi had to try.

She glanced over at the Heirs' walking sticks, which they'd left behind while they were off hunting. With cautious fingers, Usagi examined one. She could see the line where the two parts of the stick joined. She tugged it open to reveal a few inches of sharp blade. Nezu's sword. It'd be handy to have such a blade inside her bamboo pole. Or maybe Nezu would let her borrow his. But with her luck she'd probably trip and slice her own leg off. And if she leaped with it and wound up in one of her clumsy landings . . . Usagi shuddered. She put Nezu's stick back and picked up her own.

Her ears pricked at the sound of panting and rustling through the cloud forest's undergrowth. Yunja's dogs were coming. A rusty voice hummed tunelessly over the chirp of frogs and chatter of monkeys. Before long, Yunja's mossy frame shambled into the clearing, swinging his club.

"Hullo there, Rabbit Girl," said the hermit. "Where'd your friends go?"

"Hunting," she replied. The dogs gathered around and licked her hands.

Yunja showed her several fish as long as his arm, with fat silver bellies. "Look at these monsters," he said proudly. "Won't they make good eating? I thought we could eat some fresh and smoke the rest for you younglings to take on your journey."

"You're too kind, Yunja," Usagi said, admiring the fish. "First my shoes, now these fish . . ."

The hermit waved a mud-crusted hand. "Don't be silly! There's plenty to go around. Besides, I've got quite a bit put away already for me and my dogs."

"I've been wondering about that," said Usagi. "How have you managed to hide here by yourself all these years?"

Yunja puffed out his skinny chest. "I never look too far ahead. My goal is simple. Stay alive! So what do I do? Avoid the Blue Dragon's men. And how do I do that?" He waved the string of fish. "Find food around here. Never go back to the coast, which is crawling with spies. And that's it." He glanced down at the leafy branch he used as a club, deflating a little. "If I start thinking about the rest of my life—living alone, never seeing the faces of my family again—I might just lie down and let my dogs eat me for breakfast. So I don't. To survive, I take it day by day."

"Day by day," Usagi repeated. It made sense. Maybe she was looking too far ahead, worrying about what would happen to her during the Running of the Mount when she hadn't even gotten to Mount Jade yet. She gave the ground a couple of thumps with her walking stick. "Step-by-step."

"That's right." The hermit tapped Usagi's bamboo pole with his club. "Look at this fine staff! It's almost twice your size. You could take someone's head off."

"This?" she laughed. "It's just a stick of bamboo. There's nothing special hidden inside. You've seen what the others have. Nezu's got a sword, Saru calls hers a moon blade, and Inu can reach pretty far with that claw hook on a chain."

"Pah!" grunted Yunja. "Who needs any of that corrupting metal? Let a Wood Dog show you how strong a simple stick can make you." He strung up his catch of fish up in a tree and growled at his dogs, who licked their chops and whined. Then he held out a leathery hand. "Give that to me."

With a shrug, Usagi gave the hermit her pole and he passed her his club. She took ahold of the leafy branch. Its green leaves immediately withered into brown, papery curls. "It doesn't like me," she said, dismayed.

"'Course it doesn't," said Yunja. "It's been with me ever since I pulled it from a tree in my hometown." He paused and frowned at her. "Weren't you born in the year of the Wood Rabbit?" The hermit shook his head. "Never mind that. Hit me with it."

"What? No!"

"Just try," urged Yunja. "Go ahead and take a swing. Anywhere you like. Give me a good whack."

Usagi hefted the club. "I shouldn't." It was so heavy that she had to use two hands to lift it—and the hermit was gaunt and as brittle-looking as the dead leaves that adorned the branch.

Yunja looked at her with a frown and scratched his beard. "What do you mean, 'shouldn't'? Just do it. Did you want to see what your stick can do or not?" He stepped back and waited, holding Usagi's bamboo pole across his chest.

Usagi wanted to learn how to handle a weapon, but clubbing an old hermit with a tree branch wasn't what she had in mind. But Yunja looked determined, the leaves in his hair rustling as he swayed from side to side. She raised the branch. "If you insist." Usagi gave a halfhearted swing.

With a quick flick of his wrists, the hermit blocked it with the bamboo pole and batted the club away.

"Ow!" Usagi felt the impact shoot through her arms.

"Good!" said Yunja happily. "Try again. Harder."

Setting her jaw, Usagi swiped with a little more force and was rebuffed, the bamboo pole smacking sharply against the gnarled branch. A spray of dead leaves went up.

"You call that hitting?" hooted Yunja. "Keep going!"

Usagi swung with all her might and missed, spinning in a circle. Yunja gave her a gentle push with the end of the bamboo pole, knocking her on her backside. He cackled. "Get up, Rabbit Girl!"

With a grunt, Usagi came up off the ground and charged at the old hermit, heaving the club over her head. Yunja blocked the blow then deftly thrust the pole between her arms. With a firm twist he forced the club from her grasp, and it clonked to the ground.

The hermit handed over the pole with a slight bow, smiling his gap-toothed smile. "See? Your walking stick works just fine."

"Easy for you to say." Usagi rubbed her stinging hands. "No one ever showed me how to use it like that. And I'm a lot smaller!"

"Excuses!" Yunja snorted. "It's never too late to learn—and

so what if you're small? You make the most of what you've got."

Usagi squared her shoulders. "All right then. Show me."

When the Heirs returned from hunting, Usagi demonstrated what Yunja had taught her, tentatively blocking each swing of his club with her bamboo stick. She held her stick the way he'd shown her, gripping it firmly but not so hard that her knuckles were white. As the old hermit swiped at her with his knobby tree branch, newly green and leafy in his grasp, Usagi met each blow with increasing force, until Yunja threw down his club.

"I give up!" He raised his hands, chortling. "You win, Rabbit Girl."

The Heirs clapped and whistled. Breathing hard, Usagi rested one end of her walking stick on the ground and exchanged bows with Yunja, then bowed toward the others.

"This is an excellent start!" Nezu crowed.

"Start?" Usagi wiped her forehead with the back of her hand. "How much more is there to learn?"

The others laughed, including Yunja. "Rabbit Girl," he wheezed, "I'm just an old carpenter who never got past the local school in Flower Song Province. I know basics, but to be a master you'll spend the rest of your life learning—and that goes for everything, not just stickfighting." He wagged a finger at the rest. "The three of you claim to be Warrior

Heirs, but you're not doing a very good job! Shouldn't you be training her?"

Inu scowled. "We've been traveling."

"We should run drills," Saru said quickly, a flush appearing on her pale cheeks. "At least get her comfortable enough to spar."

"Yes! There are so many great stances and grips—I'll show you my favorite step sequence," Nezu told Usagi, smoothing his whiskers.

"Before you do any of that," the old hermit said, reaching for the fish he'd brought, "how about a bit of lunch? Mustn't let the hour of the Horse go by without a meal, else the horse god'll kick ya in the gut."

Everyone pitched in to clean the fish and a swamp hen brought back by the Heirs from their hunt. It was agreed that they would stay at Sun Moon Lake for another week to teach Usagi what they knew about stickfighting.

"It might be useful when we get to Mount Jade," Inu told her. "And while we're here, we've got to work on landing your leap. On the mountain, every one of your talents and gifts will be tested."

Yunja tossed one of his dogs a scrap of fish gut. "Is she Running the Mount so soon?" He let out a low whistle. "Merciful gods."

"What's that supposed to mean?" Usagi asked nervously.

The hermit shrugged. "I never tried it myself. All I know

is that the mountain goddess was never particularly easy on those who set foot on her territory, and I can't see her letting any humans on her slopes again after what happened with the Blue Dragon."

"That turncoat," Inu muttered under his breath.

Puzzled, Usagi frowned. "You've said that before, Inu. Who did the Dragonlord turn on?"

There was a pause. Inu's mouth set in a grim line and his dark eyes met Saru's. She nodded at him. He scratched his neck and cleared his throat. "Do you know how the invaders came to our shores?"

Usagi squinted at the starchy purple tubers she was cleaning, digging in her memory for all the rumors she'd heard over the years. "I—I'm not quite sure," she stammered. "I've heard different things. Like the Blue Dragon, before coming over with his men, used sorcery to awaken a dragon atop Mount Jade that swallowed up the Twelve."

Inu snorted. "That's a good one."

"I've also heard that he's half dragon and was sent from the Empire of Waya to conquer new lands," Usagi offered.

"Half dragon, eh? I wonder which half!" Yunja cackled as he scaled a fish.

Usagi rubbed the last bit of dirt off a tuber. "The most likely sounding story was that the Blue Dragon led troops from the Empire of Hulagu and joined forces with the Wayani."

The hermit stopped laughing. "Those cursed empires sent thousands of armed thugs," Yunja said bitterly. "At least nine thousand troops in two flotillas, and all of them out for the blood of those with zodiac powers. I saw their savagery with my own eyes."

Usagi gave him a sympathetic glance. "Maybe that's why everyone says the Blue Dragon vanquished the Warriors in one fell swoop." She brought the cleaned roots over to Nezu.

"A story spread by the Dragon himself, no doubt," said Nezu, scowling. He began noisily chopping the tubers on a wooden slab.

"But it's not what happened," said Saru. "History is written by those who win the war, and for those who find themselves on the losing end—well, their truth is often buried with them." She fiddled with the tie of her belt, rolling the stiff fabric between her fingers, before looking Usagi in the eye. "The man they call the Dragonlord was Druk, the 44th Dragon Warrior."

Usagi blinked and wriggled a finger in one of her ears. Did she hear that right? "The Blue Dragon was one of the Twelve?"

Nezu stopped chopping. "I wasn't at the shrine for long before he turned traitor, but he was one of the most fearsome warriors on Mount Jade. He succeeded the Tigress as the head of the Warrior Council."

"I remember that announcement," said Yunja. "It was

momentous, for a Dragon Warrior hadn't been head of the Twelve in nearly a hundred years."

A shadow crept across Nezu's face. "Not long after, the Shield of Concealment came down." He resumed chopping, faster and louder.

"At the Summoning," Usagi said slowly, "I remember the Tigress said something about a shield being created." She felt befuddled, as if she'd been told ice was actually hot and fire was cold.

Saru nodded. "From the kingdom's earliest days, neighboring nations wanted the secret behind what gave Midagians zodiac powers. Nearly eight hundred years ago, the emperor of Hulagu sent a thousand people to colonize the island and look for the cause, believing he'd find the secret of immortality and the formula for turning base metals into gold."

"There's no such thing, of course," Inu interjected.

"Luckily the Twelve led the islanders in subduing the invaders," said Nezu, "and the king decreed that no foreigners would ever be allowed onshore again."

Saru rummaged through a foraging sack for some wild onions. "The Warrior Council decided that to protect the island from further invasion, a shield would be erected. Each Warrior commissioned an item from a master artisan in one of the twelve provinces, and brought it as a votive offering to the sacred slopes of Mount Jade."

"To the Shrine of the Twelve," Inu added, and patted the spot where he carried the mirror.

Usagi understood immediately. "The Treasures," she breathed.

"The mountain goddess blessed a bond formed from the offerings," Saru continued. "As long as the Circle of the Twelve and the bond of their objects were in place, Midaga would remain hidden from the outside world."

"But when Druk became the head of the Twelve, he broke the bond," said Inu. He frowned at the swamp hen he was plucking. "He did it by crushing his Treasure—a necklace known as the Jewels of Land and Sea. It's no small thing to destroy a Treasure—it killed his Dragon Heir and triggered an earthquake and giant waves. Once the bond was broken and the Shield gone, Midaga was visible to the outside world. The invaders came not long after, swarming over the island like ants on a ripe peach."

Or roaches, Usagi thought. She remembered the first time she'd seen them, clacking all over Goldentusk in carapaces of armor, stripping fields and storehouses bare. She hadn't realized the great earthquake before the war had allowed their invasion.

"That was when a call to arms went out," Yunja said. The hermit had finished cleaning the fish and was scratching one of his dogs behind its ears. "Anyone with zodiac powers was pressed into service, with the Warriors of the Zodiac leading the charge. I never knew about the Treasures, but I did know about the Shield. Any fisherman in my town who ventured past a line of whitecaps at sea was never seen again. After the invaders got in—well, I'm not a great fighter. What Midagian would be? We were like hothouse flowers under glass—we could hardly be expected to know how to defend ourselves. When refugees from the next province said the invaders were slaughtering anyone with a hint of zodiac powers, I turned tail and came up here."

"Once, that sort of thing would have made me think you were a coward," Inu said to the hermit. "But when the royal family was killed along with our masters, we did the same." He plucked savagely at the last downy bits on the swamp hen carcass. "With our tails between our legs, we ran."

"We didn't run," corrected Nezu. He stirred the chopped tubers into a pot on the cookfire. "We retreated to regroup. On strategic orders from the Tigress. We still have a mission to locate the Treasures and keep them out of the Blue Dragon's hands. Now he might be adding those with zodiac powers to his strike force. But we'll find a way to stop him. Gods' guts, where's your Warrior spirit?"

Inu stood abruptly. "It died along with everyone else." He stalked out of the clearing, leaving a trail of feathers. One of Yunja's dogs whined and followed.

Nezu started after him, dripping spoon in hand. "Oi!" he shouted. "You think everything happens only to you? I lost

126

my master too, you know!"

"Let him go," said Saru. "He just needs to be by himself for a while." She retrieved the dressed swamp hen. "Talking about that time brings up difficult memories."

"We all lost good friends—and family besides," Nezu fumed. He returned to the pot, scowling. "You'd think he was the only one."

Usagi's heart ached. She could understand how Inu felt. Her throat tightened, thinking of her parents, deep in the turtleback grave back home. It made her want to run off too—run until she couldn't feel anything anymore, until she couldn't think anymore. She took a deep breath. It was all wrought by a man who'd been sworn to protect Midaga, and instead betrayed the kingdom and everyone in it. He now had Uma's and Tora's lives in his hands. The 44th Dragon Warrior. The Blue Dragon.

"So now what?" she asked.

"We keep to our mission," said Saru firmly. "Bring any Treasures we find to Mount Jade—and now, younglings with talents too. That means you."

CHAPTER 10

A LEAP IN THE LAKE

IN THE WEEK AT THE lake that followed, the Heirs and Usagi feverishly prepared for her ascent up Mount Jade. With each passing day, Usagi felt the distance between her and Uma growing, and her dread along with it. Her sister and Tora had surely reached the capital, and now that she really knew what the Blue Dragon was capable of doing, she wanted to go after them immediately. But her lack of skills made it hopeless.

She still hadn't mastered landing gracefully after a rabbit leap. And while Usagi was glad that the hermit had shown her how to use her walking stick as a weapon, it meant a whole new slew of drills and instructions from the Heirs.

Saru spent an entire afternoon working with Usagi just on properly holding the stick. "Relax your grip. Hands down, elbows by your sides. The stick makes a flat line, see? Feet apart. That's your beginning stance. You can do anything from flat line stance."

Usagi frowned. "The stick's just dangling. How am I supposed to attack like this?"

"You don't," said Saru. "First you learn to evade attack. In this position you can block blows easily before striking back. It looks harmless, but your opponent won't be able to guess your next move."

It turned out mastering something as simple as a stick was anything but simple. There were so many different ways to wield it: one-handed, two-handed, twisting overhead, wide grip, narrow hold, thrust grip. There were countless stances, positions, and movements. One foot forward, at attention. Feet wide, in a crouch. Down on a knee. One leg poised to kick.

You could whip the stick with a flick of the wrist, or swing it with the force of your whole body. You could strike something many steps away, or smack something a mere inch from your face. Usagi struggled to memorize all the different forms and grips, and practiced whenever and wherever she could.

"Cat! Butterfly! Snake! Crane!" she recited, arranging herself in the postures. Nezu teased her for mumbling the names of stances as she tossed and turned in her sleep. The Heirs would try to catch Usagi unawares and test her on the spot.

"Horse stance!" Inu would say as they were eating their supper. Usagi jumped into the pose, legs astride an invisible horse, still holding a half-eaten drumstick.

"Mantis!" Nezu shouted while Usagi was hauling newly washed clothes from the lake. Scrambling to get into position, Usagi threw up her arms, dropping fresh laundry into the mud. With a laugh, Nezu gathered up the tunics and helped rewash them.

"Phoenix pose!" Saru ordered as Usagi perched in a dragonberry tree picking fruit. Obediently Usagi demonstrated up in the tree's branches, losing hold of her foraging sack and sending a shower of berries raining on Saru.

But learning to fight with a stick was nothing compared with trying to land her leap. When Usagi was living in the forest outside Goldentusk, her animal talent was something to hide and use only when necessary, so she'd take bounding jumps and hope for the best. But the Heirs made clear that to make it up Mount Jade, she needed to do more than just hope. They made her practice for hours, yet her whole body seemed to resist. The more she fell, the more she stiffened upon landing.

"That's just your problem," Saru told her after several days of watching her collapse in bruising tumbles along the shore. "You lock your knees, so there's nowhere for the shock of the landing to go. You're knocking yourself down, which will keep happening if you tense up like that."

"I can't help it when I know it's coming," said Usagi. "It hurts to fall!"

Saru shook her head. "You can't learn without falling."

"Well, it's making me hate my rabbit leap," Usagi grumbled.

Nezu snapped his fingers. "I've got an idea." He grabbed Usagi by the hand and pulled her to the shore's edge. He pointed toward Wolf Snot Isle, the stony patch that peeked from the lake several hundred paces away. "Jump toward that rock. Don't try to land on it—in fact, try to avoid it. Land in the water and you won't have to worry about falling."

Usagi made a face. "I'll have to worry about swimming," she retorted. "And I don't have any special gift with water."

"That's why you've got me," said Nezu cheerfully. He plunged into the lake and disappeared. A bubbling swell sliced across the glassy waters in the direction of Wolf Snot, leaving a trail of expanding ripples. There was hardly time to blink before Nezu's head popped up by the rocky islet. "Come on, Rabbit Girl, give it a go!" he hollered. When Usagi hesitated, he lifted a ball of water, round and shimmering, out of the lake. He made a throwing motion, and before she even realized what was happening, it exploded against her shoulder, soaking her arm. Usagi shrieked.

He raised another ball of water and hurled it. She ducked, but it clipped her head and burst with a splash, dripping down her braids and the front of her tunic.

"Look what you've done!" Usagi spluttered. "I'm all wet!"

"So you might as well jump in," Nezu called.

"It's worth a try," Saru encouraged.

"Oh, all right." Usagi bent down and removed her sandals. "But I'm not ruining my new shoes for this."

Smiling, Saru set them aside. "Make sure to look where you want to leap."

"I know that much, at least," said Usagi. She squinted at Nezu bobbing by the outcropping, and dug her toes into the pebbly beach. "Here goes nothing." With a hop and skip, she flung herself toward Wolf Snot, soaring high above the glittering surface of the lake. For a moment she marveled at its wide expanse, her gaze drifting toward the other side of the vast lake. Then she remembered her target and glanced back down, spotting Nezu's head.

Too late, she realized she was hurtling straight toward the Rat Heir. Nezu's eyes went wide and he dove just as she hit the lake, right where he'd been treading water. Usagi knocked against something hard and she thrashed about until a hand closed on her arm and pulled her to the surface. Nezu had a rapidly swelling lump on his head. "That's some kick you have there," he said, touching his forehead gingerly.

"I'm sorry," exclaimed Usagi, wiping the water out of her eyes. "I didn't mean to land on you!"

Nezu grimaced. "Maybe look away from me next time." He hooked Usagi's arms around his neck and sped them back to land. As they churned toward shore, Usagi squealed and shut her eyes against the water's spray.

On her next attempt, Usagi made sure to fix her gaze away from Nezu as she plummeted. She braced herself. *Don't—it's just water.* Usagi relaxed just before plunging into the cool depths. Bubbles swirled all around her, and her ears were filled with strange underwater sounds: the gurgle of lake fish, the snap of turtles. She heard the steady swish of someone stroking toward her. Nezu grasped her arm and started pulling. Usagi kicked along, and broke through the surface with a gasp.

"Much better," said Nezu with a grin. "How did it feel?"

"It was actually kind of fun," Usagi admitted. "Can we try that again?"

Nezu towed Usagi back to shore. "Why don't we race? I'll swim and you leap. The first to get there wins."

They spent the better part of an hour competing to see who could get to Wolf Snot first, until Usagi was hurling herself into the air without giving landing a second thought, and no longer needed to take a running start. She even beat Nezu a few times. At last, Saru told them to get out of the water and dry off, which Nezu took care of with a flick of his wrists.

"Leaping into the lake is fun, but I think I know what you really need to do," Saru said. She led Usagi to a flat stone that barely came to her knee, and pointed to a patch of sand at its base. "Practice landing off this rock."

Usagi laughed. "That's easy," she said, stepping up and stepping down.

"Not like that," said Saru. "Jump using both feet." She demonstrated, hopping off the rock and landing squarely, her knees bent. He straightened. "It's just like the first stance in stickfighting—balance as if you're ready for an attack."

Stepping back onto the stone, Usagi hopped down and kept her knees bent like Saru had. "It does feel like flat line stance."

Saru seemed pleased. "Just practice that for a while."

Usagi was about to jump off the rock again when a deep clanging note sounded, as if someone had struck a giant bell. The vibrations of the note thrummed until Usagi could feel it beneath her bare feet.

"The Tigress!" Saru exclaimed. "We're being Summoned."

Saru and Nezu hurried toward the campsite, calling for Inu. Grabbing her sandals, Usagi went to follow, but Saru stopped her. "It's just the Heirs she's calling."

Feeling left out, Usagi turned back to the lake. The hum of the Summoning Bell even rippled the water's surface. As it dissipated and the lake grew calm again, one of Yunja's dogs ran out onto the shore, followed by Yunja himself, his bloodshot eyes wide.

"What in the name of the gods was that?" asked the hermit. The rest of his pack emerged and headed straight to Usagi, tails wagging.

"The Summoning Bell, up on Mount Jade." Usagi rubbed the ears of an appreciative dog, who licked her face. "The Heirs have been Summoned to report to the Tigress."

Yunja scratched his beard. "That popped my porridge, it did. A Summoning Bell, you say? Must be the size of the mountain itself, with that sound."

"I was inside a Summoning once," Usagi volunteered. "The Tigress looked like a giant tiger made of light!"

"Imagine that," marveled the hermit. He settled himself down on a rock and asked her questions, eager to hear more. Usagi was telling him about the Tigress seeing her rabbit form when the Heirs appeared, looking flustered.

"Tupa the Ram Heir just gave us news from the capital," said Saru, her pale face even paler.

Inu pulled out his mirror. "It's as we suspected. The Blue Dragon has established a school for talented younglings on the grounds of the palace." Frowning, he gazed into it and shook his head.

"Let me see!" Usagi took the Mirror of Elsewhere and anxiously examined it. She saw her sister and Tora, in new clothes with their hair neatly tied back, their expressions serious. They stood in a line with other younglings and bowed low as a helmeted Striker in heavy armor walked past. "No," she gasped. What would they be taught in such a school? What would they be forced to do? "Wh-what does this mean?"

"It means we should leave for Mount Jade now," Saru said. "The Tigress says we have delayed long enough."

Usagi handed back the mirror. "I haven't mastered my landing yet," she fretted.

Nezu flashed an encouraging smile. "But you've been practicing a lot, and I reported that to the Tigress."

"We're going into the ninth moon of the year, and the Tigress wants us back before the weather turns," said Inu. "Ascending now will be easier than when it gets colder. I tried to explain that we haven't been traveling by spirit speed, but that only seemed to make her doubt your abilities."

"I have talents," Usagi said, bristling. "Maybe I haven't been to school, but I can still learn."

The hermit clapped her on the back. "That you can, Rabbit Girl! You go up there and show her what Yunja taught you!"

Usagi looked at the old hermit. "What about you?" she said softly. "Are you just going to stay here?"

"Pah, don't worry about me," said Yunja, waving her away. "My boys and I were doing just fine before you all came along, and we'll be fine after you leave." He shook his club. "In fact, if you stayed any longer, we'd have to come round and run you off! A dog can't take intruders on his territory, y'know." He glowered at them all for a moment, then broke out in a gap-toothed smile and left them to pack up their camp.

At dawn the next day, Yunja came by for the last time, bringing smoked fish and dried fruit for their journey. The Heirs gave the hermit a small bundle. "To help protect against anyone who tries to hurt you," Inu told him. "I know metal isn't your element of choice, but there's no harm in having these on hand, just in case." Opening the bundle, Inu revealed a wood-handled knife and a string of dark metal plates. The plates had different shapes—square, round, triangular, pointed star—and were small enough to be concealed in one's palm. "Hidden blades. They're more for creating distractions than anything else, but they can really help if your opponent is out of your club's reach." To demonstrate, he threw one with a flick of the wrist, and it flew across the clearing into the trunk of a tree with a soft *thunk*.

"I'll have to practice that," said Yunja, and thanked them. "Be careful out there, y'hear? Keep out of the Blue Dragon's way."

"We can't promise anything," Nezu said with a grin. He and Yunja pounded each other on the back, and Saru gave the hermit a warm embrace. Inu growled and barked at Yunja, who wheezed a laugh and growled back. The hermit's three mountain dogs ran about in frantic circles, barking and whining.

Usagi flung her arms around the hermit, feeling the

rough surface of his mossy jacket against her cheek. He smelled like damp earth and green growing things, like the very cloud forest itself, and she knew she was going to miss him. "Thank you for everything," she whispered.

Patting her on the back, Yunja cleared his throat. "Don't ever stop jumping, Rabbit Girl," he said gruffly. "And keep practicing with that stick."

With a wave and a last round of shouted goodbyes, they shouldered their packs and left the lake. Usagi followed the Heirs out of the cloud forest, the mournful howls of the hermit's dogs echoing after them.

It had been nearly two weeks since she had to lug a backbundle across uncertain terrain, but Usagi quickly found a rhythm, marching along in her sturdy new slippers and swinging her walking stick. As the lush vegetation grew sparse, the screech of monkeys and cries of birds faded. The ground became increasingly stony, though a veil of fog remained. Usagi felt unsettled. The sounds of the cloud forest had become familiar, and Sun Moon Lake felt like a haven. She'd learned much there, but would it be enough to reach the Shrine of the Twelve? Usagi batted away the nagging worries. She had to focus on reaching the mountain. It was the first step in helping her sister.

Well into the hour of the Dragon, they emerged from the fog to a rolling landscape of scrub brush lit gold by the morning sun. Inu halted and pointed ahead. "There she is!"

Before them, the jagged horn of Mount Jade punched the sky like a triumphant fist. The massive pike dwarfed the rest of the Midagian Alps that trailed it like the ridged back of a scaly dragon. The deep green crags that gave the peak its name were powdered white with snow, which glistened in the clear light of Dragon hour.

"By the gods," Usagi said, dizzied by its grandeur. No wonder it was considered sacred.

"Beautiful, isn't it?" said Saru. She broke up a portion of dried smoked fish and offered her some. "It's been our one refuge from the Blue Dragon and his troops."

Feeling hunger catch up with her, Usagi nibbled gratefully on a salty nugget of fish. "I'm surprised he never tried to conquer it."

"Oh, he tried," Saru told her. "After the slaying of the king and the defeat of the Twelve, he returned to Mount Jade with a host of fighters to take the shrine. The Sea of Trees swallowed up the invaders and Druk barely got out with his life."

Usagi stopped chewing. She'd heard about spectacular failures of candidates who'd attempted the Running of the Mount, but a forest overcoming armor-clad invaders was something else. "Even though he was Dragon Warrior? And had troops with all their firecannon?"

"No one controls Mount Jade," said Nezu. He gazed at

the mountain, his usual mischievous expression gone. "Not even the Warriors of the Zodiac, and certainly not their traitor. The mountain decides." He took a savage bite of fish.

Usagi stared at the deep green spire, attended by a retinue of rocky pinnacles like a queen surrounded by courtiers. What would the mountain decide about her? Was she unfit? Would she be gobbled up by trees? Attacked by stone spirits? Torn apart by wild beasts? As she went through the possibilities, the dried fish began to taste like paste and her stomach churned. She caught the sound of sniffling, and saw that Saru's eyes were bright with tears. "What's wrong?" Usagi asked, alarmed.

Saru laughed a little and wiped her eyes. "The sight—it never fails to move me." She smiled at Usagi. "I can't wait for you to see Mount Jade's wonders for yourself."

"Er . . . I'm sure I'll love it," said Usagi doubtfully. "If it doesn't eat me first."

Nezu patted her shoulder. "You're the first new youngling with talent to approach the mountain in more than five years. The mountain goddess will be very pleased."

"Just remember all that you've practiced these last two weeks," Saru added.

Finishing his share of their fishy snack, Inu thumped his walking stick. "We'll be there before the day is out," he promised, his dark eyes alight with anticipation.

Saru clapped her hands, her pale face aglow. "I can't wait. Let's go home!"

Home. The word struck a jangled chord in Usagi's heart. What was home for her now? Goldentusk? A rickety forest shack, now empty? Mount Jade wasn't her home. Nothing could be called home without family. If only Uma and Tora could see the fabled majesty of the mountains, how they really looked like the undulating back of a giant sleeping dragon. Would she ever be with them again?

In silence, Usagi trudged after the Heirs. Nezu glanced back at her and a look of concern flitted across his face. He began cracking jokes and chattering about happy times at the shrine.

"Saru, remember the time that Inu put a hobbler in your seat?"

"I screamed right in the middle of a history lecture. The Tigress was so mad!"

"Yes, but I was the one who got in trouble. I wasn't allowed to go to archery practice for a week."

"Served you right, you dog! That hurt!"

"How about the time when Nezu wet all of Tupa's fire-starters?"

"Ha! It took him forever to figure out what happened, but he was pretty angry at me when he did. 'You dirty rat!'" Nezu unsuccessfully tried to imitate a deep voice. The others laughed, and Usagi couldn't help but join in. Nezu beamed. "You'll see, Usagi. The shrine is where all Warriors-in-training go—and there you'll get your rough edges smoothed off."

She wrinkled her nose at him. "Really? Looks like there's still a lot of work needed on *you*." The others hooted, and Usagi suppressed a giggle.

By the time the sun was high in the sky, they'd reached the edge of a great evergreen forest that carpeted the base of Mount Jade in dragon spruce, fire fir, and hemlock. Usagi shaded her eyes from the sun, barely able to see the peak of the mountain. High up from where they stood, jade-colored rock emerged from the darker green of the tree line.

"It's so tall," Usagi said faintly.

Nezu chuckled. "The Tigress likes to say, 'The tallest mountain anyone can ever climb is the self.' So you're fine!"

Inu gestured to the endless wall of forest before them. "Here's the Sea of Trees. It's part of Mount Jade, and your first test will be in there. Lucky for you there's no other Rabbit youngling to race to the shrine."

"Just take your time, and you'll get there," Saru encouraged.

Usagi hesitated. The spiky needled canopy repelled the bright warmth of the sun. Heavy shade darkened the underbrush, filling it with shadows. Thoughts of heavily armed Guard being swallowed by trees flooded her mind, swamping her with dread. She took a step back. "I—I don't know if I can do this."

Brushing back the hair in his eyes, Inu's gaze was steady. "You've made it this far, haven't you?"

"How will I find my way? Where is the shrine?" Usagi scanned the fortress of trees and felt the beginnings of panic. "Is it at the summit?"

"No, it's only partway up the mountain," said Inu.

"And there are many paths to get there," Saru told her. "Once we go in, you'll find the one that you must take."

"What if I don't? What I fail before I've even started?"

"The only way that happens is if you don't try," said Saru firmly. "No one who tries is a failure."

"But—"

Without another word, Inu and Saru plunged into the dense thicket. Nezu flashed a grin. "Come on, Rabbit Girl. Show the mountain what you've got." He entered the forest. Biting her lip, Usagi followed.

METAL

*"The Metal element gives strength, determination,
and persistence. But beware of the tendency toward rigidity."*

—Book of Elements, from *The Way of the Twelve*

CHAPTER 11

RUNNING OF THE MOUNT

USAGI FORCED HERSELF TO KEEP up as the Heirs led her into the Sea of Trees. Tendrils of dread crept over her in the murky gloom. Her feet dragged, wanting to go the other way. But Inu was right—she'd managed to come further than she'd ever imagined. If she made it to the shrine, not only would Usagi meet the last surviving Warrior, she would learn from her. Then she'd be able to rescue her sister.

They wound through towering, densely packed evergreens, each step sinking into the deep moss and fallen brown needles that blanketed the ground. After only a few minutes, Saru stopped and turned to Usagi, her pale face hopeful. "Do you see a path?"

Usagi peered through the shadows. The thick canopy of trees trembled, then parted, revealing a crack of sunlight. Sunbeams spilled across the ground in a path of light, weaving right through the trees like a winding golden thread.

Unspooling before her, it glowed from the forest floor. She pointed. "There!"

The three Heirs exchanged glances and smiled. Nezu clapped her shoulder. "I knew you could do it."

"Follow the path that you see," Inu instructed. "We'll meet you on the other side."

"Other side of what?" asked Usagi, alarmed. "You aren't coming with me?"

Saru shook her head. "We can't. We each must make our own way in this forest. Those not blessed with zodiac powers have never been able to pass the Sea of Trees, in part because they could never find a way through."

"This is good, Rabbit Girl," Nezu encouraged. "Just keep your wits about you, and we'll see you soon."

With a wave and a few last words of support, each of the Heirs started off in a different direction. Inu raised his chin, sniffing the air, and loped away upon catching a scent. Saru climbed high into a nearby tree and then jumped to another, then another, until she'd disappeared into the canopy. Smoothing his whiskers, Nezu jogged off with a grin, whistling a jaunty tune. In the dim light, the three of them quickly melted away into the forest, leaving Usagi utterly alone.

Her chest tightened. The trees were forbiddingly massive, their wide trunks knotty with age. Rubbing the little rabbit at her neck, Usagi took a deep breath. The air smelled of crisp evergreen needles, sharp-smelling sap, and loamy earth. Haltingly, she ventured along the sun-splashed path she saw, holding her walking stick close.

As she moved farther into the forest, a strange sensation came over her, as if her ears had gone numb, or been separated from her body. Usagi gave her head a shake. Nezu's whistling had disappeared and she couldn't hear any of the Heirs moving through the forest. She couldn't even hear her own feet shuffling across the thickly carpeted ground. The air was still. Not a single bird, frog, or insect could be heard.

She'd never been around such oppressive quiet. Just the opposite. For years, she'd heard *everything*, both near and far, and she'd quickly learned to focus on what she needed to, ignoring the rest. But now Usagi heard absolutely . . . *nothing*. Not even her own breathing, though her chest rose and fell as she sucked air into her lungs. She'd grown used to hearing her own heartbeat, but its steady presence was gone. Putting a shaking hand to her heart, she felt it pounding as if it were about to explode. But it was soundless.

Usagi tried calling out to the others, but her voice failed her. The forest swallowed every bit of noise. Disoriented, her vision began to swim and Usagi feared she might faint.

Steady, she told herself. She just had to follow the path. She couldn't turn back now.

Steady. The sooner she got through the Sea of Trees, the sooner she would pass through this unnerving quiet. Usagi broke into a run, keeping her eyes on the line of sunlight, clutching her bamboo pole so hard her knuckles were white.

Someone or some *thing* grabbed at her, while something rough and scratchy smacked her across the forehead. Usagi glanced up and froze at the sight of a hairy hand with claws. A flash of light struck her eyes, half blinding her. The stories about beasts and monsters were true! With no sound to guide her, she had no idea how large these beasts were—or how many.

Ducking and bobbing, Usagi tried to cover her head. Hairy clawed arms swooped down, trying to pluck her up from the forest floor, all in utter silence. In a burst of terror, Usagi screamed, but the sound died in her throat.

Use your stick.

Frantic, she whipped it at her attackers, cracking the bamboo pole hard against clawed, grabbing hands. She spun around and swung with all her might, batting them away as they came for her again. She could not let them take her. She would not go the way of the invaders. Usagi gritted her teeth and thrashed viciously at the arms—until one flew off and landed at her feet.

Uncomprehending, she gawked at a needle-covered branch on the ground.

She looked up to see a battered overhang of dragon spruce. She put a hand to her forehead, and felt some spruce needles in her hair.

There were no monsters. It hadn't been hairy clawed arms trying to snatch her off the path. She'd run into some low-hanging branches.

Panting, Usagi willed the fog of fear to blow away. This was just a forest, and these were just trees. How did she not see it? She felt foolish. Tentatively, she rested her hand against the rough bark of the ancient spruce, its branches torn and clipped by Usagi's stickfighting blows. The broken arms of the tree wept glistening drops of sap. "Sorry," she mouthed, still unable to find her voice.

The tree pulsed beneath her palm, as if it had a heartbeat, and a jolt of recognition seemed to flicker between them. Though the air was still and breezeless, the tree swayed gently, its branches quivering. Usagi felt a vibration, a tingle running from the tree into her fingers—as if it were trying to communicate. She pressed back against the tree, and gasped as the buzzing sensation ran up her arm and through her entire body. It wasn't painful, but it was strange. Her fingers felt as if they were sinking into the very fiber of the tree itself. Usagi glanced up to see the broken branches lengthening, new growth extending from the torn limbs until they looked whole again.

Stunned, Usagi withdrew her hand from the tree, and the tingling in her arm subsided. She stared at her hand and at the freshly grown branches. What was happening? Could she possibly have a gift with an element after all?

Excitement coursed through her. Resting her cheek against the trunk of the tree, she silently thanked it before continuing on her way. The massive trees lining her sunlit path no longer seemed threatening, and she touched several more, feeling them pulse under her touch. Usagi got a charge from each one, as if they were offering her strength to keep going. Soon she was almost skipping along the path of light, stopping from time to time to touch a tree and marvel at its response.

As the trees around her grew smaller, the path's bright golden glow dimmed, and the bubble of silence around Usagi dissipated. Her slippers began to squeak with each step, and she could hear her own pounding heartbeat returning to normal. When a cloud of gnats buzzed loudly by her head, she yelped with surprise, then giggled in relief. Her ears were back.

They pricked at the echo of several voices through the forest. The Heirs! Usagi ran eagerly toward the sound of their chatter.

By the time she entered a small clearing at the base of the mountain, the sun had dipped below the trees and the sky was a deeper shade of blue. The Heirs were sitting around a pot of bubbling porridge on a cookfire. Not even the first glimpse of Mount Jade was as wonderful as seeing them.

"You made it!" Nezu crowed.

"How did it go?" asked Saru.

With a grin, Usagi shrugged off her pack. "For a while I thought I might never see you again."

Inu leaned forward. "What happened in there?"

"I'm not exactly sure." Picking dragon spruce needles from her hair, Usagi told the others how soundless it was in the ancient forest, and how she'd fought what she thought was an attacking beast, only to find that it was a tree.

"That's a classic test—seeing how you handle yourself by taking away one of your talents." Inu nodded sagely. "People have been scared out of their wits here. But it's only because they let their fears take over."

"It almost happened to me," Usagi admitted. "But when I saw that I'd hurt the tree, I touched it—and then, something amazing happened. I felt a heartbeat, or something like it. Which sounds strange, but the tree felt so alive. Somehow we were talking to each other. Even stranger, the broken branches started to grow back. I've never done anything like that before." She examined her hand, which looked no different.

"You've discovered an elemental gift. It's the power of the mountain, bringing out what was in you all along," said Saru, her pale face alight. "It's why the main Shrine of the Twelve is here, and why the Heirs are trained here. This is wonderful, Usagi."

"Spirits be praised," Nezu said, looking pleased. He handed her a bowl of porridge. "Now eat up. You got through the first challenge, but more will come."

Laughing, Saru swatted at Nezu. "Let the girl enjoy her victory!" She then told Usagi to rest so she could tackle the next legs of the ascent in the light of day.

Usagi couldn't argue with that. If she'd had Tora's keen night vision, she might have disagreed, but she found herself suddenly very tired. She gulped down the porridge, then laid out her bedroll, quickly falling asleep under the sky as it frosted over with stars.

At dawn, the Heirs led Usagi to the base of the mountain. The ground pitched steeply and the trees grew at an angle. They scrambled over slumps of jagged green stone till they reached a crossroads.

"Which way, Usagi?" Saru pointed between two paths. They looked identical but extended in completely opposite directions around the mountain. It was impossible to see where either of them led.

Usagi bit her lip. "You're asking me?"

"When you went into the Sea of Trees, you had to find a way through, and were met by a challenge," Saru explained. "Now, by the choices you make, you'll get to the next assessment of your powers."

"Whichever path you choose will eventually take you to another challenge," Inu added. "The Warriors have created quite a few over the centuries. Don't be afraid of making the wrong choice, for there isn't one."

Usagi considered, then shrugged. "To the left is as good as any." As they climbed, the path narrowed to a winding ledge that hugged the mountain and forced them into single file. Along a particularly perilous-looking section, Usagi clung to the trunk of a nearby tree growing above the ledge. She felt it pulse under her touch, just as she'd felt in the Sea of Trees. Fascinated, she began to lay her hands on tree trunks along the path to gauge their responses. Some shivered or swayed, while one tree vigorously waved its branches. "Look!" Usagi said with glee.

"Are you sure that's not the breeze?" Nezu teased, wetting a finger and putting it in the air.

Usagi stuck out her tongue. They reached another fork in their path, a tall fir tree standing sentry over the junction.

She couldn't say how the idea occurred to her. Usagi placed her palm against the trunk of the fir tree and closed her eyes. *Which way?* she asked.

With a creaking groan, the tree leaned its pointed tip deeply to the right, and Inu's dark eyes widened. "Impressive."

With a triumphant smile, Usagi nodded in the direction suggested by the tree, and they proceeded up a thin strip of dirt that snaked back and forth across a steep slope. They came across several more junctures in their path, and each time Usagi had to choose. Whenever a tree was nearby, she would touch it for guidance, selecting whatever direction the tree branches waved.

At last they reached a track carved into the mountain, a deep groove winding up a smooth rock slope in a series of swooping switchbacks. Twelve colossal round stones sat in the turns like giant gray-green marbles. Nezu let out a low whistle. "The Bashing Boulders!"

"*Bashing* Boulders?" Usagi repeated. "That doesn't sound promising."

"Maybe I misspoke about no wrong choices," Inu muttered.

Saru shot a glare at Inu. "This particular challenge was designed by the 14th Snake Warrior. You have to go through this track and find a way to get around the stones."

"More like avoid the stones," Inu corrected. "If not . . . well, try not to look at the bloodstains."

Alarmed, Usagi goggled at the twisting trench and its twelve turns. She couldn't tell if there were any traces of blood, but the enormous stone spheres blocking each turn were too round and slick to climb.

Pressing her lips together, Saru pointedly ignored Inu. "It won't be easy, but challenges aren't supposed to be."

Usagi stalled for time. "Are you going this way too?"

"Don't worry about us," said Saru. "Just get through the boulder course."

Inu's gaze was serious. "Keep alert and be quick out there.

Remember, your talents are being tested."

She nodded, clutching her stick close. Usagi was going to have to use her rabbit leap. If only she'd had more time back at the lake to practice landing. With a deep breath, she jumped into the waist-deep trench. Halfway toward the first switchback, her ears caught a low rumble that echoed off the slick stone slope. The giant rocks sitting in the turns all began to roll, picking up speed with an earthshaking rattle.

Usagi screamed and scurried downhill. With a rolling boulder hard on her heels, she vaulted out of the trench. The boulder reached the end of the carved channel, stopping with a groaning crunch. Then with a rocky clatter, it reversed course, spinning back up the track—until it smashed into another sphere on its way down. Usagi winced at the sound. The crash sent the two spheres reeling in opposite directions. Each time a boulder hit another sphere in its path, it would change course and tumble back the way it came, only to bang into another and alter its direction yet again. Wide-eyed, Usagi watched the twelve giant spheres rolling up and down all along the snaking trench, colliding back and forth in a thunderous cacophony.

Horrified, she whirled upon the three Heirs. "I'll be crushed!"

Inu and Saru exchanged glances. Folding his arms, Inu shook his head. "I was afraid of this."

"You're not helping," Saru scolded. She steered Usagi

back to face the winding track and its rumbling stones in perpetual motion. "You have a choice, Usagi. Either use your talents and go through the course the best you can, or stop here and leave the mountain."

"Go," Nezu urged. "I've seen your rabbit leap. You can do this."

Usagi stared at the rolling spheres. "They're certainly bashing," she muttered. Steeling herself, she waited until the first sphere rolled away from the beginning of the course and jumped back into the trench. She jogged after the stone, gripping her stick with sweaty palms. There was a series of loud crashes as the stones slammed together, one pair after another, in a cascading relay. The stone she followed changed course and clattered toward her. Crouching low, she sprang straight into the air and let the boulder rumble beneath her. Landing back a little too hard, she skidded onto her bottom. "Blasted blisters," she swore. She scrambled to her feet. She'd barely escaped being squashed like a bug! But maybe Nezu was right. Even if her landing wasn't perfect, she could leap these stones. Rounding the first turn, Usagi ran straight after the second sphere.

The boulders crashed and reversed direction, and the one Usagi was chasing tumbled toward her, bearing down fast. She vaulted up and over it, and stumbled only slightly upon landing. *Bend the knees*, she reminded herself, then laughed out loud. She was past the second stone. Ten more to go.

She sprinted for the next rolling sphere, listening and counting to herself. At the sound of each collision, Usagi began counting anew, pacing the time it took between crashes and calculating how far up the path she could run before having to jump. By the fourth boulder she thought she detected a pattern: after three crashes in quick succession, she could take twelve strides and a leap before the collisions started again. But by the sixth rock she almost lost her stick when she was forced to jump after just ten steps. She barely got over, scraping the sphere with her bamboo pole as it spun past. *Spitting spirits.* The stones were moving faster and faster, and the pattern had changed. Forget counting.

With her rabbit hearing she tracked a boulder coming up behind, and waited till it was nearly upon her before leaping. She cleared it and landed safely as it rumbled up the incline. When it crashed into another stone seconds later and rolled back down, she sprang again and landed neatly on her feet. Usagi let out a little whoop, feeling a rush of excitement, and ran faster. She listened for the stones approaching behind her, and watched the ones looming before her. The pace picked up, and sometimes she had to jump the same rock multiple times. But Usagi was grinning. Dodging these rolling rocks was . . . *fun.* With each successful pass over a boulder, her grin grew wider.

Finally, she bounded over the last of the spheres and made it to the top of the switchbacks. She raised her stick and did a little dance. The others cheered from the base of the run, Nezu hopping about and pumping his fists.

To her surprise, the stones rumbled back to their initial positions and came to a stop. They remained silently fixed in place as the Heirs came up a narrow channel Usagi hadn't noticed, cut along the side of the course. "Are the boulders only for bashing newcomers?" she called.

"Pretty much," Nezu shouted back.

When they joined her at the top, Inu clapped Usagi's shoulder. "Well done!"

"Thanks," she beamed.

They set off along a dirt path that led away from the Bashing Boulders. It was wide enough to walk two abreast, at a far gentler grade than any of the trails they'd climbed earlier. Usagi was tired but proud. She'd gotten through two challenges. There might be more, but what she'd managed so far surprised even herself. Hope bloomed in her chest. She would be at the shrine soon. What would the Tigress be like? What might the last Warrior of the Zodiac teach her? Would there be anything besides hard dried fish and thin porridge to eat? As she wondered about the possibilities, she noticed a persistent roar in the distance, like the thunder of a great storm.

"Do you hear that?" she asked Nezu. He frowned and shook his head.

Uneasily, Usagi cupped a hand behind her ear. The roar grew louder. Whatever it was, it was getting closer. Her breath caught. "It sounds like a thousand horses galloping. The Blue Dragon's mounted Guard can't get up here, can they?"

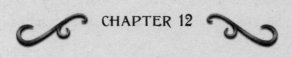

CHAPTER 12

THE TIGRESS

THE RUMBLING ROAR IN USAGI'S ears grew louder as she and the Heirs climbed farther up the mountain. She feared that Dragonstrikers were approaching Mount Jade on horseback, but Nezu scoffed. "The Blue Dragon's men can't get up here, especially on horses. Remember? They couldn't even get past the Sea of Trees."

Usagi listened again. "It's like thunder, only it doesn't ever stop."

Nezu's puzzled expression cleared. "You're probably hearing the Sage's Beard."

"The what?" Usagi asked.

"It's a waterfall with a bridge we'll be crossing."

"I've never seen a waterfall." She scratched her nose. "Why's it called the Sage's Beard?"

He flashed a grin. "You'll see."

By the hour of the Ram, with the sun tipping past its apex

toward the west, Usagi and the Heirs came upon the water-fall. It soared hundreds of feet high, with clouds of billowing pale mist spilling down a jade-green cliff. Usagi laughed, for the falls truly resembled the long white beard of an old man. Pounding rapids churned and boiled at the base, kicking up a fine icy spray that swept over them and stung their faces. Saru pointed to the cliff.

"We'll need to go up that rock face," she shouted over the crashing falls.

Usagi scanned the slick wall of green rock that framed the tumbling, swirling water. "Nezu said there was a bridge."

"Yes, but you have to climb to get to it," Inu told her. "There used to be stairs carved into the rock, but they crumbled when the Blue Dragon tried to ascend them."

"They didn't just crumble. The Tigress brought them down," Nezu yelled. "But a few years ago Saru rigged some ropes and Inu put some metal spikes up that wall, so it shouldn't be too bad."

"Is this one of the challenges?" Usagi asked, woozy at the thought of traversing the sheer rock.

Saru smiled and shook her head. "Climbing to the bridge is trickier than it used to be, but no."

Spirits. Usagi squinted. Wisps of brown webbing stretched across the jade-green wall. "Okay, I see the ropes."

"Just follow me," Nezu offered. "Watch where I put my feet."

In single file, they approached a set of knotted ropes attached to the rock at intervals. Steel spikes had been hammered into the stone, accompanying the rope lines. Saru jumped up and began to climb without the help of rope or spikes, racing up the face of the cliff like a monkey scaling a tree. Nezu grabbed a knot and stepped onto the first protruding spike, then onto the next like a ladder. Nervously, Usagi jammed her stick behind her pack.

"Use your legs as you climb—don't try to pull yourself up with your arms, or you'll tire out quick," Inu advised.

Usagi took a deep breath and grasped the rope. She put her foot on the first spike, like Nezu did, and stepped up. With her other foot, she felt around till she found a spike near her right knee, and stepped up again. Holding tight to the rope, she inched up the rock wall.

The weight of her pack shifted with each move, the straps cutting into her shoulders. Occasionally a chip of rock would rattle down the cliff face, kicked free by Saru's feet. As Nezu climbed ahead, his movements bounced through the network of ropes, keeping her off balance. Though the mountain air was cool and her hair was sodden from the mist of the falls, beads of sweat trickled down her back. It felt like they'd never get to the bridge. She reached for a knot high above her, grunting with the effort.

"How are you doing?" Inu called for the tenth time. He

was just below her, and sounded as if he were ready to push her up the wall.

"Never better!" Usagi insisted. She glanced down and froze. At this height the Sea of Trees looked like a woolly green blanket wrapped around the foot of the mountain. White wisps of cloud drifted by. In the east, Usagi could see smoking piles and great gashes in the earth that had to be the Eastern Mines. The blue of the sea striped the horizon. They were so high up. Spitting spirits, what if she fell? The forest floor began to spin and she let out a panicked cry.

"Don't look down," Inu shouted. "Look at the rock right in front of you, or at Nezu. Keep your eyes up."

Heart pounding, Usagi pressed her face against the rock wall and shut her eyes, but felt even dizzier. With a whimper, she stared at the mottled green jade against her cheek, then forced her gaze upward till she found Nezu. He seemed so far. Keeping her eyes on him, she toed around until she found another spike, and stepped up. Panting with fear and exertion, Usagi crawled along until she reached a small ledge where Nezu and Saru crouched. They offered a helping hand, and Inu scrambled up beside her. "Good job."

"I didn't think I'd make it." Usagi wiped her brow. It felt so good to be standing on something solid, even if it was only a narrow stone shelf.

"You should've seen me the first time I climbed this wall,"

Nezu told her. "Saru practically dragged me up."

"You got through the hardest part, Usagi. The bridge is at the end of this ledge." Saru nodded behind them, and then her eyes widened. "The Tigress!"

Usagi whirled. A long bridge of woven vines and bamboo planks led to a ledge on the other side of the falls. She peered through the mist. On the far ledge, more than a hundred paces away, stood a hooded figure leaning on a tall wooden staff.

Horangi, the last Warrior of the Zodiac—in her bodily form.

Tiny and stooped, she was nearly a head shorter than Usagi. Her long belted robe was the rusty hue of humble persimmon dye, the hood covering her face from view. Saru took a few steps toward the bridge, but stopped as the figure raised a gnarled hand and began crossing. The small form clutched at the ropy vines, thumping her staff slowly on the bamboo planks.

Usagi fiddled with the carved wooden rabbit around her neck, trying not to stare. *This* was the 42nd Tiger Warrior? It seemed an eternity before the hunched figure stepped off the bridge and stood before them.

"My Heirs." Creaky with age, the voice sounded just as Usagi had remembered from the Summoning. The figure pushed the hood back to reveal the wrinkled face of an old woman, her snowy hair streaked with a thick stripe of black, pulled back into a long braid. Her deep-set eyes were startlingly green, as vibrant as the jade cliffs surrounding them. Even more arresting were the pale, puckered scars on her face, three long slashes adorning each leathery cheek.

"You are late." The Tigress's words were blunt, her gaze stern. "You should have returned weeks ago."

The Heirs bowed. "Forgive us, Teacher," they chorused. Abashed, Usagi bowed as well.

"But you reported success on your mission. I look forward to seeing the return of more Treasures to the shrine." The old woman patted Inu's shoulder and reached up with gnarled fingers to smooth Saru's hair. She then pulled at Nezu's arm until he bent forward, and took him by the chin to examine his face. "Spirits be! You keep growing, ratling. Are those whiskers I see?" Nezu grinned and straightened as she released his chin with a cackle. It quickly became a dry cough that shook her bent form. As the others tried to pat her back and offer her water, she waved them off.

"We have more important matters to worry about," croaked the Tigress. Her green eyes flicked over to Usagi.

Awkwardly, Usagi bowed once more. What did one say upon meeting a Warrior of the Twelve? "G-greetings, Honored Tigress," she stammered.

The green eyes narrowed. "A youngling, unschooled and

untested, upon this sacred mount? I never thought I'd see such a thing."

Cheeks burning, Usagi dropped her head and studied her toes. It wasn't her fault she'd never had a chance to go to school.

"Unschooled she may be, but Usagi has had her zodiac powers tested," said Saru. "Her standing here is proof." The others chimed in, talking over each other in their haste to appraise the Tigress of Usagi's skills, how well she did in the Sea of Trees and on the boulder run. But Horangi held up a wrinkled hand again, and they fell silent.

"Go ahead, the three of you," said the old woman. "I will assess the youngling myself." The others hesitated, but when the Tigress fixed them with a calm stare, they bowed their heads. Nodding encouragingly at Usagi, they crossed the bridge.

The Tigress waited until they'd reached the other side, then turned back to Usagi. "I felt your entry into the Sea of Trees, but I will admit I did not expect to see you get this far. The Heirs have had the benefit of years of training." She inspected Usagi with a frown. "You have never been properly taught. You could hardly be considered a candidate for anything. What do you hope to gain by coming all this way?"

"I'm not asking to be a candidate," said Usagi. The Tigress raised her eyebrows, but remained silent. Usagi hurried on.

"Strikers took my sister and friends away because they have talents, just like me. But I won't let the Blue Dragon keep them. I want to learn whatever I can to save them." She looked at the old woman's impassive face and added, "I'm not afraid of hard work."

The Tigress stared at the bridge and cocked her head. "Very well." Her lips pursed. "Wait here. Do not cross until I give you a sign. Understand?"

Usagi nodded, wondering what the sign would be. The old woman shuffled back to the Heirs on the other side of the chasm. When the Tigress reached them, Usagi thanked the gods for her sharp ears, for she could still hear the old warrior as she spoke.

"Give me your sword, Nezu," Horangi ordered.

Even at this distance, Usagi could see confusion on Nezu's face. He pulled it out of his walking stick and handed it over. The Tigress gave him her staff and took his sword, then hobbled across the bridge toward Usagi, the ropy vines and planks creaking with each step. The blade was nearly as tall as the old woman herself. Usagi frowned. It looked too heavy for one so frail. What was she planning to do with it?

The old warrior stopped midway on the swaying bridge. Her green eyes seemed to glow. She raised the sword above her head. With a mighty swing, she cut the ropes on the very bridge she stood on.

The sound of the snapping vines was like the crack of a

whip. Horrified, the Heirs cried out. "Teacher!"

Time seemed to slow. Only one ropy vine kept the bridge suspended across the gap. The deck collapsed, swinging from the remaining rope like a set of wind chimes. The Tigress dropped the sword, which tumbled into the chasm below, and grabbed the rope. Finding the edge of the planks with her feet, Horangi clung there for a brief moment while the deck of the bridge dangled uselessly from a single vine.

But the weight of it all was too much for that last rope, and a series of ominous creaks and pops sounded until it snapped. The bridge tore in two with a loud crack. The severed pieces of the bridge swung apart, and the old warrior began to fall.

Without a second thought, Usagi sprang after her, reaching for the tiny figure. She couldn't let the last Warrior die. Leaping through the mist, she realized too late there was nowhere to really land. She flew into the Tigress and the falling end of the bridge, grabbing hold of both as it swung toward the cliff. "I've got you!" she shouted.

The bridge slammed against the rock with a shuddering bang. Usagi squealed and held tight to the worn bamboo planks and the Tigress. Heart pounding, she glanced down into the yawning gap, the rushing falls and slick green stone a swirl of color and motion. Usagi scrabbled with her feet, trying to find a toehold between the planks, but kept kicking slats off into the frothing water below. "Help!" she cried.

Horangi seized Usagi's arm with a gnarled hand. "A good effort, youngling. Hold on!" Her grip was shockingly strong.

From above, Saru's face appeared. "I'm coming!" She scrambled down the rock face alongside the dangling bridge and grasped the Tigress about the waist. The old warrior waved her off. "Take the youngling up first."

Saru called for the other Heirs to throw down a rope. She quickly tied it around Usagi and gave it a sharp tug. Nezu and Inu began to pull, while Saru had the Tigress loop her arms around her neck. She climbed up with Horangi on her back, just as the two boys hauled Usagi over the stone ledge to solid ground.

Staggering to her feet, Usagi approached the Tigress. "Are you all right? I didn't mean to tackle you, but I didn't know what else to do."

The Tigress didn't answer. She appraised Usagi in silence, looking her over with a gleam in her eye.

Inu regarded Usagi with new respect. "Forget the Bashing Boulders. I didn't expect you would do *that*." He blew the hair off his forehead with a whoosh and scowled at the Tigress. "Or that you would do . . . *that*."

With shaking hands, Nezu gave the old warrior her staff. "Here, Teacher."

"Thank you, ratling," Horangi croaked. "I am afraid I lost

171

your sword. We will get you a new one."

"Teacher, what in the name of the Twelve were you thinking?" Saru demanded. Her face was paler than the mists of the Sage's Beard.

Horangi's lips quirked. "Come along," she said simply, and shuffled away.

They picked their way along the narrow stone ledge, emerging onto a wide trail. Overhead, the bright sun seemed to shine in celebration, rapidly drying their mist-dampened hair and clothes. Usagi smiled to herself. She'd helped save the Tigress with her rabbit leap! She felt like dancing. Then she looked up and choked back a scream.

Prowling toward them was an immense cat the size of a sun bear. Its tawny fur and cloud-shaped black markings made it nearly invisible against the rocks and shadows. Usagi could see its tail twitching as it fixed its amber eyes on the Tigress, padding silently on paws as big as a man's hand. A rumbling noise from deep in its throat sounded a warning.

"Spirit's spleen, a cloud leopard!" Usagi brandished her stick. Cloud leopards were elusive, rare, and reportedly vicious. She had only ever seen a skinned pelt once when she was little, sported by a one-armed trader who'd boasted of revenge on the big cat that had taken his other arm.

Saru put a hand on her shoulder. "That's Kumo—the Tigress found him as an orphaned cub. He's been by her side for several years now."

It wasn't growling, Usagi realized with a start. "It's purring!" she whispered.

They watched as Horangi raised her gnarled hand. The cloud leopard bumped its enormous head against her palm. After a few scratches behind the big cat's ears, the old woman grasped the ruff of fur at the cloud leopard's neck and got onto the animal's back.

"To the shrine, Kumo," said the Tiger Warrior, and the great cat slinked off. Within moments Horangi and her cloud leopard were out of sight.

"With Horangi on that big cat, she'll be back at the shrine in no time," said Saru. "We should follow her at spirit speed."

Usagi hesitated. "I still haven't used spirit speed."

The Monkey Heir jumped into a nearby tree. "It's the perfect time to give it a try." She glanced down and a smile lit up her pale face. "You're on the Mount now." She took a flying leap to another tree, and then another, rustling through the treetops. "Meet you at the gate!"

"You can do it," Inu encouraged. "I'll stay with you."

"Me too," Nezu chimed in. "I'll keep in back. Just think of each rabbit leap as a step out of many, like running, but with much longer strides. You'll be at spirit speed before you know it!"

Usagi frowned, trying to picture it. Inu loped up the trail. "Try to keep up with me, and you'll see," he called over his shoulder.

"I can't promise that," she mumbled, but fell into step behind him, her backbundle jouncing awkwardly. Inu sped up, his legs scissoring faster and faster.

"Don't run, Usagi!" Nezu shouted. "Jump!"

The Dog Heir's back was rapidly getting smaller and smaller as the distance between them grew. There was no way Usagi could keep up if she didn't leap. She launched herself toward him and felt a warm rush of weightlessness as she soared through the cool mountain air. Upon touching down, she took several stutter steps instead of coming to a full stop, then sprang again after Inu.

He threw a look over his shoulder and grinned. "Good!" He increased his pace, and Usagi took another running leap. Behind her, Nezu whooped.

So this was what it felt like to go at spirit speed—all the freedom she felt while running, only each step took her twenty paces forward. It was like wearing the most incredible wings on her feet. Before long she was laughing as she vaulted through the air, covering more ground in a single bound than if she'd trekked the regular way. *The old way.*

Awash in sunlight and fragrant with evergreen, the trail passed by in mere blinks of the eye. They made their way up the mountain, following the snaking path that hugged its steep slopes. Usagi was exhilarated, the unwieldy bulk of her backbundle forgotten. She jumped so hard she nearly landed on top of Inu, clipping his flying feet.

"Easy now," he yelped. Nezu snorted with laughter behind them. Usagi wished her sister could see her, wished that she could show Tora spirit speed. She and Tora would never be able to beat Uma's horse speed, but with spirit speed they might be able to at least keep track of her. The three of them could run through the forests of Goldentusk, faster than any Guard, wild and free.

By the time they arrived in a clearing, the sun was setting, a guttering flame on the horizon that turned the sky rose gold. Before a massive shrine gate stood a smiling Saru with the Tigress, the cloud leopard by their side.

The gate was a squared portal, formed from two immense columns hewn from the trunks of ancient trees, joined by giant crossbeams lashed with rope as thick as a man's arm. Beyond it, a long, winding flight of stairs cut into the gray-green rock of the mountain.

The old warrior fixed her gaze on Usagi. "If you truly have the temperament to learn, you will reach the top. Only then may teaching begin." Without waiting for a reply, she clambered back onto Kumo. The cloud leopard passed through the giant wooden gate and padded up the stone stairs with Horangi clinging to its sleek back, carrying the elderly Tiger Warrior as if she weighed nothing.

Usagi stared after her, puzzled. Whatever did she mean?

"Almost there," said Saru, giving Usagi's arm a squeeze. The Heirs followed the Tigress, each of them reverently touching the giant gate as they passed. Nezu even hugged one of the enormous posts, though it would have taken three of him to encircle it completely.

Hitching up her pack, Usagi gazed at the winding staircase, framed by the ancient gate. As she went through the portal, she stroked the weathered wood, imagining the great trees that had been cut down to build the entrance to the shrine. A tingle ran down her spine. She was so close.

CHAPTER 13

TREASURES OF THE TWELVE

FLANKED BY AN ARMY OF trees, the staircase to the Shrine of the Twelve stretched up in a serpentine climb. Usagi couldn't see where it ended, but could hear a faint chorus of flutes at the top playing snatches of a familiar tune. Furry green moss grew thickly along the staircase and coated the edges of each broad step. The Heirs followed the cloud leopard as it glided up the stairs, the Tigress on its back.

Usagi thunked her walking stick on each step she climbed, counting to herself. One *thunk* two *thunk* three *thunk* . . . twenty-eight, twenty-nine . . . sixty-four . . . She slowed. One hundred . . . two hundred. She lost count in the three hundreds, her legs burning. "Suffering spirits!" Usagi exclaimed, and stopped. Why weren't they using spirit speed?

She launched into a hop. To her shock, she bounced against a stiff, invisible resistance. She stuck out a hand and felt nothing. Strange. Setting her jaw, she jumped again, and rebounded so violently she nearly toppled backward. With a grunt, Usagi tried once more, then kept hopping, only to go nowhere, stuck on the same step no matter how hard she leaped. It was as if she were throwing herself into an impenetrable mattress of air. Far above her, Nezu guffawed. He and Inu had turned to watch. Usagi stopped, panting. "What in the name of the Twelve is happening?" she shouted.

Snorting and clutching his stomach, Nezu wiped his eyes. "Oh, my belly. What a sight."

"She looks like a cricket in a glass box," Inu chuckled.

"By the gods, she does!" Nezu doubled over again.

Frowning, Usagi poked at the next step with her stick, and felt no resistance. She stepped up and prodded the next step. Again, no barrier. Odd. She walked up a few more steps, quickening her pace. Nothing stood in her way. Baffled, Usagi went for a leap. *Oof!* She bounced back so hard she tumbled over. Peals of laughter rang in her ears.

Her cheeks heated and she glowered at the boys. They were braying like a pair of asses and it wasn't helping. She rubbed her cramping calves. It appeared she could get up the stairs as long as she didn't try to skip any. With a sigh, Usagi grimly resumed climbing, one step at a time, while the others continued ahead. At long last, she reached the top, where the Heirs waited with the Tigress. Usagi collapsed at their feet, her muscles on fire.

"There must be a thousand steps here," she gasped.

"One thousand, two hundred, and twelve of them, to be exact," Nezu chimed, offering her his hand. Usagi scowled at him, and his face fell. "What?"

She shook her head and hauled herself up. "I'm glad you and Inu were so entertained."

"You'd laugh too, if you saw yourself," Inu protested.

"A warning would have been helpful," Usagi huffed. "That was torture!"

Horangi stared down at her from the cloud leopard's back. "To be a Warrior demands your full attention," she said, her cold eyes like hard emeralds. "There are no short cuts. The Steps of Patience are a reminder of that."

With a meek bow, Usagi followed as the Tigress led them onto a wide stone path surrounded by a stand of the tallest bamboo she'd ever seen, the dusky sky barely glimpsed through the feathery fronds. Though there was no breeze, the thick stalks swayed, and fluting melancholy notes floated above the whispering rustle of the leaves. The music Usagi had heard was coming from the bamboo itself. "You play that tune all the time," she said to Inu. "Right before we go to bed."

"You noticed?" Inu sounded pleased. "It's from the Singing Bamboo. Tonight the grove will play us to sleep instead of me."

Along both sides of the darkened path, tall figures stood sentry like frozen Guard, six to a side. Usagi peered through the fading light and saw they were stone lanterns shaped like different animals—one for each animal of the zodiac.

"They haven't been lit since the war. Horangi won't allow it," Saru confided. "I think it's too painful for her."

They reached a courtyard lit with lanterns of a far more austere style. The Tigress slid off the big cat's back and stroked its head before the leopard shook itself and slinked behind an enormous building facing the courtyard. More than two stories tall, it was built of unadorned wood, aged silvery gray by the elements. Dark forked logs protruded from the ends of the gabled bark roof.

"The Shrine of the Twelve," Nezu announced proudly. "Soul of the Mount, where the heart of a Zodiac Warrior finds its home."

The flanking buildings were long and slung close to the ground, built in the same simple fashion. A low wooden platform edged the gray-green tiles of the courtyard, connecting the buildings. Usagi hadn't expected such a legendary place to be so plain. Aside from the bamboo grove's ornate stone animal lanterns, everything looked humbler than she'd imagined.

Saru shrugged off her pack onto the platform with a sigh, then sat and looked around with hungry eyes. "It's good to be back," she said.

Legs rubbery, Usagi sat as well, allowing herself a small smile. She could hardly believe it, but she'd made it to the Shrine of the Twelve. She wanted to explore the grounds, the buildings, the Singing Bamboo. Her stomach erupted with a growl.

The Tigress turned at the sound. "Take the youngling with you and help yourselves to something to eat," she told the Heirs. "Afterward, retire to the sleeping quarters for a full night's rest. I want a complete report of your latest mission first thing in the morning."

Inu yawned. "I can't wait to sleep under a roof again."

A sharp cry jolted Usagi awake. She squinted in the sunlight from an open window. The cry sounded again. Blearily she peered at the source. A mountain thrush sat on the windowsill, calling. Usagi sat up, startling the bird away in a flurry of wings. She rubbed her eyes and looked around, disoriented.

She was at the shrine, in a room spacious but spare, with whitewashed walls and a wooden floor dark with age. Her bedroll was on a long platform covered in reed matting. Extra bedding was stacked against the wall in piles of thick blue indigo mattresses, gray woolen blankets, and pristine white sheets. A light breeze drifted through latticed windows, the wooden shutters thrown open, carrying a soft chorus of flutelike melodies and the faint perfume of sandalwood incense.

"*Ki-yah!*" Saru's shout reverberated in the courtyard. "*Ki-yah!*"

"Not bad, Monkey Girl." Inu sounded impressed. "Your form looks solid as ever. The Tigress should be pleased."

Sliding out of bed, Usagi looked out the window. Inu sat cross-legged on the wooden deck that ringed the courtyard. Saru crouched before the enormous main building, moon blade in hand. The massive wooden doors behind Saru were open, revealing a cavernous room. Usagi craned her neck. Saru twirled her curved blade by its long handle, then kicked and spun, the ribbon of her topknot streaming in a circle behind her. She lunged with another fierce cry. "*Ki-yah!*" Suddenly, she snapped to attention, then bowed. "Good morning, Teacher!"

Inu scrambled up out of his seat and bent low. "Good morning, Teacher!"

The old warrior shuffled into the courtyard, her wooden staff tapping on the stone tiles. The hood of her persimmon-colored robe was down, revealing her silver-white hair with its streak of black. "Morning." It was a statement more than a greeting.

"Nezu is making your favorite dish for the morning

meal," Saru told her.

The Tigress tsked, frowning. "I wanted a mission report from all three of you."

"Saru and I can present the Treasures," Inu offered. "We've taken them to the Great Hall."

"Did you place the Treasures with the others?"

"Of course. I'll show you now!" Inu loped through the massive doors of the outsized building, followed by Saru and the Tigress.

Anxious to see, Usagi changed as quickly as she could, flinging her bedding into a haphazard pile. She braided her snarled hair with hasty fingers and ran out of the sleeping quarters. Blinking in the bright morning sunshine, she hurried across the courtyard. The mouthwatering aroma of grilling fish was in the air. Nearby, the Singing Bamboo swayed musically, the stalks even taller than she remembered. The Great Hall cast a looming shadow across the stone tiles. Sidling to the open doors, Usagi peeked in.

A polished wood floor gleamed before her like Sun Moon Lake. Bright silk banners fluttered from the soaring ceiling. Scrolls of fine paper hung from the walls, some painted with delicate landscapes, others with graceful calligraphy. Usagi's eyes widened at the formidable assortment of weapons hung on the wall in ordered rows, displaying swords, pole-axes, moon blades, tridents, spiked clubs, and other weapons she couldn't identify. A wide expanse of thick straw mats, bordered in sturdy black cotton, were laid out before the wall of weapons—the perfect place to practice and spar.

Against the facing wall, Saru and Inu stood with the Tigress at a lacquered wooden chest. It sported a dozen drawers with brass ring pulls and designs in silver and gold leaf. They opened two of the drawers, describing to Horangi how they'd distributed rice, beans, and millet to local villagers while hunting for the Treasures. Venturing closer, Usagi listened to their account of how they'd recovered the mirror and found her with the comb. The Tigress looked up and nodded curtly as Usagi bowed, then turned her attention back to the drawers. She brought out the Mirror of Elsewhere, caressing the burnished metal with gnarled fingers, then picked up Usagi's carved wood comb.

"Indeed, this appears to be the Coppice Comb," the old warrior murmured, her green eyes glowing. She placed both items in the sleeve of her cloak. "I must inspect these more closely. Go on to the morning meal and I will join you shortly." Shuffling off, she brushed past Usagi without a word.

"Where is she taking the Treasures?" Usagi wondered. Her fingers itched to tuck the comb back where she'd carried it for five years, and she longed for a peek in the Mirror of Elsewhere, wanting another glimpse of Uma. How were she and Tora being treated at the Dragonlord's Striker school?

"Probably to the pavilion by Crescent Lake," said Inu.

184

"She'll test them both to make sure they're in good condition. It's what she did with these." He slid open a drawer to reveal a hammered metal bowl. "The Bowl of Plenty." Pulling open another drawer, he brought out a cunningly carved pillbox made of interlocking sections. "The Apothecary."

With a delicate finger, Usagi touched the bowl. "What do they do?"

Saru pointed to a scroll hanging directly above the chest. "When the Treasures were first created, one of the objects was the Pen of Truth, and the first thing it wrote was this poem." She read it to Usagi.

"Look closely at these items if one is to see their measure
These may appear quite common but they're truly gifted treasure.
Together they will help the power of the Twelve to shield
The island shall be safe from harm and never have to yield.
In turn the Twelve must keep them close and treat them with
*   great care*
For should the bond be broken then Midaga is laid bare.

The fan shall bring the winds
From every corner of the sky.

The comb will turn into a copse
Of trees that spring up high.

The belt can bridge both stream and gap
And as a raft will float.

The flute casts a beguiling spell
With each and every note.

The hammer with one strike
Will briefly bring what one might need.

The bowl can multiply its fill
So more than one can feed.

The jewels of land and sea will call
Upon the mount and tide.

The mirror is a window
On happenings far and wide.

The cloak wards off not just the chill
But any sort of flame.

The pillbox holds the treatments
For most ailments to be tamed.

The ring calls forth great clouds of mist
In which one can be hidden.

The pen writes only what is true
No falsehoods can be hidden."

"Spirits." Usagi stared at the ornate chest with its twelve drawers. "And you've now tracked down four Treasures."

"Yes, but they were the easier ones," said Inu, raking his shaggy hair till it stood on end. "We had an idea of where some might be, since our masters had carried them. Now that we have the Mirror of Elsewhere, it will help—but if you don't know where something is, you'll only get a general impression of its location. So the rest of the Treasures will still be a challenge to find. The Ram Heir has one of the toughest assignments, trying to learn what happened to the Dragon Warrior's destroyed Treasure. It could take years— he's already been away for nearly two."

"Oi!" Nezu appeared in the doorway. "Are you showing the Treasures without me?" Looking put out, he smoothed his whiskers. "Breakfast is ready. Come now, or everything will get cold!"

They followed him to one of the adjoining buildings, into a long dining room with a reed mat floor. Around a low table set with covered earthen pots, they settled on thick cushions.

Nezu lifted the lid off a bubbling pot and stirred it a few times, filling the air with an invitingly savory smell. He ladled Usagi a bowl of soup. "How'd you sleep?" he asked.

"Really well," she replied. "I barely remember getting into bed." She looked around and lowered her voice. "Where's the cloud leopard?"

"Kumo? Out hunting, probably," said Nezu. "Or sleeping somewhere. As long as he's not in here . . . that big cat makes me nervous sometimes."

"Of course he does, Rat Boy." Usagi stifled a snicker.

"Funny," said Nezu, rolling his eyes. "Eat while it's hot."

She sipped the steaming broth. Several plump white rice cakes drifted in the bottom of the bowl. Usagi fished one out and popped it in her mouth. The rice cake was warm, chewy, and filling. Her mother used to make these, pounding rice for hours to make a smooth dense paste. She poked at the remaining cakes, feeling suddenly homesick.

"What's wrong?" asked Nezu. "Too much salt?"

Usagi shook her head. "It's nothing," she muttered, trying to ignore the knot in her stomach. Was her sister getting enough to eat? Was Tora protecting them both—or would her fierce temper get them into trouble?

The Tigress shuffled into the room and settled on a cushion at the other end of the table. The others bustled about pouring her tea, handing her a pair of feedsticks, and getting her a bowl of soup, while Nezu laid a platter of hot grilled fish before her, their skins crisp and smoky. "Here, try these. Fresh from the lake out back."

The charred heads of the fish had their tiny mouths

gaping open as if calling for help. Usagi's appetite fled altogether. She pushed her bowl away and stood, anxious to explore the grounds. Maybe she could get a closer look at the weapons in the Great Hall, or check the Mirror of Elsewhere for a peek at Uma and Tora.

"Where are you going in such a hurry?" asked the Tigress with a flinty stare.

Usagi thought quickly. "I just thought I'd practice my stickfighting. After you've finished eating, I could show you all the stances Saru taught me."

"That will not be necessary," the old warrior replied. "If you intend to stay here, you must do your share of work like everyone else."

"Of course!" Usagi gathered up her dirty bowl and feedsticks, embarrassed.

"That includes washing up all dishes after meals, fetching water, airing out the bedding, feeding the goats and hens, picking up after Kumo, and sluicing the outhouses. Along with any additional maintenance or cleaning that may be required as the need arises." Horangi's wrinkled face was expressionless.

Usagi faltered. That was a lot of work. "Can I show you my stickfighting skills after that?"

The Tiger Warrior's green eyes narrowed. "What you need to show me is the ability to work hard. Nothing else."

"But I thought . . ." Usagi chewed her lip. Hadn't the

Tigress said she would teach her? "I was hoping I could learn to fight like the Heirs, and to master my gift with wood. I could demonstrate . . ."

"I'll show you where everything is, Usagi," Nezu interjected. "You'll be a huge help—I can always use extra hands to wash up after I cook!"

Dejected, Usagi collected some empty dishes from the table. She followed Nezu to the kitchen, where he helped her pile them in a washbasin.

"Don't worry," he told Usagi. "We all had to do tons of chores when we first arrived. She'll give you lessons. Horangi is a true teacher at heart."

Usagi gave him a wan smile. Rolling up her sleeves, she sighed. "I hope you're right."

The days became a blur of tasks—some of which made little sense to Usagi. Each morning, she had to rise early and fetch water from a stream that ran behind the shrine compound. But she was only allowed to use clay jars without handles, and told to carry them with just her fingers clamped around the mouths of the jars. It took at least a dozen trips with a heavy jar in each hand, and much splashing and soaked clothing before the stone trough behind the kitchen was filled.

The Tigress also had Usagi sift for things in containers filled with sand or grains. She dug through a bushel of rice to find seven chestnuts, and plunged her hands repeatedly through a deep bin of millet until she retrieved five dried beans.

"Maybe she's misplacing things in her old age," she speculated to Inu one day, elbow-deep in a bucket of fine sand. Inu raised his brows.

"Hardly," he said. "The Tigress is as sharp as the Sword of the Snake. Besides, you're not the only one with assignments. We're still working on raising the bridge the Tigress cut down to challenge you."

Mollified, Usagi worked through the thick, unyielding sand until her fingers closed around a small metal fragment. "Finally!" she gasped, holding up a steel arrow tip in her trembling hand. Her arms ached.

"Well done!" said Inu, plucking it from her fingers. "Only two more to go."

Each night she tumbled into bed and passed out, exhausted from doing nothing but strange chores all day while the Heirs trained in the Great Hall under the watchful eye of the Tigress. Usagi could hear the old warrior criticizing their movements:

"Too hard. Do not lock your elbow."

"Too soft. Keep the wrist solid."

"Where is your center? Stop leading with your face."

"You are not breathing."

"Breathing too much."

Usagi couldn't resist stopping by the Great Hall each afternoon to observe, ducking out of sight whenever the Tigress turned her way. The clatter of practice swords, the Heirs' shouts, and the thud of bodies and feet on the straw mats made Usagi wish she were with them, instead of scrubbing laundry.

One chilly autumn evening, Usagi was supposed to help Nezu and the others wrap dumplings for the evening meal—but her discouragement was growing too great to ignore. They had been at the shrine for several weeks now, and she hadn't learned a thing from the Tigress. Not even the prospect of dumplings cheered Usagi. She excused herself to get some air, afraid she would burst into tears.

She walked by the thatched wooden frame where the Summoning Bell hung, alongside the wooden log that served as its hammer. It was no small feat for the Heirs to bring it all the way from the Palace of the Clouds—the bronze bell was big enough for her to hide in. Usagi ran her fingers along the raised designs of zodiac animals cast on its surface, imagining generations of Midagian kings striking the bell to call upon the Warriors. If only she could Summon her sister and Tora and talk to them just as easily. There was so much to tell them—and so much to ask. For five years they were the only ones she spoke to every single day. Not being able to hear their voices was like losing the sound of her heartbeat.

It wouldn't do to get soft, she scolded herself. A real Warrior would carry on. She'd keep going until the Tigress taught her. Usagi turned her back on the bell and entered the Singing Bamboo. The twelve lanterns in the grove were dark as usual, giant animals frozen in the shadows. Over the silvery melodies of the swaying bamboo, she could hear the Heirs laughing and chattering as they tucked spoonfuls of seasoned filling inside paper-thin rounds of dough in the kitchen. The crescent moon winked at her through the bamboo, looking like a glowing dumpling in the sky.

Her ears pricked at a new, unfamiliar sound. She hurried to the top of the Steps of Patience, listening. Down the mountain in the distance were heavy footsteps, along with a low hum. Usagi squinted down the staircase, the footsteps growing louder, until she glimpsed a tiny moving speck of light. Someone was approaching.

Usagi whirled and raced back through the shrine compound. She burst into the dining hall and ran into the kitchen, startling the three Heirs.

"I hear footsteps on the Steps of Patience," she said breathlessly. "Someone's coming to the shrine."

CHAPTER 14

A GRIM REPORT

AT THE TOP OF THE Steps of Patience, Usagi pointed to the bright light bobbing in the distance. The heavy footsteps she'd first heard while walking in the Singing Bamboo were louder now, as was the tuneless humming. The light had become larger than a pinprick, approaching steadily. "Do you see?" she said. "Down there."

Saru and Nezu squinted down the staircase, while Inu sniffed the air, searching for a scent. The Heirs had rushed from the kitchen as soon as she'd alerted them, grabbing their weapons before following Usagi through the grove that guarded the shrine. Inu frowned. "I smell a fresh kill. Whoever it is has been hunting." He sniffed again and broke out in a smile, shouldering his bow. "I know who it is."

The bobbing light drew closer and a squeal of joy erupted from Saru. "It's Tupa!"

"Brother Tupa!" Nezu scurried down the stairs and

threw his arms around a tall figure. Usagi strained to see past a light dancing above them, wanting a good look at the Heir to the Ram Warrior. He was a young man, sturdily built, wearing a thick cloak of sheepskin over the saffron robes of a novice monk. A bronze chain was slung about his waist, while a curved horn hung from a leather strap around his neck.

"Rat Boy!" shouted Tupa, his voice deep and rich. He and Nezu climbed the last steps together, arm in arm, while a ball of flame circled about their heads, unconfined by any lantern. Usagi stared. Saru once told her that Tupa was skilled with fire, but this was impressive. If only her sister could see this. Uma was so proud of being able to start fires. She'd always pestered Usagi and Tora to let her practice, wanting to make bigger flames, wanting to see how far she could go with her fire gift, but they'd been too afraid of drawing attention, and usually insisted against it. Usagi felt a pang of regret.

Inu and Saru greeted the Ram Heir with elated exclamations, while the ball of fire, no bigger than an orange, rose above them and hovered, spitting and crackling, throwing its bright light like a miniature sun. Usagi raised her hand to shade her eyes. Dangling from the modest pack on Tupa's back was the carcass of a mountain hare, its white winter coat stained with blood. Inu's nose was on the mark, as usual.

Tupa clasped Inu's arm and pounded his back. "You've

put on some muscle! Not a pup any longer!" He caught sight of Saru and embraced her warmly. "So good to see you, Monkey Girl."

"Good to see you too, Brother Ram," Saru said, her pale face aglow.

He pointed at the whiskers on Nezu's lip. "What's this peach fuzz? Last time I saw you, it was smooth as a stone."

"I'm just trying to be like you," Nezu teased, tweaking the only significant patch of hair on Tupa's shaved head—a dark tuft of beard sprouting from his chin.

Chuckling, the Ram Heir looked at Nezu more closely. "You've managed to get some length on a few of them. Sweet sugarcane, that one's nearly half an inch!" Tupa's golden-brown eyes stood out against the tanned skin of his handsome face, and as they met Usagi's, he winked. She liked him immediately.

"I'm Usagi," she volunteered. "Born in the year of the Wood Rabbit."

"They told me about you in the last Summoning," Tupa said, and bowed in greeting. "An honor to meet you—it's so promising to have fresh blood on the Mount. Did you find it difficult to ascend?"

Usagi nodded. "It's a miracle I'm not a pancake under the Bashing Boulders."

Tupa threw back his head and laughed, his voice big and booming, and the hovering ball of fire flared a little.

"Come, let's get you inside," Saru interrupted. "You must be famished—and it's getting too cold out here!" The Heirs swept Tupa back through the Singing Bamboo and Usagi followed, longing for news or knowledge from the capital. They'd said Tupa had gone there on an extended mission. Maybe he could tell her of the Blue Dragon's school, or the new Strikers with zodiac powers—or even something of her sister and Tora.

They reached the heart of the grove, where the twelve statues stood like sentries in the dark, and were met by the Tigress and her cloud leopard, their eyes glowing green and amber. The fireball above Tupa's head floated high above the path, throwing light and shadows all about, while Kumo arched his back and growled, ears flattening along his broad skull.

"Good gracious gods, Kumo, have you forgotten me?" Tupa exclaimed. He tossed the mountain hare and the cloud leopard caught the carcass in its jaws. "Nice kitty," he crooned. He bowed deeply toward Horangi. "Teacher! I have much to report. Important matters are at hand."

"It has been too long since you were last here," said the Tigress, and the lines around her mouth deepened in a rare smile. She shuffled forward to clasp Tupa's arms. "You have reached manhood, Ram Heir. It is good to see."

With a laugh, he lifted the curved horn around his neck. "May I light the zodiac animals, Teacher? We're all together again, and we have a new candidate in our midst to celebrate," he said, glancing at Usagi with a little smile. Horangi looked in silence at the darkened path for a long moment, then gave a tiny nod.

Saru sucked in a breath. "After all these years," she whispered, eyes wide.

Grinning, Tupa put the horn to his lips. To Usagi's surprise, the fireball that had been following them floated toward the horn and disappeared into the hollowed end like a ground squirrel darting into its home. The grove fell into blackness for a brief moment, then a bright flame sprang from the horn.

The Ram Heir approached the stone figures and raised the horn higher. He took a deep breath and blew. The flame from his horn became a stream of fire that grew longer and brighter until it licked at the nearest lantern. When Tupa stopped, a flame flickered in the belly of a large stone rat. Its snarling mouth and hollow eyes glowed from the fire within. Nezu cheered.

Aiming a dazzling stream of flame around the dark forms, Tupa went along the path till light danced from all twelve lanterns, each as tall as he and shaped like a different animal of the zodiac. They reminded Usagi of the figures her father had carved for the school back in Goldentusk, though these were far more forbidding, especially with fire in their bellies. She stared at the rabbit lantern, its teeth bared with long stone ears folded back, clawed feet poised to kick. Could she ever be that fierce?

Saru clapped her hands. "How bright the Twelve look!"

"Just like when the Warriors were whole," said Inu softly.

The Ram Heir looked gratified, his broad smile widening even more. "The path was dark for far too long."

They bundled him into the warmth of the dining hall, where he was given hot tea while Nezu piled platters with plump dumplings, both steamed and fried crisp, as quickly as he could cook them. Usagi hustled them to the table.

"What a feast," Tupa declared, looking around happily.

"Like old times," laughed Saru, and she gave him a pair of feedsticks and poured everyone a round of tea. As they all gobbled up as many dumplings as they could eat, she told him about their mission to the southwest provinces, and how they'd come across Usagi and brought her to Mount Jade.

"Teacher actually cut the bridge while she was standing on it, Tupa! Took my sword and lopped it like a haircut," Nezu reported. He flashed a grin at the Tigress, who merely raised her eyebrows and took a sip of tea, then looked over the rim of her cup at Usagi. The old warrior's green eyes seemed to twinkle.

"But Usagi jumped after her," Saru added. "She was ready to save the Tigress! Talk about a Warrior Challenge. Took us days to get the bridge back up, but it was worth it."

"Tickle my toes, doesn't that beat all!" Tupa slapped his

thigh. "The bridge did seem different." He raised his tea cup. "Nice job, Rabbit Girl."

Blushing, Usagi smiled and ducked her head. She stuffed a juicy dumpling in her mouth and nearly burned her tongue.

The Tigress turned to Tupa. "Your report. You had said important matters are at hand," she said briskly. "What might they be?"

Nodding, Tupa put down his feedsticks and pushed his empty plate aside. He told them about his time in the capital, sent there by the Tigress two years prior on a long-term mission of surveillance.

"I shaved my head and disguised myself as a traveling monk, going from temple to temple in the city. I often went right by the palace gates," said Tupa, running a hand over his smooth scalp. "After months wandering as a beggar-monk, I became friendly with the head priest at the palace temple, and he took me in as a novice in their monastery."

Usagi nearly choked on a dumpling. "You were living on the grounds with the Blue Dragon?"

"Teacher's strategy lessons," Inu told her. "She says the best hiding place can be right in sight."

Tupa gave Usagi another wink. "Brilliant, no? I was just under Druk's nose! He's surrounded by his Strikers and his Guard, and the city is full of foreigners these days. No one seems to know of his previous life. It's amazing the things you can learn when people don't notice you."

"Have you learned anything of import regarding the news you shared at the last Summoning?" prodded the Tigress.

"Yes." Clearing his throat, Tupa took a sip of tea. "We've known the Dragonlord has been collecting younglings with zodiac powers for some time now." He turned to Usagi. "You know this personally."

For fear of bursting into tears, she nodded mutely. A flicker of pity crossed Tupa's face.

"And we know now that he's training them for his strike force. You've already come across a Striker with powers, right? I've glimpsed these younglings on the palace grounds, living in a new compound they're calling the Dragon Academy. But several weeks ago, I learned something horrific." His expression turned grave. "The Dragonlord plans to sacrifice the weakest ones this spring."

Nezu cocked his head. "What do you mean, 'sacrifice'?"

"Just what it sounds like. He'll execute the ones that don't meet his standards." Tupa tugged dolefully at his goatee.

It felt as if an icy wind had blown into the dining hall. The hairs on Usagi's arms stood pin-straight. "Execute?" she said, her voice strangled.

Tupa nodded. "Druk has come under the influence of the invaders and their barbarian ways. The head priest told me the younglings will be sacrificed at the palace temple come the first day of spring, to appease his new gods."

"Foolish of me to think it could not get worse," the Tigress said, almost to herself. "This is my fault. He has fallen so far." Her green eyes were cloudy and troubled.

Usagi couldn't breathe. Her greatest fear might soon be realized. Her sister was small, young, and far from strong. Surely Uma would be killed—and what if Tora was not powerful enough to survive?

"Those younglings are in grave danger," said Saru, glancing worriedly at Usagi. "How many did you see, Tupa?"

"Several dozen, though I don't know how many are marked for slaughter," replied the Ram Heir. "There are some as young as five or six—they will certainly die."

"Jago," Usagi whispered. "He's only six years old. And my sister . . . our friend Tora . . . if they're to be sacrificed . . ." She swallowed hard, unable to complete the thought. "There must be something we can do."

"I'm not sure what." Tupa shook his head, frowning. "The Warriors of the Zodiac and their Heirs, along with every Midagian adult with any powers—they were no match for Druk and the invaders. Now he's building an even more powerful army."

"That hasn't kept us from challenging Druk and his troops in our own way," Inu said. His jaw clenched. "The Blue Dragon must be stopped. We have to help those younglings."

"I agree," said the Ram Heir. "But we can't storm the palace, can we?"

Horangi's sunken cheeks became even more drawn. "It would be a suicide mission. We have had to rely on stealth and secrecy since the destruction of the Twelve. That does not change here."

It seemed an impossible situation. Feeling the dark pull of despair, Usagi clutched at her rabbit pendant. She breathed a silent prayer to the spirits of the Twelve. *Please.*

Deep in thought, Nezu stroked the whiskers on his lip. "Teacher, you've always taught us to look for opportunity in any crisis. What if we were to find a way to sneak the younglings out? We'll bring them here like we did Usagi. If anyone should be training them to fight, it's you, not the Blue Dragon."

"Yes!" Inu's dark eyes flared. "This is our chance to add to our numbers—create a fighting force of our own."

Tupa rubbed the back of his shaved head. "With the weakest younglings?"

"Why not?" Nezu flashed a grin and pointed at Usagi. "We already know it's possible to ascend the Mount without formal schooling."

"Besides, who's to decide who's weak and who's strong?" asked Saru. "These younglings could become great assets to our cause. We owe it to Midaga to try to rescue them."

The Tigress nodded slowly. "Too many with zodiac powers have already died," she said. "The slaying of innocents will never stop unless we intervene." Her green eyes cleared as they looked at Usagi. "I cannot promise that your sister or friends will be saved. But the least a Warrior can do is try."

Usagi wanted to throw her arms around the old warrior, but babbled her thanks instead. "I'll do anything you need me to do."

"This will be our most difficult mission yet," replied the Tigress. "It will require planning and all of our powers in order to be successful."

"Teacher, you aren't thinking about coming yourself?" asked Tupa. He leaned forward, looking worried. "You would be safer here at the shrine."

"I can sit here no longer when the lives of such younglings are at stake." The Tigress patted him with a gnarled hand. "Fear not, Ram Heir. The conquest of a mountain begins with the smallest of steps. Claiming back our Treasures is one. Keeping more younglings out of Druk's hands is another. We resist in any way we can."

Saru's pale face was fiercely determined. "We can't let him destroy Midaga further. What he did to his Treasure was terrible enough."

"Speaking of which . . ." The Ram Heir reached into his monk's robes and pulled out a small silken bag. He poured its contents onto the table with a clatter. "It took me months to figure out how to get to the Dragon Warrior's old Treasure after I learned it was enshrined at the palace temple.

Not that I'm proud of stealing from a temple." He broke out in a wide smile.

They crowded around to look. Two immense pearls the size of walnuts—one luminous white, the other coal black—were strung on a frayed and knotted silk cord. The cord was half burnt, and there was a charred gap between the two pearls. Several sooty fragments of jade glimmered from the table.

"The Jewels of Land and Sea," squeaked Nezu. "I can't believe you got it."

"What's left of it, you mean," said Inu. He reached out and poked at the jade fragments. "No more Land."

Usagi stared at the broken necklace. So that was what the Blue Dragon once wore. She still couldn't understand why he destroyed the Treasure he'd pledged to carry. He ruled the island now, but was all the suffering and death worth it?

Tupa looked at the Tigress. "Surely it can be repaired?"

The old warrior swept up the pieces in her knobby hand and held them to her heart. "If not, I fear Midaga itself cannot be." Her chin quivered ever so slightly. Then her mouth settled back into its usual pinched line and she poured the necklace fragments back into the silken bag.

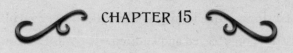

CHAPTER 15

THE BRUSH AND
THE BREATH

USAGI SLID OPEN THE DOORS to the shrine library and found the Heirs and the Tigress bent over open folios and unrolled scrolls. In the week since Tupa had returned from the capital with news of the Dragonlord's plans, they'd spent hours there arguing over the best way to carry out a rescue. A large tray of sand sat on a low table, with small wooden blocks and stone cubes set in formation. The Ram Heir knelt beside it, moving some of the cubes around and drawing lines in the sand with a long stick. He looked up and smiled. "Rabbit Girl! Come to help us figure out this mess?"

"I'd love to," Usagi said eagerly. But Horangi and the others barely glanced over from their animated discussion as she entered. The long room, smelling of old straw and dusty paper, was covered in thick reed matting with low tables and sturdy cushions. Lining the walls from floor to ceiling and crowding the latticed paper windows were shelves crammed with thousands of scrolls and bound books. Many were clearly even older than the Tigress, with yellowing edges and faded covers of silk, leather, and tortoiseshell. Usagi paused to look at some of the scrolls laid out across the floor.

There was a prewar map of Midaga, its settlements clustered along the main road that ringed the island. The capital, labeled as "Guardian City," sat at the northernmost tip of the island, where the Ring Road both began and ended. Other scrolls showed detailed maps of various provinces and towns. Usagi found one of Goldentusk, tracing her finger over the spot where her house had been.

The last scroll was the longest, spanning the length of the room. It depicted the entire palace compound, covered in colorful scenes of people going about everyday business. The king listening to a dispute between two citizens, attended by a court of advisers. Cooks plucking chickens outside the cookery. A stableboy grooming horses. A priest offering up incense at a temple altar, while shaven monks chanted. The court doctor measuring herbs, and scribes inking calligraphy. Handmaidens preparing the queen's elaborate dress as she primped in front of a gilded vanity.

"That painting's from two hundred years ago," said Tupa over her shoulder. He pointed to several figures wearing elaborate helmets shaped like animals. "See, there's warriors from the Twelve of that time in the throne hall. Raja the Monkey Warrior, Rat Warrior Zumi the Fifth, Beya the Horse Warrior. Nowadays the grounds don't look anything like that—they're full of the Dragonlord's men."

"Where would the Dragon Academy be?" asked Usagi. To her disappointment, they were interrupted before he could answer.

"Young Rabbit," said Horangi. The old warrior waved her over to an ebony table inlaid with mother-of-pearl and stacked with a pyramid of blank paper scrolls. Beside it was a thin slab of jade on which stood a brush stand filled with wooden-handled ink brushes, a pile of inksticks, a pot of water, and an inkstone.

"Painting!" Usagi hadn't seen an inkstone since the war's end days, when she traded her father's tools and supplies for food and clothing. She'd thought she'd never handle such things again.

"Not quite," replied Horangi. "Calligraphy. Are you familiar with your letters?"

"My mother taught them to me," Usagi said proudly. "And my father showed me how to prepare ink."

"Did they now," said the old warrior, raising her eyebrows. "That makes for two less things to go over. Perhaps you would like to grind the ink."

Usagi nodded, pleased but puzzled. Was she about to get a lesson—in calligraphy? She poured a little water onto the inkstone, then selected a slender new brick of pressed black ink. Clumsily, she rubbed one end against the wet stone. It had been so long since she'd done this, though helping her father prepare inks and paints was once a favorite task. Soon she was lost in the familiar scraping sound of the inkstick and the circular motions of grinding. The water thickened and grew dark. *Look, Papa.* The liquid in the inkstone's well was black and glossy. "I think it's ready," said Usagi.

The old warrior selected a brush and dipped it in the ink. She watched the drops fall back into the inkstone. "That will do," she grunted. Over a felt pad, she unrolled a blank scroll and smoothed it with her wrinkled hand, anchoring one side with a carved marble paperweight. She fixed her green eyes on Usagi.

"A good calligrapher channels movement through the body, and expresses that energy through the tip of the brush." The Tigress held back the sleeve of her robe with her left hand as her right hand glided over the paper, the brush in her gnarled fingers. "How you hold the brush, your consistency, the speed of your hand—all affect the result." Bold, even strokes of stark black appeared on the fresh white paper, blossoming into character upon character. The graceful swooping lines formed words that Horangi read aloud as she completed each one. "Honor. Duty. Courage. Truth. Respect. Loyalty. Love." Her gaze was penetrating. "These are the things that make a true Warrior. No blade can equal them." She handed Usagi a clean brush. "Make this your sword."

Placing the scroll of newly inked words in front of Usagi, the old warrior pointed with a knobby finger. "Work on the characters for 'honor.'" She sat back on her cushion. "Begin."

At the other end of the library, the Heirs continued to debate over how to get the younglings out of the palace without notice. "The problem is not getting into the palace grounds," Inu warned. "We're used to operating by stealth. But once we have these younglings with us—we don't even know how many are marked for sacrifice. What if there's more than ten?"

"We could move them out in small groups," mused Saru. "If I took them over rooftops . . ."

Nezu snorted. "You're going to make a dozen trips? I say we dig a tunnel."

Listening intently, Usagi dripped a big splotch of ink on her scroll. She longed to be sitting with them. What were they looking at over there? The Tigress rapped on the table. "Focus," she croaked.

Usagi suppressed a sigh and returned to copying the old warrior's work. This hardly seemed like something useful in battle. The Tigress watched, giving constant commentary:

"Attack each stroke without hesitation."

"I see your state of mind on the paper."

"Such poor flow and rhythm—ease your grip."

By the time the inkstone was dry, Usagi's hand ached. "Grind more ink and work on your strokes till evening meal," said the Tigress. "Repetition will make them swift and sure." The old warrior shuffled out of the library, leaving Usagi to practice with the brush.

With a groan, she put it down and rubbed her hand. Tupa came and sat down beside her, peering at her scroll. "Your first lesson with the Tigress?"

"Yes, but I never imagined it would be calligraphy," said Usagi. She reached for the water, preparing to add it to the inkstone. "And I didn't think calligraphy could hurt!"

Tupa chuckled. "Forget making more ink. Let me show you a shortcut." He pulled the slab of unpolished jade out from under the brush stand. Demonstrating with a brush dipped in plain water, the Ram Heir quickly wrote on the jade, his brushstrokes shining against the gray-green stone before evaporating away. "This way you can practice your strokes, save time *and* save ink."

"And save my hand!" exclaimed Usagi. She smiled gratefully at him, and he winked.

Over evening meal that night, it was decided that they would set out for the capital before the third moon of the new year, spiriting away the younglings just before the planned execution on the first day of spring. "There'll be so many preparations for spring festivities around the city then. We'll stand a better chance of getting to the palace

211

unnoticed," declared Tupa.

Saru nodded. "Good for the element of surprise."

"Coming back to the shrine may be slow," mused Inu. "We don't know if the younglings have been trained in using their spirit speed, and we'll have to keep in the wilderness like we did with Usagi."

"We can bring them to Sun Moon Lake for a spell," said Nezu with a grin. "I bet our hermit friend won't mind."

"But if all goes well," said Tupa, "there will be many younglings with zodiac powers on Mount Jade again. We might even anoint new Heirs!"

Horangi took a sip of tea and scratched her cloud leopard's ears. "Best not to count bowls of rice before the harvest." She looked straight at Usagi. "We still have to see how this one handles training. Young Rabbit, meet me tomorrow at daybreak in the lake pavilion for your next lesson."

In the pale dawn that marked the hour of the Rabbit, Usagi hurried through the trees to Crescent Lake, slippers crunching on the white gravel path from the shrine compound. An anxious flutter chased the pangs in her empty stomach. She'd woken multiple times during the night, scared that she'd miss the appointed time for her meeting with Horangi. Despite her nervousness, she couldn't wait to start her lesson.

Would she learn to wield a sword? Be taught archery, or

given a moon blade like Saru's? She shivered in the autumn chill, grateful for the pants and tunic Saru had found for her in an old trunk, and pulled her borrowed moth-eaten surcoat closer.

The prayer pavilion perched at the curved edge of the water, and beneath its scrolled roof sat the hunched figure of the Tigress, the cloud leopard lying at her feet like an enormous spotted rug. Usagi bounded up the stairs leading to the platform of the pavilion, and stopped short. Kumo was asleep, curled in front of the old warrior, whose eyes were also closed. Her gnarled hands were folded in her lap, and she was still. Was she napping?

Usagi cleared her throat. "Good morning?"

The Tigress opened her green eyes and fixed them upon Usagi. "Yes." She indicated a round black cushion next to her. "Sit."

Settling onto the firm cushion, Usagi admired the twelve sculpted pillars that supported the pavilion's roof. Each pillar was a different animal of the zodiac, painted in bright colors of vermilion, emerald green, yellow, deep purple, and lapis blue, and the inside of the pavilion's roof was lacquered in gold. There were a few carved jadeite stools and tables, and the floor was a mosaic of enameled tiles. It was utterly unlike the austere simplicity of the Great Hall. "There's so much color here."

"It is a relatively new structure," Horangi said. "Built

about three hundred years ago to replace one that had been damaged in a storm. The head of the Twelve at the time had a taste for showy things. Picked it up from being at court half the time." Her wrinkled lips pressed together disapprovingly.

"Oh," said Usagi, uncertain of what else to say. "I didn't bring my stick or anything," she ventured. "Shall I go get it?"

"All you needed to bring is yourself."

"Am I learning to use a new weapon?" asked Usagi hopefully.

Horangi tapped her head. "Your most important weapon is right here. And here." She tapped her chest. "So before anything else, we prepare through mind-the-mind. Close your eyes, look upward and into yourself," she instructed. "Breathe in deeply for six counts, out for six counts, and continue until your mind is where it should be. Begin."

Wrinkling her brow, Usagi considered the old warrior's instructions. Where was her mind supposed to be? How would breathing and counting get it there? "I don't understand—why are we doing this?"

The old warrior's mouth worked as if she were trying to spit out an errant seed. "It matters not whether you know 'why.' What matters is that you 'do.' That is how you will answer your own question."

That made no sense to Usagi, but the Tigress stared at her until she meekly folded her hands in her lap and shut her eyes, trying to look upward as told. But all she could see was the red of her inner eyelids as the morning sun crept onto her face. She counted silently while breathing in and out, but it seemed like every living thing in the trees was welcoming the day with squawks and shrieks, and Kumo had begun to snore. With her rabbit hearing, Usagi caught Nezu humming back at the compound, chopping something in the kitchen. Her stomach growled. What was he making for the morning meal? Hopefully those crisp sesame flatbreads— they were so good with a hot milky tea.

The Tigress reached over and tapped Usagi's spine. "Sit up straight."

Frustrated, Usagi squeezed her eyes tighter and tried counting her breaths again. Her legs went numb, but every time she twitched or fidgeted on the stiff black cushion, the Tigress tapped the offending limb. "Block outside sensation."

Finally, the Tigress told her to stop. The morning sun had barely moved, though it seemed as if she'd been sitting there forever. Usagi wobbled to her feet, legs stiff and sore.

"I will see you here tomorrow at daybreak." The Tigress closed her eyes serenely.

Each morning, before breaking their fast, Usagi joined the Tigress at the lakeside pavilion and sat quietly with her eyes closed. "Clear your mind," the old warrior would instruct. "Free it from thought." Usagi tried, but without fail she would start thinking about her sister and Tora. Winter was coming—were they keeping warm? Were they even allowed blankets? What good was sitting here? Was she learning anything? The thoughts would follow Usagi all day and into the night, leaving her tossing and turning in her bedroll.

After a week of sleepless nights and mornings of fruitlessly worrying next to the Tigress, Usagi was sluggish and befuddled, and Tupa noticed. He took her aside after breakfast. "How goes the mind-the-mind lessons?"

Usagi shook her head, exasperated. "I'm not supposed to get tangled up in my thoughts, but they won't stop."

"Let them come," the Ram Heir advised. "But try not to chase them. Practice letting them settle."

She yawned and rubbed her nose. "How do I make them settle?"

"You can't *make* them settle." Tupa picked up an empty bowl from the breakfast table. "Put some water and a little sand in this and I'll show you."

Usagi went and scooped some water from the kitchen trough and added a handful of sand. She brought it back to Tupa, who sloshed the bowl about, swirling the sand and muddying the water.

"Take a look," he said, setting the bowl down. "Imagine your thoughts as those grains of sand. Don't look at any one for too long. Just watch them as they float by in the water."

She stared at the flurries of sand in the bowl. After a bit, Usagi noticed that as the sand began to sink to the bottom, the water became clearer.

"The mind is like this bowl," said the Ram Heir. "We're not trying to make the sand stop swirling, but trying to keep still enough that the sand—or our thoughts—can settle. The next time you sit to mind-the-mind, think of this bowl."

"All right," said Usagi. But she felt more discouraged than ever. She'd been eager for the Tigress to teach her, but what sort of Warrior lessons were these? How any of it was useful remained as cloudy to her as the swirling sand.

The days grew shorter, autumn giving way to the icy cold fingers of winter. Inside the Great Hall, Usagi began working on her stickfighting techniques whenever the Tigress coached the Heirs. Out of the corner of her eye, she noticed that the Tigress was watching, and redoubled her efforts, grunting.

After nearly a week of this, the Tigress finally shuffled over, her pursed mouth a straight line. "You are holding your breath when you swing. Connect breathing to movement. I will give you breathing exercises to do in your morning mind-the-mind practice."

"Yes, Teacher." Usagi bowed.

The old warrior regarded her with narrowed eyes. "Add spirit-breath—a deep shout at the completion of a strike.

You gain power that way. Let me hear you." She swung her wooden staff at Usagi so quickly there was no time to duck.

"*Yah!*" Usagi batted the old warrior's staff away.

The scars on Horangi's cheeks puckered for a brief moment, as if she were suppressing a smile. She addressed the four Heirs, who were wrestling on the mats. "Practice with her," she told them. "We are done for now—I have repair work to do."

Tupa looked up from Saru's headlock. "On the Jewels of Land and Sea?"

Horangi nodded and frowned. "It is a riddle of a challenge, I must say."

"Is there anything I can do to help?" Tupa disentangled himself, straightening his collar.

The old warrior shook her head. "Thank you, Ram Heir, but no." She shuffled out of the Great Hall, muttering.

With a wry smile, he shrugged and turned to Usagi. "The Tigress wants us to practice together! That's a good sign—you'll be wielding a sword in no time."

Usagi grinned. "I've been waiting for her to show me how to fight with one. She's taught you everything, hasn't she?"

"Actually, I learned quite a lot from my master the Ram Warrior, as well as the other warriors," said Tupa. "They all had different powers and skills, and taught us how to handle more than one weapon."

"Like those?" She pointed to some of the more menacing

weapons that hung on the wall by the sparring mats. The Ram Heir's eyes gleamed. Tugging on his goatee, he surveyed the display.

"The flying firehammer is my favorite." He hefted a curved metal rod with flame-blackened ends. "It can knock a man down and return to your hand. But these others have their uses too." Tupa removed each weapon from its mount for her to examine. A mace covered in spikes. A boar spear, solid enough to withstand a charging animal. The winged dagger, with forked metal guards. He showed her the chain-link belt that he wore. It turned out to be a hidden weapon, with a heavy iron ball attached to one end. "It's a power chain—very useful for a monk who's not supposed to carry a sword. But if you don't have any of these, you can just use your fingers."

Usagi gave him a skeptical look. "How?"

He tucked the iron ball in his pocket and called to Nezu, who was wrestling with Inu under the watch of Saru. "Oi! Rat Boy! Come here for a second."

Nezu exchanged brief bows with Inu, then ambled over. But he stopped at Tupa's broad smile and outstretched hand. "Oh no. I know what you want to do." Shaking his head, he backed away.

Tupa sprang forward and placed two meaty fingers along the side of Nezu's neck. Nezu froze in place, eyes bulging, as still as an animal lantern in the Singing Bamboo. "Pressure points!" Tupa announced. As Nezu moaned, the others burst into laughter.

"You're hurting him!" Usagi said, alarmed.

"Fleas and fly rot! This doesn't hurt," scoffed the Ram Heir. He removed his fingers and Nezu collapsed in a gasping heap on the floor.

"Do it on yourself next time!" Nezu sputtered with a baleful glare.

Tupa snorted. "That would be like trying to tickle myself." He waved Usagi a little closer. "Here, let's show you. Don't be shy—I swear the freeze hold's not painful." He positioned her before Nezu. "Go ahead, Brother. Let her see what it feels like."

Still grumpy, Nezu placed his fingers lightly on Usagi's neck. To her astonishment, her entire body locked up as if she'd been turned to stone. She couldn't move a muscle, no matter how hard she tried. She couldn't even move her jaw to talk. The most Usagi could do was grunt, even as the others laughed and told her not to panic. It didn't hurt, and thankfully she could breathe, but having no control was alarming. When a grinning Nezu finally lifted his hand, Usagi was rather cross herself. "You don't have to look so cheerful about it," she snapped.

"When we first learned this, we'd sneak up and freeze each other in place all the time," said Nezu, his grin growing wider. "It was especially horrible if it happened while someone was peeing."

Tupa's hearty laugh boomed through the hall. In spite of herself, Usagi smiled. "Let's promise never to do that to each other."

The Ram Heir went over other holds, including one that caused fainting, one that sent limbs flailing, and one that induced vomiting. "Be careful with that one," he warned. "It's similar to a death hold." He showed her the most vulnerable spots on the body: the throat, the stomach, the eyes, the groin. "If you're attacked, then do whatever you can to hit these. Your hands and feet can be weapons enough."

Usagi looked at her hands and flexed them, then studied the wall of fearsome weapons. She'd still rather fight with any of those.

Saru called for them to finish up. "We should be getting the midday meal ready."

They gathered in the kitchen, where Nezu assigned them various tasks. Usagi was sent to collect eggs from the shrine chickens, and wash vegetables. All throughout the meal preparations, she thought about what she'd learned in the Great Hall. Upon eating, Usagi waited patiently until everyone had finished before finally asking the Tigress what had been on her mind for weeks.

"Now that I can practice with the Heirs, will I be learning to fight with weapons soon?"

The old warrior grunted. "I think your stick should be enough."

"But what about the mission to save the younglings? Won't it be better if I have a sword at least? We could hide it inside my stick like Nezu's," Usagi suggested.

Horangi pursed her lips. "You should stay at the shrine for your safety. This rescue mission carries far more risk than one of surveillance and Treasure recovery."

"No, don't leave me behind!" cried Usagi, aghast. "I can't wait around here while my sister's life is at stake."

The Tigress shook her head. "You have barely begun to study. You are nowhere close to going through Warrior Trials. How could I allow you to come?"

"What trials? Didn't I already pass them in the Running of the Mount?" Usagi was mystified.

"That's to get to the shrine," Saru said gently. "But after you've been taught by a Warrior of the Zodiac for some time, they test you on everything you've learned. You won't get a sword otherwise."

"So teach me and let me go through Warrior Trials," said Usagi, exasperated. All these hurdles. Couldn't the old warrior say yes for once?

The Tigress coughed her dry hacking laugh. "You might as well be asking for fruit from the Tree of Elements. Warrior Trials require years of study. Failure means banishment from the shrine."

"There must be *some* way I could help," Usagi persisted.

After Nezu and Inu chorused their agreement, the

Tigress held up a gnarled hand. "Perhaps you might serve as a scout with your rabbit hearing. But you are not far enough along in your lessons for anything else."

The fragile thread tethering Usagi's patience snapped. "How can I when you're not teaching me anything useful?" she retorted. There was a silence, the Heirs blinking in shock. The lines in the old warrior's face deepened.

Feeling her cheeks grow hot, Usagi fled. She ran through the compound until she found herself in the Singing Bamboo. In the midst of the guardian statues, she stopped. With their eyes and open mouths aglow from the flames flickering in their bellies, they seemed to be laughing at her. Picking up a few pebbles from the path, she threw one at the tiger lantern as hard as she could. It bounced off the tiger's stone snout and skittered into the swaying bamboo. Usagi threw one at the snarling rabbit, and then another. Its fierceness mocked her.

Her ears pricked at the approach of footsteps. She turned to see Tupa, his golden-brown eyes full of sympathy.

"I may only be an Heir, but I could teach you a thing or two," he told her. "I'll help you, Rabbit Girl."

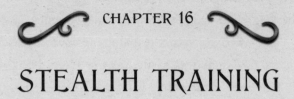

CHAPTER 16

STEALTH TRAINING

"THE SCORPION'S TAIL!" CRIED SARU, holding aloft a broad curved blade. In the morning light streaming through the Great Hall, it glinted like a sharp fang. "Inu, remember this one?"

"How could I forget? None of the Warriors would let me touch it." Inu pulled a double-bladed sword from its sheath. "Or this one, either!"

Tupa laughed. "The Twin-Tailed Snake? I doubt you should touch it *now*."

Usagi eyed the assortment of swords on the wall. Would she ever get to carry one of those magnificent blades? After she'd lost patience and insulted the Tigress in front of everyone, Usagi feared she would be sent away. She avoided the old warrior whenever possible and stopped going to mind-the-mind sessions. But to her relief and shame, the Tigress seemed to have forgotten about her, keeping away in her quarters or at the prayer pavilion, working on the Jewels of Land and Sea.

Fortunately Tupa was teaching her all he could. "We'll make it our secret," he told her. "When the moment is right, you'll show Horangi what you can do. She'll be so surprised, she won't be able to say no. We'll get you on this mission yet." They'd started practicing on her stickfighting techniques late at night after everyone had gone to bed, and had just begun working with wooden practice swords. Usagi couldn't wait to try a real blade.

"Galloping gods, is this the Tiger's Claw?" Tupa hefted a scabbard lacquered with prowling tigers. The thin curved blade hissed as he pulled it out. "The Tigress used to carry this."

Usagi leaned in for a better look. Interwoven strips of black and gold leather covered the hilt, and the steel blade had a wavy striped pattern all along its cutting edge. Tupa offered it to her with a broad smile. "Want to hold it?"

Gingerly taking the handle, Usagi was surprised. "It's so light." She heard the shuffling steps of the Tigress and hurriedly handed the sword back. "Horangi's coming."

As Tupa hung the Tiger's Claw back in its place, the old warrior entered the Great Hall, her cloud leopard padding at her heels. Usagi scurried out, not daring to meet Horangi's eyes.

But the sharp shriek of an angry bird stopped her. She

turned back and crept to the open door.

The Tigress stood before the Heirs, a fox sparrow perched on her hand. The tiny brown bird beat its wings on Horangi's gnarled finger, trying desperately to get away. It let out a shrill series of frustrated calls that echoed to the rafters. *Tschup! Tschup! Seeeeeek!* Usagi winced.

"To fly off, this bird needs resistance. See what happens when there is none." Almost imperceptibly, Horangi's arm moved in tune with the fox sparrow's movements. The bird bobbed and flapped to no avail. *Tschup! Tschup! Seeeeeek!*

Beneath the old warrior's outstretched arm, Kumo watched the frantic sparrow with interest.

"Keep your movements soft and fluid," said the Tigress. "Watch for the flow of energy and follow it. Instead of pushing back against it, you move with it—reducing your opponent's power."

Usagi craned her neck around the doorjamb, wishing she could be closer. The bird stopped beating its wings, exhausted. *Tschup! Tschup!* Horangi smiled and grew still. The bird cocked its head, then launched off her hand, speeding out the doorway over Usagi's head in a flurry of feathers. *Seeeeeek!* With a disappointed huff, Kumo slumped on his paws.

"As soon as I no longer moved with the bird, I gave it enough resistance to push off and fly," Horangi explained. "Much like a kite cannot rise unless it has an opposing wind to lift it." She shuffled to the mats and pointed to a spot in front of her. "Tupa, stand here." The Ram Heir obeyed. Horangi peered up at him. "Push me over."

"You sure, Teacher?" Dwarfing the old warrior, Tupa shifted uneasily.

"Yes, knock me down. Use your hands, feet—anything."

Looking doubtful, Tupa brought his hands up and got into a fighting stance. He pushed at Horangi's shoulder. Ever so slightly, she tilted her small frame back, and Tupa stumbled, almost falling into her. "Try again," she told him. "Faster this time."

Frowning in concentration, Tupa snapped out a kick. But before he struck the Tigress's stooped form, she glided out of the way. Tupa flailed as he missed.

"Counterattack," Horangi announced, striking him from behind. Tupa fell facedown with a thump. A small smile pulled at the old warrior's lips. "When two great forces oppose each other, the victory goes to the one who knows how to yield."

Tupa rolled over with a groan, then sat up, rubbing his shaved head. He caught Usagi wide-eyed in the doorway and gave a good-natured shrug.

Later at their midnight practice session by the lakeside prayer pavilion, Usagi asked him if he was really having trouble against the Tigress. "You're at least twice her size."

He chuckled. "Did you not hear what she was saying? I

wish I could say I was pretending, but I wasn't. Pure force is great—but technique helps too. Now let's work on yours."

Tupa handed Usagi a practice sword made of strips of bamboo and wood bound with leather, and had her begin drills. The night air was lit by several hovering fireballs from his firehorn, but they did little to warm the frigid air. Usagi's hands felt like frozen claws around her sword handle.

After attacking a straw bale with repeated hits, Usagi stopped shivering. Left cut, right cut. Her breath came out in puffs of steam. Head strike. Torso strike. Tupa stopped her.

"Where's your voice?" he asked. "Don't forget to use spirit-breath like the Tigress said. Let it come from the depths of your belly. *Ki-yah!*"

Usagi struck the bale. *"Ki-yah!"* she tried.

"Louder! Find your voice!"

"Ki-yah!" she shrieked, hitting with all her might.

"Hounds and horses, there you go!" said Tupa. He picked up a practice sword and faced her. "All right, Rabbit Girl. Come at me. Head strike."

Usagi raised her sword and moved toward Tupa. She swung at his head. *Thwack!* The wood and bamboo blade glanced off Tupa's skull with a loud crack. "Spirits!" she cried, horrified. "I'm so sorry!"

"I'm fine!" His booming laugh echoed through the frigid air. "You've never seen one of my animal talents, have you?" Tupa took the straw bale and set it by the edge of the frozen lake. He took a few steps back, then lowered his head and butted it with a thump. The heavy bale flew into the air and landed a good twenty paces away, skidding across the hard icy surface. Usagi's mouth fell open. Tupa turned and knocked his forehead with a broad smile. "Now you know why I'm Ram Heir!"

After sparring for a while longer, Usagi helped retrieve the straw bale and stash it in the trees. They walked back to the shrine, Tupa shouldering their practice swords.

"You have talent, Rabbit Girl. Maybe the Tigress doesn't see it right now, but I'm sure she'll come around."

"I don't know what I'll do if she doesn't," said Usagi, glad for the Ram Heir's confidence. She told him that she was still sleeping poorly. In frequent nightmares, Uma's face loomed before her, asking what would happen if the Blue Dragon's men came for her. *I would never leave you*, Usagi would say, right before the dreaded clacking of Dragon-striker armor drowned out Uma's reply. All too often, Usagi would wake up in a cold sweat, half out of breath from chasing her tied-up sister in a speeding cart. "It's the last thing I said to my sister, and then I went and *abandoned* her."

"We'll make this right," Tupa told her. "You'll be on the mission, with a weapon like the rest of us. If you're not— well, may the Tree of Elements fall on me."

"Is that a real tree?" Usagi teased.

Tupa stopped in his tracks. "You don't know? It's not far from here."

"I thought it was just an expression when the Tigress mentioned it," said Usagi. "What is it?"

"It's a sacred cypress at a spring of burning water. Iron-stone fragments grow out of its trunk, forming the Circle of the Twelve. It's got all five of the elements, see? Some say the mountain goddess planted it there, but more likely one of the first Warriors put chunks of ironstone in the trunk—they're these beautiful pieces of tiger iron . . ." He cocked his head as Usagi stifled a yawn. "I'd take you to see it, but I think you'd better get to bed."

Winter storms buffeted the top of Mount Jade and blanketed the shrine in snow. Usagi had to don a shabby coat of bear fur whenever she stepped outside, pulling the hood up against the biting cold. Saru found her sturdy sheepskin boots to replace her rope slippers.

Tupa filled small metal boxes with burning coals, wrapping the boxes in felted wool to carry in a pocket or pouch. Whenever Usagi's fingers grew too stiff from the chill during their late-night practices, she would wrap her hands around the pocket warmers to thaw.

He insisted that she continue to practice mind-the-mind and calligraphy. "A proper Warrior knows both. The Tigress was right to teach you those things." So Usagi would sit in the warmth of the library with her jade slate, working on her strokes with a brush and water. The Heirs welcomed Usagi into their practice sessions, and both Nezu and Inu commented on how much she seemed to be improving. Usagi had to hide her smile when Tupa winked at her behind their backs.

But her fears for her sister were never far away. For the first time, Uma's birthday had come and gone without Usagi there to find her a special treat, like a piece of honeycomb. Now that Uma was nine, might the Blue Dragon spare her? Usagi checked the Mirror of Elsewhere as often as she dared, waiting till the Great Hall was empty. She'd sneak a peek and catch her sister and Tora in uniform, marching, running, or doing exercises. Sometimes they carried wooden swords, stabbing the air in unison with others. Usagi had never seen Uma so grim-faced. What was happening to her?

On the last day of the year, Usagi was at the chest of Treasures, about to take out the mirror when she heard Nezu coming. She stepped back and pretended to be stretching when he entered. Greeting her with a flashing grin, he went to the chest and removed the Bowl of Plenty.

"My master carried this," he told her. "Want to see what it does? I've got to make more rice for our New Year's feast." He took a pinch of rice and dropped it into the metal bowl. Cradling the bowl in both hands, he swirled its contents around three times, then placed it carefully on the ground.

The bowl vibrated, the grains tinkling against the hammered brass, and the amount of rice in the bowl began to rise until it was full to the brim. "See? As long as this bowl's around, we'll never go hungry."

"Sweet spirits, that's useful," Usagi marveled. If only she'd had that back in Goldentusk. They'd never have had to eat bugs.

That night, Nezu outdid himself preparing the feast to mark the turning of the year. In addition to mounds of hot fluffy rice, there was roasted fish, meaty grilled mushrooms, glazed squash, winter greens braised with herbs and onions, spicy pickled cabbage and turnips, bubbling bean curd stew with egg and smoked wild boar, and a savory clear broth full of chewy rice cakes and tender green spruce tips. There was even dessert—slices of poached pear and persimmon floating in honey syrup.

It was the most food Usagi had seen since before the war, and it put everyone in good spirits. When she accidentally made eye contact with the Tigress, the old warrior's green gaze was good-humored—she didn't seem angry with Usagi at all. The meal felt like a reprieve from the training and mission planning that had consumed them since Tupa's arrival from the capital. Despite the cold outside, the chatter and laughter around the table warmed everyone from head to toe.

"Here's a riddle," Nezu shouted. "'When set loose, I fly

away, never so cursed as when I go astray. What am I?'"

"Easy," Inu scoffed. "An arrow."

"No, guess again!" Nezu looked at each of them, grinning, until he could hold it in no longer and chortled, "A fart!"

"That you are," Inu told him, and guffaws rang out. Even Horangi laughed, coughing her odd, hacking chuckle while her cloud leopard purred in the corner.

The next morning, Usagi made her way to the lakeside pavilion, where she found Kumo pacing while the Tigress stared at something in her hands. Usagi stood at the bottom of the steps, fiddling with her rabbit pendant. "Teacher? May I speak to you?"

The old warrior looked up, and her gaze sharpened. "Young Rabbit." She gave a short nod and her cloud leopard settled on its haunches beside her. Two sets of eyes, one pair green and the other amber, watched as Usagi climbed up to the platform. "What is it?"

Usagi nervously cleared her throat then bowed low. "I—I just wanted to say that I'm sorry. I never meant to insult you and I didn't mean to be ungrateful." The words poured out in a rush, bottled up for weeks. "I know it's an honor to be taught by you. I've been practicing everything you showed me, and I'll work hard on anything else you teach me."

Horangi raised an eyebrow. "Control yourself in one

moment of anger, and you will save yourself a hundred days of sorrow." Her wrinkled lips pursed, then quirked at the corners. "I accept your apology. Perhaps our next lesson could be on patience."

The cloud leopard got up and bumped its head against Usagi, nearly knocking her over. With a relieved laugh, Usagi scratched Kumo's back, feeling lighter than she had in a while. She saw that the Tigress was holding a piece of jade. It was the size and shape of a giant bear claw, with a hole bored through the wider end. Usagi pointed at the polished green stone. "What is that?"

"A replica of the Land Jewel in the broken necklace Tupa brought back," said Horangi. She rubbed a gnarled finger over the jade bead. "I made it from memory, using a piece of the mountain's heartstone. But will it serve?" She sighed and shook her head.

Usagi had never seen the old warrior look so uncertain. Maybe this was the time to ask. "Teacher, the mission is fast approaching. I know you said that I might scout, but couldn't I also try going through Warrior Trials? I want to help fight—with a proper weapon."

"Fools in a hurry use feedsticks to drink. Patience really *should* be our next lesson." The Tigress frowned, forgetting the stone for a moment. "It is not enough to fight with weapons or fists. To cross a river without learning the currents and depths could get you killed." Her gaze was piercing as she looked at Usagi. "You are standing at the edge of a rushing river, thinking you can simply wade across."

"I'm just trying to help Uma," Usagi protested. "Her life is in danger, and all I can do right now is worry."

The cloud leopard began to wash its giant paws with its blue-gray tongue.

"Worry and doubt can be more cruel than reality." The creases around Horangi's mouth deepened. "When the birds of worry fly over your head, do not let them nest. You cannot help your sister otherwise."

Usagi shook her head. "I can't help anyone if I'm not taught to fight back."

"Do you know what happens if you fail Warrior Trials?" Her glowing green eyes bore into Usagi's. "You fail as a candidate for Heir and are banished from the shrine. Is that what you want?"

"No, but it's a risk I'll take." She bowed and started down the steps. "I'll ask the Heirs to teach me what they know. They've already been doing that anyway."

"Stop right there," the Tigress growled. She pocketed the jade piece and picked up her staff, leaning heavily as she got up. The old warrior sighed and stared over the frozen waters of the lake. "The Midaga I knew was lost along with the Twelve. The last thing I expected was to teach our traditions to a new youngling—the fighting arts least of all, for those take many years of practice and training. But one plants trees so that the next generation can enjoy the shade." She shook her head and grimaced, puckering the slashing scars on her face. She looked at Usagi. "You are right. It would be irresponsible of me not to teach you as much as I can. Time is too short to prepare for a full-fledged Warrior Trial, but if you can show me your competence with a single weapon, you will be given it—and allowed to come on the mission."

Usagi felt a lump form in her throat. She tried to thank the Tigress, but no words would come.

"Now, now. Give me your arm, Young Rabbit." Horangi's green eyes were soft. She put a gnarled hand in the crook of Usagi's elbow, and began shuffling out of the pavilion. "We have a lot of work to do."

CHAPTER 17

WARRIOR LESSONS

BITTER WINTER WINDS LASHED THE shrine and bent the Singing Bamboo nearly to the ground, its usual soft melody a loud, protesting moan. Usagi was so intent on all she was learning that she stuffed cotton wool in her ears and carried on. She huddled with the others in the drafty Great Hall, where the Tigress drilled them on the art of escape—crucial for the mission. "A successful escape is not only about speed or stealth footwork," she told them. "It may also require distraction, hiding, misdirection, and camouflage." She pointed at Usagi. "Using the Five Elements as a guide, name some escape methods."

"Wood: hide in nearby trees or bushes," recited Usagi confidently. "Fire: use smoke bombs for cover, and firecrackers to distract and direct attention away from your location. Earth: keep low to the ground, use stone-form to hide among rocks, and throw dirt to temporarily blind your pursuers. Water. Um . . ." She looked up, as if the answers were on the ceiling.

Nezu jumped in. "Water: use waterways to hide, with a hollow piece of bamboo for a breathing tube. Throw rushes or duckweed on the water's surface to escape under the cover of floating greenery. Metal: hidden blades, throwing stars, and ground spikes can distract or slow down anyone giving chase."

The Tigress nodded. "Correct."

Usagi bit her lip. She knew all that. This was no way to show readiness for her Warrior Trial. She would have to study harder.

The old warrior continued. "Now, if you have an elemental gift, you may use the elements in more unusual ways." She raised an eyebrow. "Nezu, for example, could use water to distract or impair. Every power you possess gives you an added advantage."

Puffing out his chest, Nezu smoothed his whiskers. Usagi wondered what she might be able to do with her wood gift. Maybe she could get a tree to drop its leaves on command, or knock a Guard down with whipping branches. She vowed to do some experimenting.

To practice escape, they took turns throwing a handful of chestnut spikes—pieces of metal shaped like the spiky seedpod of the water devil chestnut—across the floor. The Heirs had nicknamed them "hobblers," which Usagi agreed was an apt name when she accidentally stepped on one, the hard iron nub sending shooting pains through her heel.

"You're supposed to run in the *opposite* direction from where you throw them," Inu told Usagi as she hopped about, rubbing her stinging foot.

Saru gave her a sympathetic squeeze. "Forget these. Just find whatever's at hand to slow a pursuer. Throwing pebbles underfoot can work—even the reflection of the sun on a knife blade can compromise their vision long enough for escape."

Nezu flashed a grin. "Once I tied the ends of some long grass together—it tripped five Guards!"

Everyone laughed, except Tupa. "Our lives have become nothing but stealth and secrecy." He shook his head sadly. "We didn't always have to use underhanded techniques."

The Tigress sighed. "If we are to survive, we must learn to bend with the winds."

As the days passed, Usagi learned more and more from the Tigress. She was taught the basics of archery, of swordwork, of handling a moon blade. The old warrior instructed her in ways to move about without making a sound, and after watching the Heirs demonstrate, Usagi stopped walking normally around the shrine. Instead she crept about in a crab-walk or some other stealth walk, scuttling along walls or from tree to tree, practicing for the rescue mission.

To demonstrate her progress in calligraphy to the Tigress, Usagi used the shrine's entire courtyard as her slate. On the gray-green stone, she painted the words "honor," "duty," "courage," "truth," "respect," "loyalty," and "love" in extra-large strokes with water, which quickly froze into shiny slicks of ice.

The old warrior gave her a withering stare. "Use ink and paper properly. You are making the way treacherous."

Chastened, Usagi enlisted the help of Tupa. With his firehorn, he blasted a stream of flame across the courtyard tiles, melting the ice into puffs of steam.

During all her lessons, Usagi became accustomed to Horangi's critical eyes and exacting evaluations. It was a change from her secret lessons with Tupa, who'd become like the older brother she'd never had. The Ram Heir gave her steady encouragement, often telling her how well she was doing.

But the Tiger Warrior's constant corrections were taking hold, for Usagi now wielded her practice sword with ease, could twirl the long handle of a moon blade almost as smoothly as her stick, and even hit a straw target a couple of times with a bow and arrow. In stealth drills, none of the Heirs could sneak up on her, no matter if they used the crab-walk, fox-walk, or light-walk, thanks to her rabbit hearing. Usagi would pretend to be unsuspecting then whip around with a demon face. Seeing Nezu or Inu jump in surprise made her laugh every time.

It all began to feel natural to Usagi, and her confidence was growing in all her skills—except her wood gift. She'd neglected it while trying to keep up with chores and lessons. She decided to look for the Tree of Elements, and see for herself what Tupa had told her about. Surely the most sacred tree on Mount Jade would help enhance that power.

Using her rabbit hearing one wintry afternoon, Usagi listened for the sound of running water and eternal flame in the trees surrounding the shrine compound. It didn't take her long to locate a burbling, whooshing sound in the frosty air. She followed it until she came upon a hollow in the mountainside. There, out of a fissure in the rock, orange flames danced as a stream of water poured into a small pool. An ancient cypress, as gnarled and bent as the Tigress, stood beside the burning spring, buttressed by a sturdy wooden pole.

Usagi drew closer, feeling the warmth of the fire in the hollow, and wrinkled her nose at the pungent smell of rotted eggs. Embedded in the twisted trunk were a dozen rocks that might have once formed a circle, but now looked more like a deformed teardrop. They were vividly striped red, gold, and black. Tiger iron, the Ram Heir had called it. With a tentative finger, she stroked the rough bark of the tree and poked at the ironstones. It had been a while since she'd tried to communicate with a tree. This one was even older than the ones in the Sea of Trees, its wispy tufts of feathery green needles like an elderly man's balding pate.

She laid a hand on the trunk, and detected a faint hum, as if it were vibrating. But though she tried, Usagi was unable to get the tree to respond to her. It stood immobile and silent, next to the hissing roar of the flames and the trickling water.

Back at the shrine, she told Tupa that she'd found the Tree of Elements. His face lit up and he tugged excitedly at his goatee. "You should get a piece of that tiger iron. It's a powerful stone, much like jade. Wouldn't that be perfect for convincing the Tigress of your abilities?"

"I suppose," said Usagi. "But how? I don't dare chop one out, if that's what you're thinking."

"Of course not! It's a sacred tree." Tupa looked indignant. He handed her a round, unshelled walnut. "Your hands are stronger now, aren't they?"

Usagi squeezed the hard knobby shell till it shattered with a satisfying crack. She grinned. "I'd say." All the odd chores that the Tigress had assigned her, like carrying heavy jars of water and sifting through bins of rice—not to mention all the training—had certainly strengthened her grip.

Popping the shelled nut in his mouth, Tupa smiled back. "So use the strength of your fingers! Like I've told you—your hands can be weapons enough. Combined with your wood gift, the Tree ought to release some of that tiger iron."

The next day, Usagi returned to the ancient cypress and set upon a large chunk of ironstone buried in the wood. She pulled with all her might. She wiggled and tugged. She braced a foot on its trunk for more leverage—and immediately fell on her backside. No matter how hard she tried to pry a piece of ironstone loose, nothing would budge.

Discouraged, she reported this to Tupa, who shrugged and patted her shoulder. "It was worth a try. Maybe Teacher was right and there's no getting anything from that Tree." He winked. "Don't worry. You'll impress her in other ways."

Unsatisfied, Usagi wandered through the trees surrounding the shrine, and placed her hands on their trunks, hoping to feel them pulse, alive and knowing, as they had for her when she first came up Mount Jade. But they were nearly as unresponsive as the Tree of Elements. After some experimentation and not a few splinters, she found that if she hugged a tree in the biting cold, she'd just barely detect a connection.

She was doing that one morning, embracing a leafless maple, when she heard the Tigress shuffle up.

"What are you doing, Young Rabbit?"

Usagi glanced over her shoulder. "I'm trying to see if the tree will respond to my touch. It's been hard to work on my wood gift since they all seem to be asleep for winter."

The old warrior pursed her lips and pointed. "Practice on those evergreens," she advised.

Usagi switched to a lacebark pine and tried to get it to move, frowning with the effort.

"Listen to it first," said the Tigress. "No need to wrap yourself around it in that unseemly manner. Think of what you do in mind-the-mind—you notice what is happening in your mind and body as you sit, without trying to force or control anything. The same with your wood gift. Find the heart of the tree and feel what it is saying—and you will become one with the tree."

Nodding, Usagi placed her chilled hands against the pale silver-green bark and shut her eyes. After a few breaths, she felt a slight tingling beneath her palms, and then a slow, languid pulse that briefly warmed her hands as it ran through the trunk. Her eyes popped open. "It's awake!" Hastily she closed her eyes again and continued to focus on the tree's sluggish energy. She sensed the heavy snow on its branches, weighing down the needles. *Shake it off,* Usagi thought. A shudder ran through the lacebark pine, and then a shower of icy snow came down on her and the Tigress. "I think it listened to me!" Usagi exclaimed.

The Tigress pushed back her hood and brushed off the fallen snow. "Indeed. Or you listened to the tree. If you continue to cultivate such a dialogue, you will find it easier and easier to access your wood gift."

"My father—he was a carver who made the most amazing shapes come out of wood," said Usagi, running a hand along the pine's trunk. "They even came to life in his hands. But that never happened for me."

Horangi nodded. "He had a gift for bringing wood to life. Your gift is with the living trees. The gift of each person is different—as are talents."

Clear as day, Usagi remembered her father's hands coaxing a graceful horse with flowing mane and tail out of a piece of wood for baby Uma. Whenever he held it up, it would flick its ears and its legs would gallop, and little Uma would laugh and laugh. She could still smell the wood shavings and resin on his smock if she closed her eyes. Overwhelmed with memories, Usagi leaned back against the tree. "I wish he were still here to see me do this." Her throat grew tight and she turned her head away. There was a long silence, and then she felt Horangi's hand on her shoulder.

"To love is to remember, Young Rabbit," said the Tigress softly. "And one who is not forgotten is not dead."

After that, when Usagi placed her hands on a tree, she felt doubly connected, to both the living wood beneath her palms and to the memory of her father. He'd be so proud to know she had a wood gift too. As the weeks wore on, the bitter cold seemed to ease, and the trees were increasingly responsive to her touch, though Usagi wasn't sure if it was because she was mastering her gift or because the trees were waking up.

Then came a morning when Usagi heard a new sound—the *drip, drip, drip* of melting ice from the eaves of the Great Hall. The trickling music of running water led her to investigate, and she found that the stream that ran behind the compound to the lake was no longer frozen solid. Spring was coming, and when she saw the Tigress at breakfast, the old warrior's eyes glowed green. "It is time for your Trial."

FIRE

"The heat of Fire can temper and strengthen—
if it first does not destroy."

—Book of Elements, from *The Way of the Twelve*

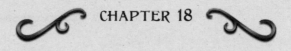

CHAPTER 18

THE BLADE TRIAL

USAGI AND THE HEIRS GATHERED around the sparring mats in the Great Hall, studying the weapon wall.

"Are you sure you want to do this, Usagi?" Saru asked, her pale face creased with concern. "If you don't pass . . ."

Tupa waved her off. "You worry too much, Monkey Girl. Usagi's got this. She's been working hard." Smiling broadly at Usagi, he gave her the barest wink. Usagi smiled back.

"I've got to—for Uma and for Tora," she insisted. "And for all of you too. I don't want to weigh down the mission by having to be protected all the time."

Inu twisted the archer's ring he wore on his thumb. "You wouldn't be weighing us down."

There was a low grunt as the Tigress entered the Great Hall, Kumo slinking in beside her. Usagi and the Heirs bowed, and the Tigress gave a brisk nod. She pointed her staff at the wall of weapons. "What will it be, Young Rabbit?"

She'd been thinking of this moment for weeks. Usagi glanced at Tupa, who nodded. She took a deep breath. "The sword."

The old warrior raised an eyebrow, and Kumo stopped washing his face to stare at Usagi.

"Are you sure you wouldn't want to try the moon blade or your stick?" Nezu's voice cracked. "Or maybe archery?"

"Have you seen her shoot?" Inu muttered.

Usagi shot him a look. "I heard that." She lifted her chin. "I'd like to be tested on my swordwork, please." Spirits, were they going to be surprised.

"Very well," said the Tigress. "Face off against Nezu. You will both wear sparring armor and use blunted blades in order to get in the full range of cuts and strikes without harm."

Usagi had never worn armor, but once she gripped the sword Saru handed her, it seemed like a good idea. Though the metal blade was blunt, it still looked like it could do real damage. Saru helped her into a black lacquered bamboo breastplate, a protective apron with leather panels, padded gloves that ran up her forearms, and a padded helmet with a metal grille over her face. It was all terribly bulky, and hard to see clearly with the helmet on. She peered through the grille and saw Nezu in the same equipment. Faceless and armored, he looked uncannily like a Striker, a nightmare come to life. Unbidden, the image of her sister tied up in the

250

back of the Striker cart flashed in her mind's eye.

Feeling dizzy, she asked for a moment and knelt by the side of the mats. Closing her eyes, Usagi breathed deeply and evenly, concentrating on the air moving in and out of her lungs and minding the mind. *Focus.* When she opened her eyes, she saw the Tigress looking at her approvingly.

Calm again, Usagi faced Nezu on the mats, with Inu acting as their referee. They exchanged bows.

"Let's go, Usagi! You can do this!" Saru and Tupa clapped from their seats at the edge of the sparring area. The Tigress sat nearby, observing in silence, her cloud leopard lying at her side.

Inu shouted, "Begin!"

"Ki-yah!" Nezu howled, and lunged. Usagi faltered. *Thwack!* Nezu's blade glanced off her helmet. Too late, Usagi ducked and hefted her blade with a grunt. The blade was heavier than she was used to.

Clang! Usagi took a step back. *Clatter!* Another, as Nezu shoved at her. *Crash!* With a thump, Usagi landed onto the padded straw flooring, her sword skidding away. She grimaced and lay unmoving as Nezu pointed his blade at Usagi's throat.

"Halt!" Inu called. "Point goes to Nezu!" He helped Usagi up. She got back into position and adjusted her helmet, suddenly grateful for its bulk.

"Begin!"

Setting her jaw, Usagi charged. *Crack!* Nezu's sword crashed against Usagi's breastplate. *Oof.* Another point to him. In the next round, he struck her gauntlet, then her helmet. *Ow.* Usagi shook out her arm and glanced at the Tigress. The old warrior's pinched expression had yet to change. Kumo blinked sleepily beside her, his head on his giant paws. Anxious flutterings started up in her chest. *Don't fail Uma again.*

"Stop giving him points!" Saru cried.

Tupa gestured at his torso. "Spirit-breath!" he reminded. "Use your voice!"

Nodding, Usagi got into position. Sweat stung her eyes. She gripped her sword with damp palms and squinted at Nezu.

"Begin!"

Usagi lumbered forward and swung, shouting with all her might. *"Ki-yah!"* A resounding crash filled the hall as her sword crossed Nezu's, the blades rattling as they pushed at each other. With a growl, she pulled away and swung again, catching him squarely on the helmet.

"Halt!" Inu called. "Point goes to Usagi!"

Finally. Usagi pumped her fist. But for the next round, the harder she tried, the more she struggled. Her limbs felt leaden, she could barely see, and she was gasping for breath. Usagi could hear her heart beating a panicked drumbeat as she fended off Nezu's blows, unable to get in a strike of her own.

She spotted an opening and swung her sword. Nezu parried, hard, and aimed a hit at her wrist. Usagi jerked away and felt a searing pain as Nezu's blade slipped over the edge of the gauntlet. He'd cut her arm, right where it was exposed. She dropped her sword with a cry of surprise.

Blood quickly seeped out, a darkening patch of red that soaked her sleeve. Usagi fell to her knees, light-headed. Tupa rushed up and caught her as the other Heirs gathered round. They took off her armor and examined the cut.

"No visible bone," Inu said, looking relieved. "It's not too deep."

Usagi couldn't say anything—the cut felt deep to *her*. She squeezed her eyes shut and moaned, biting her lip to keep from screaming.

"I'm so sorry," babbled Nezu, his face paler than Saru's.

"What was that?" Tupa roared at him. "You should have been more careful!"

"Stand aside, Ram Heir," said the Tigress. She knelt beside Usagi with the Apothecary in her gnarled hands. Sliding open its various compartments, she mixed several powders with drops from a few tiny glass vials until she had a pungent mud-colored paste. She applied it to Usagi's cut. A soothing warmth stopped the pain and bleeding immediately. Usagi sighed with relief.

As the tense expressions on the Heirs slackened, the Tigress bound Usagi's arm with a strip of cloth. "Leave it on for a bit." The old warrior stood. "As I suspected, you are not ready." Behind her, Kumo yawned and shook himself, then began licking his hindquarters. "But I will not banish you from the shrine, as this was never a full-fledged Trial. Consider yourself fortunate for this exception."

"Please, let me try one more time." Usagi clutched at Horangi's gnarled hand. "Tomorrow?"

The Tigress pulled from Usagi's grasp. "Enough. We have no more time to waste on your notions. We leave in three days."

"I'm sorry, Usagi," Saru whispered.

Tupa gave her a sad smile. "You did really great, you know."

Crushed, Usagi stumbled to her feet. She bolted out the door, even as the Heirs called after her. She ran through the trees, crunching across slushy snow, until she reached the prayer pavilion. She stared out over Crescent Lake, eyes hot and dry, too angry at herself to cry. How could she help her sister and Tora now? Usagi pounded a clenched fist against the gilded railing. When she heard Inu and Nezu coming, she slipped away. At the Tree of Elements, she heard Tupa calling and got out of the hollow before she could be discovered. She moved constantly, avoiding everyone. She looked for refuge in the Singing Bamboo, in the kitchen, in the sleeping quarters—even the goat shed.

Finally she ducked into the library, where her calligraphy

work was laid out. Usagi picked up a sheet of paper on which she'd written the seven words she'd practiced for months. They seemed to taunt her. *Use the brush as your sword*, the Tigress had once said. But what use was all that practice when she'd failed the Trial with a real one? Gritting her teeth, Usagi crumpled the paper and threw it across the room, just as the Tigress appeared in the doorway with Kumo. The cloud leopard lunged for the ball of paper and batted it across the floor.

"We can still use you as a scout, Young Rabbit." The old warrior's gaze was steady as her green eyes met Usagi's. "You need not stay behind."

"Maybe I should. You saw what happened." Usagi stared at her hands.

"There is no time for dwelling on what you cannot change." The Tigress checked Usagi's arm and grunted in approval. The cut had already healed completely. But Usagi still felt the agony of it somehow.

"I thought I could do more. I *want* to do more." Her voice quavered. "But I keep failing."

"Failure does not predict future failure. It is simply a delay, not defeat. Failure is the seed from which success springs," said the Tigress. She picked up the ball of paper and smoothed it out. "There is more to being a Warrior than just carrying a weapon. While your calligraphy has a fine quality of line and movement, I fear that you have not absorbed the meaning of these words at all." The old warrior let the paper fall onto the table, and Kumo laid his furry muzzle over it. "Your talents are still needed. Serving as a scout does not diminish your importance on this mission. Now, will you come help save the other younglings or not?"

Sniffling, Usagi rubbed her eyes until she could see clearly. The cloud leopard nudged her with a gentle bump of its head. She gave a faint smile and rubbed Kumo's velvet nose, then squared her shoulders. "I'm coming."

The morning of their departure from the shrine arrived with a warm breeze. Usagi hauled the last of the packs to the courtyard and collapsed on the wooden platform. Kumo stopped his agitated pacing and sniffed her. The Tigress had forbidden the cloud leopard from accompanying them. "He would attract far too much attention," she'd said. He snorted, blasting Usagi with hot breath, then resumed stalking about the courtyard with a glower.

For two straight days and nights, they'd prepared in a fever of activity. Usagi helped Nezu pack rice balls, dried fruit, salted fish, and other food for their journey. She assisted the Tigress and Saru in going over their supply of medicines and ointments, using the Bowl of Plenty to restock. She oiled blades and inspected arrowheads with Inu, and patched and mended their traveling packs alongside Tupa. In everything they did, Usagi offered up a prayer to the spirits of the first

Twelve, asking them to bless the mission.

With a sigh, she got up from the platform and joined the others in doing a final check around the compound, securing doors and windows, and making sure they hadn't forgotten anything. Gods be good, the next time she was back here, her sister and Tora would be with her. She itched to check the Mirror of Elsewhere and see them. If only she could bring it on the journey. She would take one last look before they set off, just to make sure Uma and Tora were still okay. Usagi slipped into the Great Hall.

But the room wasn't empty. Tupa stood before the chest of the Treasures, his back to her. As she drew close, he turned, startled. "Rabbit Girl!" He gave her a broad smile. "I'm glad you're here." Waving her over, he pointed to the opened drawers, four Treasures nestled inside. "I really think we need these with us on this mission," he confided. "Packing extra medicines and food is well and good, but this is our most dangerous assignment yet. What if we're caught in a bind?" He picked up the Coppice Comb. "Wouldn't this be useful?"

"I used that to hide once, when the Guard was chasing me," Usagi said. "It definitely helped." She hesitated. "What does the Tigress say?"

The Ram Heir shook his head. "I haven't asked. What if Teacher says no? We'd waste time arguing. We should bring them in case we get in a situation where we need the

Treasures. Think about it—we could use the Bowl of Plenty to help feed all the younglings, and the Mirror could help us keep an eye on the Dragonlord even when we're on the grounds of the palace."

"That's true," said Usagi. "I was just wishing we could have the Mirror with us." She glanced up at the poem describing the Treasures, then at the four open drawers. "But it seems risky to take them from the shrine. You've all spent so much time hunting these down."

Tupa handed her the mirror. "All the more reason to keep them close. I've thought about this for years—what if the Twelve was weakened because they didn't make full use of the Treasures after the Shield came down? On this mission, we need every advantage we can get." He pulled out the comb. "Take this too," he told her. "I'll keep the Bowl and the Apothecary in my robe. Believe me, we'll be glad of them if we run into trouble."

Usagi rubbed her thumb over the back of the Mirror of Elsewhere and stared down at the comb, feeling its familiar weight and shape in her palm. This was perfect—she could easily check on her sister and Tora until they were rescued. And she'd kept the comb safe for five years, so what would it hurt to carry it once more? She took a deep breath, her heart skipping a beat. "All right." She slipped the Treasures into her belt, tucking them snugly in the spot where she'd always kept the comb.

"Excellent," said Tupa happily. He secreted the bowl and pillbox into the voluminous folds of his robe, and slid the chest drawers shut. "It's a shame the Tigress hasn't found a way to repair the Jewels of Land and Sea."

"I think she has," said Usagi. "I saw her with a piece of jade—she made a new bead for the necklace."

The Ram Heir's eyes widened. "Really?" He stroked his goatee, thinking. "Do you know if she keeps it on her?"

Usagi shrugged. "I think so. At least she did the last time I saw it."

"Perfect," Tupa said. "If Horangi's carrying it, we'll have the powers of five Treasures with us." He gave her shoulders a squeeze. "All right, Rabbit Girl. Let's go get your sister."

They stepped out of the Great Hall and fastened the doors, then joined the others in putting on their packs. "What took you so long?" asked Inu with a scowl.

"We got sidetracked in there, talking about arming ourselves with powerful weapons," Tupa said with a laugh.

Horangi frowned. "The most powerful weapons are . . ."

"The mind and the heart," they all chorused. Usagi and the Heirs exchanged grins.

The old warrior sniffed. "As long as you do not forget." She gave her unhappy cloud leopard a few last scratches. "Guard the shrine well, Kumo." Horangi looked at them all and nodded. "It is time."

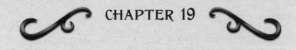

CHAPTER 19

PEARL GARDEN
ENCOUNTER

THEY LEFT THE SHRINE, Tupa carrying the Tigress on his broad back, traveling at spirit speed down Mount Jade and on through the wilderness, heading north toward the capital. Leaping, sprinting, and springing across remote woodlands, meadows, and hills, they covered the miles in hours instead of days. Usagi thought of her arduous trek to Mount Jade six months prior, and thanked the gods. She'd come a long way since then.

At the end of the third day, they reached the Ring Road. Few other souls were about. In the safety of the trees, Usagi and the Heirs changed into entertainers' clothing, with the exception of Tupa, who kept on his monk's robes. They donned bright patterned coats and belts over white pants and tunics, with the plan to visit a particular inn just outside the capital. Everyone traveling on the Ring Road stopped there, and the Heirs believed they could gather useful information.

"Now that we have Usagi," said Saru, "we'll hear so much more than we could before."

Inu nodded. "People like to talk—it's how we tracked down the Treasures."

Uncomfortably, Usagi adjusted her belt, feeling for the comb and mirror. It felt strange to be carrying them without the others knowing, but Tupa caught her eye and smiled. "The right word at the right time can open all sorts of doors," he agreed. He stuck a hand in his pocket and gave Usagi a conspiratorial wink. Hiding her smile, she winked back.

The sinking sun washed the sky in purpled pink. In the distance, rows of paper lanterns lit a sprawling three-story complex against the night. They had reached the Pearl Garden, the largest and finest inn outside the capital. A babble of voices, clinking cups, and uproarious laughter floated through the air.

Usagi stared at the curved eaves and elaborately carved columns in wonder. Two stone lions with dishes of salt in their snarling jaws guarded the entrance. The rich scent of grilled meats and long-simmering stews wafted through the door, shielded by a heavy indigo curtain. Her stomach growled.

Inu raised his head, sniffing. "I smell their famous Peddler's Noodles."

"Well, let's go get some," Nezu said. "I'm famished."

"Just a moment," said the Tigress from Tupa's back. He let her down and handed over her staff. Grasping it in a gnarled hand, she gazed at them with stern green eyes. "Remember, we are going in to glean the latest information. Only engage with someone if Usagi hears something of interest. Order the bare minimum and focus on your surroundings."

They murmured their agreement, Nezu with some disappointment. Usagi tugged her ears nervously as they approached the door. An old battered sign above the threshold proclaimed the strict no-weapons policy held by inns all across Midaga. An ugly gash, likely from a Guard's sword, obscured where the "No" once was.

"A relic from before the war," Tupa chuckled. "No one except the Guard carries weapons nowadays. Right?" He adjusted the power chain around his waist and winked.

Saru shrugged innocently. "All I have is my walking stick."

"I wouldn't dream of wearing a sword," agreed Nezu, holding up the staff that concealed his blade. He flashed a grin.

Inu thumped his hollowed stick on the ground, jingling the chain and claw hook inside. "Same here. Just my stick."

Usagi glanced at the faint scar on her arm and felt the sting of her failure all over again.

They pushed aside a curtain flap and ducked into the

inn. Usagi's mouth dropped open.

She'd never seen such a place. The inn's rooms were built several stories high around a central courtyard that held the tea garden. Amid potted plants, a cascading water fountain, and tiny dwarf trees arranged in miniature landscapes, dozens of tables were crowded with all manner of travelers eating, drinking, and talking—peddlers, blacksmiths, and farmers, as well as merchants dressed in strange foreign clothes from the neighboring empires of Waya and Hulagu.

The sounds of the inn were overwhelming after being in the quiet of the shrine and wilderness for so many months. Songbirds hopped about in bamboo cages that hung from the balconies overlooking the tea garden, their chirps competing with a trio of musicians on a raised dais in the corner, playing an exotic-sounding Wayani song with flute, lute, and zither. Multiple conversations in many accents filled Usagi's ears. A few younglings carried trays of tea and rice wine to tables, and cleared empty dishes as a red-faced woman in a stained apron snapped her fingers and ordered them about.

They found themselves an empty table, and sat facing the bustling courtyard. The flood of noise swept over Usagi, and she struggled under the barrage of new sounds, unable to home in on anything. How would she manage to listen in such a racket? A boy who looked to be about Nezu's age walked by with a tray of sizzling fish, their fragrant sauces jumping and spitting off the hot iron plates. Her mouth watered, and Nezu's eyes widened. "That's a new sort of dish—I think it's from the Amami Islands. I'll have to try making that," he muttered.

"Please do," said Inu, inhaling appreciatively.

Tupa smiled. "In the capital, there's a newfangled way to serve soups and stews," he told them. "They heat stone bowls till they're red-hot, and your food cooks at the table. Apparently that's how they do it in the Kingdom of Solongos."

The red-faced woman made her way over to them. "What'll you have?" she barked in a thick Hulagan accent.

"A pot of tea, if you please, and five cups," said the Tigress calmly.

"And?" prompted the red-faced woman.

"Some of your traditional meat buns," said the Tigress. "That will be all."

As the red-faced woman waddled away, grumbling to herself about stingy Midagians, Saru nudged Usagi. "Hear anything interesting?"

It was time for her to get to work. Usagi closed her eyes, reaching for the tiny wooden rabbit at her neck. Rubbing its carved body, she scanned the snippets of conversation around the noisy room with some difficulty. After a while, she could pick out a pair of voices here, a trio there, and caught fragments of arguments, joke-telling, and negotiations.

There was a table of peddlers laughing at a story: *"He expected rice and got a mouthful of maggots!"*

"Ha! Serves him right for being such a toad!"

A wife berating her husband: *"How could you bet our last gold mon on a six sticks game?!"*

"I was on a winning streak!"

Foreign merchants haggling over a deal in heavily accented Midagian: *"Have you lost your senses? Two bolts of silk for five bricks of tea is robbery!"*

"I'll give you one more brick of tea if you add a bolt of cotton, then."

None of it seemed to be of any importance to their mission. "I'm not sure what I should be listening for," Usagi said with a grimace.

"Just continue to use your ears," said the Tigress. "You will know if and when you hear it."

Usagi squeezed her eyes tighter still and sifted through the cacophony. There was a slap and a shout from the red-faced woman, berating a hapless youngling. *"Worthless empty dumpling skin! Never bring back an empty tray!"*

A petulant young man whined to his traveling companions. *"That tailor had better be finished when we get back to the city. I refuse to attend the spring festival celebrations in these old rags."*

Then a different sound. Usagi's eyes popped open—it was the rattle of armor and clopping of horse hooves. "A mounted patrol is coming," she hissed. "Should we go?"

"No need to panic," said Tupa. "We might get good

information from them if we stick around and listen."

"We'll break out in a song and dance if we have to," Nezu said stoutly.

Saru's face grew a shade paler. "What if they're Strikers?"

"Maybe we should leave," Inu frowned.

A young boy came by and delivered a platter of meat buns and their tea. Nezu poured a cup for the Tigress, who calmly took a sip. "We shall be fine. Do not draw unwanted attention to yourselves and remain alert." She picked up a meat bun and took a bite. "Quite good."

Nezu passed Usagi the platter of buns. The soft white bread was warm and steaming, but she barely nibbled, unable to focus on anything but the whooshing breath of approaching horses and squeaking clank of armor. *"There's the inn!"* a man's voice shouted.

"Sounds like regular Guard—at least eight of them," Usagi reported. "And they're definitely headed here." The music and bustle of the tea garden swirled around them, while she and the Heirs sat watching the entrance.

At last the Guard burst through the door, all raucous laughter and coarse jokes. They swaggered into the inn wearing their swords, while the tea garden immediately quieted. Only the birds continued to sing.

The tallest Guard looked down his long nose around the inn. He spotted the musicians, who'd frozen in the midst of their performance. "What're you lookin' at?" he roared.

"Play!" He swept a glare over the tea garden and glimpsed the Heirs and Usagi in their entertainers' garb. He pointed at them. "You! Entertain us! Give us a show!"

Slowly, Inu stood up, followed by Nezu and Saru. Usagi made to get up too, but Inu cast a dark look over his shoulder. "Stay put and keep listening," he muttered. "But be prepared to run if need be." She shrank back, clutching her rabbit pendant.

As Inu, Nezu, and Saru made their way to the musicians' corner, the Guard settled themselves at a table near the door, blocking the way out. They heckled each other as they removed their helmets and put up booted feet, ignoring the furtive glances of other travelers. The festive, bustling mood of the inn had disappeared.

The trio of musicians struck up a lively tune, and Inu, Nezu, and Saru began a juggling routine, grabbing items from nearby tables: a pair of empty cups, three plates, a set of rice wine bottles. Despite her anxiety, Usagi smiled as they threw them into the air, spinning and catching everything with ease. The atmosphere around the tea garden lightened and conversations started up again.

Usagi glanced at the Tigress. The old warrior patted her hand. "Carry on, youngling. There is nothing to be afraid of."

"We'll be on our way soon enough, after our jugglers finish their routine," said Tupa, cramming down the last of his meat bun and swigging some tea.

With a tiny nod, Usagi relaxed. The Tigress was right—what was there to be afraid of? Although she would feel a lot better if she'd had a weapon like the others. She sipped her tea and took a bite of her bun, straining to hear the Guards' conversation. Over the music, twittering birds, and trickling fountain, the hum of other patrons talking and laughing, the clink of feedsticks on plates and bowls, and the shouts that Saru, Nezu, and Inu made while tossing cups and bottles back and forth, Usagi could barely make out what the Guards were saying. She craned her neck, trying to read their lips.

The tall one with the long nose leaned forward. *"We have orders to be in Dragon City as soon as possible. The Dragonlord has a big execution planned."*

Usagi's heart slid up to her throat. The younglings—Uma! She swallowed hard and listened, catching only some of the words through the din, the rest a muddled garble.

"Is this . . . garble garble . . . *new Striker captain?"* asked a grizzled Guard. *"I heard he* . . . garble garble . . . *Captain Wono for the post. The Dragonlord thinks he'll do a better job, especially with* . . . garble garble . . . *involved."* He picked up a glass of wine and tossed it back. Wiping his mouth with the back of his hand, he said something else Usagi couldn't quite hear. Blast all this noise. She needed to get closer—she couldn't afford to miss anything.

Frowning, Usagi got to her feet and looked around. She

stopped a youngling with a tray of full glasses. "Here, let me help you with that," she said, and hefted the tray out of his hands.

"But I don't need any help," said the befuddled boy.

"What are you doing?" hissed the Tigress as Tupa's eyebrows shot up.

"There's talk about important things," Usagi told them, not wanting to say too much in front of the young server. "I won't be long."

Before anyone could reply, Usagi had wound her way around the tables to the Guard. "Tea or wine?" she asked, a little too squeakily.

"Wine all around, and two cups of tea," said the tall Guard. As nonchalantly as she could, Usagi began putting drinks on their table.

A squat Guard belched. "Those younglings at the palace—freaks with demon abilities. I can't believe he's keeping them there."

"It's like his own little zoo," said the grizzled Guard. "Unnatural things. They should be exterminated."

On Usagi's tray, the remaining cups and glasses clinked like chattering teeth. She fought to steady herself.

The squat one leered at her. "What's the matter, little doe? Never seen warriors before?" His smile looked like a chewed-up corncob. Usagi wanted to dump the tray of drinks on his head.

"Leave her alone," said the tall Guard in a bored voice. He waved Usagi away. "That's enough for now."

She put the last glass down and turned straight into the red-faced woman. The boy who was supposed to serve stood forlornly next to her.

"How dare you interfere with my servers?" demanded the woman, hands on her hips. "You don't work here."

"I—I just meant to help . . ." Usagi stammered. She shoved the tray back at the forlorn server. "You all seemed so busy. . . ."

A fat, hairy hand closed around Usagi's wrist. It was the squat Guard with the corncob teeth. "Hullo, Madam . . . is this youngling giving you trouble? I'm happy to send her to the mines, if you like."

The woman's glare gave way to a sickly smile as she turned her attention to Corn Teeth. "Thank you, sir," she simpered. "My apologies for the interruption—it's so hard to find good help these days!" She frowned at the serving boy. "Go get these gentlemen a round of wine on the house." The boy bobbed and ran off.

"Free wine—how kind." A gleam appeared in Corn Teeth's beady eyes. "I'm always in the mood for something sweet." Loosening his grip on Usagi's arm, he moved closer to the red-faced woman, who tittered and smoothed her frizzy hair. Usagi was pressed uncomfortably between their bellies, all but forgotten as they made eyes at each other.

The smell of his breath and the sweat and grease on the woman's apron made Usagi gag.

Usagi ducked out of the Guard's grasp and slipped out from between them, falling to her hands and knees. There were legs everywhere—chair legs, table legs, people's legs. She crawled as fast as she could through the forest of legs.

Bumping a table, she heard cups rattle and the splash of tea. "Oi!"

She brushed against a calf and a woman gave a startled squeal. "Stars!"

"Get her!" shrieked the red-faced innswoman.

The squat Guard grabbed Usagi by the scruff of her neck, hauling her to her feet. "Not so fast."

His grip hurt. Usagi tried to stomp on his feet. "This one's got some spirit," laughed Corn Teeth. "The mines will break it nicely!"

Usagi glanced around frantically. People were staring. Tupa and the Tigress were on their feet, while the other Heirs had stopped juggling. Nezu made a discreet motion with his hand, and a squirt of water flew from the fountain and hit the Guard from behind.

"What the . . . ?" Corn Teeth wiped the back of his head and scowled at his wet hand. Usagi saw her chance and yanked free. She was hemmed in, tables of diners crowded around them. She clambered onto a tabletop, sending dishes and cups scattering and crashing to the floor. "Sorry, so sorry," she babbled, and scrambled to another table, squashing a steamed bun. She stepped to a third table, knocking the hat off of an old farmer. "Beg pardon!" Usagi hopped again.

"Come here, little brat!" Pushing people roughly aside, the squat Guard headed for Usagi, his hand at the hilt of his sword. Screams and squeals went up as tea garden patrons launched out of their seats and scurried out of the way.

Usagi spied a broom leaning across the next table, dropped by one of the servers. Grabbing it, she swatted at Corn Teeth with its bristles. He laughed. "You can't sweep me away that easily."

He swung his sword, and Usagi raised the broom to block the blow. The curved blade sliced off the bristles, leaving her with nothing but a stick. Usagi yelped.

"Oh ho," Corn Teeth chortled. "Keep it up and your foot'll be next!"

Shorn of the broom head, the thick wooden handle was more balanced, almost like her walking stick. In desperation, she flipped the cut end up at the Guard, hitting him squarely in the nose. He grabbed his face and roared angrily. Usagi swung and jabbed once more, shoving with all her might. He sprawled back into an abandoned table and chairs, knocking them over.

The other Guards rushed her, swords drawn. Nezu raised his hands and scalding hot tea rose out of cups all around. With a quick pushing motion, he hit them full in the face. Howling in pain, they stopped in their tracks. The tea garden patrons looked around in bewilderment as Usagi jumped down and ran toward Tupa and the Tigress.

"No, no! To the door!" shouted Tupa. Raising his fire-horn, he blew a giant plume of flame that made everyone duck. He snatched a wisp of fire from the plume and lit a firecracker. As it sparked and flared, he threw it up. There was a loud bang and a shower of sparks, followed by a cloud of smoke. As people shrieked and ran about, he and the Tigress slipped out.

The tall Guard, his face dripping with tea, came at Usagi, brandishing his sword. In desperation she heaved herself toward the inn's entrance. Leaping high, she sailed through the inn's courtyard over the Guards, the red-faced woman, the smoke, and the diners. Shouts and astonished cries filled the tea garden. Landing neatly at the open door, Usagi glanced back. The other three Heirs were on her tail, while the tall Guard pointed their way. "It's a pack of freaks! After them!"

They ran out of the inn and onto the Ring Road. "They saw us use zodiac powers," Usagi gasped. She was still clutching the broom, her walking stick left behind in the chaos.

"What were you thinking?" Horangi's green eyes glowed furiously in the dark.

"No time to talk," Tupa warned. "We're going to have company soon." He pointed to the lights of the inn twinkling in the distance. The Guards were mounting their horses, and one had started galloping toward them.

With a flick of his wrist, Inu scattered a jangling handful of chestnut spikes across the Ring Road, where they lay gleaming in the moonlight. "That should slow them down some," he said. Then they raced off for the capital as fast as their spirit speed would allow.

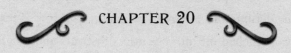

CHAPTER 20

THE PALACE OF
THE CLOUDS

THEY SLIPPED THROUGH THE GATES of Dragon City just as dusk was falling.

Jostled by crowds of people entering and leaving the city walls before the gates closed, Usagi gawked at a place she'd only heard about. For centuries, the capital was known as Guardian City, filled with sprawling temples to the gods and tall shrines that celebrated the Twelve. The temples remained untouched—and unlike in the provinces, the invaders had refrained from razing the shrines honoring various Zodiac Warriors, for they served as excellent watch-towers.

Tiered towers with soaring metal spires and curving tiled roofs rose over the city like armored sentries. A grid of streets stretched out before them, paved in the famed white stone of the island's Marble Gorge. The buildings lining the streets were bigger and finer than anything in Goldentusk, with multiple stories, swooping eaves, glazed ceramic ornamentation, and filigreed windows. Narrow lanes and byways branched off into countless districts and neighborhoods. And all about, people were hanging garlands of paper flowers, sweeping doorways, and hurrying with packages in preparation for the spring equinox.

"It's so big here," Usagi said faintly. She leaned on the broom handle from the Pearl Garden, overwhelmed by both the sights and the sounds. The din of the inn was nothing compared to the capital city. The force of it was almost painful, like when she was little and first began noticing her animal talent.

"If you ever get lost, just look for the Phoenix River," Tupa told her. "It runs the length of the city, starting from the hills where the Palace of the Clouds sits." He scowled as someone bumped him, and turned to the Tigress. "Teacher, let me carry you on my back—there are far too many people here."

The old warrior patted his arm. "Thank you, Fire Ram, but I can walk just fine. I must say, the capital streets are the busiest I have ever seen."

Crowds pushed by, men and women shouting, arguing, talking, while laughing younglings ran after each other. The hum and buzz of city folk going about their lives made

Usagi's head swim. Dogs barked and snarled in the alley-ways. Horse-drawn drays and ox carts clattered through the streets. There were even small two-wheeled pullcabs drawn by men instead of animals—Usagi had heard about this invention from Waya but had never seen one before.

The residents of Dragon City didn't wear the same haunted look as those in Goldentusk. People here weren't as thin, and while the streets reeked of animal dung, sewage, and the sweat of far too many bodies, many seemed downright happy, dressed in colorful silken gowns and exotic-looking costumes, chattering in unknown languages.

Usagi caught the lilting cadence from the Empire of Waya, the hissing lisp that Hulagans affected when they spoke, and strange tongues she couldn't identify. While there were plenty of ordinary Midagians about, a good many people appeared foreign—ruddy-faced men with beaked noses and frizzy clouds of golden facial hair, those with dusky skin and eyes a startling icy blue, ghostly pale people with flame-colored hair, and some with blue-green tattoos inked in swirling patterns on their faces.

She saw tributes to the Dragonlord everywhere. Above doorways, on stall posts, and even from towers were hung paintings of a stern-faced man with handsome features, dressed in the regalia of a king in formal silk robes, with a dragon crest on prominent display. Statues of the man guarded city wells and fountains, and little carved dragons sat on window ledges or perched on the roofs of pullcabs and palanquins, as if keeping a close eye on everyone. The Guard were all around, patrolling the streets, standing watch up in the towers, spilling out of teahouses reeking of rice wine.

"There must be thousands of Guard here," Usagi observed nervously, tugging at the collar of her tunic. With the spring equinox less than two days away, it felt almost too warm, especially coming from the slopes of Mount Jade.

Saru scanned the streets and gave Usagi a half smile. "The good thing about being around so many people is that we hardly stand out. Especially with all the visitors from other lands."

"Since becoming Dragon City, more outsiders have come with their odd customs and speech," Inu agreed. He pushed the shaggy hair out of his eyes. "You can hardly understand half the people in the capital these days."

"Oh, I don't know about that," said Nezu, flashing a grin. "As long as they bring good food, what's not to understand?"

Inu shook his head, frowning. "They're not bringing us anything—they're taking. You've seen it yourself—most ordinary Midagians aren't getting rice."

The Ram Heir clapped Inu's shoulder. "Enough talk," he said briskly. "Let's get to the riverwalk—a seldom-used path there will take us to the palace district. Follow me."

He led them down a broad avenue, the white marble

paving stones reflecting the purpling sky. As the sun sank behind city walls, workers lit oiled paper lanterns hanging from lampposts and buildings, illuminating the streets.

Inu sniffed the air. "I smell the night market!" he exclaimed.

"You mean paradise," said Nezu, smacking his lips. "Gods' guts, leaving the Pearl Garden without tasting their Peddler's Noodles was torture."

Tupa gave Nezu a little shake. "Focus. We aren't going on an eating tour of Snake Alley—we're only going to cut through."

Nezu rolled his eyes but nodded, while Inu took a deep whiff and sighed. In the distance, Usagi caught the calls of market vendors hawking their wares.

"Cabbage pancake! Onion pancake!"

"Puffed rice, puffed rice—light and crispy! Sweet or savory, take your pick!"

"Grilled chicken hearts! Grilled duck livers! Five to a skewer!"

As the calls grew louder, the scent of smoky charcoal and hot griddles grew stronger, filling the air with delicious smells. In spite of herself, Usagi walked faster, as did the others. Even the Tiger Warrior's shuffling pace quickened.

They rounded a corner and Usagi stopped short. Stretched before her was a covered maze of crooked alleys, crammed with stall after stall. The profusion was dizzying. In Goldentusk you could count food vendors on one hand.

"Stay together," Tupa reminded. "The river's on the other side."

Customers squatting on low stools nibbled at delicate fried fish cakes, picked at glistening cubes of stewed pork on rice, or gingerly unwrapped steamed triangles of sticky rice from bamboo leaves to get at fillings of sweet bean paste or savory mincemeat. Stall workers stood beside roaring cook-fires, assembling dumplings, frying long rashers of dough, and noisily chopping heads of cabbage. Usagi's mouth watered with sudden craving, and she gulped.

Not even the New Year's feast at the Shrine of the Twelve compared to this. What bounty! How many times had she and Tora risked capture and beatings as they scrounged for fallen grains in the fields back home? How often had she given Uma her own share, then lay awake all night from hunger? Now Usagi saw where all the crops of the Western Plains were going. Her stomach groaned loudly in protest.

They passed by a noodle stand, where a few customers hunched over steaming bowls of soup. A Hulagan woman with her hair tied back in a white cloth folded and pulled strands of dough until they were thin as pine needles, while vats of fragrant broth bubbled. Licking her lips, Usagi took a whiff.

The woman caught her gawking. "Bowl for a copper. A copper more to add meat."

Usagi shook her head and kept after the others. A few

stalls down, a small crowd gathered around a Wayani man making elaborate candy sculptures, his movements swift and sure. Eyes wide, Usagi slowed. Pulling and twisting at a glob of heated sugar syrup on a wooden stick, the man used scissors and metal feedsticks to poke, clip, and mold the hot taffy before it hardened into the shape of a crane, feathered wings stretched in flight. He held it up and the spectators applauded.

"Nezu, do you think you could do that?" Usagi asked, enchanted. He didn't answer. "Nezu?" She turned and the bottom dropped out of her stomach. He and the others were nowhere to be seen. Usagi looked up and down the row of stalls, buffeted by a stream of people squeezing past. She was alone. Fighting a spasm of panic, she waded through the crowded market, searching for Nezu's excited squeak, Tupa's deep voice, or the Tigress's croak over the shouts of vendors.

At times she caught someone calling her name, and headed in the direction of the voice, only to come up empty. Heart pounding, she wandered down one lane, then another, getting hopelessly lost in the twisting maze of stalls.

She shouldn't have stopped to watch that candymaker. Why did she let herself get distracted? Would the others go on without her? How was she to get to the palace? Usagi commanded herself to stay calm. *Think.* They had gone into the market to . . . of course! They'd been headed for the riverwalk. *If you ever get lost, just look for the Phoenix River,* Tupa had said. She'd be sure to find the others there.

"Excuse me," she said to a woman crisping turnip cakes on a smoking griddle. "Which way is the river?"

The turnip cake vendor wiped a hand on her apron and pointed. "Down five stalls, turn left at the fishmonger, then right at the custard apple stand—the one by the fan and parasol repair. Make another right at the Snake shrine. You'll see the river from there."

Usagi thanked her and hurried through the night market, following the vendor's directions. Exiting Snake Alley, she found herself on a wide path edged by a low wall, from which came a dull, watery roar. Peering over, she saw the Phoenix River, a wide, rippling ribbon that glimmered from the rising moon and the lanterns of the city. Flowering trees lined its banks and perfumed the air. The murmuring river seemed to wash away the cacophony and pungent smells of the capital.

But where were Horangi and the Heirs? Usagi walked further from the frenetic shouts and activity of the night market, listening for their voices and scanning the riverbanks. The streets were emptying as the night wore on, and Usagi's dread grew. Tupa had said they'd be following the river. Had something happened to them? Her hand strayed to her rabbit pendant and she worried it between her fingers.

"Tupa? Saru?" she called, leaning over the river wall.

"Inu? Nezu?" A couple of young women in pale silks and embroidered coats strolled by. They gave her strange looks, then exchanged glances and giggled. Usagi scowled and slinked along, smoothing her hair self-consciously. Was there something on her face? If she had a mirror . . . Usagi stopped with a gasp. How could she forget? She had the Mirror of Elsewhere.

Fumbling for it, Usagi moved under a street lantern. She held up the mirror and thought of the Heirs. It grew cloudy, fogging over for a moment, then cleared to show Inu, Saru, and Nezu walking along a busy alleyway, the three of them looking in all directions. They were searching for her! She peered at the mirror, disoriented, trying to make out exactly where they were. The Heirs stopped before a little street shrine bedecked with garlands of rice straw and flowers. That looked familiar—she'd passed it exiting the market. Inu sniffed the air, then pointed.

Usagi pocketed the disk and hurried back toward Snake Alley. As she drew closer, she could hear Nezu's voice, then Inu's. *"She's this way!"* They burst out of the night market entrance just as she was about to go in.

Saru hugged her, hard. "Oh, Usagi, we were looking everywhere for you!" She put her hands on Usagi's shoulders and gave her a tiny shake. "Where did you go?"

"I got distracted watching the candymaker," Usagi said in a small voice.

Nezu gave a knowing nod. "You're not the first to fall under that sugar magician's spell."

"Come on," said Inu. "Tupa and Teacher are waiting."

They followed the path overlooking the river until they reached a break in the wall where a set of stone steps led down to the riverbank. There, in a grove of blooming cherry trees, stood the Tigress with Tupa. "Here she is," said the old warrior with a grunt of relief.

"Thank the gods," Tupa said. "What happened?"

"Candy!" said Nezu cheerfully. A sheepish Usagi started to explain, but Inu interrupted, pointing to the moon.

"It will be the hour of the Rat soon," he observed. "We've got to get to the palace by dawn."

They set off along the riverbank, keeping hidden beneath the flowering trees, avoiding the use of spirit speed. Tupa hung back to walk with her. "Everything okay, Rabbit Girl?"

"Now it is," said Usagi. "I stopped to watch a candymaker and the next thing I knew, you all were gone. I was so lost, but then I remembered the Mirror of Elsewhere. Thank the gods I had it!"

"Didn't I tell you it would come in handy?" Tupa exclaimed.

Usagi smiled. "You were right."

He slowed so that they lagged even farther behind the others, and lowered his voice. "While we're at the palace, it would be helpful if I had the Mirror to help us keep track of

284

the Dragonlord's whereabouts."

Nodding, Usagi reached for the mirror and sneaked it into his palm. "Here."

"Thanks, Rabbit Girl. Just stick closer next time," the Ram Heir said with his broad smile. "Shall I keep the Coppice Comb for you as well?"

She placed a protective hand on her belt. "Er . . . that's okay," Usagi said. "I can handle it."

"As you wish," said Tupa, and winked.

As the sky lightened, birds above them began to sing. Ducks and other waterfowl roused themselves, their quacks and calls echoing along the riverbank. The Phoenix took a gentle turn, and as they followed the curve of the river, a sprawling complex of ornate, brightly colored buildings came into view. In the dawn light, the palace nestled in the misty hills overlooking the city, as if hovering on a bed of clouds.

Usagi's jaw dropped. Though she'd seen paintings of the Palace of the Clouds in the shrine's library, the view took her breath away. Even from afar, the elegant lines and swooping tiled rooftops of the palace made the grand towers around the capital seem like brutish giants. The buildings were covered in elaborate carvings painted in riotous colors and gilded trim. A high white marble wall encircled the compound. This was once the seat of wise leadership and gracious governance. Generations of Midagian kings had ruled there, advised by the Council of the Twelve.

Now the Dragonlord had installed himself in that citadel. Somewhere behind its walls were her sister and Tora, and little Jago. She was closer to them than she'd been in months. What would they think when they saw her?

The sun was over the horizon by the time they arrived in the palace district, burning off the mist enveloping the hills around the Dragonlord's lair. The narrow, winding streets around the palace came to life as residents emerged from their homes, beating bedrolls from windows, sweeping doorways and sluicing their front steps with buckets of water. Tradesmen opened their shutters. Carts of firewood, rice, and other supplies rattled up the hilly cobblestoned lanes toward the palace gates. The great wooden doors swung open with a groan and creak, their bronze fittings glinting in the morning light.

"As planned, we're going to walk right through the main gate like we belong here," Tupa muttered. He straightened his monk's robes. "I'll tell the Guards that I'm taking you to the palace temple to perform for the spring festival."

Inu gave a curt nod. "Teacher, your cover is that you're a fortune-teller who reads tea leaves."

"If only I actually had such foresight," said the Tigress dryly. She gazed at the palace, her green eyes almost black, then pulled her hood over her head with a sigh.

Usagi's grip tightened on her broomstick and she lifted

her chin, striding after the others toward the palace wall. Built of the same white marble that lined the streets, the wall encircled the hilltop and dwarfed the enormous doors of the main gate.

They passed the line of delivery carts waiting to be inspected. One of the Guards on duty eyed them as they approached the gatehouse. He had tremendously bushy brows and a firecannon slung against his shoulder.

"Oi, monk," said the bushy-browed Guard. "What's your business here with the rubbish folk?"

"I've fetched them for the festival tonight," Tupa said smoothly. "They'll be performing at the Temple of the Immortals, by the request of Head Priest Chantangu."

The Guard's bushy brows worked like two hairy caterpillars boxing. He looked them over. "Why haven't I heard about this?"

Tupa cocked his head. "Does the head priest tell you everything?" He chuckled. "All I know are my orders."

"Well, *my* orders . . ." began Bushy Brows, but the Guard inspecting the carts looked over and waved.

"Well, if it isn't the wanderer! Haven't seen you in a while!"

The Ram Heir waved back. "I was on an errand," he boomed, then looked at Bushy Brows triumphantly.

"Fine," the Guard said at last, and waved them through.

Usagi let out her breath and followed Tupa onto the

287

grounds. Tupa had told them the palace compound was divided into three sections: the Outer Court, which housed the palace temple, guard barracks, the royal mint, and an armory; the Central Court, with all its grand ceremonial halls; and the Inner Court, where the royal family's residences were once located. Bright murals of richly glazed tiles adorned walls everywhere, and dozens of sumptuously embellished figurines lined the sloping ridges of gleaming roofs. Just as depicted in the scroll paintings, there stood the Court of the Wisdoms, the Gallery of Song and Beauty, the Hall of the Golden Throne, the Royal Library, and countless smaller buildings, courtyards, and gardens. It was like nothing Usagi had ever seen. But there was only one thing she really wanted to see.

Holding tight to her rabbit charm, she listened, hearing the activity all through the compound. From the cookery came the sound of sizzling oil and rapid chopping. There was a chiming clang of metal on metal from a blacksmith. The rattling clack of Dragonstriker armor. A cracking whip in the distance, and a shriek—whether animal or man, it was hard to tell. Usagi gave an involuntary shudder at the piercing cry.

They approached the eastern side of the Outer Court, anchored by the Temple of the Immortals, which vibrated with the low chants of temple monks. The temple's garishly colored facade seemed to scream danger. Here was where

the Blue Dragon planned to execute innocent younglings—
and her sister could be among them. Usagi's stomach roiled
at the thought.

She turned her head and caught her breath at the sound
of younglings' voices. They were coming from somewhere
in the Central Court. It had to be the Dragon Academy.

CHAPTER 21

DRAGON ACADEMY

THE TEMPLE COMPLEX LOOMED BEFORE them, thrumming with the droning chants of monks praying. In his monk's robes, Tupa led them toward a hiding place he knew from his time there. Yet Usagi's feet were rooted to the spot, unable to follow the Heirs and the Tigress. She couldn't, not when she could hear the laughter of younglings coming from somewhere else on the palace grounds. Tears came to her eyes. After all these months, her sister was near.

"Tupa, wait," she croaked. But he and the others didn't turn. Usagi cleared her throat and tried again, afraid to call too loudly. "Teacher? Saru? The Dragon Academy is this way!"

No one heard her. Usagi watched the others slip behind the Temple of the Immortals. None of them really understood. They didn't have family in danger like she did. Usagi wanted—no, *needed*—to see her sister, now.

She glanced around. No one was about. This was her chance. Usagi dashed toward a garden grove of flowering plum trees and paused, checking for the sound of young-lings' voices. Darting behind a wall, she scurried along until she came across a stately building with dozens of windows opened to the morning air. She ducked into a crouch and scuttled past.

With her ears leading her, Usagi ran from building to courtyard, past stables and a laundry, till she arrived in the Central Court at a cluster of squat structures. Large stone dragons guarded their entrances. She hid behind the rough flank of one of the dragons and peered through its legs. Usagi caught a glimpse of several younglings dressed in indigo, but they disappeared around a corner. She hurried after them then halted at a lilting whinny of a laugh—just like her sister's when she was excited during a game. It had to be Uma. Usagi's heart began to gallop and she clutched her broomstick with sweating palms. A stampede of running feet ended in a flurry of shouts, ringing out from a nearby courtyard.

"I won, I won! The extra bowl of rice is mine! Fire Horses rule!"

A lump formed in Usagi's throat at the sweetness of the sound. She glanced about then moved toward the laughter, squeezing into the blooming forsythia bushes that lined the walls of the surrounding buildings. She parted the bright yellow flowers and peeked in.

Her heart tripped at the sight. Uma was in the flesh, dressed in a tidy blue tunic and pants, her hair in a long, neat braid. Her sister stood with a knot of other uniform-clad younglings, teasing and bantering. She was smiling and her pink cheeks were surprisingly round. It had been years since Usagi had seen her so well fed. She felt a spark of hope. Perhaps her sister wouldn't be sacrificed after all.

The sound of marching feet caught her attention, and soon a line of younglings paraded into the courtyard. Usagi stifled a gasp at the sight of a girl with amber eyes and slashing scars on her arm. Tora. Her unruly hair was cropped short and slicked back, but she moved with the same stealthy grace she had in the forest, slinking at the end of the line behind everyone else. Uma stopped talking, suddenly serious, and stood at attention as several dozen younglings formed into rows alongside her. She turned every now and again to glare at someone until they inched into place.

Before long an elderly man in gray robes joined them. Bald but sporting a flowing white beard that reminded Usagi of the waterfall on Mount Jade, he was even more wrinkled and stooped than Horangi. He faced the rows of boys and girls of varying ages, sizes, and shapes, identically clad in dark blue.

"All hail Master Douzen!" said Uma in her clear, high voice, and led the younglings in a bow.

Master Douzen bowed back. "Hail to the Chosen," he

said in a Hulagan accent, voice quavery with age. "I bring good tidings. The Striker captain has arrived for spring festivities. Later today he will review your progress, and more importantly, Lord Druk will be accompanying him."

"The Dragonlord is coming!" Excited murmurs rippled through the rows.

The students quieted as Uma held up a hand. "It's rare to be graced with his Lordship's presence, so we must be at the top of our form!"

"Yes, Cadet Uma!"

"All hail the Dragonlord!" said Master Douzen.

The students shouted back with fervor. "Long live the Dragonlord!" Usagi gaped in astonishment. They seemed to adore the Blue Dragon—Uma and Tora included.

The wizened old man smiled, showing a set of gold teeth. "To the training hall!" he quavered. He left the courtyard, cadets marching behind him two by two. Uma joined the line and Usagi nearly cried out. The younglings were leaving and would soon be out of sight. She couldn't let her sister and Tora disappear again. Panicked, she cupped her hands around her mouth and whistled.

Twee hee, hoo hoo.

A birdcall, the one they always used to announce that all was clear. Uma stumbled, falling out of step. She glanced around briefly, then kept marching, her back straight as a spear. Tora brought up the end of the line as she had before, skulking toward the exit with a small boy by her side. Desperate, Usagi tried again. *Twee hee, hoo hoo.* She followed it with a different call they used—the hooting of an owl. It was midmorning—an owl hoot *had* to get attention.

Tora turned, a puzzled look on her face.

The small boy noticed and stopped midmarch, the crest of hair on his head bobbling. "Cadet Tora, are you coming?" It was Jago. If Aunt Bobo could see her son now! He'd been crying and snot-covered the last time Usagi saw him, but even he seemed to have grown, appearing serious and composed.

"Er . . . I'm going to inspect the main quad before the Dragonlord arrives," Tora told him. "Go ahead—I'll be there in a minute."

Jago nodded and left. Frowning, Tora glanced about then moved cautiously toward the line of bushes.

Usagi whistled once more as Tora drew near. There was no one left in the courtyard now but the two of them. Swallowing hard, Usagi emerged to stand before her friend. "Hello," she said softly.

Tora's eyes widened and she clapped her hand to her mouth. Then she threw herself at Usagi. With a half sob, Usagi hugged Tora with all her might. Her friend laughed, squeezing tightly before stepping back to look at her. "I can't believe it," said Tora. "I wasn't sure I'd ever see you again."

"Me too," Usagi confessed. "I've been so worried. I . . . I

ran. I've never been able to forgive myself."

Tora shook her head. "I told you to run! But I wish I hadn't. I didn't know we'd end up here."

"Neither did I," said Usagi, examining her friend closely. Though Tora was still lean and muscular, her face and frame had filled out and she no longer looked haunted by hunger. Her tunic had a small dragon embroidered on the left side, and a tiger on the right. She stood ramrod straight, in split-toe shoes of leather and felt. Usagi felt almost shabby in her entertainer's costume.

She heard a gasp, and turned to see her sister standing across the empty courtyard, dark eyes wide with shock. "Uma!" Usagi cried. She ran over and threw her arms around her. Uma stiffened, making no move to hug her back. Confused, Usagi let go. "It's me!"

Her sister's gaze was cold. "What are you doing here?" It was a punch to the gut.

"I—I'm sorry," Usagi stammered. She reached for Uma's hand. "You're angry, I can see that. You have to know I never meant to leave you."

"But you did." Pulling away, Uma frowned. "You said you wouldn't, but you disappeared."

Usagi flushed with shame. "It wasn't intentional, truly it wasn't. It just happened." She looked at Tora and her sister pleadingly. "I've been thinking about you all these months, wanting to find you. It's why I'm here now."

"Dressed like that?" Tora cocked an eyebrow. "How did you even get in here?"

"It's a long story," Usagi said. "But friends of mine—they brought me." As her sister and Tora exchanged glances, Usagi hurried on. "I heard your voice, Uma, and I had to come looking for you. I haven't been able to stop thinking about how to save you since the day the Strikers took you away."

Her sister rolled her eyes. "You don't need to save us, Usagi. Lord Druk saved us. Isn't that right, Tora?"

Tora nodded. "We went from starving in the forest to living in a palace." She looked at Uma. "And now Usagi's finally here with us."

After a pause, Uma's forehead smoothed. "That's true, I suppose. You've seen the error of your ways and have come. I'm sure you'll be welcomed, especially if we vouch for you."

"What? But I'm not here to . . . I came to take you away from this place," Usagi protested. "You're in danger! The Dragonlord means to kill you at the festival of the spring equinox."

There was a stunned silence as Tora and Uma stared at her, then at each other, before they burst out snickering. Usagi's cheeks burned. This wasn't turning out how she imagined.

"Where did you hear such a thing?" gasped Tora, trying to stifle her giggles. "The Dragonlord kill us? Why?"

"He means to sacrifice the weakest younglings," insisted Usagi.

"We're not weak," Uma snorted. "Besides, Lord Druk would never do that."

"Would never—the Dragonlord's the reason for the war! He's why Mama and Papa are dead. All those with zodiac powers, killed. Do you not remember the giant turtleback grave? Come to your senses!"

"How do we know that it really *was* a grave? Maybe those are lies spread by the Dragonlord's enemies," scoffed Uma.

"You were too young to remember, but I do, and so does Tora," said Usagi firmly. "So many died. All because of the Blue Dragon."

Uma squeaked in dismay and Tora waved a frantic hand. "He doesn't like to be called that," Tora hushed, glancing around. "You don't understand, Usagi. It was different during the war, but now he values our talents."

"He says I'm a star, and that having powers so young is proof," declared Uma. "My fire gift will bring glory to Midaga."

"Lord Druk has a vision for Midaga—and he's good to us," Tora continued. "Look at where we get to live! We eat three meals a day—three!—and go to school. We're to become Dragonstrikers even greater than the ones he has now."

Usagi shook her head, trying to clear it. She thought of all that the Heirs had told her, and all that she'd seen. The Blue Dragon's men had defaced and removed every sign of the Twelve in the kingdom. "No. He betrayed our country . . . he's a traitor."

Furious tears filled her sister's eyes. "Are you really trying to get us to leave the palace? If you thought we were suffering, you're wrong. We're actually quite happy here." She paused. "Happier than we were with you."

Usagi felt her heart crack. "But the war," she said weakly.

"We're prepared to ask Lord Druk to accept you as a cadet, but only if you give up these wild ideas," said Tora with a frown. "Uma's right. We're fine here. You haven't seen what we've seen, and you're only repeating the lies you've heard."

"If you don't want to stay, then leave," Uma sniffled. "After all, you've left us before."

At that, Usagi faltered. She'd promised her father she'd take care of Uma, swore to Uma she'd never leave her, and failed horribly on both counts. Her sister wiped her eyes and turned away. Maybe it was all a big misunderstanding. She had to stay and see for herself what was true. She clutched Uma's arm. "I'm not going anywhere."

Her sister softened. She squeezed Usagi's hand. "All right then."

Tora smiled with a glint of her snaggleteeth. "Now let's find a way to get you into the Dragon Academy."

They led her to a hulking building nearby. Stone dragons flanked the entrance, and emblazoned on the doors was a twisting dragon—the same one stitched on both Uma's and Tora's uniforms.

Uma looked at Usagi's brightly colored outfit and frowned. "You can't go in looking like that. You'll stand out like a frog in a squirrel's nest."

"Wait here," said Tora, shoving her behind one of the stone dragons. "Stay out of sight. I'm going to get help." She cracked open the double doors and slipped inside.

Usagi caught a glimpse of activity and moved closer, peering through the crack. A couple of boys spun and twirled on their heads like a pair of tops, surrounded by a circle of others cheering them on. Another boy ran about holding a flaming practice sword aloft, chased by two girls throwing orbs of water. Several girls were attacking burlap sacks lined against the wall, landing their kicks with fierce cries, then sinking their hands deep into the heart of the sacks and tearing out fistfuls of straw.

"Get back," Uma hissed, and pulled her toward the stone dragon.

Tucking herself behind its scaled back, Usagi looked up at her sister. "They haven't mistreated you?"

Uma gave an impatient sigh. "Lord Druk built this for us!" she said with a grand sweep of her arm. "Imagine, an entire school devoted to younglings with zodiac powers, right in the palace. What do you think?"

Usagi bit her lip. Would the Blue Dragon go to such lengths with these younglings if he meant to execute any of them? What if Tupa was wrong? What if the rescue mission they'd planned all these months was for nothing?

The double doors opened and Tora emerged, followed by a great giant of a boy, as tall and wide as two grown men. He carried a rolled-up rug over his arm as if it were a towel. He unfurled the heavy woolen rug and snapped it a few times, unleashing clouds of dust. "Anyone need a ride?" he drawled.

Uma hustled Usagi from her hiding place. "Cadet Goru, my sister, Usagi."

"Born in the year of the Wood Rabbit," Usagi said, bowing. She noticed the ox embroidered on his tunic.

"No time for that." Tora pushed Usagi toward the rug. "Lie down—we're going to sneak you in."

Usagi obeyed, lying across one end of the dark brown carpet. Goru smiled down at her. "Hold tight," he said, and began rolling until she was snugly inside a scratchy wool tube. She felt herself hoisted up, and heard the doors opening. With the rug draped over his shoulders, Goru entered the building.

Peering down the narrow tunnel of the rug, Usagi caught sight of an expansive wooden floor, straw practice mats, and a wall of weapons. The room echoed with activity and shouts. No one seemed to pay attention as Goru carried the rug into a dim room. He set Usagi down on the ground.

"Stay here—Rana and your sister will be coming in," he muttered, and shut the door.

Usagi waited, an anxious flutter in her chest, cramped and hot in the heavy, musty rug. The flutter soon turned into panic and she squirmed, trying desperately to escape her cocoon. She managed to push her head out and gasped for air, lying on the floor of a crowded storage room lit only by the light filtering through a high, narrow window. The walls were stacked with sparring pads that smelled of souring sweat, racks of practice swords, and various boxes and bins. Wiggling her arms free, she dragged herself out of the rug. *Whew.*

Creeping to the door, Usagi cracked it open. She peeked through and saw a room that reminded her of the Great Hall at the Shrine of the Twelve. But the hall at the shrine didn't have a portrait of a grim-looking man taking up nearly an entire wall.

It was the most elaborate likeness of the Dragonlord Usagi had ever seen. He was dressed in black armor trimmed in gold, looking like he was covered in dragon scales, with a longbow and quiver of arrows strapped to his back. His hooded eyes stared out beneath a black helmet featuring the golden head of a snarling dragon. The Dragonlord was mounted on a black warhorse, its long face covered with a dragon-shaped gold helmet.

Beneath the portrait, the giant boy, Goru, stacked stone blocks as if they were wooden toys. Little Jago climbed on a stack and launched himself in the air, where he hovered with a grin. He circled gleefully around Uma and a girl wearing dark braids coiled about her head. They appeared to be arguing with Tora. Listening carefully, Usagi homed in on her sister's and Tora's voices.

"Time is wasting, and no one is cleaning," fretted Tora. *"You want Lord Druk to see this mess? Where'd Master Douzen go?"*

Goru turned. *"He went to fetch Lord Druk and the captain. Said he'd be back in the next hour. We've got time."*

"The whole hall must be in order before they come back!" Tora anxiously rubbed at the scars on her arm.

"Afraid of another haircut from him?" asked the girl with coiled braids.

Uma crossed her arms. *"Your punishment could've been worse."*

"I deserved what I got." Smoothing her short hair, Tora bit her lip. *"But we've got to get everyone cleaning—now."*

"Leave it to me," said Uma, and she clapped her hands loudly. The other cadets stopped what they were doing and stood at attention. "Fellow Chosen," Uma called. "Lord Druk and the captain will be here soon. Everything must shine for inspection. Including our hearts and minds!"

"Yes, Cadet Uma!"

Looking smug, Uma clapped her hands again, and the cadets sprang into action, dropping practice equipment into baskets, sweeping up the straw that had come out of the sack targets, and putting the room back to order. With cleaning rags, they lined up against one end of the room, then bent and crossed the floor in unison, polishing the wooden planks in an industrious row. They turned at the other end of the room, repositioned their rags, and swarmed back across like a line of ants. Usagi stepped away from the door as some of the cadets scooted by.

Her sister and the girl with coiled braids entered the storage closet. At the sight of Usagi, the girl with braids stopped short, her eyes widening. She shut the door quickly behind them. "I thought you might be joking," she murmured to Uma.

"I don't joke," snorted Uma, and she introduced the girl to Usagi. "Rana, meet my sister."

Rana folded her hands in greeting. "Born an Earth Snake. Welcome to our little corner of heaven."

Her wry smile made Usagi want to smile back. "I'm Usagi. Year of the Wood Rabbit."

"We'd better get you something else to wear," said Rana, her sharp eyes looking over Usagi's outfit. She began rummaging through boxes of uniforms. Uma went to help her, and Usagi drifted back to the door and peeked out, impatient to see more of the Dragon Academy.

She noticed several maps and paintings on a nearby wall. Bright red ink circled Mount Jade on a map of Midaga. Beside the map hung a painting of twelve ordinary objects arranged in a circle: a bowl, a pen, a fan, and a mirror, among others. Usagi recognized them immediately as the Treasures, the comb looking exactly like the one she was carrying.

Turning, she nudged Uma. "What's the meaning of all those maps out there?"

Uma held up a wrinkled tunic and sniffed it. She made a face. "They're part of our training. We must memorize everything about Midaga, especially its geography and riches."

"What about the scroll with the items on it?"

Her sister stuffed the tunic back in a box. "Those are the Twelve Treasures—they're ancient objects of great power that belong to Midaga. They're all lost now, but Lord Druk says we're going to find them." She brushed off her hands. "Now that you mention it, I wanted to ask—do you still have that comb Papa gave you?"

"Why?" Usagi tried to sound casual, but suddenly felt as if the comb was sticking out of her belt. Sneaking a glance, she saw nothing.

Uma shrugged. "I remember it looking so much like the one in the painting. I thought it might be worth taking a look."

"I—uh, lost it, actually," Usagi said, squirming. She'd never lied to her sister before, but the maps on the wall and the painting of the Treasures left her on edge. The Heirs and the Tigress were right—the Blue Dragon *was* after the Treasures. "But Papa probably just carved a replica. He must have heard about it or something. I mean, the only power that comb had was to take the tangles out of your hair."

Looking disappointed, Uma shook her head. "That's a shame. You carried it like it was something special. Papa would be so sad that you lost his comb."

"I feel terrible," Usagi agreed.

"Here you go." Rana handed her a uniform. Her dark eyes were apologetic. "I couldn't find one with a rabbit on it."

Uma smiled. "I'm sure Lord Druk will see that you get one after he meets you." They left the tiny room so that Usagi could change.

With shaking hands, she took off her small rucksack and stripped out of her entertainer's costume. The Academy tunic was thankfully clean, and had dragons embroidered on both shoulders. Usagi slipped it on, feeling like she was in the wrong skin. She emptied everything that was in her old belt and secured them into the wide cloth belt of the uniform, tucking the Coppice Comb away with special care. Wearing the Dragon Academy uniform was just another form of stealth, she told herself, and stuffed her own clothes in her pack.

Click clack. Click clack. The dreaded clatter of the Dragonstrikers' armor filled Usagi's ears and she froze. She wished she had her broomstick still. But in the excitement of seeing

Tora and Uma, she'd left it in the courtyard. Examining the sparring equipment in the dim, stuffy space, she wondered if anyone would notice if she took a practice sword. As the clacking grew louder, Usagi fought the urge to run. She sidled to the door of the closet and peeked out. The Academy doors burst open and a phalanx of black-armored Strikers marched in. A murmur of excitement swept through the hall. "Lord Druk is here!"

CHAPTER 22

THE BLUE DRAGON

USAGI PEERED THROUGH THE CRACKED door of the storage closet, watching the Strikers file into the Academy. Younglings scurried into rows beneath the giant portrait of the Blue Dragon, chests puffed in their indigo uniforms, their expressions matching the stern face on the wall. Her sister and Rana ran to join Tora and the other cadets in welcoming the Dragonlord.

His elite strike force formed two lines and stood at silent attention. Their horned helmets sat low on their heads, obscuring their eyes. Another Striker, presumably the captain, clacked through the doors with Master Douzen, escorting a man dressed all in black into the Academy. Though his face couldn't be seen from where Usagi stood, the man in black's broad shoulders radiated strength and power. She leaned against a bin of practice spears and craned her neck. Was that the Blue Dragon? There was no armor, no weapons, no kingly robes or regalia. His dark hair was gathered in a simple topknot, his clothes utterly plain. Yet there was something arresting about the way he walked—as if everything and everyone would wait for him. He halted for a moment before Uma, who bowed deeply. With a nod, he strolled up and down the rows with the Dragonstriker captain, each student bowing as they passed.

When the man in black turned, Usagi stifled a cry. The man's set jaw and dark, hooded eyes were the same as in the portrait, but his face—she could see it clearly now. His skin was a pale grayish blue, his lips almost purple. The Blue Dragon was actually *blue*. None of the portraits of him had shown it.

Was he sick? Diseased in some way?

No wonder Tora hushed her when she called him the Blue Dragon. The name was a reminder of something the warlord wanted everyone to forget. Something he wanted no one outside these walls to know.

Usagi stared at the Blue Dragon's face. Because of him, the Twelve were no more, their powers scattered to the wind. Because of him, the island had been invaded and plundered for gain. Because of him, so many were dead, snatched from their homes, taken from families and friends. And now her sister and Tora—the only family she had left—were in his thrall. They were following the Blue Dragon's every movement, their eyes shining with admiration. It made her stomach turn.

In his high, quavering voice, the wizened Master Douzen addressed the cadets. "To the fortunates who have caught Lord Druk's favor. Receive all that he says and you will be rewarded beyond your greatest dreams."

"All hail the Dragonlord!" cried Uma. Usagi flinched. How strange to see her little sister giving commands—as if she were the Blue Dragon's star pupil.

"Long live the Dragonlord!" the students shouted back.

The blue-skinned man gave a curt nod. "Thank you, Master Douzen." The Dragonlord's voice was deep and commanding, like a barrel drum. "Your reports of the Chosen Ones' progress have been encouraging, and the Dragonstriker captain is looking forward to the day they join his ranks. I can see for myself how they are growing in strength and skill."

The cadets all seemed to stand straighter, lift their chins higher at the Blue Dragon's words.

"As future guardians of Midaga, you should know the great news. Midaga's last enemy has been captured." Excited whispers rippled through the assembly of uniformed younglings. He waited till the room was still again. "The witch of Mount Jade was lured from her lair and will no longer stand in the way of our progress. Thanks to the captain of the

Dragonstrikers, who delivered her to the palace this morning, we can all rest easier," said the Blue Dragon. "Dragon Academy, all hail the captain!"

As the students cheered, the captain stepped forward and doffed his helmet. Usagi cracked the door a bit wider, and almost fell out.

Tupa stood there, accepting the cheers of the assembled younglings. *He* was the captain of the Dragonstrikers.

"No!" she whispered.

Blindly, Usagi shrank into the farthest reaches of the closet. She thought of all that Tupa had taught her. He'd shown her how to wield a sword, pushed her to use her voice, demonstrated how to fight back, encouraged her in everything she did. He'd been so concerned when she'd gotten hurt in the Blade Trial.

Yet here he was, captain of the Blue Dragon's prized force. Which meant the Ram Heir had come to the shrine and lied. To the Heirs, and the Tigress. To her. And brought them all here to the palace like a special delivery. The bitter taste of bile rose in Usagi's throat and she retched. She closed her eyes, breathing hard. *Get ahold of yourself.*

Usagi crept back to the closet door and peeked out. Tupa stood beside the Blue Dragon, smiling broadly and smoothing his goatee. He'd changed out of his monk's robes and wore a suit of black lacquered leather armor, with a black helmet sporting large beetle-like horns tipped in gold, indicating his rank. His face was flintier, colder, despite his smile. Around his neck was his firehorn, and a firecannon was slung behind his back. "Future Dragonstrikers," Tupa boomed, "it's good to be back. The final pocket of resistance has been brought to heel. We have them safely behind bars here at the palace, and several precious Treasures they stole have been recovered. Behold!" He held up the Bowl of Plenty to cries of awe.

Usagi's hand flew to her belt, where she'd tucked the Coppice Comb. "Farting firehorns," she groaned. No wonder he'd insisted on bringing the Treasures. Not only did she not stop him, she'd *carried two of the Treasures for him.*

"At the festival of the spring equinox, we shall celebrate—and see the last remnant of old Midaga submit to the new," said Tupa. "And now, Lord Druk and I look forward to your demonstrations of progress." He raised his voice. "All hail the Dragonlord!"

"Long live the Dragonlord!" shouted the younglings. They broke into groups and began preparing for their demonstrations, while Tupa snapped his fingers at a couple of the Dragonstrikers. Clicking and clacking in their plated black armor, the roaches fetched stools for the Blue Dragon and Master Douzen, while Tupa stood with his arms folded. He surveyed the hall, frowning, and when his gaze swept past the closet door, Usagi jerked back. Tupa had said the others were behind bars. Were they somewhere on the grounds? She had to get out and find them. But how? She couldn't just walk out without being noticed.

She looked down at her uniform and thought again. Could she?

Usagi undid her braids and pulled her hair down over her face. She grabbed a tall stack of sparring pads. Her cheek pressed up against them, and she nearly gagged again at the sour stink of old sweat. Peering out, she saw that Tupa had his back turned. She nudged the door open and slipped out of the storage room, face hidden behind the sparring pads.

"There you are!" Tora said. "Uma and I were just coming to fetch you. That uniform fits perfectly!"

Swiveling to peer around the stack of pads, Usagi gave them both a strained smile. "Thanks," she muttered.

"Let me take those and we'll introduce you to Master Douzen, Captain Tupa, and Lord Druk," Uma offered. "How lucky that all three of them are here!" She started to take the pile, but Usagi resisted, keeping a firm hold on the pads.

"That's all right, Uma," she said hastily. Through the curtain of her hair, Usagi saw the line of Strikers standing at attention by the front entrance, while the first group of younglings began a demonstration with straw dummies. To her alarm, Tupa glanced their way. Usagi ducked her head. This wouldn't work—she needed to get out of sight. "They're awfully heavy. Maybe we don't need so many? I can take some back." Usagi gave her sister several pads, then spun around with the rest and headed rapidly back to the storage room, resisting the urge to break into a run.

She slipped back into the cramped closet and shut the door quietly behind her, heart pounding. There was no way she could walk out of there without attracting attention— not with a squad of roaches at the exit and certainly not with Tupa around. He knew she still had the comb—he had to be looking for her.

Her ears pricked at Tupa's booming voice. *"Cadet Uma, who was that girl?"*

"Captain," her sister piped. *"You're just the person I wanted to talk to. My sister is here. She'd make a great addition to the Dragon Academy—she's got zodiac powers and was born in the year of the Wood Rabbit."*

"A Wood Rabbit, you say?" Tupa's voice grew keenly interested.

"Yes—she has the talents of hearing and jumping. I wanted to introduce you, but she just went to the storage room with some equipment."

Usagi scanned the closet frantically. She could hear Uma telling Tupa about how surprised she was when her older sister had appeared at the palace that morning. Glancing up, she spied the narrow window. It was high up, close to the ceiling, with stacks of boxes and chests in the way. *Click clack, click clack.* Tupa's armor rattled and clattered as he walked across the hall, Uma chattering by his side. Usagi had to get out now.

Palms damp with sweat, she grabbed her pack and threw it on, then clambered up piles of boxes, which swayed and creaked in protest under her weight. Standing atop the tallest stack, she found she could just reach the window's wooden frame. She stretched on tiptoe and pushed until it popped open with a groan. Grasping the windowsill, Usagi scrabbled with her feet and wriggled halfway out. The small pack on her back snagged. Her sister's voice and Tupa's were getting close. She pulled, grunting, until her pack came free. Swinging outside, she hung from the frame. As they opened the closet door, Usagi's sweaty hands slipped. She dropped to the marble tiles of the walkway below, the window closing with a soft thump behind her.

"I don't understand—she was just here!" Uma's perplexed voice floated after Usagi as she dashed away. It pained Usagi to hear it. But she couldn't let Tupa see her. He was captain of the Dragonstrikers! There was no telling what other deceptions he'd fed them. Usagi ducked into the courtyard where she'd left her broomstick, retrieving it from beneath the forsythia bushes. Now to find the others. They were locked up somewhere, but where? By the gods, if only she still had the Mirror of Elsewhere. At least she had her rabbit hearing.

Usagi rubbed her wooden rabbit and listened carefully.

314

She filtered out the sounds of the Academy, the stables, the cookery, the barracks. Was that the voices of the Heirs? It was muffled, but she could have sworn she heard the squeaky crack of Nezu's voice. It was coming from the Outer Court, which was where she'd left them.

She hurried toward the Temple of the Immortals, passing ordinary Guards and palace workers, her head held high. *Be a Striker cadet.* Usagi's stomach was clenched in knots, but she glared haughtily at anyone who glanced her way. She retraced her steps until she found herself back by the palace temple, where she could see a flurry of activity in the center of the complex. Monks and palace workers were stringing up garishly festive lanterns and raising a platform. Usagi shivered. Something told her this was where the Tigress and the Heirs were going to be forced to submit to the Blue Dragon. And if she weren't careful, she would be too.

There it was again—the squeak that Nezu's voice made when he was excited. Usagi walked behind the temple where she'd seen Tupa leading the others. A raked gravel path led through a wooded park that surrounded the temple complex. Her feet crunched on the white gravel path, which sported trails of footprints. A spray of scattered gravel on the ground caught her eye, marble chips kicked off the path in all directions. Something dark and polished gleamed amid the white gravel. Usagi poked at it with her stick, then bent and picked up a curved jade bead of deep green—the one the Tigress

315

had made to fix the broken Treasure.

A muffled voice shouted and cracked. *"Usagi! Are you there?"* She turned around, heart leaping in her chest. It was definitely Nezu.

A female voice joined in. *"Usagi! Can you hear us? We're in the stone cellar! . . . Are you sure you caught her scent, Inu?"*

"I'm sure, although she might not be alone," came the reply. *"I smell something of the palace with her."*

Usagi looked down at the Academy uniform she was wearing and sniffed it. If it smelled like those stinky sparring pads from the storage closet, she couldn't detect it. But Inu would—and he and the others were somewhere nearby. She looked around wildly. Where was this stone cellar?

"Keep calling," Nezu suggested. *"She'll hear us with her rabbit talent."*

With her ears guiding her, she turned toward a hillock of trees, where the voices seemed to come floating out of the earth. Drawing near, Usagi saw that part of the tree-covered mound was a mossy wall. A narrow ramp led down to a hidden wooden door. By her feet there were mesh-covered slits in the wall that could barely be called windows.

"She's close!" Inu said, and shouted her name.

With a rush of relief, Usagi crouched and called into one of the narrow openings. "I'm here! I heard you!"

"Thank the gods!" Saru sounded overjoyed. "Are you all right? You have to get out of here—Tupa . . ."

"Led us into a trap," Usagi finished. "I know. He's the captain of the Strikers."

There was a shocked silence, and then exclamations poured from the cellar vents. "That no-good two-faced billy goat," spluttered Nezu.

Usagi glanced around nervously. No one was around but she didn't want to raise her voice. "Is the Tigress with you?"

"No," said Inu, sounding defeated. "The head priest escorted the Tigress elsewhere, and then Tupa led us here and locked us in—to hide us, he said. He told us he had a special way to locate you."

Alarm ran through Usagi. "He has the Mirror of Elsewhere," she confessed. More exclamations and a stream of questions burst from the cellar. "It's all my fault but there's no time to explain! I have to get you out. If he's looking for me, then he or one of the Strikers could be here any minute. What did he tell you before he left?"

"Just that he'd be back when the sun went down," said Nezu. There was a faint pounding sound that echoed out the vents, and he yelped. "Ow! The door is solid wood a foot thick."

"The whole cellar is nothing but stone—even the ceiling is stone slab," Inu reported. "And the windows are too small to squeeze through."

Usagi jumped into the trench concealing the cellar entrance. An enormous beam barred the door and was

317

secured by a heavy iron lock. She had no key, and had never learned to pick a lock. How could she break them out of such a place? She stood back, looking at the cellar and its protective mound of earth crowned with oak trees. Her eyes narrowed, and she ran back up the ramp to the cellar vents.

"I have an idea," she told the Heirs.

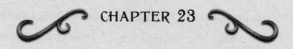

CHAPTER 23

TRUE COLORS

USAGI GLANCED ABOUT, MAKING SURE no one was in sight. The Heirs' prison was crowned with a hill sporting several stately swordleaf oaks. Their roots spread across the mound like a tangled network of silvery snakes. She leaned toward the cellar vent.

"Prepare to move quickly," she warned the Heirs. Usagi climbed the mound of earth hiding the cellar, and headed for the largest tree. "Gods help me," she muttered.

She'd barely explored what her wood gift could do—had never tried anything like this before. She knelt by the base of the majestic oak and took a deep breath. On Mount Jade, Tupa had advised using force on the Tree of Elements, and it had gotten her nowhere. Usagi placed her hands on the pale gray bark, closing her eyes. *Listen to it first . . . feel . . . become one with the tree*, the Tigress had told her. For a tense moment, all Usagi could feel was her heart pounding in her chest. Then a deep, slow pulse shuddered through the broad trunk. With a sigh of relief, she felt the tree's energy surging beneath her palms.

Usagi connected to it, and focused on following the tree's pulse down to its roots, which were blocked by the cellar. She envisioned the roots reaching through the soil and prying apart the stone slabs of the ceiling, wedging between the stone blocks of the walls, forcing their tendrils through until the cellar was filled with cracks and holes. *Please,* Usagi thought. *I need your help. Claim the earth that is yours. Free my friends.*

The tree's pulsing quickened, and the twisting, exposed roots at her knees shifted. A deep rumbling grew and shook the tree-covered mound. Usagi gritted her teeth and pressed hard, her fingers growing as warm as if they were cupped around a bowl of hot tea.

There was a muffled shout by one of the Heirs. Usagi opened her eyes to see a crack open up in the ground. Loose earth crumbled into a growing split between two stone slabs, into the cellar itself. Thick roots expanded their reach into the space till the gap between the slabs was wide enough that she could see right in.

"Boils and blisters!" Usagi exclaimed, and pulled away from the tree, shaking her overheated hands to cool them. She crouched at the edge of the hole and peered in. "Everything all right?" The cellar seemed to be filled with a snarled web of roots, looking as if a wayward giant spider had gone on a rampage.

"A little cramped," said Inu, "but otherwise impressive."

"You really had that tree going," Nezu called up.

Saru scrambled up the ropy network. Her head popped out, hair coated in crumbs of soil and her cheeks smudged with dirt. But her pale face glowed. "My stars, look at what you did!" There was just enough space between the stone slabs to shimmy through. She had the boys pass her their packs and walking sticks. Then they followed Saru through the split in the cellar ceiling. When Inu got stuck halfway, Saru and Usagi each took an arm and pulled until he emerged like a reluctant radish from the earth.

"Thanks," he grunted. "That's some gift, Wood Rabbit." He pointed at the cellar vents. Roots had pushed through and grown so long, they dangled to the ground like ragged drapes. Inu tousled his shaggy hair to get rid of fallen soil, while the others brushed off their clothes. Their entertainer whites had become a dingy ocher.

Nezu pointed at Usagi. "Nice outfit. Where'd you get that?"

"From the Dragon Academy." Usagi grimaced. "My sister got it for me, and then she went to ask 'Captain Tupa' to let me join. I slipped out of there just in time." She worried her rabbit pendant with her fingers. "What do we do now?"

"Find the Tigress, of course," said Inu.

321

"I heard Tupa say there would be some sort of celebration tonight, where they'd make their captives submit to the Blue Dragon," Usagi recalled. "And there are preparations going on right now at the temple."

"Then Teacher must be nearby," said Nezu. His face darkened. "I still can't believe Tupa led us into this. How did the Blue Dragon get to him?"

Saru slapped hard at her dirt-crusted sleeve. "I can't even imagine. He fooled us all." She shook her head. "We can't pass as entertainers like this—and if Tupa planned this whole trap, no one will believe us anyway. Time to change our disguise." The Heirs took off their brightly patterned entertainers' coats and turned them inside out, displaying the indigo lining instead. With dark blue coats over their dun-colored clothing, they could pass for groundskeepers or stablehands.

In the distance, Usagi heard feet crunching on gravel. "Someone's coming this way." She listened carefully. "Not a Guard—maybe a palace worker. We can't let them see what's happened here. I'll hold them off while you go hide."

She watched the Heirs disappear into the wooded park behind the complex. Tightening her grip on her broomstick, Usagi marched away from the destroyed cellar. A temple monk, slight of build with a shaved head, approached. He frowned at the sight of her. "Young one, whatever are you doing here? Shouldn't you be at the Academy?"

Thinking fast, Usagi raised her chin. "The captain asked me to check on the entertainers for the festivities. I'm going back now to give him a report."

The monk shook his head. "No one should be back here. Come with me." He grasped Usagi firmly by the arm and hustled her toward the front of the temple complex. His grip was surprisingly strong for such a skinny-looking man. Usagi stumbled trying to keep up with his quick strides. They rounded the corner into the temple courtyard, and she stopped short.

"Hello, Rabbit Girl." Tupa stood there waiting in his Striker captain's armor.

Yanking herself from the monk's grasp, Usagi whirled to flee, but Tupa was on her in a flash. With a meaty hand, he swiftly pressed his fingers in the freeze-hold pattern against her neck. Usagi's entire body went rigid. Her stick dropped and clattered away out of reach. Around the courtyard, the monks and palace workers preparing for the spring festivities stopped to stare. Frozen and unable to move, Usagi glared at Tupa.

"If only you'd stayed at the Academy," he said softly. "Your sister was so excited about it. To tell the truth, I was hoping that you and the others might see the benefits in joining us. We're building a new Midaga. But now . . . I wonder if maybe you're all beyond persuading." He snapped his fingers and two monks brought over a bamboo cage, like what she'd seen

323

Strikers use for captured younglings. Tupa stuffed her into the cage and slammed it shut. As he snapped an iron padlock around the bars, Usagi felt a tidal wave of fury sweep in, along with the ability to move and speak again. Glowering, she shook the cage door as hard as she could, making the metal lock jump and rattle.

"You traitor," she rasped. "You lied to us this whole time. How could you? You're no better than the Blue Dragon himse—"

"Quiet!" Tupa slammed a fist against the bars. "Think carefully before you speak. You have some fine talents, Usagi. It'd be a shame to waste them on a losing proposition." He bent down and gave her his familiar broad smile. It was so fake, Usagi couldn't believe she'd ever thought it real. "I know you have the Coppice Comb. Hand it over and I'll set you free right now. I'll even go easy on the Warrior Heirs."

"I'm not giving it to you," Usagi spat. "You don't deserve to even *touch* the Comb."

He straightened, his smile gone. "Fine. You'll give it to me later—don't think that you won't."

"I won't," Usagi vowed. "And the Heirs are gone—I freed them!"

"You think I don't know that?" Tupa's smile returned. He gestured to the monks. "Put her in lockdown while we find the others. By the gods, we'll have them when festivities begin tonight." Turning back to Usagi, he leaned in close. "Your dear sister really wanted you to join us. Remember that, and remember the Heirs. You all still have a chance."

Tupa strode off, clicking and clacking in his roach armor. Several monks hoisted the cage. They took Usagi through a temple outbuilding to a dusty bare room. Opening a trap-door in the floor, they lowered the cage and shut the door, blanketing Usagi in darkness. A padlock clicked as they locked it, leaving her in a cold, damp space. How was she going to get out of this? What would happen to the Heirs? Usagi bit back a despairing moan. She wouldn't give her captors the satisfaction. After their footsteps faded away, she became aware of another sound behind her—someone breathing. She was not alone. Could it be?

"Teacher?" Usagi whispered.

A pair of green eyes glowed in the dark. "Young Rabbit!"

"Oh, Teacher! Are you all right?" How overjoyed she was to see the glow of the old warrior's gaze.

"Thank the gods," croaked Horangi. "I am unharmed, youngling. Did they hurt you? By the time I realized you had disappeared, the Heirs and I were already separated."

"No, I'm fine," said Usagi. She hesitated, wondering if Horangi knew about Tupa. Then it all came out in a rush, about how she'd heard her sister's voice and followed it to the Academy, about what she'd seen, the visit from the Blue Dragon and the shock of Tupa by his side in Striker armor, holding aloft the Bowl of Plenty. "What are we going to do?"

The Tigress sighed. "I have let you all down terribly." Her strained voice trembled. "I was supposed to protect our last bastion of hope. I let our small successes in recovering some of the Treasures blind me." There was a long silence, and her green eyes blinked shut. "I have failed."

"Don't say that," Usagi pleaded. She squinted, but it was pitch-black. She closed her eyes and listened to the Tigress—her uneven breathing, the rustle of her clothing, the faint creak of the cage bars as she sagged against them. Usagi stuck out her arm. Her hand brushed against smooth bamboo bars, then found the bony form of the Tigress. Gently, she patted her shoulder. "Teacher, don't give up. I freed the others before Tupa tracked me down."

The glow of Horangi's eyes returned. "You did?"

Usagi couldn't help but feel a rush of pride. "There were some nice-sized oaks growing above their holding cell. I tried my wood gift on one, and it worked pretty well, if I do say so myself."

She told the Tigress that the Heirs managed to slip away when she revealed herself and was brought to Tupa. "He had the Mirror of Elsewhere—because I helped him take it from Mount Jade." Usagi's cheeks grew hot with shame as she confessed what she and Tupa had done with the Treasures. "I'm the one who's let you down."

The old warrior grunted. "What is fated to be yours will

always return to you. The Treasures belong to the Twelve. It just may take longer than we thought to see their return."

"I've still got the Coppice Comb on me, and when I was looking for the others, I found this." Feeling in the dark for the jade bead, Usagi reached out and pressed the cool gem into Horangi's warm palm.

"The replacement Jewel," exclaimed the old warrior. "But . . . I threw this away."

"You did?" Usagi was confounded. "Why?"

"When the head priest led me toward the temple, I sensed danger in carrying it and let it slip from my fingers. It is clear now that Druk sent the Ram Heir to Mount Jade to obtain a new Jewel for the Treasure he destroyed." Horangi's croaking voice became a whisper. "Bad enough that he is capturing those with zodiac powers to exploit for his own gain. If Druk manages to obtain all the Treasures, his power will be unparalleled."

"He won't," Usagi declared. "As long as there's hope, the fight goes on. And I still have hope."

The Tigress laid a gnarled hand over Usagi's and squeezed it tight. "Young Rabbit. I cannot ask you to succeed where I myself have failed. But you are right. One can fight as long as there is still hope." She was quiet for a moment, then continued. "All I ask now is that you trust me. Do you trust me?"

Usagi squeezed the old warrior's hand back. "Of course."

"If I were to give a command, would you still follow?" Horangi asked, sounding strangely timid.

"What a thing to say," said Usagi, disconcerted. The Tigress she knew was fierce and steady—not lost and unsure.

"Answer my question," growled the old warrior.

That sounded more like Teacher. Usagi smiled to herself but replied meekly, "Yes, I would follow your command."

"Good," said the Tigress, relaxing her grip. "Whatever happens, know that you are a true Heir of the Twelve, and will make a fine Rabbit Warrior someday. You have proven yourself beyond any Warrior Trials. Inu, Saru, and Nezu were right to bring you to Mount Jade. I knew from the moment you leaped to save me at the bridge."

Usagi's heart swelled. "Thank you, Teacher."

They leaned against the bars of their cages, huddling together as best they could in the cold damp, periodically clasping hands or patting an arm, whispering encouragement to one another. Usagi shared what little food remained in her pack. She even took out the Coppice Comb and debated with the Tigress about using it, to call forth a grove of trees that might break open their prison, but the Tigress insisted that she hold off. So Usagi ran it through her undone hair instead, rebraiding it into two neat plaits again, before tucking the comb away.

Mostly they waited. Usagi rubbed the wooden rabbit at

her neck, thinking of what Horangi had told her. She was worthy of being called an Heir. No less than the last Warrior of the Zodiac said so. She vowed to herself that if she ever became Rabbit Warrior, she would fight to keep the Blue Dragon from gaining more power, in service to Midaga and the memory of her parents.

After what seemed like hours, Usagi finally grew exhausted enough to drowse in the dark. A loud boom startled her awake, followed by an insistent thumping. It was a deep, pulsing beat that vibrated through the temple complex.

The Tigress stirred. "Drums," she said. "The hour of the Rat is upon us. Spring is come."

More booms replied in the distance. It was a response to the palace temple from temples around the city, filling the air with their calls to the gods of spring. Before the war, all Midagians would head to their local temple from sunset to dawn to give offerings of food and money to the gods for a fruitful new season. They'd burn incense and set off firecrackers to ward off angry spirits, and head home to play games and eat flower cakes for a sweet spring. Usagi knew the Blue Dragon would not be doing any of that. She recalled what she'd overheard at the Pearl Garden—the Guards there had spoken of an execution. So had Tupa, before his betrayal. Would it be of the Tigress? And since Usagi was locked up with her, was she about to die too? Her heart thudded in tandem with the drums.

The marching of dozens of feet filled the temple complex, in time to the drumbeats. The clacking of Striker armor sounded nearby, and Usagi tensed. "I think Tupa might be back."

The reedy voice of the old bearded Academy master called out. "Good and Bountiful Spring, Chosen Ones," he quavered in his Hulagan accent.

"Good and Bountiful Spring, Master Douzen," chorused a host of younglings.

Just then, the trapdoor above them swung open with a bang, and Usagi blinked in the sudden harsh light from a lantern. "Bring them up," ordered Tupa.

Armored Strikers thumped down and heaved the cages out as if they held livestock. The roaches dropped them before Tupa, who crouched and gave Usagi a broad smile.

"So, have you had a chance to think things over?" He sounded as if she'd had a choice between flower cakes and iced fruit pudding.

Usagi stared in disbelief. "Yes, and if you had any honor you would know my answer without asking."

His smile quickly disappeared. Horangi raised her head, her scarred cheeks drawn and sunken. Her green eyes were glazed with sorrow. "What happened to you, Ram Heir?"

The old warrior's tears shocked Usagi. She glared at Tupa, wanting to reach through the bars for his stupid chin beard and pull until he begged the Tigress for forgiveness. But he was unrepentant.

"I was to become the next Ram Warrior," Tupa said forcefully. "I studied and trained for years. But for what? Hiding and spying? It made as much of a difference as flies on a pig." He raised his voice till he was nearly shouting. "History is made by those who seize greatness!"

"Greatness? You're the pig," accused Usagi. "No true Warrior of the Twelve would do what you did. You aren't worthy of being Ram Warrior!"

Tupa's face darkened. "Shackle this one and take her outside," he commanded, handing a Striker a set of keys. "As for the old woman, bring her out when Lord Druk calls for her. Tonight we have our sacrifice."

The Striker smiled thinly. His face was mostly covered by his helmet, but Usagi could see some nose hairs sticking out of his nostrils. She stared at them with distaste.

"With pleasure." He unlocked Usagi's cage and dragged her out. She did her best to give him a good kick before another roach grabbed her and held her still. They fastened wood and metal restraints on her wrists and ankles and forced her to march. Usagi could barely walk, let alone leap. With mincing steps, she hobbled into the courtyard.

Monks were chanting prayers inside the temple, along with a few kneeling beside the enormous barrel-shaped drums just outside its doors. Younglings in Academy uniforms were lined up in the temple courtyard, where lanterns and torches illuminated their solemn expressions and the blades they carried. Usagi searched for her sister and Tora and located them in the first row. Next to her sister was little Jago, who fidgeted with the short steel sword sheathed at his side. Alongside the giant Goru and Rana, the sharp-eyed girl with coiled braids, they faced the raised platform overlooking the courtyard.

On the platform stood Master Douzen and Tupa, an altar covered in rich brocade between them. There sat the Bowl of Plenty and the Apothecary on silk cushions, while the Mirror of Elsewhere was propped on a lacquer stand, its decorated back on display. There were empty cushions on the altar, waiting for missing Treasures. Usagi brought her bound hands close, trying to shield the comb in her belt.

"Future Dragonstrikers!" Tupa boomed. "We celebrate spring's arrival with the return of several Treasures. And, we have a potential new addition to our ranks who's brought us yet another." He gestured and the Strikers brought Usagi before the platform. She heard gasps and turned. Tora and her sister stood just a few feet away, staring at her with wide eyes. Jago looked bewildered. "What's Usagi doing here?" he whispered to Uma. Usagi slumped as Nose Hairs unlocked just her wrists, pushing her before Tupa.

He stared down at her. "I'll give you one more chance, Usagi. After all, you volunteered to bring the Coppice

Comb all this way. Hand it over and I'll let you go. You can join your sister, right over there."

But Uma was glaring, her eyes fiery. She shook her head in disgust. "You lied to me," she snarled. "I asked you about the comb and you said you didn't have it."

"No, I——" Usagi tried to explain, but her sister turned away. Her heart sank. The silence in the courtyard grew as the crowd waited for her response. With fumbling fingers, Usagi pulled the comb from her belt. The former Ram Heir leaned down with an eager hand. The gilt-trimmed horns of his black helmet gleamed in the flickering torchlight. Usagi hesitated.

Would surrendering the Treasure fix anything? She thought of what the Tigress had said. If the Blue Dragon had all of them, his power would be unparalleled. She clutched it to her heart and shook her head wretchedly. "I can't."

With a frustrated growl, Tupa leaped from the platform. He grabbed Usagi's wrist and yanked the comb from her hand. "Too late," he said.

"No!" Usagi cried. She struggled against his strong grip, but there was no getting the comb back.

He pushed her at Nose Hairs. "Bind her. She's made her choice clear." Tupa jumped back onto the platform and took the comb out of its silk wrapping. "And now we have the Coppice Comb!" He held it up for all to see.

As the Academy cadets cheered, Strikers locked Usagi's

wrists again and she fought not to cry. They pulled her away from the foot of the platform as Tupa raised a hand to quiet the crowd.

"It's an honor to present these found Treasures to our dear leader, as well as an even bigger prize," he announced proudly. "Lord Druk, your loyal forces await!"

The Blue Dragon strolled into the courtyard, still dressed in simple black robes, though he wore a sword at his side. He ascended the platform and looked out over the throng, his gray-blue face pale and sickly in the lantern-light.

"All hail the Dragonlord!" shouted Tupa.

"Long live the Dragonlord!" The air reverberated with the shouts of the cadets, the temple monks, and the dozen or so Strikers who stood watch along the edges of the courtyard. From the foot of the platform, Usagi looked up at the Blue Dragon with dread.

He nodded brusquely at Tupa, then turned to the altar where the Treasures were displayed. The hint of a smile played across his purplish lips as he lifted each item, caressing them with long-nailed fingers. He lifted the Mirror of Elsewhere and looked into it for a moment, then laughed a low, amused chuckle. "Captain Tupa, you've proven yourself admirably," the Blue Dragon said. As Tupa bowed, the Blue Dragon waved a hand. "Bring out the witch of Mount Jade! It is time for the sacrifice."

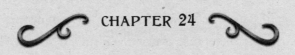

CHAPTER 24

SACRIFICE

THE FAINT THUMP OF TEMPLE drums all across the city pulsed in the air, heralding spring's arrival. But a hush fell over the palace temple as two Dragonstrikers brought out the Tigress, her gnarled hands tied before her. Her long hair had unraveled out of its braid, hanging around her wrinkled face like a ragged striped curtain. The Strikers dragged Horangi onto the platform and unceremoniously dumped her before the Blue Dragon. Usagi yelped in outrage. How dare they treat the last Warrior of the Zodiac that way?

A strange expression crossed the Blue Dragon's face. He bent down and helped Horangi to her feet. "Hello, Teacher," he said quietly, steadying her. He looked around, his black eyes gleaming. "Where is her staff? Bring it here now—we aren't barbarians."

As he placed it in her hand, the old warrior gazed at him

and sucked in a breath. "By the Twelve, what have you done to yourself, Druk?"

"I have become my true self." The Dragonlord straightened and stared down at Horangi. "By taking precious metals, I am stronger than ever—the ultimate Metal Dragon. Ingenious, is it not? The Hulagans believe that metal begets metal. No one has ever tried strengthening their elemental gifts in this way—except me."

"Drinking silver and gold will not fortify you in the way you think," said the Tigress severely, as if he were a youngling still.

Master Douzen turned his rheumy stare toward Horangi. "On the contrary," the stooped Hulagan quavered. "Look who is the most powerful man in the kingdom. Metal has only increased his talents."

Horangi's eyes narrowed. "I know of medicine and talents, you charlatan," she growled. "Do not think you can peddle your false magic for long."

Usagi tensed as the Dragonlord reached a blue hand for the Tigress. With a long-nailed finger, he touched a pale scar on her wrinkled cheek and smiled. "These have healed nicely. So happy you've had something to remember me by. Especially since you nearly killed me the last time we met. I'm sure you thought Mount Jade would finish the job you started. Making the steps by the waterfall crumble beneath my feet was quite a show."

"It was for the protection of the shrine," retorted the Tigress.

The Blue Dragon gave a delicate shrug. "I survived, thanks to Master Douzen." He swept a hand across the temple courtyard. "Now I thrive."

The old warrior didn't flinch as she stared up at her former student. "Druk. I know you have not forgotten all you were taught. What is broken can be repaired. It is never too late to repent, my son."

His nostrils flared. "I'm not your son," he hissed, clenching a fist.

"Once one is a teacher, one becomes a parent for life," Horangi replied softly. "You were my best student—and I had hopes for you as I would my own child."

The Dragonlord snorted. "What meager hopes they were. You're blind, old woman. You always have been." His upper lip curled. "The only thing you can see is the past. Clinging to your traditions—refusing to consider new ideas! You never understood. The one who refuses to look ahead will remain behind." His gaze flickered over Usagi for a moment. "She's got you under her spell, hasn't she? Pity. Midaga has a glorious future ahead—beyond just the island. Join us. Your talents will wither away otherwise."

Usagi shook her head. "You're wrong," she said weakly, but her thoughts eddied around what he'd said like water around a river rock. The Dragonlord spoke with such

337

certainty about the future. Was it bad to hold on to the past? To remember and try to honor it?

He clapped a hand on Tupa's shoulder, rattling the plates of his armor. The former Ram Heir stared straight ahead as the Dragonlord smiled. "No matter. Even those who've been in her thrall the longest can be made to see the light." He nodded down at Usagi. "Everyone has a choice."

Turning to the Tigress, he pulled her to the front of the platform. She clutched her staff, gnarled hands trembling. Her green eyes were cloudy and she looked even more shrunken beside the Blue Dragon. "Behold Mistress Horangi, the witch of Mount Jade!" he exulted. The blue of his skin deepened to the color of twilight—to the very color of the sky as Usagi remembered on her seventh birthday.

Her father had presented her with the rabbit pendant he'd made. He'd placed the wooden carving on his palm, and his elemental gift brought the little figure to life. It bounded about in his hand until Usagi's mother plucked up its leather cord. "To celebrate the showing of your animal talent," her mother had said. "May the spirits of the Twelve guide and protect you." She'd fastened the rabbit, frozen in midleap, around Usagi's neck, while her father beamed.

Now a raucous cheer went up from the Academy younglings, who raised their fists and shouted into the night. They all believed in the Dragonlord, and would follow whatever he said. But Usagi wouldn't. She couldn't.

Not after what had happened to her parents, to Gold-entusk, to the Twelve. Not after being on Mount Jade and living at the Shrine of the Twelve steeped in centuries of history. Her talents hadn't withered there, despite what the Blue Dragon said. Quite the opposite.

She searched about the complex for some way out. Monks in their saffron robes knelt inside the temple, praying to the gods of spring. About a dozen Strikers stood along the courtyard perimeter in their lacquered black armor, helmets pulled low. Though Usagi was dressed like the cadets, they all carried swords, while she had nothing. She glimpsed a stray wooden stick beneath the platform. Was that *her* broomstick? If only her hands and feet weren't bound—she would leap to get it in an instant. She squirmed and pulled at her bindings to no avail. Nose Hairs prodded her with the butt of his firecannon. "Stop that," he growled.

Tupa searched through the pockets of Horangi's robes. The former Ram Heir pulled out the small silken bag he'd first brought to Mount Jade and smiled in triumph. "My Lord, you must see the restored Jewels of Land and Sea." Eagerly, he poured the contents into his palm, then frowned. He held up a silk cord with two pearls dangling from it. "Where's the new Jewel?"

"She doesn't have it," Usagi said impulsively. Raising her voice, she repeated it. Maybe the Tigress could hide the Jewel, or find some way to keep it from Tupa and the Blue

Dragon. Usagi thought fast. "I found it on a path by the temple." That much was true.

Scowling, Tupa jumped down and held out a hand. "You should know by now the futility of trying to hide it."

She shook her head, stalling. "I threw it in the trees. Release me and I'll go find it."

"You think I'll fall for something like that?" Tupa scoffed. "All I have to do is put you in a freeze hold and have you searched." He reached out and Usagi cringed, but the Tigress spoke in a terrible voice.

"Stop, Ram Heir. Usagi does not have the Land Jewel. I do." She raised a hand, the dark green bead gleaming from her gnarled fingers. "Leave the youngling alone."

Tupa sneered at Usagi. "Nice try." He looked up. "My Lord, I fear this youngling may be a lost cause, however talented she may be."

The Dragonlord waved an absentminded hand. "We'll find a use for her," he said, eyes fixed on the jade bead in Horangi's hand. "Even if it's just for Master Douzen's experiments." He knelt down before the Tigress, his expression softening. His voice turned coaxing. "Teacher. I knew you could fix it. You wanted to, didn't you? It's why I sent the Treasure back to Mount Jade, for only the shrine guardian would have a chance at restoring the Jewels of Land and Sea. Marvelously done, Teacher. Give me the new Land Jewel, and all will be right again." He smiled, his

340

teeth white against his purple lips.

"Don't give it to him," cried Usagi.

Very deliberately, the Tigress brought the jade bead to her mouth and put it between her wrinkled lips. Pressing them together, she stared straight ahead.

"Don't even think about swallowing, for if I have to cut you open, I will," warned the Blue Dragon. "You can't stop us. We shall have the Treasures." His black eyes narrowed and he stepped toward Horangi, hand on the hilt of his sword.

Yelling and a commotion erupted all along the edges of the courtyard. Two Strikers ran about throwing clouds of yellow dust. Fellow roaches clawed at their faces before slumping to the ground. As younglings shouted in confusion, another Dragonstriker turned and lobbed firecrackers into their midst, causing the assembled rows of students to break and scatter.

"What's the meaning of this?" roared the Blue Dragon.

Tupa stared at the three rogue Strikers as they ran toward the platform. His face twisted into an ugly mask. "It's the Heirs."

Tears of relief sprang to Usagi's eyes. She called out, but Nose Hairs clamped his hand over her mouth. Tupa lunged toward the Warrior Heirs. Somehow they'd managed to disguise themselves in Dragonstriker armor, taking the other Strikers by surprise and disabling them with sleep powder. There was only one left to deal with.

Usagi jerked her bound hands overhead at the Striker's exposed face, and poked Nose Hairs hard in the eyes. Bellowing, he loosened his grip enough for her to break free. She hobbled frantically toward the platform to grab her broomstick, and tripped. Hitting the ground with a thud, she rolled herself over and over until she was beneath the platform. She looked up to see Tupa blowing a stream of fire at the Heirs with his firehorn. Inu yanked his helmet off and used it as a shield, exposing a shaggy head of hair, while Saru, clad in heavy black armor, leaped high in the air and landed behind Tupa, holding her moon blade at the ready.

Nose Hairs recovered and wedged his armored bulk beneath the platform, trying to get at Usagi. She jabbed at him with her stick, but he grabbed it and jerked her forward. Usagi screamed. Nezu broke away from Tupa and came charging, rat-tail braid swinging from beneath his horned helmet. He pulled Nose Hairs away and slugged him before shoving a handful of sleep powder up his nose. The last standing Dragonstriker collapsed.

Nezu helped Usagi up. "Are you okay?" he shouted.

Usagi leaned over the knocked-out Striker and scrabbled at the keys on his belt. "Help me with these!"

He grabbed them and unlocked her restraints. "We're going to get the Tigress."

"I'm coming with you." Usagi glanced behind Nezu. "Watch your back!"

Several Academy boys charged at them, their blades raised. Nezu spun and whipped out a curved Striker sword from the scabbard at his side. He smashed his blade against theirs, disarming them with swift strokes, hitting their swords so hard they had to drop them. Yelping, they fell back, nursing their sore hands.

"Nothing but pups." Nezu flashed a grin. "Who's next?"

Tora and Uma rushed up, their blades drawn. "Usagi!" cried Tora. "Get away from him! These aren't Dragon-strikers—they're impostors."

"It's no use, Tora," Uma cut in. "She's clearly made her choice." She raised her sword.

Nezu raised his in turn, but Usagi stopped him. "No. Leave them to me," she said.

With a quick squeeze of Usagi's shoulder, Nezu charged off to help Inu and Saru, fighting both Tupa and a scrum of cadets who'd joined in the fray. Usagi sank into a crouch, holding her wooden broomstick across her chest. "Stay back, both of you. Those are my friends, and they're the last Heirs of the Twelve. I've been trying to tell you, the Blue Dragon is the real impostor. His so-called witch is the 42nd Tiger Warrior."

Her sister shook her head angrily. "I won't listen to the lies they've told you. Look around. You're outnumbered! If you don't give yourself up then you're as good as dead."

What her sister said was true. A gaggle of Academy

students had joined them, surrounding Usagi on all sides. But not all of their swords were pointed at her. Some had even left them sheathed, including the giant boy, Goru, the girl Rana with coiled braids, and little Jago, who craned his neck anxiously. Maybe they'd listen to her.

"Numbers aren't everything," Usagi said. "I bet that old Master Douzen never taught you about the first Ox Warrior. Kalbi the Archer. He fended off a thousand men by himself—all because he had the advantage in skill."

"And position," retorted Uma. "I know the story. The Archer sat high in a narrow mountain pass, so the men were trapped like fish in a barrel. But that's no bow, and you're certainly not sitting high."

A figure streaked through the air and landed by Usagi's side. Saru! The Monkey Heir swiped her pole arm in a wide circle, pushing the crowd of cadets back.

Usagi stared at Uma. "I may be outnumbered. But I'm not alone."

Her sister's face twisted and she lunged at her, just as several other younglings charged with drawn swords. Saru swung at the attacking students, keeping their swords at bay with her moon blade, its curved edge gleaming in the torchlight. Raising her stick, Usagi gave Uma's arm a good whack, then stepped aside and swung in the other direction, catching her on the back. Uma spun about, rubbing her arm with a glare.

344

"Uma, what are you doing?" Tora shouted. "Usagi's family."

"Not anymore," Uma spat. "Family tells the truth. Family sticks around." She heaved the sword up over her head with a grunt and charged again.

Usagi ducked as the blade came down and feinted with her stick, deflecting the blow. "Please, Uma," she begged. "I don't want to fight you."

"Family doesn't abandon you," Uma raged. She paced around Usagi, looking for an opening to attack. Her hands erupted into flame, which engulfed the sword she held. "Fire beats wood in the end."

Usagi felt something in her harden. She'd come too far and learned too much to let anyone break her. Not even her sister, for whom she would have done almost anything. "Maybe," Usagi agreed calmly. "But wood can split flesh."

Eyes flashing, Uma sprang with her flaming blade raised. Usagi swung and hit the flat of the sword hard. The blade trembled with a loud vibration and sparks flew. Adjusting her grip, Uma lunged again with a determined cry. Again Usagi repelled her attack, and ducked from the shower of sparks.

Each time her sister came at her, Usagi would meet her sword with a sharp crack of her stick, then flip the wooden pole to smack Uma's leg, or arm, her back, or stomach. It was almost like a dance, the two of them circling each other, stepping in to exchange blows, then stepping out. Wood rapped against metal, in rhythm with the beat of distant temple drums. One-two, *crack-smack*. One-two, *crack-smack*. But Usagi could feel her pole disintegrating with each strike against the hot steel of her sister's sword. Uma swung again and Usagi moved to block the blow. Upon contact with the blazing blade, her broomstick shattered into pieces that caught fire.

Uma smiled triumphantly. "Fire beats wood."

The shouts of the cadets and their yelps of pain rang in the air, as wave after wave of them attempted to attack Saru. Some tried to throw sputtering fireballs and streams of water at her, but timed their aim badly, their assault colliding into swirling clouds of steam. Others used their talents to fly at her with their swords drawn, only to see her somersault safely out of the way before disarming them with her sweeping moon blade.

Usagi dove for one of the dropped swords and scrambled back to her feet. "Then let's give metal a try," she told Uma. Out of the corner of her eye, she saw that Inu and Nezu were standing back-to-back, taking turns fighting with Tupa and a group of cadets. From his canteen, Nezu had created a shield of water to deflect Tupa's firehorn attacks, while Inu threw hobblers beneath the younglings' feet. As they doubled over and howled, Inu threw his metal claw on a long chain, yanking their weapons from their hands.

A flaming sword flashed before her face and Usagi ducked just in time. "Pay attention to me!" shouted Uma. Her sister was getting angrier and angrier, but also beginning to tire, her nostrils flaring as her breathing grew labored. Usagi watched carefully. All she had to do was keep sparring until the moment was right, and then she'd relieve her sister of her blade.

Usagi hefted the sword in her hand. It was wide and flat, with a double edge, and even heavier than the one she'd used in the Blade Trial. But she could not fail this time. Her lessons came back to her. *Movement, strike, spirit-breath.* She met her sister's next blow with one of her own, and shouted at the top of her lungs. *"Ki-yah!"*

Sparks flew as Uma's fiery sword met her own cold blade, again and again. Usagi shuffled and swerved, looking for an opening. Finally, her blade locked against Uma's, and they stood straining against each other, neither giving the other an inch. Usagi remembered the words of the Tigress. *Victory goes to the one who knows how to yield.* She yanked herself back, and Uma lurched forward. Usagi gave her sister a quick kick in the behind, and Uma sprawled against the marble tiles of the courtyard.

Leaping on her sister's back, Usagi kicked the flaming sword out of Uma's hand and sent it spinning away. She kept the flat of her own sword pressed against her sister's shoulders. "I'm sorry, Uma."

347

Around them, the remaining younglings were scrambling to get away from Saru and her swooping, flying moon blade. Inu and Nezu had knocked out the cadets helping Tupa and were trading blows with the former Ram Heir, roaring with determination all the while. As her sister glared helplessly, Usagi allowed herself a tiny smile. She and the others were doing well. Then she heard a shout.

"Oh no," Saru gasped.

Up on the platform, the Blue Dragon towered over Horangi, pointing his sword at the old warrior's heart. All she had was her walking staff.

The Tigress fixed her green eyes on Usagi. "Remember your promise. I command you to go. Get back to Mount Jade as quickly as you can."

Inu and Nezu started toward Horangi but she put up a gnarled hand. "No. This is my battle to fight."

"So you think you have one more in you?" the Blue Dragon said pityingly. "Stubborn old Tigress. You should have been called the Mule." He lowered his sword and bent down, leveling his gaze with Horangi's. His nose nearly touched hers. "You never know when to give up."

"As long as one can struggle, there is still hope," the Tigress replied. The Dragonlord chuckled, his smile mocking. The old warrior gently raised knobby fingers to her former pupil's face, tears in her eyes, as though she longed to stroke his cheek. Then she slapped him with a sharp smack.

The Blue Dragon jerked back, eyes blank with shock. With a collective intake of breath, the courtyard grew so silent that the only sound was of flames guttering in the torches. Against the blue skin of the Dragonlord's cheek, the white mark of a hand appeared. Without saying a word, he brought up a long-nailed hand to his face and touched the mark, which seemed to throb. No one moved, breathed, or even blinked.

In the next instant the Blue Dragon lashed out with his blade, bellowing in fury. Horangi threw up her wooden staff, meeting his flashing sword with a mighty crash, her lined face impassive. Only the set of her jaw and a grunt indicated the effort it took.

"We have to help her," Saru said urgently. She sprang at one of the buildings along the courtyard, bounding off its wall toward the Tigress and the Blue Dragon.

At the same moment, Tupa blew from his firehorn, surrounding the platform in a ring of fire. Saru shied from the flames in the nick of time, somersaulting in midair. She turned on Tupa and tried to knock the firehorn out of his hands. As Inu and Nezu joined the Monkey Heir in trying to subdue Tupa, the ring of fire continued to burn around the Dragonlord and his former teacher. Usagi's heart was in her throat as the Blue Dragon slashed at Horangi with movements so quick, she could hardly see the blade.

Yet the Tiger Warrior met his attack blow for blow, her

wood staff whirling and spinning as she turned and twisted. The pulse of distant temple drums was drowned out by the clash of their weapons. Every eye in the courtyard was turned toward the fiery duel.

With a roar, the Dragonlord heaved his sword across Horangi's torso.

"Teacher!" Usagi cried. The old warrior leaped out of the way with surprising agility. She glanced at Usagi and smiled briefly, then threw her staff up as the Dragonlord's sword came down with a bone-rattling crash. "All of you, go! Now!" the old warrior ordered, her voice ringing with authority.

"Hold on!" Saru called to the Tigress, her voice breaking. "We're coming!"

Horangi straightened and her green eyes blazed. "I said, *RUN!*"

She turned and looked right at the Blue Dragon as he raised his sword and plunged it over her head. As he struck the Tiger Warrior, a blinding flash of white light and a walloping boom blasted outward from the last member of the Twelve, shaking the earth and the very air around them, knocking down anyone still standing. Usagi was thrown back.

Ears ringing, she lifted her head from the ground. For a long, disorienting moment, Usagi couldn't hear anything but a high-pitched whine, even as the earth continued to tremble beneath her. As her hearing came back to her, Saru's horrified cries grew louder and louder. They echoed through the courtyard as the Monkey Heir tried crawling to where Horangi had been standing. But Inu and Nezu held Saru back, for the Tigress was nowhere to be seen. The Blue Dragon stood amid the wreckage of the platform, roaring in triumph.

Where had Horangi gone? The ring of fire had disappeared, while black blast marks streaked out in all directions from the collapsed platform, striping the courtyard and temple walls. As the Academy younglings picked themselves up and saw the Blue Dragon holding his sword aloft, they began to cheer. Across the city, fireworks popped and flared, shrieking into the skies as if joining in their celebration. "No," Usagi whispered. Tears filled her eyes.

But the earth had not stopped shaking—the shuddering was getting worse. Squinting, Usagi saw that the Treasures had been knocked from the altar, and the Coppice Comb lay quivering on the ground. The marble tiles of the courtyard cracked and split as dozens of trees rumbled out of the earth. Cadets screamed and tried to scurry out of the way. Usagi spied an opportunity.

Scrambling to her feet, she leaped high in the air, reaching the fallen Treasures in a single bound. She lunged for the Mirror of Elsewhere and snatched up the Apothecary, stuffing them both inside her tunic. Her hands grasped at the Bowl of Plenty when someone slammed into her, knocking her aside. "Oh no you don't!" her sister snarled.

Usagi tried again to grab the bowl, but Uma hurled herself at Usagi, pulling at her sleeves, her arms, her collar, reaching for the Treasures she'd hidden in her top. Usagi hunched over and batted away Uma's hands. She felt a hard tug and a stinging snap at her neck, and then Uma stepped away, holding up a broken leather cord with Usagi's wooden rabbit.

"Give me that!" cried Usagi. She reached for it, feeling as if she'd been stripped of her own skin.

"If you want this," said Uma, "then hand those Treasures back."

Usagi shook her head helplessly. "I can't. Let me explain."

"There's *nothing* to explain," Uma flared. "You lied to me!" Her voice grew louder and louder, until it was a near shriek. "You had a choice—Lord Druk and Captain Tupa both gave one to you—and you chose strangers over me!" The wooden carving caught fire, and Usagi squealed as if she were on fire with it. The leather cord blackened and shriveled, giving off an acrid smoke. Uma's face was filled with fury, and her fist turned white-hot as she burned the rabbit pendant to ash.

A horrified wail burst out of Usagi. "Papa made that!" she cried. "It's all we have left of him!"

The briefest flicker of regret crossed Uma's face before she opened her hand and let a blackened fragment fall to the ground. "You did this to yourself. Now give me the Treasures!"

"No!" Usagi snatched up the burnt sliver of wood, still hot and smoking. She searched for the Bowl of Plenty, but in the wreckage of the wooden platform and emerging copse of trees, Usagi couldn't see it. As the grove of trees continued to grow, over the rumbling earth and screams of confusion, she heard Saru calling. Standing at the courtyard entrance with Inu and Nezu in their Striker armor, the Monkey Heir waved frantically at her to join them.

Uma lunged at Usagi, trying to get at the mirror and pillbox stashed in her tunic, but Usagi shook her off and stared into her sister's face, so twisted with anger that she hardly recognized her.

"I'm sorry," she told Uma, her voice shaking. She tucked the burnt remains of the rabbit carving away, her palm blistered. "I still love you." Usagi turned and sprang into the air, high over the copse of trees crowding the blast-streaked courtyard, away from her sister, leaping toward the Heirs.

"I hate you!" Uma screamed.

The words struck Usagi's heart like ice. She glanced back for a dizzying moment and saw her sister standing near the wreckage of the altar for the Treasures, small in the chaos but nearly glowing with rage. Averting her gaze, Usagi plunged toward the entrance to the temple complex and felt her legs buckle. For the first time in months, Usagi fell.

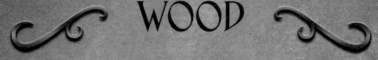

WOOD

*"The season of the Wood element is Spring—a time
for planting seeds, new beginnings, and fresh growth."*

—Book of Elements, from *The Way of the Twelve*

CHAPTER 25

THE TIGRESS'S NEST

USAGI TUMBLED INTO A HEAP outside the entrance to the temple complex, hitting the ground with a bone-rattling jolt. *Spit and spleen.* It had been a long time since she'd landed so badly. The Heirs rushed to haul her to her feet. They'd put their Striker helmets back on, looking for all the world like the Blue Dragon's elite forces.

"Are you all right?" asked Inu, his dark gaze full of concern.

Wincing, she nodded. "What happened to the Tigress? Did you see?"

Saru shook her head, red-rimmed eyes bleak. "Just a flash of light and then the explosion. I don't know what the Blue Dragon did, but . . . she's gone." Inu patted her arm, his mouth drawn in a tight line. He sniffled and pushed his helmet over his eyes. Heaviness settled in Usagi's chest.

"I—I couldn't get them all, but I grabbed a couple of the Treasures," she said, searching for something good to tell them. "Though the Coppice Comb's still back there, and I lost the Bowl of Plenty."

"It's amazing you got anything at all," Nezu said with a wan smile. "We should get out of here before they realize we have some."

Usagi looked back at the temple courtyard, bursting with trees and echoing with the shouts of the Academy cadets and a jubilant Dragonlord. "How?"

The Rat Heir pulled his helmet lower. "We're all in palace uniforms. If we don't run and call attention to ourselves, we can walk out. Quickly—before an alarm is raised."

They hustled away from the temple, heading through the grounds to the palace's front gate. Usagi stopped and pointed. "It's closed. That means the smaller gates will be locked too." She looked fretfully up at the spring moon, hanging high in the sky like a round temple lantern. "It's already the hour of the Ox—they won't open till morning."

"Don't panic," said Inu, steering them away. "The garden at the edge of the Central Court overlooks the Phoenix River. We'll scale the wall there and swim if we have to. We can use spirit speed once we're out." They hurried through the palace's Outer Court, which was relatively deserted, though they twice crossed paths with patrolling Guards. At the sight of them Usagi grew light-headed, but she joined the Heirs in exchanging stern salutes with the patrols without breaking stride. They passed the armory, where, Nezu confided to Usagi, the Heirs had broken in and obtained their Striker armor.

The drums and fireworks across the city had ceased, and the only sounds were from the pounding of their feet and the clatter of the Heirs' armor. Then Usagi heard a birdcall.

Twee hee, hoo hoo.

She turned. The call came again, and then someone hissed her name. Crouching in the shadows of the Royal Library was Tora. She stepped out with her hands raised. "I'm not trying to stop you."

"Wait!" Usagi told the Heirs. She ran to her friend. "What are you doing here?"

"We want to come with you," Tora said, nervously smoothing down the shorn ends of her hair.

Usagi's heart leaped. "'We'?" Was Uma with her? Had she changed her mind?

An enormous boy came out of the shadows, along with a slip of a girl, her braided hair coiled about her head. She had a hopeful look in her dark eyes. "Usagi," said Rana. "Goru and I have been looking for a chance to escape from the day they captured us."

"When someone's taken you from your home against your will, it's hard to believe anything they tell you," added Goru with a raised eyebrow.

Rana bowed. "If you let us, we'd like to come with you and your friends."

Startled, Usagi turned to Tora, who nodded. "It's not that we didn't try to fit in. And I thought I was starting to. But it wasn't always easy to forget." She rubbed the scars on her arm. "Then you showed up. And I couldn't do anything but remember."

"We've been sticking together. Goru always says there's strength in numbers," Rana said. "Even though he's probably stronger than all of us put together. If we may join you, maybe we'll have a chance at a different fate."

"I—I'd have to see what the others say," Usagi stammered. The three Heirs came clacking up behind her, weapons drawn, and she quickly apprised them of the situation. Glowering, they inspected the Academy students suspiciously.

"Peace, friends," Goru said, and bowed. "I know of a spot for escape. It's through the garden of the Inner Court. It'll take us straight into the hills. I didn't want to try it alone, because it's not far from the Dragonlord's quarters. We'll have to hurry before he returns from the temple."

Inu frowned. "We've been betrayed once already. How do we know this isn't a trap?"

"You don't," said Goru. With slow and careful movements, he removed the scabbard at his side and laid it on the ground, while Tora and Rana followed suit. "So we offer you our swords."

"As a sign of good faith," added Tora. Her amber eyes

were steady as she gazed at Usagi. "But if you don't trust us, then tell us now and we'll leave you be."

"I trust you," Usagi burst out. She looked at the Heirs pleadingly. "Tora's as much a sister to me as Uma is. She's saved me so many times. If it weren't for her I'd probably be here—forced into the Academy too. None of them chose to be brought here."

After exchanging glances with Inu and Nezu, Saru motioned to Usagi to gather up the younglings' weapons. She brandished her moon blade. "Show us this spot. If there's any hint that you've lied to us, I won't hesitate to use this."

"Fair enough," said Goru with a nod. He led them through the grounds to the Inner Court, where there was a garden with immaculately sculpted trees and a pavilion by a pond that reminded Usagi of Crescent Lake. The garden was quiet and dark, lit only by the ghostly light of the moon. With the help of Tora's tiger vision, Goru guided them to a remote, secluded corner. There, the palace wall loomed high, separating the manicured grounds from the wild brush of the hills that overlooked the city.

"Now what?" asked Nezu. He smoothed his whisker-less lip, singed bare by the explosion that took the Tigress. "The four of us can leap or climb over this wall easily enough, but what about you?"

"Oh, there's no need to go over," said Rana. She stepped to the base of the wall and placed her hands on the ground.

Her forehead wrinkled in concentration as she pushed against the earth like she was kneading dough. Before long a hole appeared beneath the wall, the dirt falling away from Rana's hands. "We can use this tunnel."

Goru chuckled. "Nice work, Earth Snake, but it's a little small for me." He stuck his thick fingers along a marble block in the wall directly above Rana's tunnel, and wiggled and pulled, gritting his teeth. The block came free and he yanked it out with a heave and a grunt. It was nearly as long as Usagi was tall. He placed it easily on the ground as if it were an old, dry sponge, then tried to squeeze his shoulders into the hole left in the wall. "One more," he muttered. He pulled out another block in a spray of mortar dust and stone chips.

Nezu grinned. "You've made your point."

One by one they squeezed to the other side. As Goru and Rana restored the wall and the earth to cover their tracks, Tora gave Usagi a firm hug. "I'm sorry about Uma," she whispered. "She'll find her way to us again."

Usagi's eyes prickled with hot tears as the failure of their mission hit her. They'd been betrayed by Tupa, the Tigress had been vanquished by the Blue Dragon, and her sister . . . now *hated* her.

But not Tora. She blinked away her tears and hugged her best friend back. "I thought I lost you both."

"They gave us these swords for the spring festival. The

Dragonlord said they're from Waya, but . . . something about them made me realize we were being lied to."

"What was it?" asked Usagi. Then she stiffened at the sound of frantic clanging. "Bells. I think they know we're—"

Inu interrupted. "We need to get out of here, and fast. Have you younglings ever tried spirit speed?"

When Tora and the other cadets shook their heads, he smiled. "Then we'll teach you on the way to Mount Jade." In the darkness, Inu hurried them away from the palace wall and straight into the underbrush. They ran through the hills until they could no longer see the lights of the city below them and were deep in the wilderness, leaving the Blue Dragon and his Academy far behind.

A warm breeze blew into the Great Hall at the Shrine of the Twelve, wafting the scent of spring's last blossoms around Usagi and Saru. They circled each other on the mats, Usagi watching warily as Saru paced about. Without warning, the Monkey Heir lunged.

Ducking, Usagi kicked and caught her heel on Saru's sleeve. Saru shook her off and punched rapidly at Usagi's head and torso, unable to land a single blow as Usagi deflected her fists with swift movements of her own. Then Usagi darted forward and flipped Saru, thumping her onto her back.

"That was a good one!" Saru beamed. She sat up and

turned to her audience. "It's all about defense. Got that?"

Tora, Rana, and Goru watched closely, sitting cross-legged by the sparring area. They nodded. Though the three former cadets still wore the indigo uniforms with their respective ruling animals—tiger, snake, and ox—stitched on the right shoulder, the dragon embroidery on the left side of their tunics had been ripped out. Rana's dark eyes were thoughtful as she chewed on the end of a braid that had come uncoiled. Goru stretched and flexed his large hands as if he couldn't wait to spar.

Tora slipped her fingers into the thick fur of Kumo's pelt and scratched the cloud leopard's neck as he dozed. Upon returning to the shrine, they'd been greeted by an agitated Kumo, who lashed his tail from side to side, looking for Horangi. He'd paced the grounds yowling, and only Tora seemed to be able to settle him down. Since then, the cloud leopard trailed after her much as he'd followed the Tigress.

Nearly a month had gone by since returning to Mount Jade. The newcomers were settling in nicely, after an ascent that took them through challenges created by the Warriors of old. Goru had impressed everyone when he went through the Bashing Boulders like Usagi had. Instead of leaping over the rolling stones, he'd stopped them in their tracks and lifted them up and out of his way.

And despite the younglings' lack of training in areas like breathing, mind-the-mind, calligraphy, and other subjects that the Tigress had drilled into Usagi and the Heirs, they were quick to learn and never complained. Usagi especially liked having them help her with chores—Rana could clean a room in seconds, gathering all the dust in piles that tumbled themselves out the door.

Now the three leaned forward eagerly as Saru told Usagi to prepare for an attack. Usagi got into a ready stance and waited. The Monkey Heir sprang, feet aimed squarely at her head. Usagi let out a cry and whirled around, sweeping one leg behind her to knock Saru to the ground. She grinned at the awed looks on the others' faces.

"At the Academy, even with all the equipment and grand uniforms, you were never taught defense?" The moves she and Saru were demonstrating seemed basic to Usagi now. She caught herself. Once it had all been new to her too.

"They told us defensive maneuvers were a waste of time. It was about the attack," Goru explained. "Having a strong offense was more important than anything else."

Saru frowned. "If you can properly deflect a blow, it doesn't matter how vicious the attack."

The memory of Uma swinging at her with her fiery sword flared in Usagi's mind. She flinched. Would she ever forget the look of hate on her sister's face? She glanced over at Tora. For the most part, Tora was adjusting well to being at the shrine, but there were times she would seem distracted or sad, and she didn't like to talk about her months at the

Academy. Usagi smiled at her friend, but Tora was staring into the distance, a faraway look in her eyes.

Shaking her head, Saru looked at the chest of Treasures, empty except for the two relics Usagi had saved. "Now that Teacher's gone, it's only a matter of time before the Blue Dragon tries once more to conquer the only part of Midaga that won't bend to him."

"Which part is that?" asked Rana.

Goru tweaked her stray braid. "Mount Jade, of course," he said.

"Not if I can help it," said Usagi. She raised her chin, feeling fiercely protective of their little band and their haven. "We can't let him win."

Saru smiled. "Which means it's of the essence to be good defenders," she said. She had the newcomers face off against Usagi, who threw punches and kicks for them to practice deflecting. Usagi was wiping the sweat off her brow when her ears pricked at the sound of Nezu's footsteps. He appeared in the open doorway to the Great Hall.

"Oi! I've cooked up something special, and I don't want it to get cold." He flashed a grin and waggled a finger at Usagi. "Especially for you."

"What's that supposed to mean?" asked Usagi, but Nezu's grin only grew. They filed out and washed up for the midday meal. When they walked into the dining hall, Usagi stopped and stared.

"This is a banquet," she said. The table was laden with the best of Nezu's cooking—the most since the New Year's feast. The others were wreathed in smiles. Usagi laughed, confused. "What's the occasion?"

"You'll see," said Saru cheerfully. "Sit, everyone!" They plopped down on cushions around the table, exclaiming over the dishes.

Usagi looked around. "Where's Inu?"

"He's finishing something," Nezu said, while Tora and Rana giggled and nudged each other. Saru poured cups of wolfberry tea, but before Usagi could take a sip, the door to the dining hall slid open. The Dog Heir entered with a cloth-wrapped bundle and a long, polished stick. All chatter ceased as everyone looked up at him expectantly.

Inu's eyes crinkled and his usual serious expression gave way to a grin. "Rabbit Girl, would you do us the honor of standing for a moment?"

Mystified, Usagi got to her feet. Saru steered her toward Inu. He unwrapped the bundle and held up a finely wrought silver chain. A silver rabbit figurine no bigger than her thumb glimmered from the chain, its paws outstretched in midleap. Chips of grass-green jade formed its eyes. Heart pounding, Usagi couldn't take her eyes off the necklace. It looked just like the wooden rabbit her father had carved for her, the one she'd worn for years until Uma burned it. Only this one was of metal and jade, and would be far harder to destroy. Inu must have been working on it ever since they returned to the shrine.

"It should really be wood," he admitted shyly, "but I don't have a gift with that element. Anyway, we wanted to give you something to officially mark you as the Rabbit Heir. Do you accept the title, promising to uphold and defend the Way of the Twelve?"

Had Horangi been here, she would have been the one to ask the question. Usagi felt a lump come into her throat, remembering the Tigress's words. *You are a true Heir of the Twelve.* She swallowed hard and stood straight as a spear. "Yes, I do."

To loud cheers, Inu placed the chain around her neck. Then he picked up the polished rod and presented it ceremoniously to Usagi. "To replace your lost walking stick." Usagi bowed and accepted it. She turned the stick in her hands. It was made of phoenix tree wood, fine-grained and strong. Running her fingers along the smooth surface, she came across a tiny groove in the wood. "Open it," urged Inu. "If you'd rather a moon blade or a spearhead, I can change it out."

She pulled the stick apart to find a straight, long sword blade sheathed in the wood, similar to Nezu's. Her very own hidden weapon! She looked around at everyone, feeling more fortunate than she had in a long time. "Thank you," she managed.

Saru raised her cup. "To the new Rabbit Heir!"

They all raised their cups of sweet wolfberry tea. "The new Rabbit Heir!"

Overcome, Usagi ducked her head, fingering the chain around her neck. Her new necklace was beautiful.

"Now let's eat!" Nezu ladled Usagi's favorite soup, thick with rice noodles and dandelion greens, into bowls. He carved the crisp skin off a golden roasted pheasant, and folded it into steamed buns with wild onion, bits of juicy pheasant meat, and dabs of sauce. There was braised venison, so tender it was melting off the bone. Platters of fried fish and sautéed mountain vegetables were passed around, and sour pickled plums to go with heaps of steaming hot rice.

"I haven't seen this much food since the Palace of the Clouds," Tora remarked. She looked at Usagi, poking at a pickle on her still-full plate. "Aren't you hungry?"

"I was just wishing . . ." Usagi trailed off, unsure she could say more without bursting into tears.

Tora nodded and squeezed her hand. "I know. I wish Uma were here too."

"I just worry," said Usagi. "What will become of her?"

"Maybe she'll come to realize that you were right," said Tora. She turned and lowered her voice. "There's something I never got to finish telling you. Those Wayani swords that they gave us at the Academy? They were new, and I know it sounds crazy, but it looked like . . . my father's work."

"But your father's dead," Usagi said. "He's buried with mine in the turtleback mound."

Tora shook her head. "That was what I thought. But did you actually see your parents placed in that grave?"

"No," said Usagi slowly.

"It just made me think," said Tora. "What if rice and minerals aren't the only things being taken from Midaga?"

After the feast, Usagi went to the lakeside prayer pavilion. They had taken to calling it the Tigress's Nest, and Usagi kept a little vase of flowers there, changing out the blossoms whenever they began to wilt. The afternoon sun filtered through the trees, dappling the pavilion with light and illuminating the little cushion that Horangi liked to sit on during mind-the-mind.

"Hello, Teacher," Usagi said softly, hoping that the spirit of the Tiger Warrior could hear her somehow. She knelt beside the cushion and touched it, then placed a hand over the new rabbit figurine around her neck. "Thank you for believing in me." Usagi remembered the Tigress's glowing green gaze, and how she'd told her she would make a fine Rabbit Warrior. "I promise I won't let you down."

Her fingers brushed against a little ridge on the rabbit's underbelly. Pressing the minute bump, she heard a click and the figurine opened, revealing an empty hollow. It was a locket. Usagi raised it into the sunlight to get a better look. The space within was just big enough. She reached into her belt and pulled out the burnt sliver of wood that had once been the carved rabbit from her father. It was a perfect fit.

She thought about what Tora had said. Could it be that Tora's father was still alive? Could that mean that *her* parents were still alive? The notion filled her with more hope than she thought possible. The green waters of Crescent Lake lapped and swirled around the pavilion pilings like the emotions running through her. Grief for the Tigress. Sorrow and worry over Uma. Wonder, that their parents might not be gone.

And she was happy for the addition of Tora, Goru, and Rana. Their training was coming along beautifully. Surely they would become Heirs. New Heirs would be found for every branch of the zodiac.

Usagi was an Heir now, in line to become the Rabbit Warrior, her duty to the Circle of Zodiac Warriors and Midaga. The struggle over the Treasures would continue. Though the Tigress was gone, the Circle would form again, and the Twelve would be reborn. She'd be just the first of many more Rabbit Warriors to come. Of that, Usagi felt certain. She heard a familiar birdcall in the distance—*twee hee, hoo hoo*—and turned to see Tora crunching down the gravel path.

"Inu's looking for you," Tora reported. "He wants to finish that last game of six sticks. He promised to show me he could beat you."

Usagi grinned. "All right."

"Last one back has to do the other's chores," said Tora with a glint of her snaggleteeth. She turned and ran off into the trees.

Usagi blinked. For a moment it felt like they were back home in Goldentusk. Then she realized they *were* home—a new one. Standing on the steps of the Tigress's Nest, bubbles of joy swelled in her chest till she laughed.

"Here I come!" she shouted. And then Usagi leaped.

ACKNOWLEDGMENTS

In bringing this story into being, I am beyond fortunate to have my own special Warrior Council, of which there are many more than twelve to thank.

My deepest gratitude to Josh Adams, agent extraordinaire, for seeing promise even when this novel was in its early stages and championing it with unflagging enthusiasm from the very first pages. Your endless patience and whole-hearted encouragement means the world to me, and I wouldn't be holding this book in my hands without you, Tracey, and the rest of the Adams Literary family. You are a true Warrior, and I am so thankful for your great talents and gifts.

To Kristen Pettit, the best editor a writer could have—thank you for loving Usagi and her friends from the jump, and for your fabulous eye and incisive pen. You really know how to find the beating heart of a tale, and what gives a story the power to roar. How grateful I am for your guidance and how it's made me grow. I couldn't ask for a better Tigress to watch over this book.

Eternal thanks must go to the team at HarperCollins: to Kate Morgan Jackson, queen of everything; to editorial assistant Clare Vaughn for being so amazing on the front lines, to designers Molly Fehr and Alison Klapthor for the gorgeous book; to artist Sher Rill Ng for incredible cover art that brought tears of joy; to production editors Jessica Berg and Gweneth Morton for your much-needed attention to details; to copy editor Veronica Ambrose for your gimlet eye; to marketing directors Robby Imfeld and Emma Meyer for your genius; and to production manager Kristen Eckhardt for making it all happen. You are dreammakers, every one of you.

There have been many over the years who've read my attempts at this story and offered encouragement and support along the way. I must give thanks to Hilary Hattenbach, Josh Hauke, Lilliam Rivera, Elizabeth Ross, Mary Shannon, Jason White, and Frances Sackett for cheering even my baby steps; to the beloved sisterhood of Elizabeth Barker, Aurora Gray, and Arti Panjabi Kvam for faithfully reading countless pages and drafts; to Jim Thomas, for showing me the way; to Laurie Zerwer and Lisa Gold for your feedback and friendship; to Ryder LinLiu for being the first youngling to read a full manuscript; to Kristen Kittscher, Brandy Colbert, and Elana K. Arnold for your counsel; to Ken Min and

Erin Eitter Kono for shoring up spirits; to Helena Ku Rhee and Sherry Berkin for the writers' lunches; and to Oliver Wang and Erin Kieu Ninh for the disciplined work sessions. To Joven and Leslie Matias, for asking about my biggest dream—and nudging me to go after it. To Stefanie Huie and Roger Fan, for never blinking at my fanciful notions of writing a novel. To the SCBWI, for giving me a place to learn and develop—and to Kim Turrisi for her effective matchmaking. To them and so many others I've met on this writing journey, I am indebted.

To all my teachers—especially Paula Yoo, my first creative writing instructor and constant source of inspiration; Leslie Lehr, who urged me to pursue the more challenging story; and Francesca Lia Block, punk faerie queen and insightful, generous coach—you have taught me so much, and I will forever be your grateful student.

Finally, to my family. To my sister, Wendy Chang—you are my heart. You and Dennis are Warriors for fighting off my fears and doubts, and for celebrating every milestone. To the rest of the Chang family, especially my nieces and nephew—you make life a joy. Special thanks to Amanda, Nicole, and Lindsey for asking, "And then what happens?" with genuine, endless curiosity, and to John Paul for your energetic cheer. To Koo and Rosa Pak, and the memory of Steven, thank you for your loving presence. To the Hou and Lin relatives, this American cousin appreciates you. And last but not least, to my parents, Paul and Martha Lin—you have given me the world. There are no words to express my gratitude for your unconditional love and support. I can only hope to make you proud by trying my best every day, just as you have shown me. *Kám-siā*.

TURN THE PAGE TO READ
AN EXCERPT FROM

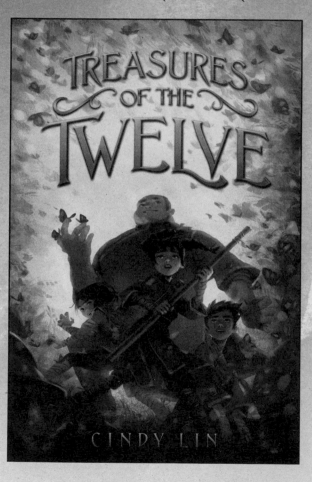

TREASURES
OF THE
TWELVE

CINDY LIN

CHAPTER 1

THE PEN OF TRUTH

USAGI WINCED AT THE SCREECH of seabirds and hurried along the harbor's busy waterfront, squinting against the reflection of the morning sun as she followed her target. A crisp spring breeze, sharp with the tang of salt and fishrot, threatened to blow off her headwrap and expose her dark braids. She shifted the pole across her shoulders, empty baskets dangling from either end, and tugged the white kerchief down more securely. While there were girl porters working the docks here in Port Wingbow, they were few and far between, and the last thing she wanted was to call attention to herself.

"To your left, Rabbit Girl," said a familiar voice, twenty paces back. Most passersby would think that Nezu was just muttering to the other young porter hauling a basketload of packages beside him, but Usagi could hear the Heir to the Rat Warrior loud and clear, thanks to her ability to hear as

well as a rabbit. She didn't dare risk trying to reply to him and her friend Tora, neither of whom shared that particular animal talent. Raising her arm, she scratched her shoulder to show that she'd heard, then veered across the crushed-shell path toward the main pier.

"*Tell her the Guards have arrived,*" hissed Tora, who was keeping a lookout with her sharp tiger vision. "*It's too late. We'll have to wait till the harbormaster's done for the day and his Guard detail goes away.*"

"*You can tell her yourself,*" said Nezu. "*Are you forgetting she hears us?*"

"*I've known Usagi a lot longer than you—I know exactly how well she can hear. You're the one who insisted on a protocol. 'Everything must go through the head of the mission!'*" Tora mimicked. Usagi could hear her best friend smugly stroking imaginary fuzz on her upper lip, something the Rat Heir often did when he was pleased, nervous, or deep in thought.

"*Because I've been doing this for a few years now, Tiger Girl.*"

"*Doesn't mean you know everything, Rat Boy.*"

"*You're just upset about not wearing the belt, but I'm telling you, it fits me better—and as head of the mission, why shouldn't I?*"

Usagi groaned. In all her thirteen years, she'd never known anyone to squabble as much as this pair. She turned and retraced her steps, pretending to look for something she'd dropped, until she bumped right into them, knocking some of their decoy parcels to the ground. Usagi yelped a false apology, and as they all bent down to collect the scattered packages, she glared at them.

"What's wrong with you two? We're close to getting one of the Treasures back, and you're arguing!"

Looking abashed, Nezu reached up and tugged at the barest wisp of whiskers on his upper lip. It didn't help them get any longer, but he'd been doing it since he first sprouted peach fuzz, and now it was a habit. "Sorry, Rabbit Girl. You're right. We're just on edge after waiting for so long—and now we have to wait some more." He flashed an apologetic smile, his usual grin dimmed somewhat. At sixteen and the seniormost Warrior Heir on the mission, he was responsible for leading them, and the difficulty they'd had securing their target these last few days was wearing on him.

"If you'd only trusted me the first time I said I saw the harbormaster, we might have gotten to him sooner." Tora's amber eyes flamed with indignation. She was a year older than Usagi but wasn't yet a Warrior Heir. She was hoping to become one by proving herself on this assignment.

Long before Usagi had become the Rabbit Heir, before ever meeting Nezu and the other Warrior Heirs, Tora had been by her side. For years after the Dragonlord's overthrow of Midaga's king and the Warriors of the Zodiac, she and Tora had been orphans in the forest. Along with Usagi's sister, Uma, the three of them had been just trying to survive and keep their zodiac powers hidden. Until—

Until . . .

Usagi pushed the painful thought of her little sister away and handed over a stack of parcels to her friend. "Can the two of you please behave?"

"Of course," said Tora, baring her sharp white canines. They were snaggleteeth that stuck out from the rest of her smile, making her look extra fierce even when she wasn't annoyed. When she was truly furious, they would grow till they protruded from her upper lip. Thankfully they were currently in check. An angry youngling sprouting long fangs would draw attention—too much attention on a mission to steal back the Pen of Truth.

One of twelve Treasures that once belonged to the Warriors, the pen was now in the possession of a man who ran the kingdom's only seaport—and he was using its powers for profit.

"You said you saw the Guard?" Usagi asked Tora. Her stomach clenched at the thought of the armed troops who kept order for the ruler of Midaga. Though she'd bested one in a fight once, it was always better to avoid tangling with the Dragonlord's men.

Her friend nodded. "Two of them, right as the harbormaster got to the dock."

"So we wait until he's alone again. Might as well stick together till that happens." Usagi straightened. "My apologies!" she said loudly. "Let me help you." She made a show

4

of taking some of their bundles—mostly just straw wrapped in squares of cloth—and putting them in her empty baskets. She hoisted her pole over her shoulders, making sure the sword hidden inside was secure. Nezu's walking stick also hid a blade, as weapons had been forbidden for all but those serving the Dragonlord. Since Tora was not yet an Heir, her pole was just solid wood. She was eager to earn her place as the Tiger Heir, and with it, a hidden weapon of her own.

Together they headed toward the largest pier in port, where the harbormaster's station was perched. Weaving between rumbling ox carts, they ducked and dodged as bales of wool, cords of exotic woods, bundles of sharkskin leather, and other imports were unloaded from the myriad ships docked along the piers built all throughout the cove. Though they'd been on Feather Island for nearly a week, Usagi was still dazzled by the sight of all the boats. Who knew there could be so many types of vessels to travel across water? There were ships with battened sails that folded like fans, sloops with white canvas billowing from the masts like puffed-out frogs' throats, flat-keeled boats propelled by paddlewheels, longships that sported rows of oars manned by oarsmen, squat boats with chimneys that belched smoke, armored ships bristling with firecannon.

Before the fall of the Shield of Concealment, the kingdom of Midaga had never seen so many visitors to its shores. It had remained hidden from the rest of the world, safe and protected by the Warriors of the Zodiac, until Druk the Dragon Warrior betrayed his oath to the Circle of the Twelve. He shattered the Shield, allowing invasion and war to devastate the land, and seized the throne as Dragonlord.

Now, seven years into his reign, ships from lands near and far came to Midaga, eager to see and trade with the kingdom that had been but a myth for hundreds of years. The port in the Bantam Islands, once the only part of Midaga that the world was allowed to see, had been expanded by leaps and bounds, per the order of the Dragonlord. A harbor that had received at most four ships a year when the Shield was up now saw many times that each week. And from his spare wooden lean-to on the main pier, the harbormaster ruled over it all.

They drew close and saw the line of ship captains and various agents waiting to report their cargo to the harbormaster. The front of the shanty was wide open, flanked by two armored Guard. They glowered beneath metal helmets that sat on their heads like overturned cookpots. Their burly torsos were shielded by iron breastplates, and their leather-sleeved arms cradled firecannon. At the sight of them, Usagi quailed. It was an old reflex. She forced herself to hold her head up. She was the Heir to the Rabbit Warrior, after all. She'd spent months training and could handle them both if need be!

She spotted the harbormaster's bulky form and tall

official's hat but was unable to see the Treasure. Fortunately, they had Tora's tiger vision, just as Usagi's sharp ears listened for them all. "Is it there?" Usagi whispered.

Tora's eyes narrowed. "There's a pen on his desk, in a brush stand beside the cargo registry. It's bigger than an ordinary ink brush, with a gold handle decorated with the twelve animals of the zodiac. It's got a gold cap, but he's taken it off. I see the bristles. They look like ox hair."

"Ox—the animal embodying truthfulness," Nezu said. "That's the Treasure, all right." They continued farther down the pier until they came to the last ship, which looked nearly deserted, its cargo unloaded, most of its crew likely in one of the port taverns. They set their baskets down. Nezu took his headcloth off and wiped his face, then retied it around his close-cropped hair, taking care to tuck in the long, thin rat-tail braid at the base of his skull. He flashed a smile at Usagi. "How are your rabbit ears from here?"

She tilted her head and squeezed her eyes shut, listening. Out of habit, Usagi reached for the pendant she wore around her neck and rubbed the little silver rabbit with its chips of green jade for eyes. Over the cries of seagulls, the shouts of dockworkers, the splash of seawater against ships and dock pilings, the creak of wooden hulls, the clattering of wheels on cobblestones and planks, Usagi located the gravelly voice of the harbormaster, which she'd come to recognize after several days of surveillance. He was interrogating his latest

7

quarry in the line of ship captains and cargo masters waiting to report to him.

"*Name and vessel name?*"

"*Captain Golae of the* Fleet-Finned Whale."

"*Home port?*"

"*Port Busana in Solonos.*"

The harbormaster would always ask about the cargo, and then hand over the Pen of Truth to sign off. That was the part that always made Usagi feel a little sorry for the harbormaster's prey.

"*Oh! Wait! I—I didn't mean to write that! Th—that's a mistake!*"

"*Is it really, Captain? You aren't trying to skimp on paying your import duties, are you? If I have the Guard go to your ship right now and search it, do you swear on your life we will only find* ten *bales of cotton for trade instead of* fifteen?"

After some threats detailing what could happen to those caught trying to cheat the Dragonlord, the harbormaster would then offer the hapless victim an opportunity to buy his way out of trouble. In this way, Usagi noticed, the harbormaster was becoming a very rich man.

"He's up to his usual tricks," she reported. "Just got a Soloni ship captain to hand over five gold mon for lying about his cargo."

Nezu whistled. "That's more than some people make in a lifetime." He peered into the water. "Anyone getting hungry?"

Glancing around to make sure no one was looking, he made a little swirling motion with his hands until a small cyclone of water rose from the sea. Knitting his brow, he gestured sharply upward, and the cyclone spat a silvery fish onto the pier, where it flipped and flopped at their feet.

"Mealtime!" Tora exclaimed. She pounced on the wriggling fish and dispatched it with a quick thump against the dock. With his knife, Nezu cleaned the fish, slicing it into neat filets. He portioned it out between the three of them and pulled out fist-sized balls of salted rice wrapped in seaweed.

"It's too bad none of us have a fire gift," he remarked. "A little blast of flame would sear this fish nicely."

Usagi couldn't help but think of Uma at that moment. Her sister was able to conjure fire with her bare hands and had used her elemental gift to cook whatever they could scavenge, back when they lived with Tora in the forest outside Goldentusk. Now Uma was part of the Dragonlord's troops, a prized cadet in a corps of younglings with zodiac powers, her fire gift and horse speed to be used by the Dragonlord as tools in maintaining order over all Midagians. Usagi's rabbit locket felt heavy at her neck, and she rubbed its hollow belly. It contained the charred remains of the wooden rabbit she used to wear—until Uma had burned it in a fury. That was the last time Usagi had seen her sister.

With a sigh, she sat with the others on the edge of the

dock, dangling their feet over the swirling seawater. Clumps of kelp drifted on the surface while a pair of black-tailed gulls bobbed alongside, staring up at their meal with hungry yellow eyes. She was about to take a bite of her rice ball when Tora stopped chewing and squinted down the pier.

"There's the harbormaster's daughter," she muttered. Usagi turned and caught a bit of movement as a small figure ducked behind the railing of a docked ship. Since coming to Port Wingbow, they'd seen the girl hanging around the docks—the only youngling who wasn't a porter, though she might as well have been one, dressed as she was in a ragged tunic and pants, a grimy white kerchief tied over a frizzled braid.

Nezu draped a piece of fish over his rice ball and took a bite. "Are you sure she's his daughter? Seems like more of a servant to me. He's always ordering her around."

"And slapping her if she's too slow," said Tora with a frown. They had witnessed the harbormaster boxing the girl about the ears when he wasn't in his shed extorting payment from ship captains. It had disgusted Usagi—the girl couldn't have been more than seven or eight and was spindly with large dark eyes that reminded her of Uma.

Usagi got to her feet. "I'll be right back."

"Where are you going?" Tora cocked her head.

Waving a vague hand, Usagi headed for the ship, eyes on where she'd last seen movement. As she drew closer, she heard the growling of an empty stomach—only for once it wasn't hers. She stopped at the base of the lowered gangplank. "Merciful spirits! What a lot of rice and fish," Usagi exclaimed. "I can't eat all of this by myself! What to do?" As a dark head with wide eyes peered out, Usagi smiled. "Oh, hello!" She held up her rice ball. "I've got a little too much here. Would you like some?"

The girl hesistated, then nodded. Usagi waved at her to come down, and she crept down the gangplank. Her face was smudged with dirt and soot, and she smelled like she'd been sleeping in a pile of fishnets. Usagi broke her rice ball in half and gave her most of her raw fish. Shyly, the girl took it, then stuffed everything in her mouth all at once, as if she were afraid Usagi would change her mind. Usagi laughed. "Slow down! You'll give yourself a bellyache." She took a bite of her own and then looked at the girl chewing mightily, eyes half-closed in relief. It reminded Usagi so much of Uma that a lump came into her throat. Swallowing hard, she held out the rest of her food. "Here, why don't you have some more?"

Eyes shining, the little girl took it. She bobbed her head in thanks.

"What's your name?" asked Usagi, and pointed to herself. "I'm Usagi, born in the year of the Wood Rabbit."

The girl paused in her chewing and mumbled through a mouthful of rice. "Ji. Year of the Rooster."

"I knew a boy back home who was born a Metal Rooster," Usagi said. "Jago was always full of energy, as Roosters often are." She took care not to mention that little Jago had developed the talent of flying or had been hauled away by Strikers to serve the Dragonlord. She waved a casual hand at the harbormaster's station. "So, is that your father in there?"

Ji stopped chewing, startled. Slowly, she nodded.

"You know that gold pen of his?" Usagi pressed. "It's so pretty. Do you know where he got it?"

Shaking her head, Ji backed away, eyes wide.

"No, wait!" Usagi hadn't meant to alarm her, but the girl turned and ran back up the gangplank, disappearing onto the ship. She'd said too much. *Spit and spleen.* Usagi stood there a moment, cursing herself, then returned to her friends.

Nezu looked at her curiously. "What were you trying to do there?"

"I remember what it's like to be hungry," said Usagi with a sigh. "And I thought maybe she could tell me a little bit about the pen. But she ran away before saying anything."

"Better to leave her alone," Nezu advised. "The fewer people we talk to around here, the better. We don't need anyone recognizing us after we've lifted the pen." He polished off the last of his rice ball and licked his fingers. "Spirits. I could've eaten five of those." He tightened the leather belt at his waist. Decorated with silver, wood, and horn fittings, the Belt of Passage was a precious heirloom passed down from

12

warrior to warrior in the Circle of the Twelve. That was, until the war had decimated their ranks and scattered their treasured artifacts around the kingdom. The belt had only recently been recovered, and the other Warrior Heirs had insisted that Nezu wear it on this mission, in case its powers were needed.

Tora stiffened. "The harbormaster's leaving his station and dismissing the Guard. He must be off to the teahouse for midday meal. Should we try for the pen now?"

"Is it on him?" asked Usagi. From where she stood, more than two hundred paces away, she saw the harbormaster closing the doors to his shed but couldn't see much more than that.

Narrowing her eyes, Tora nodded. "He's sticking it in the back of his belt, just as he has for the last three days. He's consistent, at least."

"Perfect." Nezu rubbed his hands and flashed a grin. "I think we've watched and waited long enough."